I0671048

GEORGIA BURNS

PUBLISHED AD 2011
Genre: Fiction

Tommy Davis

RUMORS OF WAR:

GEORGIA BURNS

A POLITICAL THRILLER
By
Tommy Davis

Copyright © 2009 Tommy E. Davis
All Rights Reserved
ISBN # 978-0-9825522-3-0
Genre: Fiction

Tommy Davis

War is a mere continuation of politics by other means.
-Carl von Clausewitz

All politics is local.
-Tip O'Neill

War is the health of the state.
-Randolph Bourne

All warfare is based on deception. Hence, when we are able to attack, we must seem unable; when we are near, we must make the enemy believe we are far away.
-Sun Tzu

Tommy Davis

For Angie and our children.

PROLOGUE

He had promised the people *Hope*, but hopes were still unfulfilled in the year that President Abraham Soloto began his re-election campaign.

It had been the devastating near-collapse of the economy that helped sweep Soloto into the office of the President of the United States only three years before. And it was that same as yet-to-be corrected recession, along with brooding resentment of the endless trickle of body bags from the overseas wars in which the U.S. was bogged down that now threatened Soloto's chances of winning a second term at the hands of the American electorate.

Throughout his first term, President Soloto had sought to re-inflate the economic balloon by spending massive amounts of money. Though change had been slow in coming Soloto soldiered on, ignoring the doomsayers who warned that over-spending coupled with the over-printing of new money could put more pressure on the U.S. Dollar than the old Greenback could withstand.

Yet Soloto would not be deterred. He considered himself a left-of-center moderate who had won the White House in a center-right country, a very difficult task and a great achievement. But the economy was in a nose dive; Soloto saw but one course of action, like a fighter pilot under pressure--gun the throttle and dump raw fuel into the engines to re-ignite them until the nose of the plane pulled up and leveled off.

And he knew of but one fuel for the economy--fresh money. There would be time to deal with the debt created by the spending, but that task would have to wait until his second term. To get to that term and finish the work he had started meant Soloto had to get himself re-elected.

With the economy still in the dumpster, the opposition party felt that their candidate would be a sure bet to win, denying Soloto a second term.

That improbable party nominee turned out to be Faron Y. Huxtable, a former Methodist preacher who had once been the Speaker of the State House of Arkansas. When the sitting Governor and Lieutenant Governor had died together in a plane crash, Huxtable stepped into the top office unopposed, and from there had made the improbable leap to become a major party candidate for President of the United States.

Soloto's team at first thought Huxtable's nomination a laugher, dismissing Huxtable as too goofy to gain widespread popularity. But to their surprise Huxtable hit the road running, kept flashing a big toothy smile, and ran a self-styled race with such focus and purpose that by June the polls showed him pulling ahead of the President, with the election only five months away.

It was looking as if the same economic factors that had propelled Soloto into the White House would now rob him of a second term. Things were looking bleak for the President. But then two things happened that Huxtable never saw coming.

First, the economy took a sharp turn in the right direction. The ocean of money printed and pumped into the financial system finally made its long slog through the pipeline of bureaucracy; and in the middle of the summer of the election year those trillions burst upon the economy like a flood of ice-cold water on a blistering hot summer day.

Unemployment began to drop a full point per month while at the same time investors watched the Dow Jones rise rapidly. Factories were receiving new orders again and began to hum along at full capacity. Each week brought another piece of good news for the economy, and for President Soloto. Waves of new car and home loans were made available to families who could now begin to purchase and fill up the neighborhoods across America that had become weed infested ghost towns. Mailboxes were once again full of weekly credit card offers.

If there was one thing Soloto knew about the voters, it was that they would most often vote their pocketbooks.

Ben Rothfellow, the head of the National Bank Reserve, the private banking cartel that controls the nations money supply, gave Soloto a big boost by going to the Senate floor in September to testify that with "wise, measured, and time-tested responses to the economic challenges of the past few years, another 'Great Depression' has been averted, and the crisis is now officially over!"

On the same September day that Rothfellow testified before the U.S. Senate, Gallup published a poll that showed that Soloto had closed the gap with Huxtable--the race was now dead even.

But if the change of fortunes in the economy had brought Soloto to even, it was the second unexpected event, an October surprise to end them all, which proved to be the knockout punch landing squarely on the jaw of Faron Y. Huxtable. And it was provided, not by some high-ticket Chicago political schemer, but by a little old lady from rural Arkansas.

Her name was Beulah Mae Deal and she was ninety-three years old, but her mind was still clear as a bell. She still lived on her own, and on a fixed income asking help from no one, thank you very much.

One September morning Beulah Mae had slept late, to nearly 7:00 in the morning. Still dressed in her cotton nightgown, she went for the mail, creeping gently to the postal box out by the road to collect her Social Security cheque.

Pulling the brown envelope from the mailbox, her small wrinkled fingers pried it open along the seal. As she looked the cheque over, a blood-red anger began to creep visibly up her neck and over her face, threatening to overwhelm the white of her very thin hair. Belle, her cat, watched with growing worry as Beulah's face changed colour.

There by the mailbox, Beulah Mae read the accompanying letter, a letter which explained why her cheque had been cut by more than sixty dollars. But the explanation only made her more angry. It explained that the cut was due to the 'recent actions of Congress.'

"Recent actions of Congress," Beulah Mae repeated in a sarcastic tone that made Belle take an anxious step back.

Beulah Mae Deal had out-lived the Great Depression, a World War, two husbands, three of her eight children, and twelve dogs. One lazy cat survived, the one that followed her to the mailbox every morning. And though she wasn't overly interested in politics, she did at least give President Soloto's party credit for saving the country from the Robber-Barons back in the day.

Beulah Mae tried to be at least indifferent to Huxtable, whose name she could only pronounce 'Huckleberry.' He was, after all, from her home state. But in her heart she knew she would end up voting for Soloto, because *that* was who Bill Clinton supported.

As she was glad to explain to any who would listen, Beulah Mae Deal loved Bill Clinton. She had proudly voted for Clinton every time his name had appeared on the Arkansas ballot, whether for Congress, Attorney General, Governor or for President of the United States. Fourteen times in all, through primaries, run-offs and general elections, Beulah Mae had traveled to her local fire station that doubled as a voting place, and pulled the lever beside the name of Bill

Clinton. She often wondered how many other living souls could make such a claim.

"Back in nineteen an' seventy-nine," she had bragged to her friends in Sunday School, "I got me a hug from Bill Clinton his-self!" And it was true, for at the young age of sixty Beulah Mae had once met Clinton at a local political barbecue, and the tall and handsome man took time to notice her and to stoop over and hug her neck.

Since that moment, Beulah Mae had believed every word the man had uttered. She believed him when he wagged his finger at the television camera and said "I did not have sex with that woman"; and she believed him when he looked sadly into that same camera and said, "I did." Sex or no sex, Beulah Mae trusted what Bill Clinton said, though she did despise the one she called "that Yankee Hillary," whom she believed to be her Bill's only real mistake in life.

And she remembered that Bill Clinton had said to watch out for that other party because they were going to try to destroy Social Security! If she rightly remembered--and her memory was good yet--she had heard Franklin Delano Roosevelt utter the same warning over the radio when she was just a girl. For her, those two taken together made it gospel.

And at that moment, standing out by her mailbox in her nightgown, Beulah Mae was suddenly mind-struck by a long-buried memory, a memory that turned her anger to the giddy excitement of a schoolgirl. And how often, she thought, can a nonagenarian say that happens?

Back in her living room, Beulah Mae dug through dusty stacks of church bulletins that were curled yellow by time and sunlight. She had lived through the Great Depression and did not believe in throwing anything away.

After a moment and a few determined tugs, she pulled free an aged cassette tape. The tape had also yellowed with age, but she did not blow the dust off, only to have to breathe it again. Using the hem of her gown, Beulah Mae wiped the dust from the cassette so she could read the label. Faded and barely legible, the label of the cassette read:

Big Oak Methodist Church
September 17, 1972
Sunday Morning Sermon by
Reverend Faron Y. Huxtable

Oh boy, thought Beulah Mae with a smile, *this will be interesting*.

After making her way back to her rocking chair, she sat down slowly and turned on an ancient stereo. She opened the cassette deck and inserted the tape. Beulah Mae worried that the old machine might mangle the aged tape, destroying it forever, but she figured she would trust God with such details.

She mashed PLAY. Her rocking chair creaked gently as it rocked back and forth over the heartpine floors her granddaddy had cut and sawed ages ago.

The cat had made its way in through an open window, for in all of her ninety-three years Beulah Mae had never seriously considered buying an air conditioner, though she cursed the Arkansas heat just as well as the next person. Belle curled up next to the rocker, being sure to pull its tail in when the chair began to rock.

Together the two listened as the tape rolled along through hymn singing and Sunday School announcements. And then the voice of a young minister began to bark from the speakers. The inflection of his voice, noticed Beulah Mae with a grimace, was that of a young, inexperienced man trying to speak with authority to an audience much older and grayer, if not wiser, than he.

"Turn in your Bibles to Proverbs 14:34." The sounds of the ruffle and crackle of crisp Bible pages were heard turning on the pulpit. Again, the young preacher Faron Y. Huxtable's voice bellowed forth.

"Hear these words from the text: 'Righteousness exalts a nation, but sin is a reproach to any people.'" Amen, at least to that part, said Beulah Mae to herself. The cat, as bored with the sermon as an old deacon, yawned widely as it dozed off to sleep. But Beulah Mae listened patiently to the message delivered by the then-young preacher.

"If we are ever going to take America back for Righteousness, we must realize the power of these words!" 'Amen's' that must have been shouted by the original audience sounded forth from the speakers in Beulah's living room. She kept listening and kept rocking.

It was about twenty minutes into the sermon when Beulah Mae stopped rocking the chair. The young preacher, who had been running down the sins he felt were bringing reproach upon the nation, had introduced a point about how those who were 'forcing the mixing of the races through school desegregation' were destroying the moral fiber of America.

Yes, anticipated Beulah Mae guiltily, *now lets hear him preach the white supremacy.*

"To dare to mix what God has left unmixed," Huxtable's voice cried out, "to dare to mix the White race of men with that of the Negro, a race which of all of Adam's offspring is the most base, unfortunate and undisciplined...that mixing is a sin that will not be winked at! And until we repent of desegregation, this nation will continue to suffer the punishment that comes to those who refuse to protect the purity of our education system!" Hearty 'Amen's' were again heard in the background.

Beulah Mae leaned over and mashed STOP. She pulled her Social Security cheque from her gown pocket and looked it over again, this time grinning as mischievously as a teenager.

Rising carefully from the rocker she removed the cassette tape, and made her way lightly across the pine floor to her roll-top desk that sat in the opposite corner of the room. She then retrieved a simple white envelope from a desk drawer marked ENVELOPES. Beulah Mae put the cassette tape into the envelope, drew several long strips of Scotch Tape from a dispenser, and secured the cassette inside. After reaching for a pen from a drawer marked PENS, she hesitated. Beulah Mae was considering to whom she might send the tape. She knew that she would send the tape to either CNN or ROX News, since she regularly split her T.V. time between the two networks.

Now, she thought, CNN is owned by that Ted Turner fellow, and she had heard that he did not even believe in God, so why trust him with it? But what about ROX? She did enjoy watching that Cal Limkey fellow, who seemed like a fair minded person, though his arrogance had begun to grate on her as of late. Still, something gave Beulah Mae pause about ROX News, but what was it? Oh yes, of course, now she remembered, it had to do with Bill Clinton. She recalled a memory of an interview that Bill had granted to ROX News, but that Chris Waller fellow had been very rude to her Bill.

"Uh huh," Beulah Mae said loudly enough to wake Belle, who gave her an annoyed stare before going back to sleep. Beulah Mae then put pen to envelope and wrote "*CNN*," and then under that she wrote "*To the attention of Mr. Wolf Blitzer.*" Under Blitzer's name she wrote in bold letters, ***IMPORTANT: HUXTABLE CLOSET RACIST, PROOF INSIDE.***

After adding an address and the words "Certified Mail" on the envelope, Beulah Mae Deal began her slow trip back to the mailbox. It had been decades since she had made two trips to the mailbox on the same day, but the Social Security Cheque in her gown pocket made her somehow feel lighter on her feet, almost as if she could dance a jig. She moved slowly and carefully, inexorably toward the mailbox--and history.

As soon as CNN had verified the recording as authentic, the network began to loop the recording, with complete sub-text, every hour for a solid week, and several times a day thereafter. Most other major networks followed suit. The old sermon was soon posted to YOUTUBE, going viral almost immediately with millions of hits within a few hours.

The Huxtable campaign was caught like a deer in the headlights; flatfooted, clueless, confounded, and about to be run over. Unable to explain why he had hidden the fact that he had been a staunch segregationist as a young man, Huxtable spun it as best he could and took on the demeanor of a semi-penitent. And though he soldiered on for the remainder of the campaign, his once winning smile now seemed forced and insincere. It was over.

Come election day, Huxtable still carried most of the 'Red States,' including most of the deep South, Utah, and Alaska. But that was about it. Soloto bested him in the critical, Electoral Vote-rich states of Ohio, Florida, California and New York. It was not quite a landslide, yet Soloto's victory was secured well before midnight.

Secure--but not complete.

Because there was another factor at work on election night. A month before the election, with Huxtable stumbling more every day, Soloto had had to face the issue of a bankrupt California.

Due to massive State debts built up over decades, the State of California had stopped paying its bills, first to contractors, then to unionized State employees and retirees.

The outcry was loud enough to be heard in the White House, and Soloto, realizing he could not take a chance on losing California and its fifty-five Electoral College votes, signed an Executive Order that guaranteed the debt of the State of California to be paid in full, backed by the Full Faith and Credit of the United States Federal Government.

California was pacified, but the 'Red State' voters went ballistic, claiming that all U.S. taxpayers were now saddled with the debt of the 'Left Coast Californians.'

Rebellion against what was dubbed the 'California Bailout' was seen and heard across the fly-over hinterlands of America and throughout the South.

Leading the outcry was the 'Revolution Party,' a grass-roots series of gatherings that had swept across the nation soon after Soloto was first elected President.

Called the 'Rev. Party' for short, these angry, rowdy millions called for a hopefully blood-less Revolution that would overthrow what they believed to be the Socialization of America.

Soloto's bailout of California gave the Rev. Party just enough momentum in the Red States to boost their candidates, and on election night the Rev. Party incredibly captured a full one-third of the seats in Congress.

But it was in Georgia that the fury over the California Bailout, like the weather in summer, seemed hotter than anywhere else in America. The Rev. Party voters in Georgia were so disgusted that they threw their entire support to a man named Jim Cummins, an underdog candidate for Governor of Georgia.

Jim Cummins won their hearts by making a solemn vow that, if elected, he would see that not one red cent of Georgia taxpayer money would go to pay for the California Bailout, even if it meant that the D.C. government not be allowed to collect any Interior Proceeds Taxes within the State!

And to add fuel to the fire, Cummins further promised to have the California Bailout, along with all other unconstitutional laws, declared 'Null and Void' within the borders of what Cummins called the 'Sovereign State of Georgia.'

Finally, Cummins promised that if Soloto and the feds tried to force Georgia citizens to ante-up for the 'Bailout' or other 'Socialized Schemes' then that would be the signal for him as Governor to call a Convention to Consider the Secession of Georgia from the Union!

And so, on the same night that saw Soloto retain the White House, the people of Georgia, by one half of one percent, put Jim Cummins into the Governor's Mansion in the State of Georgia.

So there it lay. Before Soloto and the whole country lay the promise of a newly elected Governor to resist, by all necessary means, the Will and Power of the federal government of the United States. Though few outside of Georgia believed Cummins would carry out his threats, President Soloto saw no other choice except to confront this bold challenge to his administration and to the very foundation of the Nation.

PROLOGUE
PART II

After any election, the winning politician begins to consider which campaign promises he intends to keep, and to get busy keeping them, or at least appearing to keep them.

Soloto knew that promises were one thing, but deals are quite another. A promise is vague and political, a thing soft enough to be reshaped and adjusted. But deals were hard, specific commitments that were much more difficult to ignore. Deals made with powerful, influential people were ones that could not be ignored or merely dismissed with political double-speak.

And Soloto *had* made a deal to ensure his re-election. It was a deal concerning campaign money, as is usually the case since campaigns had become so expensive in the U.S.

In a secret, un-logged Oval Office meeting six months prior to the election, Soloto had met with Ken Rothfellow, Chairman of the National Bank Reserve, the private banking cartel that controlled interest rates and the money supply in America, and therefore in much of the world.

Also present at the meeting six months before was Soloto's Treasury Secretary Tag Tower, as well as Jim LeGrant, the head of the nations largest investment bank, Silverfox Capital Investments.

Before coming to Treasury, Tower had been the CEO at Silverfox. And LeGrant, before taking the helm at Silverfox, had been a deputy at Treasury.

Tower and LeGrant were only two of the figures who moved back and forth through the revolving door connecting Wall Street and the Washington D.C. Government. The financial regulators who were supposed to flag this conflict of interest had also been enriched by the cozy relationship between the big banks and D.C., so they looked the other way.

Everyone at that meeting had needs. Soloto's campaign needed a large influx of cash for a final push for re-election, and the National Bank Reserve needed value-security for the US dollar.

The Wall Street bank, Silverfox, was a necessary part of the scheme to funnel the money through the financial apparatus, lending it a veil of legality. For its participation in the deal, Silverfox stood to make huge profits, much of which would be divided among its top executives as bonuses. The bonuses would attract some unwanted attention but were necessary as hush money to keep executives from blowing the whistle on the deal. By the time the public found out what had happened, all the major players would have long since bailed out with golden parachutes.

The NBR actually had the greatest need, and it involved regime change, or at least regime dissuasion, in the Middle East. Because the NBR had created so much new money during the recent financial crisis, it was running the dangerous risk of hyper-inflation, which occurs when there are too many dollars chasing too few goods and the money loses its value rapidly.

The only thing still supporting the value of the dollar was that foreign nations needed dollars to purchase oil. Most of the world's oil trades were denominated in U.S. dollars, or 'petro-dollars.'

With the dollar holding this world-reserve status, America had wildly printed money since World War II, artificially boosting her own standard of living. That is why the National Bank Reserve could not afford to allow any major oil-producing nation to stop trading oil for dollars.

When Saddam Hussein had attempted that very thing in the year 2000, it was only a few years before American tanks rolled into Baghdad and Saddam found himself dangling from the end of an executioners' rope.

Bush had taken care of Iraq, but what about neighboring oil-rich Iran, which was now taking actions to end its own oil-for-dollar sales? Iran had to be dealt with, lest America become another Weimar Republic.

And so the NBR, America's lender of last resort, needed to cut a deal with the US military to put a stop to Iran's plan to sell their oil in a different currency. The very standard of living in America depended on it. The commander-in-chief of the military had to be persuaded to effect the change in Iran. Fortunately for all involved, it was an election year, a time for deals to be cut. After serving the guests drinks, Soloto was ready to get down to business.

"Gentlemen," began the President, "though this meeting never took place, I think we should get on with it." There were chuckles all around the room. Soloto remembered to turn on the scrambler sitting on his desk, a device that made it impossible for any voice recording to be made of the meeting.

"Fellows, as you know, I'm in a very close and heated race for re-election. My pollsters tell me that I can still pull it off, provided I have enough cash to flood the country with television ads for the next six months. But T.V. time is expensive, and that is why we are here."

"We understand, Mr. President, and speaking for the NBR, we want to see you re-elected. I personally think you deserve four more years, and as always, 'The Bank' is ready to do its part to help," said Rothfellow.

Soloto knew there was something 'The Bank' wanted in return for their 'support,' and was waiting for the quid pro quo. "How much money will it take to help you reach your goal, Mr. President?"

The President was sitting on the edge of his desk, at a higher level than the bankers who relaxed on sofas. Soloto looked down at the floor, hesitating before spitting out the amount needed.

"My people tell me it will take about six hundred million to cover all the production and broadcasting costs of the infomercials we need to get our message across. I am told that we can keep about a third of that off the books through, shall we say, creative methods of purchasing. Our friends in the non-profits will help us with that. That means about four hundred million will be on record with the FEC, but it will take six hundred to crack the nut. I know that is a lot, but this economy is a tremendous drag on my campaign."

Six hundred million dollars. The amount seemed staggering to Soloto, but to the man with the money machine, it wasn't that big a deal. It only had to be created out of thin air; it wasn't as if the money had to come from trade or earnings.

"Mr. President, we can handle that figure easily," replied the Bank Chairman, "but the dollar is our stock. Actually, it's the stock of the country as a whole. And we do have a *problem* we need help with. What we have is a viable threat to the value of the dollar coming from the Middle East. Sir, as you already know, the rogue, terrorist nation of Iran is about to finalize its plan to open an Oil Bourse, or Trade-Center, on the island of Kish. Since Iran is floating on an ocean of oil, they have leverage. With the help of their Russian and Chinese allies, Iran can soon begin to double their pumping capacity, flooding the market with a high grade of sweet crude.

"Mr. President, if the Iranians combine over-production with trades made in Euros and other non-dollar currencies, our dollar is going to take the worst hit it has had since the Civil War. The bottom line is that we at the Bank realize the danger Iran now presents to our country. We need the Iranians to be made to feel the consequences of opening this anti-

American trade center, and of their attempt to destroy our currency. Their hatred of our freedom and prosperity seems to know no bounds." Soloto nodded his head with understanding approval.

"Ken, I want you to know how much I appreciate your willingness to work with us on this thing. I can assure you that we are all concerned about Iran and its desire to have nuclear weapons" said Soloto, though Rothfellow has said nothing about nukes. "My administration believes that Iran must be dealt with. I have talked with the Secretary of Defense and others at the Pentagon, and they are definitely on board with our view of the situation. But before we discuss that, I want us to iron out the details of funding this campaign. Now, Tag, will you and Mr. LeGrant of Silverfox explain how this process will work?"

"Certainly, Mr. President," said Tower. "Jim and I have already discussed the nuts and bolts of the process. The money will be secured from the Bank, part of it in cash--about a third. The other two-thirds will be moved through Silverfox as part of reinvestment funds." He meant bail-out funds but knew that the President did not want the words 'bail-out' used in the Oval Office.

"Mr. LeGrant," asked the President, "what type of compensation would Silverfox need to get this done?"

"Mr. President, sir," responded LeGrant nervously, "normally, we could handle something like this at ten percent. But given the current atmosphere, and considering the regulators that will need persuasion to overlook these transactions, we will need to be at twenty percent on this deal."

Wow, thought Soloto, *twenty percent of two-thirds of six hundred million dollars!* If the President had his math right, that would be eighty million dollars that the executives at Silverfox would be able to pocket, minus a few percent that would go to bribe regulators. But Soloto knew he could not raise the money any other way, and he had to have it to get re-elected.

"Sounds fair," replied the President. "And now, about the Iranian problem. As you know, our ground forces are already spread thin holding down Iraq and Afghanistan, not to mention our other commitments in over a hundred countries around the world; therefore, I have asked the Pentagon to prepare a plan of attack that would utilize attacks from the air only, using a combination of bombers and cruise missile strikes. We have targets identified in Iran that they are using in their nuclear program. Now, we will need some extra funding to get political cover from our contacts at the International Atomic Energy Agency, and from a few key Heads of State at the UN. This will ensure that we have confirmation of the Iranian nuclear ambitions."

"We can handle that, Mr. President," replied the Bank Chairman. "But, sir, we must have an iron-clad commitment on Kish. That is where the Oil Bourse is being set up. We need that island razed, sir. In fact, we were hoping that a tactical nuclear weapon might be used on Kish, just as a--shall we say-- a way of adding an exclamation point to our conviction that petro-dollars must continue to be used in the Middle East and throughout the world. Nothing like a mushroom cloud to give shade to the dollar...and remind the world who runs things."

The room went silent for a moment as it sank into the minds of all present that the NBR had just suggested using a nuclear weapon against a civilian target.

Tag Tower saw a look of shock on the President's face, but did not want him to have to respond to the powerful Bank Chairman's suggestion.

"Ken, I'm sure Kish can be dealt with," injected Tower quickly, "but should we not let the military guys decide what ordnance is best to fit the situation? Besides, no one really wants to open the nuclear Pandora's box again." Tower added a sheepish, unconvincing chuckle. But Tower's attempt to save face for Soloto was not enough, and the President felt the need to brush the Bank Chairman back a bit.

"Mr. Chairman, the Bank is not actually suggesting that I authorize the use of a nuclear weapon against Iran, now, is it?" said Soloto with a strong hiss of challenge in his voice.

At that the Chairman simply rose from the sofa and walked casually over to the beverage table sitting near a window as the others in the room sat amazed that he would dare turn his back to the President of the United States during a conversation. Who did this guy think he was, the money god? But Rothfellow seemed unfazed, and the others, including Soloto, suddenly realized that this was not the first geo-political deal that the NBR had made with a sitting President. After all, it *was* the Bank and not Congress who actually controlled the purse strings of the American empire, as well as interest rates, so who could say that the Chairman was not the most powerful man in the room at the time?

"Abe," the Chairman said, calling the President by his first name amidst the clinking of crystal as he poured himself a drink, "I want to emphasize how important it is to the Bank that Kish be dealt with. Iraq was important, but the people in that region can be quite dull, and few seemed to get the message we were sending."

Rothfellow turned now and walked over to where the President was sitting. Pausing to take a drink, he looked Soloto in the eye and continued.

"We want Iran to be given such a blow that the other oil rich nations--Venezuela, Saudi Arabia, even Russia--will have any and all doubts removed as to the consequences of failing to trade their oil in Dollars. We are coming to a major crossroads in World History. Things are changing fast, and if this new century will be ours, then the dollar must be protected by *all necessary means.*" Rothfellow punctuated those last three words by punching the air with his glass, the ice cubes clinking with each thrust.

Tower grew more worried when he saw his boss Soloto stiffen with anger, preparing to defend his own power and position as the most powerful man in the room. Tower started to speak up again, but the President beat him to it as he stood to face Rothfellow squarely.

"Mr. Chairman," Soloto said with a stern, unpleasant voice, "please understand something; Yes, I want to win this election, and I need the Bank's help to do it. But that does not mean that I will be given orders to detonate a nuclear device. I will not open that door!"

"We had Truman to open that door in 1945, Mr. President," replied Rothfellow with no hesitation. Everyone heard what Rothfellow said, but no one knew if he meant 'we' the U.S. or 'we' the NBR, was responsible for Nagasaki and Hiroshima. "It cost a lot of money to load the Enola Gay. Mr. President, where do you think that money came from?"

Soloto seemed at a loss for words. He walked over to study a picture of Lincoln hanging on the wall. Looking at it helped him remember that Lincoln had been willing to do anything, no matter how morally or legally questionable, to win his war and his elections. Soloto turned slowly back to face the other three men.

"Mr. Chairman, Mr. Tower and Mr. LeGrant will work out the details of the exchange with you. I assure you that Iran will feel the painful consequences of attacking the U.S. currency. And I further assure you and your Bank that

21

the island of Kish will be left a smoking pile of rubble, whether it be bombed conventionally or otherwise. Thank you Gentlemen," he concluded sternly. "That will be all."

Soloto turned back to face the Lincoln portrait, signaling that he would have the last word. The other men rose and began to shuffle towards the door, but they could hardly believe that the NBR Chairman paused and turned, daring to speak again. But what he had to say sent chills up every spine, including the President's.

"Fine, Mr. President, the NBR will cooperate. We at 'The Bank' believe in supporting our Presidents. We have been supportive of every one of them since Woodrow Wilson--all except Kennedy, that is. JFK was such an unimaginative man, and died so poorly. He never did understand the role of 'The Bank'--America's Bank. What a pity!"

Chapter One

The Oval Office
The White House
Washington, D.C.

With his re-election now behind him and his second term beginning, President Abraham Soloto gathered his ten most senior and trusted advisors with him in the Oval Office for an important strategy session. It is time, he told them, to set the tone and establish my legacy as President, and that means making bold moves. The meeting dragged on late into the evening, the longest and most intense meeting anyone present could recall.

There were many concerns on the Presidential radar screen-- the wars dragging on in the Middle East, the situation with Iran, the response to global climate change. And while all of these items were important, the red-button issue foremost on everyone's mind was the situation in the State of Georgia, where a loud mouthed Governor was making trouble for the President, and the nation.

Every political hack in the room agreed that major political moves had to be made by Soloto, and made quickly, though no one agreed on what those moves should be. The noise from Georgia grew louder everyday, and everyday the authority of the President was being challenged by that man in Atlanta, Jim Cummins. Something had to be done to quell him, and assure everyone who was in charge of the country.

After nearly three hours of discussion, the President finally pushed his chair away from his desk and rose to his feet, a sign that he had come to a conclusion. The room became silent. Looking around at every face in the room, he spoke with finality:

"I'm going to Atlanta! There I will deliver a major policy speech aimed directly at this belligerent Governor Cummins."

Soloto began to pace the room now as he spoke, his hands locked behind his back.

"I'll use this major speech to announce that the CIA has uncovered a plot by the nation of Iran to smuggle a nuclear weapon into the United States." Soloto paused to let that sink in. Jaws were dropping all over the room as eyes widened at what the leader of the free world had just said.

23

"In this speech," continued Soloto, "I will announce that our intelligence agencies have further learned that the Iranians are only days away from obtaining weapon's grade uranium, and that they are planning to hand the bomb off to their terrorist friends in Hamas. I will also say that Hamas has a terrorist cell there, in that very city of Atlanta, and that we have discovered plans that Hamas wants to use that cell to smuggle the nuke into the country and..." Soloto stopped pacing to deliver the next phrase..."to detonate it right there in the capital city of Atlanta, Georgia."

Cheers and clapping erupted throughout the Oval Office as the gathered brain-trust of the Soloto administration realized what a political masterstroke their President and leader had just announced. They saw immediately that Soloto would, in one fail swoop, neutralize the arrogance of the Governor of Georgia by proving that only the power of the D.C. government was able to prevent the destruction of his own State, and at the same time unite the rest of the country behind Soloto as Commander in Chief with his stand against Iranian terror. He would accomplish all of this in a speech delivered at the Georgia Governor's very doorstep!

The group quieted as Soloto continued to outline what was soon to be dubbed his 'Atlanta Strategy.'

"I'll deliver the speech on the most patriotic day of the year, the Fourth of July. People, we are aiming for the perfect spot for the speech, the perfect venue, as well as the perfect time. We have the perfect base of support in the city, with its millions of African Americans; and we can emphasize the civil rights history, where King got his start, even emphasize the Civil War history, where Lincoln and Sherman secured freedom with the March to the Sea. I'll follow right in the wake of those great freedom fighters, and I'll paint this ridiculous Governor Jim Cummins fellow as just another racist, neo-confederate who is bent on destroying this great country. And by doing it in Atlanta, it will show the whole country and the whole world that I am firmly in control of this country and that no challenge to this government's authority has a chance, whether that challenge comes from without or within!"

Soloto's advisors hummed with praise. They loved the idea and realized afresh why this man, who only a few years ago was just a community activist in Detroit, had risen like a blazing meteor. His natural political savvy and insight were simply amazing to behold.

The President's Chief of Staff, Eli Brandenburg, felt it was his place to be the first among the group to add follow-up suggestions.

"Perfect, Mr. President! And the best part about it is that there is nothing that this Cummins person can do to stop you. You'll make him look like the fool he is, in the eyes of the whole country. And we can bring the Vice President on stage with you, some of our party's Congressional leadership as well. It will present a front of solidarity that will reinforce a strong image and thoroughly embarrass this nut case Governor Cummins."

"Nice touch, Eli," complimented the President. Brandenburg smiled brightly, proud of himself.

"I agree with the idea; but Eli, let's not call it a 'front' or an 'image,'" replied Henry LeBeau, a rival advisor. "This President and his administration are constitutionally elected and legally sound through and through. No need to put up any front or façade."

It was none other than Henry 'Hank' LeBeau offering this correction of Brandenburg's ideas. LeBeau was the President's top campaign and political advisor, and a bitter rival to the Chief of Staff.

Chief of Staff Brandenburg, offended by LeBeau's insinuation, glared at the other man with zero attempt to conceal his contempt for the man.

Those two had some bad history between them. Brandenburg, the younger of the two rivals, was a former congressman whom the President had chosen as his COS for his ability to move legislation through the House and Senate, and to maintain party discipline. No one played that game of pork-barrel payoffs better than Brandenburg. So competitive was Brandenburg that in his off-time he competed in mixed martial arts, keeping himself in great shape. As COS, he suggested the Presidential schedule from day to day, as well as screening all requests for face-time with The Man.

LeBeau, on the other hand, was a sixty-three year old career political advisor, a pure and brilliant political animal, often called the 'Carl Rove of the left.' LeBeau had been the director of Soloto's stunning Presidential campaign victories, both of them come-from-behind wins. He considered himself very close to the President, but he had already had many run-ins with Brandenburg, a man he considered to be a rude and obnoxious upstart.

On several occasions during Soloto's first term in the Oval Office, the COS had denied LeBeau's requests to see the President in off-schedule, impromptu meetings that LeBeau considered politically urgent. Hard looks and harsh words had passed between the two rivals, and though he could not be sure, LeBeau suspected that Brandenburg had advised the President to dump LeBeau from his team now that the re-election campaign was over.

There was a time when LeBeau had considered Brandenburg a friend, but that time had long passed. The COS had sought to push a very strong leftist agenda through Congress during Soloto's first term, a mistake LeBeau had advised against as both arrogant and foolish. LeBeau's views were as liberal as anyone's, yet he felt that the second term was the time to push hard with that agenda, not the first term.

And because of that, LeBeau had had to work doubly hard to portray the President as more of a centrist so that he *could be* re-elected.

As campaign manager, he had worked upwards of seventeen hours a day, every day, over the past six months to get this job done. The result was that LeBeau had barely seen his family in months, and his marriage was strained to the point of separation. His health had suffered along with his personal life and there was often a tightness in his chest, though he had told no one about it in fear of losing his position to a younger man. Brandenburg was the easiest target of blame for LeBeau's trouble, and now the two men neither liked nor trusted one another.

Soloto had noticed the snipping back and forth between the two which grew worse by the week. The fact was that both men had hinted that the President should let the other go. Soloto knew he might have to solve the problem by dumping one of the men, but he considered them both irreplaceable members of his team. He would try, as Lincoln had done ages before, to hold together a team of rivals.

There, in the Oval Office, the air between the two remained tense, and Brandenburg could not let LeBeau's challenge go un-parried.

"Henry, don't be stupid! You know I did not mean to imply that the President put up a façade," said the COS to LeBeau. To Soloto he said, "Mr. President, I simply meant a 'front' as in the frontal assault while in battle. And this is certainly a political battle we are in with this rogue Governor of Georgia."

LeBeau rolled his eyes at what he considered the lameness of Brandenburg's rhetoric. But the President had had enough, staring both men down with a disapproving glare.

"Gentlemen, let's work together! Remember, we are all on the same team here, and it's *my* team! We *will* all work together and in unison; and if not, I will find people who can. Is that understood?" asked Soloto harshly.

The room was very quiet now as both the COS and political advisor bowed their heads sheepishly, like children scolded by a father. Soloto, for his part, left no doubt as to who was running the show. Having re-established control of the meeting, the President continued.

"All right then, I am meeting in the Situation Room downstairs with the Directors of the NSA and the CIA to craft the Iranian evidence. I want the rest of you to be back at your desks by six in the morning working on the Atlanta event. People, understand me: I want this Atlanta speech to be, not just a speech, but an EVENT! I want perfect coordination between the Travel Office and the Press Office. I want this to be the most perfectly planned event of my Presidency to date. I want bands and bunting; I want children and balloons; I want it all. My entire legacy as President hangs now on this one event, and if there is even the slightest glitch, from a malfunctioning teleprompter to a missing hors d'oeuvre, I want resignations on THAT desk within hours," said Soloto as he pointed to his executive mahogany.

"From this moment until the Fourth of July, each of you will make this event in Atlanta, Georgia, the very focal point of your entire career." He paused to let the room digest it, then added, "Call all the networks and cable providers, including Al-Jazera. Let them know I want this speech to go out to the entire nation and the world. Now--make it happen. Good night."

With that everyone rose and filed quietly out, leaving the President alone. He wasted no time, calling his evening secretary for a fresh pot of coffee. His wife would have to turn in without him tonight. Soloto sat down at his desk, reached for his keyboard, and began to compose perhaps the most important Presidential address of his career.

Chapter Two

Air Force One
In the skies over the State of Georgia
Nearing Atlanta

President Abraham Soloto loved traveling on Air Force One. The converted jumbo jet was unique, and uniquely American, a feat of technology that featured the finest of everything.

Hundreds of millions of dollars had been spent to convert the Boeing 747 into a flying office-fortress-luxury hotel that had every tool that the President of the United States could possibly use to perform his duties while in the air. Costing more to operate per hour than most Americans earn in one year, this was a ride fit for an Emperor, much less a President. It even boasted an operating theatre and gym.

And on this beautiful July morning, Air Force One was cruising through the airspace over the State of Georgia, its destination the capital city of Atlanta.

Seated behind his desk in his comfortable office located midway of the fuselage, President Soloto was enjoying that sense of accomplishment that few men in history had been privileged to feel, that which belonged to an American President who had fought through a first term and been re-elected by the American people.

Soloto pondered those thoughts as he leaned back in his high-back leather swivel chair, his hands folded behind his head. And he thought of the business he had in Atlanta, business ushered on by the recent election.

From his lips hung a Marlboro cigarette. He took a heavy drag, holding the smoke in his lungs a moment before slowly exhaling. Smoking was a bad habit he had honestly tried to quit, but Soloto had discovered, much as his political ally Bill Clinton before him, that just because they call you President doesn't mean you lose all your bad habits.

So, at least for the moment, Soloto allowed himself to enjoy the nicotine rush as he meditated on the events of the past few months and on what he would say in Atlanta. He had the script of the speech, the final of nearly a hundred drafts and re-writes, on the desk before him and was now going through it yet again, reading it out loud to make sure he had just the right inflection on each word and phrase.

In the cockpit of the massive aircraft sat Colonel Dick McGrudder, a veteran pilot who had been at the controls of Air Force One for nearly twelve years.

The airplane of the President of the United States is by far the most sophisticated and expensive airliner in history and not just anyone is allowed to fly it. But McGrudder was a special kind of pilot. If measured by experience and training, McGrudder would rank as one of the top four or five pilots in the world. He had flown every kind of aircraft under every condition, including in heavy combat zones.

Few other pilots as professional and polished as McGrudder could come off as jocular and friendly, but McGrudder was known to all those on the Presidential travel detail as both highly competent and a lot of fun to be around.

McGrudder did not have to be there, he could have retired years before. But for a man who had flown both fighter and bomber missions in the skies over battlefields everywhere from Vietnam to Kosovo, McGrudder now had the best pilot seat in the world. So, he reasoned, why give it up until they forced him to?

This day found him guiding Air Force One towards Atlanta. From his first day at the Air Force Academy in Colorado Springs, McGrudder had been known for his coolness under pressure. Yet at this moment in the cockpit of Air Force One, there was a slight tremble in his hand as he fingered the stubble on his chin. He could hardly believe the exchange he had just had with someone at his destination; Hartsfield-Jackson International Airport in Atlanta.

The co-pilot had also been privy to the conversation, and wanted to weigh in on it.

"I'm not believing this—" the co-pilot started to say, but McGrudder's hand snapped in the air, stopping the other man mid-sentence. McGrudder was not generally short with people, but he needed a moment to think without interruption, and his co-pilot was too often a windbag.

McGrudder took a deep breath, steadied himself, and thumbed his mic switch to call Vince Jones, head of the Secret Service detail responsible for the hour-by-hour safety of the President. Jones was also designated, at the President's request, as the Personal Protector to the President, which meant Jones was the agent who stayed closest to The Man in all his public movements. If anyone ever took a shot at this President, it was most likely to be Jones that would be the sponge to absorb it.

"Vince, we have a situation here," said McGrudder, surprising himself with the calmness of his voice.

"Mechanical?" replied Jones's voice in the pilot's earpiece.

"No, the bird is fine, but I've just received a strange call from the airport in Atlanta. You better come up here right away."

Vince Jones, stationed just outside the President's office, hesitated to leave the President's side even in a secure atmosphere like Air Force One. Yet something in the pilot's voice, taken with the news that had been coming out of Atlanta lately, made him excuse himself from the corridor area where he had positioned himself.

Jones was not the only security person who had been just a bit nervous about this Atlanta trip since the President had insisted on making it. It was rumored around the White House that the President felt that he would be left looking weak and irrelevant by recent events if he did not create positive momentum going into his second term. Jones cared little about the politics of the situation as his concern was with the security and safety of the President alone.

He knew that the 'Revolution Party,' or Rev. Party as it was being called, had ramped up their rhetoric to pure fever pitch, and even some of Soloto's supporters had expressed concern about his safety.

As an African-American President, Soloto had decided that this speech had to take place in Atlanta, which had become a kind of black-capital of the New South. And though the particulars of the speech had been closely guarded, Jones knew that it was designed to both cool down the President's opposition and at the same time encourage his base of support.

The address would be given before an audience of over fifty-thousand conventioneers gathered at the annual meeting of the League of Urban Growth and Renewal. And though Georgia was considered a very 'Red' State with what some were calling an 'unbalanced' Governor who spoke of Nullification and even Secession, the Atlanta City Government was solidly in the control of Soloto supporters. Atlanta had promised the President both a warm welcome and an extra measure of security.

The Secret Service ran its own show and paid the barest attention to the promises of the city governments, yet the Service had detected no actual threats to the President's safety in the Atlanta area despite the blusterous talk.

Before he left his post to walk to the cockpit, Jones looked in on the President, but Soloto was busy with a phone call and did not look up at Jones. He left the President uninterrupted this time, though he usually informed him when he had to temporarily leave his post. Jones turned now towards the airplane's cockpit, moving with a quicker gait than normal, though not so quick as to call attention or cause alarm.

As he approached the cockpit door he noticed an agent standing guard there, this one a female agent named Tamara Underhill.

Underhill had been with the Service for seven years and her service record was nearly spotless. She was a fine agent, and seeing the look on Agent Jones's face as he approached caused her to step aside without having to be asked to do so.

Despite the fact that the cockpit door was reinforced, bulletproof and triple hinged, Jones could hear excited voices from within. Unlocking duel locks with his personal set of keys, Jones was perhaps the most professional personal protector in the world, yet was growing more concerned by the second.

There were always minor concerns on these Presidential flights, but something felt out of place. Something eerie was in the air. Yet he knew that whatever it turned out to be, he must not let his concern morph into anxiety. *Manage this*, he ordered himself, *from beginning to end manage yourself.*

Jones had often meditated on the difference, subtle yet drastic, between the concern due a thing versus the kind of worry that bred panic. Agent Jones was extremely well trained, as fit as in his days as an Army Ranger. He was dead-on accurate with three kinds of firearms. Fluent in Arabic, the language spoken by many well-intentioned people but also by the most dangerous of terrorists, Jones could pick up cross-talk in a crowd that might indicate a threat--a phrase uttered out of place, a nuance of extremism.

This senior agent was known as a control freak around the Service, fanatic about being able to determine every detail of his environment whether at work or at home.

Such was Jones' devotion to discipline that it was whispered within the Service that he even had a bathroom scale that digitally measured his weight to the nearest quarter of a pound, which he could manipulate with precision through exact portions of food, exercise, and sleep.

Though he was the master of many disciplines important to his trade, Vince had found his own emotion, his passion, the toughest thing to master.

Emotion is often useful, he had been taught by his psy-ops instructors. It is most useful when it fuels ones cause. But let it seep into the workings of the mind and it was like pouring sand into an engine. Things then would not work as they should, the mind would betray you. Presently, he was through the door and in the cockpit.

"O.K.," said Jones, speaking with a no-nonsense tone directly to the pilot, ignoring the co-pilot who had started to speak out of turn again. "What is the concern here, Dick?"

"Vince, thanks for coming up. We just received a call from Hartsfield-Jackson over the secure frequency telling us that we are not cleared for landing. Let me play the exchange for you." McGrudder ordered the co-pilot to roll the tape and then monitor current radio traffic in case someone tried to contact them while the tape rolled. The co-pilot hit a few buttons to re-set the compact disc for play, then slipped his own head-set over his ears to monitor radio traffic.

The tape began to play. The first voice to be heard was baritone and unfamiliar to Jones, yet unique in that it carried a southern drawl so thick that it fairly dripped with cane syrup.

"Air Force One, be advised that y'all are hereby denied clearance for landing. I say again, you may not land at Hartsfield-Jackson Airport today. Now don't have a hissy fit, fellers. Just simply make the necessary flight schedule changes...now."

The next voice was that of McGrudder with the good-natured reply that the pilot had made in response.

"Hartsfield-Jackson, this is Air Force One, and we can tell you good ole boys are having some fun today. But they don't give us much leeway for joking around, so please be advised that we will be landing on schedule within thirty minutes at your front door. I need runway assignment." It was at this point that things began to turn ominous.

"Air Force One, be advised that the State of Georgia hereby denies you clearance to land at Hartsfield-Jackson Airport in Atlanta, Georgia, on this Day of Our Lord the Third of July. This, sir, no-sir, is not a joke at all--this, I repeat, is neither a prank nor a jest of any kind. Sir, you will not put that bird down hear today!"

The voice had spoken with authority and seriousness, and McGrudder's reply showed that the pilot was upset by its tone and content.

"This is Colonel Dick McGrudder, pilot of Air Force One of the United States of America. We bear the President of the United States. I request that you state your name and the situation on the ground there."

McGrudder's voice was as hard and sharp as a cut diamond, but the response that followed bore no less of an edge.

"McGrudder, this is Governor Jim Cummins, duly elected Chief Executive of the Sovereign State of Georgia. You are denied permission and access to our airport, Hartsfield-Jackson, in Atlanta, a city which I remind you is IN the Sovereign State of Georgia. Now, that is the situation on the ground. The situation is none other than I have just stated. Y'all are not welcome here and will not be allowed to land here today. To ensure the safety of your President I advise you to change course immediately. Have I made myself perfectly clear?" Then there was a pause on the tape, because McGrudder had not made immediate reply. The voice from the airport hesitated a moment longer, then ordered with a strain of anger, "Acknowledge! Acknowledge that you have received my clear instructions!" Then another short pause before the pilot's voice answered more slowly and darkly.

"Air Force One acknowledges your transmission."

That last reply was obligatory and had been uttered by McGrudder in a low and bitter tone, one that you would expect from a former fighter pilot when challenged and angry. McGrudder looked up at Agent Jones, signifying that had been his last transmission.

As the tape ended, Jones's face was poker and ash. The words of Governor Cummins--"for the safety of your President"-- hung in the air of the cockpit like acrid stench. Jones clinched his teeth, causing the muscle along his jaw to tighten and protrude, his lips drawn to a pucker. His eyes were cold as they stare out of the cockpit's front glass. The sky was blue and beautiful, but the plane was still at cruising altitude and his eyes could not yet make the outline of the city of Atlanta.

Behind those eyes his cool mind was deep in thought, already reviewing different courses of action and the consequences of each to the third or fourth step. That is the difference, Vince had been taught, between common men and exceptional men--thinking not just of a reaction, but reasoning its consequence, and what subsequent consequences would be generated at step three, four and five.

Think it through, he commanded himself.

The co-pilot again opened his mouth to offer his opinion but was cut short yet again, this time by the sharp snap of Jones's hand. Jones was the kind of man who could stop you in your tracks in a number of different ways, and didn't dread doing it.

In the silence of the moment it took Jones precisely seven seconds to mentally map out his next six actions in response to the situation--contact the fighter jets that always escorted Air Force One and notify them of the possible change in flight schedule, brief the President on the situation and get his orders, gather the security detail on the plane and brief them, relay a message to his own people in D.C., contact the lead team on the ground at Hartsfield-Jackson, and finally, upon the President's approval, unlock the weapon's bay and issue the assault rifles to his team.

The last step he thought probably unnecessary but demanded by Service protocol. If a possible threat to the President exists, every agent must be fully armed. And having a single handgun was not considered fully armed.

Throughout the history of the Secret Service, there had been many serious threats to the life of the President. The public would never learn about most of them, but Jones had never even heard of, much less been confronted by, a situation like this.

The voice transmitting from the airport had definitely come over the frequency used exclusively by Air Force One. It was the most secure frequency in the world, carrying dialogue using the world's most advanced encryption technology. And the voice claiming to be that of the Governor of Georgia was very serious about denying the President's plane clearance to land.

In Jones's opinion the voice contained some man's sense of honour, and had the ring of a man who meant to keep his word. Yet how could all this be happening? The lead team at Hartsfield-Jackson had sounded no alarm as to any situation on the ground. But even if that well armed team managed to secure the airport for landing, a jumbo jet like Air Force One makes for a big target to any maniac who meant the President harm.

"How far out are we from the airport?" asked Jones.

"About twenty-three minutes," replied McGrudder.

"Stay your course for five more minutes, and slow us down a bit if possible to give us a little more time. If I have not called you back in ten, change course for your secondary landing choice--no, wait, what is your second landing choice for this flight?"

McGrudder checked his itinerary.

"The airport in Macon, Georgia." Jones was not happy with that information.

"Look further down the list. Find an airport within our reach but not in Georgia. Make that your second choice. And please transmit a copy of the taped conversation to Langley for analysis. And, let the decoy bird know our situation." That last command referred to the decoy 747, painted identical to Air Force One, always flying within a few miles of the President's plane.

"Done," replied the pilot. Jones turned, unlocked the door and walked quickly out, instructing Agent Underhill to lock it behind him.

Though McGrudder was the senior pilot of Air Force One and officially the plane was his, he knew that Jones, as the senior Secret Service agent aboard, had command-control with authority coming directly from the President himself.

If McGrudder had found Jones's orders to be unworkable, he would not hesitate to make his concerns known. Thankfully, Jones's decisions were right in line with what McGrudder would have done in this situation, and there should be no need for a crisis of authority on board today, at least between the pilot and the Service.

McGrudder quickly scanned his list of nearby airports again, then said to the co-pilot, "Prepare a heading to the airport in Nashville, Tennessee. I'll tell you in a few minutes if we are going there today."

Nashville, thought McGrudder, *the home of Country Music.* For some unknown reason an old Merle Haggard tune came to mind--*'When you're runnin' down my country, you're walkin' on the fightin' side of me.'*

Jones, having left the cockpit, moved quickly back towards the center of the aircraft where the President's office was situated. As he walked he lifted his wrist to his mouth and spoke into his wrist mic, sending a message to his advance team on the ground at the airport, but there was no reply.

As he arrived at the still open door, the grave look on his face alarmed the agent stationed there. But Jones made no eye contact with that agent, walking directly into the President's office. The President was still on the phone, engaged in a jovial conversation with a man who had given healthily to his election campaign. This President did not enjoy being interrupted, but seeing the pallor on Jones face was enough to make him cut short even an important call.

"Larry," said the President into the phone, "I'm sorry but I'm being interrupted. Can I call you back later? Sure, my love to Jan and the girls. O.K., talk to you soon." He hung up the phone and looked blankly at Jones. "What is it Vince?"

"May I close the door Mr. President?" asked Jones.

"Yes, of course, what's going on?" Jones closed the door and turned back to the President.

"Sir, we have a situation." Jones felt a wave of surreal sweep over him. He could hardly believe he was about to say the next sentence, but he forced the feeling from his mind with pure will. "Sir, we have received a transmission from Hartsfield-Jackson Airport in Atlanta that this plane is not cleared for landing. Air Force one has been formally denied permission to land, sir."

The use of the words 'formally' and 'permission' implied an authority and determination beyond any mere practical or logistical concerns, such as another airplane blocking the runway. The President was a highly intelligent man and he could keep score as well as anyone. He immediately stood, bolt upright, to his full height of well over six feet.

"What? Who? What's going on down there?"

"Sir, we are currently trying to raise our advance team, who has sounded no alarm as of yet. Agent Jenson is leading that team and he contacted us twenty minutes ago saying all was well, but we are now having trouble contacting him. Sir, the transmission we received did come over the secure frequency. There is no way to fake that, sir. And sir, he claimed to be the Governor of Georgia."

The President's mouth gaped slightly and his eyes bore the hollow look of disbelief for a second before he regained his composure. He was known above all for being a cool character but was clearly taken aback by the news. After a short pause and a deep breath, the President had fully recovered himself.

However, agent Jones noticed that along with keeping his cool the President's face bore another look, a new one he had not seen in this particular President before. Jones had been around the halls of political super-power long enough to spot the gleam of opportunity when he saw it. And he was certain that he was seeing it now in the eyes of the man before him, and the worry crept in anew.

Understanding the urgency of the situation, Jones spoke up again.

"Mr. President, we are some twenty minutes out from the airport. The pilot is contacting alternate landing sites outside of Georgia. I advise that we go to the cockpit and choose one." But at those words the President's face grew stern and his neck stiffened.

"Alternate landing site? No, no way! I am landing in Atlanta, Georgia! I am the President of these United States and I will land in Atlanta as planned!" His voice had risen steadily through that last sentence, spilling into the corridor even with the office door shut.

Seated in the wide corridor not far from the President's office were several men, including the President's Chief of Staff Eli Brandenburg and the President's chief political advisor Henry 'Hank' LeBeau. Both men looked up from copies of the Atlanta Journal-Constitution that they had been reading. The Journal/Constitution had been very supportive of the President and his agenda, and it was generally a pleasure to read, especially the Pulitzer Prize winning political cartoons of Mike Lukovich, a man whose pen could satirize his political opposites with savage glee.

Both now sensed that something was amiss and both rose to their feet, eyeing one another as they moved closer to the office door. As they approached, the door was opened by Agent Jones. The Presidents' voice boomed through the door, calling for Brandenburg.

The COS hurried to move through the door, brushing roughly against LeBeau as he passed. LeBeau, already bristling at the fact that the President had not called first for him, now bristled further at the perceived physical insult from Brandenburg. A short wave of pain passed through LeBeau's chest, but he would not sit down, hovering outside the open office door as Brandenburg went in.

"Eli, we have a situation and we don't have long to make a decision," said Soloto, who now noticed LeBeau standing awkwardly outside the door. Soloto decided it would be good to have his political advisor in the room as well. "Hank, please come in. I want to get your input on this as well." LeBeau's face had flushed with the chest pain but was starting to regain its normal color. Soloto noticed the tension in LeBeau's face but had no time to ask about it.

"Vince, give these two a quick, no-bull account of the situation," ordered Soloto.

"With your permission Mr. President, I will have the transmission from Hartsfield-Jackson patched directly in."

"O.K. Let's get on with it," said Soloto with less patience. Jones spoke into his wrist mic and within seconds the

Bose speaker's mounted in the corners of the President's office crackled with sound.

The transmission began to play, each man in the office listening wide-eyed and carefully. Only LeBeau bothered to take notes. It was generally known around the White House that Brandenburg had a memory bordering on total recall, which allowed him to take notes only when it was needed for show. After the transmission ran through once, Soloto asked that it be run through again.

"Does anyone need to hear it again...we don't have all day on this thing," said the President. All said 'no.' Jones spoke up before the others could.

"Gentlemen, the transmission came over the secure frequency. It certainly originated at Hartsfield-Jackson. Voice analysis is being done as we speak. My gut tells me this guy, the Governor, is deadly serious. I advise we divert to another airport immediately," stated Jones succinctly.

"Are we sure this isn't some kind of prank?" LeBeau asked.

"You heard what Agent Jones said about the frequency Hank," said Soloto. "Eli, your assessment."

"Mr. President, this idiot claiming to be the Governor of Georgia is crazy. He knows he cannot get away with this. He cannot turn away the President of the United States." Soloto turned to LeBeau.

"Hank, what do you think?" LeBeau saw his chance to outshine Brandenburg.

"Mr. President, Eli is right that we are dealing with a nutcase, but he is wrong to suggest we challenge this guy from the air. I agree with the Secret Service," he said, nodding to Agent Jones. "Let's follow those fighter escorts out there to another location and deal with this maniac then."

LeBeau was happy with his advice but not sure how Soloto took it. Judging from the look on his face, the President was only growing more angry. The President looked over as if to study a wall of the office. Then he said as he snapped his head back around,

"I want to talk to this guy at the airport. Agent Jones, see if we can raise him on the radio."

"Mr. President, we will try, but we are only a few minutes out now. Let the pilot turn the plane and that will give you plenty of time-" This time it was Agent Jones who was cut short mid-sentence by the President.

"No! No hick Governor from Georgia is going to turn us back. We are going to Atlanta. I will not be denied and embarrassed by some nut who thinks he can bully the federal government."

"Mr. President," began LeBeau, "there is no embarrassment in diverting to another airport. Who knows what this guy is capable of? Politically, I don't think it will hurt-" LeBeau was cut off now by the COS.

"I like your stand, Mr. President. I think this idiot is bluffing. He would not dare turn back the President of the Unites States of America!"

Agent Jones, the consummate professional protector, now felt a pang of worry shoot through his mind. He realized things could now get out of hand, emotion beginning to trump reason and drive the situation out of control. He felt he had to assert some control over the situation, for the President's own good.

"Sir, with all due respect, I am prepared to order the pilot to divert to the airport in Nashville, Tennessee. If this man in Atlanta is as determined as he sounds, as crazy as he sounds, then he means you harm--he may very well mean you harm, Mr. President. Our advance team is not responding and may have been compromised. I cannot allow your aircraft to get anywhere near him. Service protocol allows for no other course of action than to divert."

There it was. Jones had put it all on the table, even suggesting that he was ready to over-rule the President and divert with or without permission. But Brandenburg took offence at Jones's forwardness.

"Agent Jones, you are speaking to the President of the United States. Just who do you think you are? You do not over-rule the leader of the free world!" Brandenburg was pointing his finger towards Agent Jones's face, but it was Brandenburg's face that was now flushed red in rage. Jones had his hands folded in front of him over his buttoned suit-coat, standing in an at-ease position. He merely regarded Brandenburg with a cold face, refusing to be baited into an argument. Jones would not deal in opinion, he operated only by fact and protocol.

"Let me make it clear to everyone here," boomed Soloto's voice. "I and only I will decide what course of action we take. The decision is mine and mine alone!" Jones kept his face blank but knew that if the President insisted on taking command-control, he would be hard pressed to stop him, even if it put all their lives in danger. Still, it was his job to protect the President's life, perhaps even from The Man himself.

The President turned away in confused anger as LeBeau started to back up the obvious prudence of what Jones had advised. But the voice of Dick McGrudder sounded now from the loud speakers.

"Sir, this is Colonel McGrudder. Be advised that the fighter escort is very concerned. They want to know what we are going to do and when. They are raising cane about this, sir."

Soloto, allowing anger and pride to overcome his natural calm sense, moved quickly to his desk and picked up his direct line to the cockpit.

"McGrudder, this is President Soloto, and we are going to land in Atlanta as planned. Do you understand Colonel?" That last phrase was more command than question. But the pilot was only more confused now.

"Mr. President, I...I... Sir, I cannot land without clearance from the tower there." But the President's face only grew more dour. He was the most powerful man in the world, but was now being bucked by men he trusted to serve and obey him: his body guard and his pilot.

"Colonel McGrudder--no bottom feeder from Georgia is going to divert this plane. Call their tower now and tell them I want to speak to them!" Brandenburg saw his opportunity.

"Mr. President, we all know about the emergency special ops brigade stationed near the airport," the COS said excitingly. "You can order the brigade to secure the runway and we can land there no matter what this nut-case Governor says! I still say he's bluffing anyway." These remarks drew a blood-curdling look from Agent Jones, as another hand-full of sand fell into the engine. He had to again try to insert some sanity into the situation.

"Brandenburg!" barked Jones in a full-throated military voice as if back in the Rangers, "all you are giving is your opinion, and your opinion on matters of the President's safety has no bearing on this situation."

Suddenly everyone was acutely reminded that agent Jones was the only armed man in the room. Shocked at being yelled at by what he considered a hired hand, Brandenburg started to reply but the President barged his way through the group of men and out the door. He seemed to need some air, and some space, but once out of the office he kept on walking with heavy steps up the corridor.

Agent Jones followed close behind instinctively, motioning for three other Service agents to gather around the President. They were followed by the COS and the LeBeau. The group was moving with quick deliberation, keeping pace with the long striding President.

As the party pass by both White House staff and members of the press those folks began to nudge one another and whisper as to what they were witnessing. As the men moved through the corridor, Jones pulled a senior agent close and whispered to him,

"Mike, quietly have everyone except our team confined to their seat and buckled up. Take my keys and open the weapon's bay, issue the BPS's with light-load ammo to our people, and don't forget to lock the bay when you're done. I want you to get the entire bird under lock-down, and then join me in the cockpit. And bring your shotgun with you."

Everything aboard Air Force One was well thought out, like using the Browning Pump Shotguns with light-shot ammunition that would stop a man but stray shot would not be heavy enough to penetrate the hull of the aircraft. Agent Simisky never imagined he might actually have to use one of those weapons while airborne, and he could hardly believe the command he had just been given. But his training took over and he broke away from the group to carry out the instructions to the letter. He would get the job done, but he knew when sand was in the engine as well as anyone. For a reason unknown to him, a phrase ran through his mind; "To get to hell, you've got to go through Atlanta."

Agent Underhill, at her post by the cockpit door, spotted the President's group as they headed towards her. She grew nervous at what she knew to be very inordinary, she yet maintained a stiff posture and a cool demeanor. At least outwardly.

As the President approached it was clear that he meant to enter the cockpit. The agent did not step aside, Soloto noticed.

"Open the door, please," ordered the President. The female agent, still standing with hands folded behind her, looked from the President of the United States over to her immediate boss, Agent Jones. Underhill wanted Jones to giver her instruction, but Jones simply stared at her, forcing her to fall back on her training. She would have to follow protocol.

"Mr. President, sir, per the Secret Service Code, I need the permission of the Senior Agent to open the cockpit door."

Soloto had a blank and empty look now on his face. He knew that Jones had purposefully allowed a Presidential order to be disobeyed by not immediately duplicating the order to Underhill. Soloto knew that Jones knew that Agent

41

Underhill would follow protocol in absence of an order from a senior Agent. Soloto turned to look at Jones. Jones made brief eye contact with the President, but also gave Underhill a look that said, 'Well done.'

Jones nudged his way to the cockpit door himself and pulled his own key. Underhill backed away as the locks clicked open. He was taking his time with the locks, hoping the extra few seconds would give tempers time to cool. Time, he had been taught, was the most necessary element for cooler heads to prevail. Yet he also knew that unlimited time was the one thing you did not have in an airplane at flight. They would soon be over Atlanta, and Governor Cummins.

The other Service agents now received calls to come to the weapons bay and headed back down the corridor, leaving the COS and LeBeau there with Agent Underhill.

Jones opened the door for the President to walk through, and then stepped in front of Brandenburg and LeBeau, barring their entrance. He quickly pulled the door closed to say to the others that they would not be allowed into the cockpit. Once his point was made, Jones opened the door slightly ajar and calmly issued orders to Underhill.

"Agent Underhill, remove your firearm and disengage the safety. Stay here with these two gentlemen until we are finished in the cockpit."

'Oh my Lord' Underhill said in her heart, but at the same time reached within her jacket and pulled a Glock 9mm, grasping the weapon with both hands in the ready position, with the business end of the gun pointing towards the floor. The two political hacks were aghast at this action, and stepped back a bit so as to keep their toes out of the gun's line of fire. Neither was sure exactly what would happen next.

Though the plane was adequately cooled by powerful air conditioners, round pellets of sweat began to pop out on the foreheads of both Brandenburg and LeBeau. There spittle turned pasty in their mouths as they tried to swallow. The ever so slight trace of a grin ran unnoticed across Agent Underhill's lips as both men cursed at Jones refusal to allow them into the cockpit where they knew the decision would be made as to whether or not to attempt a landing in Atlanta.

In the cockpit, the President had already ordered the pilot to raise Hartsfield-Jackson on the secure frequency. The pilot turned the head-sets off, putting the radio traffic on the loud-speakers. A drawled voice eased from the speakers.

"Air Force One, this is Governor Jim Cummins and I am speaking to you from the control tower at Hartsfield-Jackson Airport. I have you on radar, and you should have diverted by now. You are in-bound to an airport for which you have no clearance. Colonel McGrudder, do you consider that a wise course of action considering this is the single busiest airport in the world?"

The President had walked off some of the anger on the way to the cockpit but was instantly more angry than ever.

"Listen to me Governor Cummins, this is Abe Soloto, President of the United States. I WILL land at Hartsfield-Jackson today, in just a few minutes. If anything is done to hinder our landing, I will take it as an attempted assassination of the President of the United States. I have a powerful escort of fighter planes with me Governor. They are not armed with heavy bombs, but I can imagine what a Side-Winder missile could do to your control tower. Do you really want to push this thing?"

"Soloto, you will not be visiting us in Atlanta today, Side-Winders or no Side-Winders. I have you in check-mate, and even you are smart enough to know that. By the way, making terrorist threats against an airport sounds like something Osama bin Laden would have done."

Cummins was baiting the President, and it was working.

"Listen you sorry bag of dirt, this is the President! You WILL give control of that tower to the regular traffic people now and you will get out of the airport, or I will have you arrested and thrown in jail for the rest of your pathetic life! Do you hear me!"

"Soloto, you don't understand. The air traffic people *are* my people. You may be President somewhere, but you certainly are not *my* President, and I don't take orders from a Usurper and a Tyrant! I advise you to seek friendlier skies elsewhere. We don't want you here. Georgia is not a colony of the D.C. government, and you don't own us, or our airport!"

"Cummins, you crazy freak, you cannot tell me where I will and will not go! Clear us for landing or I will have my fighters blow you away!"

Soloto had fairly screamed this last command at the microphone. Now all was deathly silent as the cockpit waited for the next reply. It did not come immediately. A strong wave of static now filled the airwaves, and no one in the cockpit was sure, but it sounded to Soloto like a one word reply;

"Bang."

Soloto squinted and turned his ear toward the speaker, trying to understand what he just heard. He then noticed through the cockpit window, out of the corner of his eye, one of the fighter escorts that had drawn uncomfortably close to Air Force One. It was an F-22 Raptor, the worlds most advanced tactical War-Bird, and Soloto was seeing but failing to comprehend why the fighter jet was suddenly engulfed in a brilliant orange-crimson ball of flame. As the fighter jet disintegrated the force of the explosion barreled into the port side of Air Force One. The special aluminum skin of the mammoth plane helped absorb the concussion, a shock-wave of energy running in ripples across the flexible metal that covered the fuselage.

Still, the fighter had drawn much closer than normal because of the current situation and the blast-power pushed the President's plane hard to starboard. Air Force One began to roll, losing two thousand feet of altitude almost instantly as the fireball that had been a multi-million dollar jet-fighter burnt out and extinguished itself, its smoldering debris falling helplessly earthward where the Smokey Mountains of north Georgia reached up as if to receive the burnt offerings.

Everyone aboard Air Force One who had not been buckled in their seats was thrown into a wall or onto the floor. Many in the press core had sensed that something was up, and had refused to stay buckled in their seats, afraid that they were going to be denied coverage of an important story.

These were now sprawling all about, some knocked unconscious, others shouting, some crying and bleeding from banged up heads and shins scrapped to bone. A few even had suffered open fractures out of which bubbled deep shades of red speckled with white bone fragments. Utter chaos now reigned throughout the plane.

In the cockpit, Jones had been thrown violently about before landing on the floor. The President had fallen on top of Jones, and by instinct Jones grasped Soloto in his muscular arms in a protective effort. But Soloto, still conscious and unhurt, felt that he was being constrained and this only added anger to the fear he already felt. He tried to push himself away from Jones, trying to break his grasp. But Jones, unsure what had happened, would not let his charge go and there the two lay, struggling on the cockpit floor.

McGrudder and his co-pilot had been strapped firmly in there chairs, fighting the roll of the airplane. They now had regained control of the aircraft, correcting its attitude.

Warning buzzers and lights were going off across the multiple control panels, contributing to the disorder.

Voices were now screaming over the radio. One was the voice of the other escort who had been flying close to starboard. The pilot of that Raptor had no line of sight to the other fighter when it exploded, and knew nothing until he saw the President's plane rolling towards him. He had to pull his craft hard right and away from the jumbo jet to avoid collision with it. When he caught his breath, the fighter pilot screamed into his mask,

"What the crap just happened?" It was the excited yet cool voice of Dick McGrudder that answered.

"An escort has been hit. I repeat, a Raptor is burning and down. I see no chute in the air. Someone circle back and check for a chute." But no parachute would be found. The Raptor pilot never knew what hit him and had died instantly in the fireball. A few charred limbs would later be found by Georgia mountain hikers alongside a little path known as Rigdon Trail.

Within minutes, twenty other Raptors would come seemingly out of nowhere to surround the President's plane in a defensive maneuver carried out to utter perfection. Ironically, the Raptor is made in nearby Marietta, Georgia, by Lockheed-Martin.

In the meantime, outside the cockpit, Agent Underhill had taken a hard spill, dropping the Glock as her head smashed into the grill of an air vent. Her scalp took a wide, nasty cut which she instinctively clutched as pain and blood blinded her eyes. The two men, Brandenburg and LeBeau, were sprawled across her legs, one atop the other.

Emergency lights and buzzers were going off, filling the air with chaos.

Brandenburg managed to roll off the pile. He felt an object underneath him. Having climbed near the top of the political ladder with quick thinking, he employed it right then. A secret gun enthusiast, he recognized the feel of a Glock on his belly and, reaching under him, took the gun in hand. He quickly tucked the gun into his pants, but forgot to pull his shirt-tale out to cover it, the black grip of the Glock left exposed to view.

Crawling over to Underhill, the COS grabbed her arms and tried to pull them down so he could look her in the face. He asked her if she could hear his voice. Her pupils had dilated and her mind was groggy. She never felt his right hand reach into her coat pocket and remove her set of keys.

Brandenburg looked over at LeBeau, who was out-cold on the floor. LeBeau would have to fend for himself, Brandenburg decided.

The COS made it to the cockpit door and quickly got the keys in the proper locks. *I need to get into this cockpit before the Secret Service makes my President look like a cowardly fool.*

Opening the door, he saw the President on the floor and hurried to his side. Agent Jones, still a little disoriented from his fall, had by this time gotten to one knee and was positioned between the seats of the pilot and co-pilot. His head was still pounding and his mind so jogged that he did not think to stop and question how Brandenburg gained entry to the cockpit. He rubbed his eyes hard with both fists, fighting to keep his wits.

Jones regained enough presence of mind to issue an order to McGrudder to immediately divert to the airport at Nashville. McGrudder responded that he had already started his northward turn and, he added, Air Force One was now surrounded by at least twenty Raptors in a protective screen.

In the corridor outside the cockpit, agent Mike Simisky had made it back, pump shotgun in hand and at the ready. Seeing Underhill down and her head bloodied made him pause to check on her. LeBeau was opposite her in the corridor and had managed to sit up. Seeing no blood on him, he knelt beside the female agent.

While holding his BPS in one hand, he pulled a handkerchief from his pocket and put it to the gash on her head, instructing her to hold pressure to it.

"Tamara, is your weapon secure?" She dropped one hand to her holster but felt no weapon, then remembered having it drawn moments before.

"I must have dropped it," she said, trying to look around on the floor for the missing Glock. Simisky looked around himself, saw no gun, and really began to worry. A loose cannon aboard Air Force One was not an acceptable situation.

Inside the cockpit, Jones looked up as the cockpit door quickly swung open and agent Simisky entered with the muzzle of his shotgun at head level, the guns' stock held firmly to his right shoulder.

"We have a missing firearm," Simisky said as he scanned each man in the room. Jones's hands dropped to his own Glock which he pulled and grasp in a two handed presentation. Jones had recovered enough of his senses to notice the handgun grip protruding above the belt of the Chief of Staff.

The Senior Agent pointed his Glock at Brandenburg's head as the COS's eyes widened with fear. He had never had a loaded gun pointed at him by a man who would not hesitate to use it.

Following the lead of his senior agent, Simisky now swung the business end of the BPS around to point at Brandenburg as well.

Now in the cockpit of Air Force One were the pilot and co-pilot, the President, his Chief of Staff with a gun in his waist and his hands raised, and two Secret Service agents with guns aimed point-blank, and no slack in their triggers.

Jones was momentarily at a loss for words. He had never arrested a member of the Presidential Staff, but he knew it was a federal crime for unauthorized persons to be near the President with a gun. No one spoke for awkward seconds until the President, seeing the guns pointed at his COS, looked down to see the Glock in his waist.

"What are you doing with that?" asked Soloto of Brandenburg.

"Mr. President, it--the girl outside dropped it and was out-cold. I could not just leave it on the floor." The President had a dumbfounded look on his face. Agent Simisky now took a couple of quick steps towards the COS, placing the muzzle of his shotgun firmly to the man's sternum. A look of utter disbelief mixed with terror appeared on the man's face as Simisky reached down and pulled the Glock out of his waist. His bladder involuntarily functioned.

Simisky stepped back a few feet, but his shotgun was still trained on Brandenburg, center-mass.

"Gentlemen," said the President, "for goodness sake, this is my Chief of Staff. Put the guns away." But neither agent lowered his weapon.

Jones gave a blunt command to his fellow agent.

"Mike, escort Chief of Staff Brandenburg to the holding room and secure him there. Guard the door until I relieve you personally--no one in or out."

Simisky, weapon held high, stepped back to allow the COS room enough to get to the door.

Brandenburg, appalled that he was being arrested, looked helplessly to the President. To be marched at gunpoint through the halls of Air Force One, on display to staff and reporters alike, would likely be the end of Brandenburg's promising career. The President spoke up for his old friend once more.

"Agent Jones, this is uncalled for. You men have done your jobs. Now we need to work together to deal with this animal in Atlanta." But Jones never took his eyes off the COS.

"Sir," Jones said to the arrested man, "move along, now!" Brandenburg let out a gasp of frustration then stomped quickly to the cockpit door and out into the corridor with agent Simisky trailing closely behind. Jones, unsure what the days' events would do to his own career, nonetheless soldiered on as he looked finally back at Soloto.

"Mr. President, your safety comes before all else. Mr. Brandenburg brought a loaded weapon into your presence, and he will be held responsible for it. I cannot allow the personal feelings of the President to compromise the safety of the President. Colonel McGrudder now has us on a heading to the airport at Nashville, Tennessee, sir. May I escort you back to your office or living quarters at this time, sir?"

Soloto did not know what to say; he was the President of the United States, but both his order to proceed to Atlanta and his order to overlook the harmless actions of his Chief of Staff had been ignored and contradicted by Agents of the Secret Service.

It was an angry, grim faced President who exited the cockpit. But before he stepped out ahead of Jones, Soloto put his face up to Jones' face and said through clinched teeth,

"Agent Jones, when this day is over and we are back on the ground, you will have learned that the 'personal feelings' of the President of the United States are the very things that you will respect."

With that, Soloto began his march back towards his office, his freshly reprimanded Personal Protector close on his heels. Other agents, armed with their shotguns, quickly coalesced around Soloto and Jones. The pack of men moved together as one through the corridor with stern bearing, having to step over and around the wounded staff and reporters littering the floor.

There was a television mounted on the wall in the corridor not far from the President's office door. As Soloto approached it he glanced up at the screen. What he saw drew him to a quick stop. CNN was broadcasting a live feed from what looked to be an airport. *This can't be happening*, he thought.

The President quickly read the caption at the bottom of the screen:

GEORGIA GOVERNOR CUMMINS CLAIMS
TO HAVE TURNED AWAY AIR FORCE ONE
FROM HIS HOME STATE. PRESIDENT SAID
TO BE ABOARD THE PLANE FORMERLY
INBOUND TO ATLANTA AIRPORT, NOW
RETREATING TO NASHVILLE, TN.

In the background of the camera shot Soloto saw a man
dressed in a suit, surrounded by armed men in what looked to
be blue Georgia State Patrol uniforms. The suited man was
giving orders and people were running about, some shouting
inaudible words.

Jones looked at Soloto and noticed that his mouth had again
dropped open. The President was obviously aghast at the fact
that Governor Cummins had actually taken a cable news crew
into Hartsfield-Jackson Airport to broadcast the aftermath of
the event. Jones did not feel comfortable with Soloto remaining
in the corridor, so he put his hand on the President's shoulder
to gently urge him forward. Soloto did not resist, but moved on
towards his nearby office.

Arriving at the office, he walked through the door, then
slammed it shut loudly within an inch of the face of the trailing
Agent Jones.

Jones tried not to take it personally. He knew he had to do
his job, no matter how angry the President became, no matter
how unpleasant it was for the President. That was what he had
signed up for and trained for. Jones decided then and there
that he would never regret the actions he had taken to protect
the President that day, even if it cost him his job. He simply
turned on his heels and took up his position in front of the
President's office door.

The President sat down hard in his chair, put both elbows on
his desk, and tried to rub the stress from his face with both
hands. He did not realize that the secure frequency was still
patched into his office speakers. Soloto jerked his head around
as the speakers crackled with a now familiar voice.

"Air Force One, our radar shows that you have prudently
chosen to divert. That is a wise choice, for tyrants shall not
enter this Free and Sovereign State unmolested. Any other
uninvited incursions into our airspace shall be regarded as an
act of aggression. Mr. Soloto, keep out." The transmission
ended.

The President felt a rage overcoming him again. He hurried over to his water cooler for a cool drink, but noticed for the first time that it had fallen over and spilt on the floor, no doubt from the impact of the exploded Raptor. About that time there was a knock on the office door.

"What is it!" shouted the President towards the door. It was LeBeau who opened the door and stuck his head in.

"Mr. President, we need to talk about the events of the day."

"Not now Hank, can't you see I need some time?"

"Of course, Mr. President," LeBeau said sheepishly as he backed out and closed the door to the President's office. Soloto plopped down in the huge, leather upholstered chair that had been a gift from the Israeli Ambassador. This cannot be happening, thought Soloto. That Governor in Georgia must be insane. First he takes over an airport, then he interferes with the work of the Secret Service lead team, then he threatens me, the President, if I try to land. And then there's the explosion of the Raptor escort fighter jet. How could he have pulled that off?

But wait, thought Soloto, *that Governor never claimed to have shot down the Raptor*. Insane perhaps, but a cleverly insane man as well--crazy like a fox. Soloto realized that in turning away Air Force One and The President of the United States, Cummins had won a victory of sorts without ever actually laying a hand on the President.

Soloto searched his memory for a moment. He thought he remembered hearing the word 'Bang' just before the explosion of the Raptor, but that by itself did not prove anything. A three hundred million dollar fighter jet does not just explode in mid air by itself. It had to be connected to that nut down there in Atlanta, he knew. If it proved to be so, then the Governor of a State in the Union would have to be arrested by federal authorities for the murder of the pilot as well as an attempt on the life of the president. *This will get messy. Need our friends in the press to spin this one strongly our way. I'll put in a call to Cris Matthews myself, he thought. If we play our cards right, we might even get Cal Limkey on board, which would help neutralize the ROX News/Red State/Rev-party crowd. Maybe just a little*, thought Soloto, but that crowd will probably be screaming for my head till the Second Coming.

The President's mind now turned to his Chief of Staff and the trouble with the Secret Service. Agent Jones, he thought, had definitely overstepped his bounds on this one. I am the President, he thought, no one should be able to over-rule me aboard my own airplane. The Secret Service had their job to do, but they serve at my pleasure, not the other way around. Agent Jones will have to be made to regret his actions, and serve as an example to the other agents. And I must save Brandenburg, somehow, even though he picked up that weapon. He says he was just trying to protect me, anyway. I must show loyalty to him or none of the staff will believe in me and we will all be intimidated by those who are supposed to be protecting us, thought the President.

Soloto took a deep breath. He could not hide in his office forever. It was time to gather close to him those he trusted and begin to make some decisions. The Press would be all over this one, and he had to have a ready, carefully constructed response prepared.

The Governor of Georgia had just gone 'all-in' in the biggest political game in American history since 1860, the year that South Carolina seceded from the Union.

Secession. Surely that man down there in Atlanta wasn't crazy enough to try something like that, something that could lead to another civil war?

Soloto knew that his next move, like Lincoln with Fort Sumpter, had to be perfect. It was time to dial up an old friend and ally, Benny Lefever, Speaker of the House of the Representatives of the State of Georgia.

ROX News Headquarters
New York City

The newsroom was bustling in frantic activity. Conflicting news accounts out of Atlanta about the events surrounding Air Force One were continuing to come in, and the production people, writers and news anchors were all scrambling to put together major segments of their broadcast that would give viewers a full, blow by blow account of everything that had taken place. ROX News needed crews camping out at Hartsfield-Jackson International Airport and outside the compound of the Georgia Governor's Mansion, interviewing anyone who would go on camera. The ROX reporters were good at scratching for every detail available, but because CNN was based in Atlanta itself, ROX found itself outmanned if not outclassed on the coverage of this particular story. The ratings war between the two networks had created an intense rivalry that caused a tension one could feel when the reporters for each organization butted heads while covering the same news story.

Both networks had been built by rich, powerful men who ruled financial and business empires with ruthless efficiency. For CNN, Ted Turner had been the founder of the world's first twenty-four hour news channel, becoming a legend in the broadcast and communications world for his efforts. Above all things, Turner was known as a competitor and he did not tolerate losing. Turner would create an Atlanta based network that would claim, as do all news outlets, to be objective in its coverage, though, like Turner himself, it clearly pulled to the left politically and socially. Though claiming to run things up the middle, Turner had always admitted that his network could be challenged from the right. If someone could put together a network that played to the more conservative notions of middle class America, even Turner knew that it could mean trouble for CNN.

Enter Ryper Minchow, a Chinese media mogul who would provide just such a challenge. Minchow, who had clawed his way up the business and communications ladder, created the ROX news channel and began broadcasting in 2001. Based in New York City, ROX News quickly rose in prominence, offering viewers red meat content that its detractors would call rightwing political pandering. Whatever it was, it had worked, and ROX eventually overtook CNN as the most watched news network in the world. Minchow proved to be every bit as competitive as Turner had been, and had the deep pockets to hire the personalities he needed to make ROX News work.

Now CNN and ROX were in open, hostile competition for the trust and viewership of people worldwide, but especially in the U.S. market. Now in the lead, the producers of ROX News had no intention of allowing CNN to overtake them in market share, no matter what.

Presently in the New York news room of ROX News, producers were scrambling to catch up to CNN in the coverage of the biggest story to hit America in a long time. Not used to coaching from behind, the ROX people were uptight and tensions were running high. Everyone was feeling the pressure. Walter Goble was the head producer for ROX News in New York, and Walter was not a happy man. He dialed Jill Lasiter on the phone.

"Tell me, Jill, why are we not up to speed in Atlanta yet? I ordered those crews down there the moment this thing broke." Jill Lasiter was his assistant and the frequent target of his tirades when things did not go swimmingly.

"Walter, those crews received their instructions on time. One crew had flight delays, which could not be helped. Two of the technicians on the second crew had grandparents to die on the same day and had to be with family. These things happen," responded the assistant.

"With all the flights leaving New York, are you telling me we could not find another flight to Atlanta?"

"Walter, you know we always fly directly into Hartsfield-Jackson, but since it was the sight of a major event, the FFA shut it down for two full days. It's one of the busiest airports in the world and shutting it down threw a wrench into the flight schedules of every major airport in the southeastern United States. There was just no way around it."

"Jill, the crews could have driven down there by now. It's not like I was sending them to China!"

"You ordered an extra fifty people and a tractor trailer load of equipment to Atlanta. Do you really expect to get all that down there at the same time by driving?"

"Jill, I don't care how you get them to Atlanta, by train, by bus, by land, sea or air, but you better get them there now. I don't care if you have to rent pack mules and walk them there yourself, just get it done!" The phone was slammed dead in Jill Lasiter's ear. A coworker was standing beside her and overheard part of the conversation.

"What is it Jill, is Walter wigging out again about Atlanta?"

"You might say that a jackass just put in an order for fifty pack mules," said Jill to the now confused coworker.

Chapter Three

The Situation Room in
The White House
Washington, D.C.

FBI Director Rodney Bound had received a call on his cell phone to attend an emergency meeting at the White House. A few hours before, Bound had been in his office located in the J. Edgar Hoover building on Pennsylvania Avenue not far from the White House when a deputy called him, asking him to turn on CNN. He watched the live report from Hartsfield-Jackson Airport in Atlanta and had immediately ordered his secretary to clear his calendar for the next entire week. The Georgia situation was going to be to deal with, and the FBI would likely be near the eye of the storm. *Wow Jim, what are you trying to do down there?*

Arriving at the White House, Bound was escorted directly to the Situation Room located in the basement of the White House. Bound was anxious to see who all was invited to this particular party. As a young man, Bound had been taught by Hoover himself that one could determine the purpose of a meeting with the President simply by identifying who was invited. As he entered the room he began to make mental notes of who was present.

Many of the men there were what Bound would have called the 'usual suspects.' The Vice President was there, at which Bound concluded that there were no funeral's of foreign dignitaries for the man to attend on that particular day. Attorney General Lawrence Kabill was there, as expected, as well as Secret Service Liaison Andrew Vincent. Bound was surprised as well as a bit concerned to see the Joint Chiefs of Staff of the Armed Services at this meeting, especially since it concerned a domestic law enforcement situation like that in Georgia. Even more troubling was the presence of National Security Agency head Dennis Click.

Bound had had run-ins with Click before, and he considered the man devious and opportunistic, even dangerous. Bound had once discovered advanced electronic listening devices in the restrooms of the Hoover Building--bugs too advanced to be Soviet or Chinese. He could not prove it, but he would swear the bugs must have been planted there by the NSA spooks, though Click had denied any involvement by his agency whatsoever.

Bound knew one of the Joint Chiefs. That man was General Case Garrett, Secretary of the Army, whom Bound had served with in Vietnam.

"It's a little early to be declaring war against Georgia, isn't it Case?" said Bound to the General in a half-joking way. But the stone-faced Garrett did not crack even so much as a half-smile.

"We're gonna take this guy in Georgia down hard, I can promise you that," replied Garrett. *Wow*, thought the FBI Director, *Garrett is wound tight.* And from the grim looks on the other faces in the room, so was everyone else.

Of course, Bound knew that the situation was serious and involved the loss of a pilot, though everything surrounding the incident was not yet clear and still needed investigation. Yet he hoped the purpose of this meeting was to not let a bad situation get out of control. Moderation should rule the day, he knew.

Bound and his people had discussed nervously amongst themselves for years about how divided the country was growing, the people pitted against one another by greedy career politicians, and how that could lead only to trouble. One flashpoint could cause real, intense unrest across the United States.

Governor Cummins of Georgia, whom Bound knew personaly, had definitely crossed the line. Still, Bound's idea of leadership was to contain a crisis, not to escalate it. He hoped that President Soloto would agree.

All those present had taken seats around the large table in the center of the room. Hearing someone announce the President's arrival, all rose to their feet as Soloto entered the Situation Room. No one dare show disrespect by remaining seated when POTUS enters a room of the White House. Trailing Soloto were COS Brandenburg and political advisor Hank LeBeau.

Soloto marched directly to the head of the large table. Positioning his six foot-three inch frame between the table and the President's chair, Soloto asked the others to be seated with him. The President then opened the crucial, historic meeting.

"Folks, we are here to get a handle on the situation that took place in Georgia yesterday. As you know, I have to address the nation this evening, so we need to make sure we have our facts in line, and that we come up with a measured response to what has happened.

"First of all, I want to play a tape of the exchange that took place between Air Force One and Hartsfield-Jackson Airport. Roll the tape."

The room sat in an eerie silence as the voices of Governor Cummins, Colonel McGrudder and that of the President talked back and forth. Gasps were heard around the room at the sound of the exploding Raptor, followed by the noise of chaos aboard Air Force One. Some in the room were thinking that they might be hearing the first resistance of the federal government by the Governor of a State since the antics of Alabama Governor George Wallace in 1963.

When the tape ended, red complexions and angry expressions dominated the faces around the table. The President then ordered a tape of the Vice Presidents' press conference held earlier that day to be played on one of the flat-panel video screens. When that ended, the others in the room wisely waited for the President to speak.

"Now, I will take fact-based reports from several of you in order. I do not want any opinions as to our next course of action at this time other than what is specifically dictated by the facts. I will ask for opinions when I am ready. Let your minds speak first, your emotions second. First of all, Larry, as Attorney General, I want you to tell me what federal law has been broken by this Governor Cummins with this stunt of his."

"Mr. President, I am ready to seek indictment of this maniac in Georgia, based on the content of this tape, for making terrorist threats against the life of the President. Pending our investigation of the downed fighter jet, we can upgrade that charge to the attempted assassination of the President of the United States as well as the murder of the Raptor pilot." Soloto let those words hang in the air a moment as he tapped his fingers with a pencil he was holding.

"And what federal judge will you approach for signing the arrest warrant," asked Soloto.

"Mr. President, under current law, we can seek an emergency Warrant from the Judge of the federal circuit over either Georgia or D.C."

"Threats, murder, attempted assassination of a sitting President. O.K. I agree that these charges are merited," said Soloto, "but making charges and enforcing them are two different things. Director Bound, what can the FBI do to serve any warrants issued against this Cummins person?"

"Mr. President, I am prepared to bring the available assets at our disposal in and around Georgia and the Southeast to enforce any federal warrant that is lawfully issued."

"Define available," said Soloto coolly. It was already evident that the rumors of Soloto's disdain for Bound and the FBI were true. But Bound was just as cool a customer as Soloto and responded to the question without hesitation.

"Nearly two hundred field agents, sir, are in that area and-"

"Two hundred? Is that all! I thought your agency had several thousand agents at your disposal," said the President, raising his voice. Bound paused a few seconds as if to gather himself before answering. He felt the tension in the room tick-up a few notches.

"Mr. President, due to the emergency budget cutbacks imposed by congress, we have laid off several thousand agents. We still have over six thousand active agents, but they are spread all over the country and the world. You yourself ordered a team to Iraq and two more teams to Afghanistan to investigate the bombings in Kabul last month. Our resources are thin, but our people are dedicated and well trained."

"I don't doubt your agency's training or dedication, Director Bound. But we have got to make a statement here, and it will take overwhelming force to get it done," said Soloto, pounding his fist on the thick tabletop as he spoke. It was one of the first times anyone had seen a crack in the man's cool demeanor.

"Sir," responded the FBI director, "if given more time we can have as many as a thousand to fifteen hundred agents converge on Atlanta."

"We don't have unlimited time, Director. We have to act decisively and quickly. Every moment that this rogue in Georgia gets by with what he has done is a moment of insurrection against my administration." The two men had locked eyes and neither would look away or show weakness.

"Rodney, why don't you share with us what kind of man we're dealing with in this Cummins person? I understand that you know him personally," interjected Dennis Click, head of the super secret National Security Agency.

Bound snapped his head around at Click, giving him a hard stare. Indeed Bound did know Cummins, and even considered the man a friend, though they had not spoken in a few years. But that was something Bound had shared with no one outside his family, and it was unlikely that click could have known unless he had put his snoops on Bound's trail for some reason. Again, the tension level ticked up another notch.

"Wait a minute, you know this clown down in Georgia?" asked the President of Director Bound.

"I met Jim Cummins on a hunting trip down in Georgia about twenty years ago and have hunted with him a handful of times since then. He's a very personable guy, an ethical hunter, never poaches or takes too much game." President Soloto, a member of PETA, grimaced at the talk of hunting wild game, but Bound just kept talking. "I've never discussed politics with Jim Cummins, so I don't know where he's coming from in that regard." Bound was obviously irritated that his friendship with Cummins was being made an issue.

"If you know him, we might be able to use that friendship to set him up for an easy arrest, maybe save some lives? I'm surprised you did not suggest it first," stated the NSA head.

"It doesn't change anything that the man is an acquaintance of mine. I will arrest him the same as I would any stranger, or my own brother for that matter, if a warrant has been lawfully issued!" Bound's face was grave as he answered Click's question, a question that bore more than a hint of accusation.

"No offense, Rodney, I just want to make sure you're not too close to the situation," added Click. But Bound took even more offense.

"Listen Click, don't you ever question my professionalism, or that of the Bureau!"

"Director Bound," said the President firmly, "the NSA is a trusted part of this government. Director Click's concerns are valid, and he was not out of line in voicing them." Click grinned slightly at Bound to let him know who had won the skirmish.

"Now, let's move on. General Garrett, is the U.S. Army prepared to defend its Commander in Chief?" Garrett's chest full of military medals puffed up all the more as he started to answer the President. But when he opened his mouth to speak, FBI Director Bound cut him off.

"Mr. President, you need to be careful. Using the Military against private citizens is a serious line to cross. There is no widespread insurrection going on in Georgia, but you will create one if you are not careful. Remember that Posse Comitatus says-" Bound was then himself cut short by NSA Director Click.

"Bound, you of all people should know that Posse Comitatus was over-ruled under Bush. After 9-11 the rules changed, and we have the authority to do whatever it takes to get the job done!" The President looked pleased with what Click had said.

"Go ahead General," said Soloto to the Army Chief of Staff, giving Bound a nasty glance.

"Mr. President," began General Garrett, "the United States Army is indeed prepared to defend its Commander in Chief. And we have been forward-looking on Domestic Terrorism. We have had several Brigades with the Third Infantry Division stationed in Georgia for several years, training for just such a Homeland Security emergency. These soldiers have urban combat experience in both Iraq and Afghanistan and could travel from their base at Fort Stewart, Georgia to Atlanta in a matter of hours. We stand ready, sir." Garret was still sitting at attention, sounding like a man bucking for a fifth star.

"Outstanding, General. I had no idea we had home-guard units in Georgia. This is an unexpected blessing. Did you say you could have those soldiers in Atlanta within hours?"

"Within eight to twelve hours from departure from base, sir."

But the FBI Director would not be ignored.

"General Garrett, are you sure you want to roll the U.S. Army through the streets of America?" asked Bound.

"Come on, Bound!" snapped Click, entering the conversation again. "It's not like we're rolling through downtown New York. Most of those hicks in Georgia will probably cheer at seeing a good military parade." That remark drew laughter from around the table, but Soloto was not laughing. He looked with unkind eyes upon the FBI Director.

"Bound, you and everyone else in this room had better get on board with what I'm trying to do. I'm not going to let this country fall apart on my watch!" the President almost shouted across the table. "Now, I want to stress that no plan of action has been decided upon. Right now, all we are doing is contingency planning."

"I can take care of this problem with one wing of Stealth Bombers, Mr. President." That was the loud and craggy voice of Lief Rorakson, COS of the Air Force. Scattered laughter followed, and even Soloto smiled and said,

"Leave it to Lief to come up with a delicate approach--Curtis LeMay's got nothing on this guy!" Now the whole table erupted in laughter, as usually happens when a President attempts humor. "For now, Lief, we will keep those Stealth Bombers on the ground and hope we don't need them. But I want to ask you if you have an updated report on the Raptor we lost?"

"Mr. President, as you know we lost a good pilot in the explosion of the Raptor. We have sent teams to try to recover any debris on the ground, but the mountainous terrain makes the task nearly impossible. Radar tracking your group of planes over Georgia recorded no missile being fired at the Raptor, so we really need to reconstruct the bird to determine how it was brought down. Also, our recovery teams have encountered local Sheriffs, who have threatened our people with arrest if we come into their counties without permission." That last bit of information was new to most of those around the table, including Soloto.

"What was that about the locals?" asked the President.

"In Georgia, as in most States, Mr. President, the county Sheriff is the chief law enforcement officer and has supreme jurisdiction," replied Rorakson. "Legally, no one from any level of government can over-rule a local Sheriff, and these local guys in Georgia know the law. So they have given our people some grief."

"I disagree with that! No one has a higher authority than the President of the United States! It's in the Constitution. Anyway, what kind of grief have they given us?"

"In two instances, sir, our search teams, having identified themselves, were threatened with arrest by local law enforcement. In one of the cases, guns were drawn. It is not clear who drew weapons first, but I am told that it was pretty tense for a few moments, though no shots were fired. They claim that we have to pass all search requests through their local office for approval of the Sheriff."

The Attorney General spoke up at this point.

"Mr. President, if I may--it is true that under normal circumstances a local Sheriff has supreme jurisdiction in his county. However, as Director Click eluded earlier, under an Executive Order signed by then-President George W. Bush, during times of national emergency, federal law enforcement agents acting under the authority of the President can over-rule any other officer in the land, including local Sheriffs. Mr. President, I advise that you quietly sign an Executive Order declaring that a national emergency exists, at least in the State of Georgia."

"Mr. President, if you designate Georgia as being under an emergency order, then you might as well cover the whole deep south," said Director Bound with perhaps more boldness than he intended. "Our field offices in Alabama and Tennessee, as well as in the Carolinas, have been receiving an elevated number of both neighbor awareness reports and anonymous threats since Cummins was elected. And these events spiked when he turned your plane away."

"With all of your agents doing other things, I'm surprised you have anyone to answer those calls, Bound," replied Soloto, obviously not interested in what he had to say.

"Mr. President," COS Brandenburg cut in excitedly, "I can have our legal team draw up the Executive Order and place it on your desk no later than tomorrow morning. We can box-in this idiot in Georgia legally and enforce our will with one stroke of the Presidential pen!" LeBeau, the political advisor whose head was still hurting from the fall he had taken aboard Air Force One, had been waiting for an opening and now saw his chance.

"Speaking of being boxed-in Brandenburg, it's good to have you out of the lock-up." A couple of muffled laughs were heard in the room, which drew a hard look from Soloto.

"Mr. LeBeau," said Soloto, "do you have anything of substance to add to this conversation?"

"Yes, sir, I want to issue a word of political caution against over-playing this hand. All this brash talk of 'Executive Orders' and 'Stealth Bombers' can lead to a group-think mentality resulting in a solution that is out of proportion to the problem."

Brandenburg was livid now, his face flushed red with anger at LeBeau's mention of his detention aboard Air Force One, so he fired back.

"Well Hank, you may think the attempted assassination of our President to be a small matter, but the rest of us think it calls for more than just a slap on the wrist. Maybe you should trade in your political panties for a good dose of patriotism!"

"Now you just wait one minute! I'm not the one who stole a Secret Service weapon aboard the President's airplane!" shot back LeBeau, whose face was even more flush-red than Brandenburg's' now. Both men rose from their chairs and stepped towards one another, though the other men seated near them were quick to grab and separate them before blows could be exchanged.

"Gentlemen!" shouted Soloto. "Everyone calm down and please, sit down! I won't have these kinds of outbursts at our meetings. We have a serious situation on our hands and I need everyone to be thinking with cool heads! Now, Hank, as for what happened aboard Air Force One, it was a misunderstanding and the Secret Service was out of line to detain Eli. Eli was just trying to protect me because he saw a loaded weapon belonging to an incapacitated agent. That is the end of that and I'll not hear more about it!"

"Yes, Mr. President," said LeBeau, but he shot a look that could kill in the direction of Brandenburg. Brandenburg knew that feud between he and LeBeau was not going away, and he knew that LeBeau would try to use the Glock incident against him. The President had just issued a gag order on the subject, including to those who had witnessed it aboard Air Force One. Still, Brandenburg made a mental note to watch for leaks that LeBeau could feed to his many contacts in the media that would be glad to tarnish Brandenburg. He knew that if LeBeau went down, he would surely take Brandenburg with him if he could.

It had already been a wild meeting, but then something else unexpected happened. Andrew Vincent, the liaison between the Secret Service and the White House, spoke up.

"Mr. President, on behalf of the Secret Service I would like an opportunity to address this subject." But Soloto was in no mood for other opinions on the subject, especially from the Secret Service.

"That won't be necessary, Vincent."

"With all due respect, Mr. President, the Secret Service feels that we need to make clear the rules that we will enforce in terms of those who are in the physical presence of the President." Soloto felt he was being pressed.

"Mr. Vincent! As I told you before, you can send out a memo to all staff members and to anyone else you like concerning my security and your protocol. Other than that, the subject is not on my agenda today!"

Vincent had taken a real chance in broaching the subject and had just learned what it was like to get shot down by the President. He merely nodded his head in compliance and said nothing further. But inside, Vincent was seething.

Though the Service prides itself on agents keeping their personal feelings hidden and detached from professional behavior, the events on Air Force One had been on everyone's mind at the Service. Many in that agency were livid that Brandenburg had been exonerated by the President and that Agent Jones had been forced to apologize to Brandenburg upon arrival back in D.C.

Every agent knew that Jones had acted in perfect obedience to his professional duty to protect the President's life at all times, and to never allow anyone other than a fellow agent near the President with a weapon. Yet Jones had had to suffer the humiliation of apologizing for doing his duty and it was rumored that Brandenburg had cursed the agent to his face after receiving the apology.

Adding even more insult was the fact that the President had ordered that Jones be immediately reassigned to a desk job and replaced as Personal Protector. Did the President feel more loyal towards Brandenburg than to the agents who risked their lives to protect him? There was a lot of whispering going on among Service agents within an agency known for being circumspect.

Vincent realized that none of this was good, not for the Service nor for the President. A President does not need people guarding his life who feel he is ready to undercut them to cover the mistakes of his political hacks.

It was at that point that Click of the NSA spoke up again.

"Sir, if I may make a suggestion? I think I see another option you can utilize. As you know, my agency is nearly ten times the size of the FBI. And a larger percentage of our people are tactically trained for armed operations. In fact, our record of armed engagements is impressive. We have no Waco's or Ruby Ridge's to haunt us." That was a brick-bat thrown at Bound and the FBI that did not go unnoticed. Click continued. "Our strike teams are motivated and decisive, and will fulfill any mission you give us. We are militarized but not the Military, so we can carry out in-country duties without crossing the lines that Bound is so worried about. And if things escalate, we will always have the General's troops out of Fort Stewart to roll in behind us if necessary, Mr. President, though I doubt that will be necessary."

Soloto looked pleased. Click had just given him an option that would give him cover from the civil libertarians and at the same time give him a militarized force to take down Governor Cummins.

"Director Click, I think you might be on to something here. How many men can you bring to bear within a week or two?" said Soloto, taking his seat again.

"Seven to eight hundred, sir, all armed and ready." Bound was not sure of the number but exaggerated in order to get the President's attention.

"Outstanding! I'm hereby authorizing you to take charge of this operation. The Attorney General will supply you with the necessary warrant. General Garrett will have his men on standby to back you up if necessary. Bound started to speak up again but the President hushed him by standing up to close the

meeting, "Bound, your FBI will provide backup to the
NSA. You will work under Click and the NSA on this matter."

"One more thing, Mr. President," Click added. "I understand
that Governor Cummins may be about to make his move on
Nullification in the next few days. Do we want to take action to
prevent that from happening?" Everyone realized that Click
was suggesting something that had not been done
since Lincoln had disrupted the Maryland State Legislature just
before the Civil War. The President hesitated a moment, then
said,

"No, Dennis. We can't be seen as interfering in the local
workings of democracy. But I do have a friend in the State
Legislature in Georgia whom I believe can help us with that part
of the problem."

As the meeting broke up, FBI director Bound was the first
one out the door. He was met there by two of his assistant
directors, and they saw the look on his face and knew that the
meeting did not go well, at least for the FBI.

"Sir, is everything alright." Bound looked at him coldly.

"No, Larry, everything is not alright. The President is getting
bad advice and is about to act on it. I thought he was more
level-headed, but he is taking this thing very personally."

"Well," replied Larry, "it was *him* who was disrespected,
maybe his life even threatened from what I hear." Bound
stopped in the White House corridor through which they were
walking and turned to his assistant director.

"Larry, I know Jim Cummins personally, and I know the
people of Georgia. They are good, hard working folks, but if
they feel you have pushed them around, they will push
back. Yes, the Governor of Georgia has gone too far and must
be dealt with, but the way it is carried out is more important
than anything else. This is a molehill that could grow into a
mountain overnight." Bound turned and continued walking
down the corridor.

The Oval Office in
The White House
Washington, D.C.

President Soloto chose to broadcast his address to the nation
directly from the Oval Office while seated behind his executive

desk. As is normal for a Presidential address, it would go out live across all the television networks, cable services and satellite feeds. All of America and much of the world would be able to see and hear it.

Soloto was seated and dressed in a dark suit over a pearl colored shirt with a red tie, all standard for Presidential dress. As the broadcast began, America saw the President with his hands folded on the desk before him. Obviously unhurt by the recent events aboard Air Force One, Soloto wore as grim a face as he could muster to emphasis the seriousness of the situation.

My fellow Americans, good evening. As many of you have already heard, yesterday morning there was a seditious and illegal act perpetrated by the Governor of Georgia, Jim Cummins. Mr. Cummins, armed with the knowledge that I was flying into the airport in Atlanta, Georgia, did unlawfully enter the airport with men and weapons and subdue my advance team of Secret Service agents, and commandeer the control tower of Hartsfield-Jackson airport. Cummins then contacted my pilot in the cockpit of Air Force One and refused clearance for my plane to land. After that, events turned deadly as I personally witnessed, out of the cockpit window, the explosion of one of our Air Force fighter jets that flew alongside of my airplane as an escort. The pilot of that fighter jet, Lieutenant Joey Davenport, was killed instantly, leaving behind a grieving wife and family. The shock wave from that explosion nearly caused Air Force One to go into a nose dive, and only the skilled and brave determination of my pilot, Captain Dick McGrudder, kept Air Force One from spiraling out of control. Even so, nearly all the staff and reporters aboard suffered some kind of injury, though thankfully none of them lost their lives. I was not injured. As your President, I want to assure you that Governor Cummins of Georgia and his accomplices will face swift and sure justice for his outlandish, unprecedented, and illegal actions. I will use every power at my discretion to arrest and punish all of those responsible. Again, let me say that your President is safe and uninjured, and let me assure you that the rule of law still holds in the United States of America. We will never let a rogue Governor, or anyone else, intimidate and disrespect the lawfully elected government of the United States. Good night, and may God Bless America through these troublesome times.

As the President signed off, hundreds of TV talking heads began their chatter, explaining to America what it had just heard, each putting their own spin on Soloto's words.

Chapter Four

The State Capital Building
Atlanta, Georgia

The heavy oak gavel rose and fell with deliberate, forceful swings. Its echo bounced off the marble walls of the cavernous House Chamber of the Georgia State Capital building where the Georgia State Legislature was holding a joint meeting of both the State House and State Senate. A heated debate over the Governor's Nullification Bill had run on for more than nine hours, and things seemed to finally be coming to a head.

As bodies grew tired, tensions continued to rise. The nerves of even those lawmakers known for cool-headedness were fraying at the edges, causing tempers to flare. The outlines of debate, often heated but usually stable and often predictable, had taken an unfamiliar shape, and those who had in the past controlled the debate felt themselves quickly losing control. This worried the veteran lawmakers who were present and trying to keep things in line.

With all the fresh blood present, these newly elected, un-experienced firebrands had unbalanced things to a level no one expected. And with that fool now in the Governor's office, some were thinking, there was no stopgap measure to fall back on; if this body passed irresponsible legislation, there would be no veto firewall there to protect the state, and the people, from it.

The gavel, still pounding, failed to quell the contentious murmuring which was now being punctuated by angry and accusing shouts and curses. Finally, Speaker of the State House Benny Lefever, who had been down on the floor working members that he thought might still be persuaded to vote his way, now climbed back onto the stage that supported the massive Speaker's podium. Leaning over to touch a button controlling the volume of his microphone, Lefever punched it up to its highest, loudest setting. He did not bother with the gavel that his stand-in had been pounding on the podium to no avail, choosing volume over protocol.

"Order, order--order Ladies and Gentlemen!" The volume was so loud that some representatives winced at the voice booming from massive Peavy speakers ceiling-mounted all about the room. The room began to quiet as everyone realized that the Speaker was off the floor and back behind his podium, which, standing underneath a massive Georgia State Seal inset into the thick marble wall behind, endowed the Speaker with a special sense of authority when he occupied it.

"Please quiet down...the Speaker recognizes representative Hartwell from Decatur."

Now rose Cal Hartwell, as seasoned a politician as had existed in the State of Georgia in the past fifty years. Hartwell was the longest serving member of the Legislature, the survivor of countless political battles and the broker of countless backroom deals. He had spent years building up his political network throughout the State. Not one veteran member of the legislature did not owe him a favor; even the Speaker himself held his seat only because he had received the blessing of Cal Hartwell.

Hartwell's political weight was rivaled only by his physical bulk, the three hundred and forty pounds of which he now heaved up a short set of steps and behind the podium. Speaker Lefever smiled as he gave way to the one man he knew had the political heft to crush this debate once and for all. Lefever knew that the keepers of the old guard such as he and Hartwell could not allow the newly elected political novice of a Governor to carry out ridiculous plans--plans which bordered on madness!

For years the State of Georgia, with its business hub of Atlanta, had been growing by leaps and bounds. Jobs had come in by the thousands, and money with it. People with new ideas were moving here in droves.

Industry. Business. Progress. Moving forward at warp speed, seeking to leave behind what many considered a shameful and stagnant past. Lefever and Hartwell had been there for the whole thing. They had watched this deep-south State, once an anchor of segregation racism, grow and develop and transform itself from a back-water into the most progressive of all its neighbors.

But then along came Jim Cummins with his neo-confederate populist campaign that had a redneck crawling out from under every log to register to vote for and elect this fool as Governor. Cummins' had not run an overtly racist campaign, but Lefever knew a closet racist when he saw one. And he knew that a closet radical was more dangerous than one that would show his cards early in the game.

Lefever had been part of the push led by former Governor Roy Barnes to change the Georgia State Flag by removing what they saw as the outdated and hideous Confederate Battle symbol from it, a symbol that had offended blacks and other progressives. That, along with other reforms, had been a great leap forward and a welcome leap away from a backward past.

But Cummins now threatened to undo all of it with his demagoguery, thought Lefever, playing to simple minded gun-rack-and-six-pack crowds that followed him around the State hooping and hollering for a return to the past, demanding respect for their so called 'heritage.'

Lefever never ceased to experience a wave of heartburn when he thought back to that awful election night that found Cummins celebrating a narrow victory and, even more foreboding, many of his surrogates winning in district elections for legislative seats.

Cummins' freak win of the Governorship had been bad enough but could be overcome as long as proper majorities held in the legislature. But they had not held, and today's circus sideshow had been the pathetic result.

Well, Cummins and his followers and their heritage would be consigned to the nethermost regions of hell if Lefever and his ally Hartwell had anything to do with it. They were not going to allow these blind leaders of the blind to destroy a State they had worked so hard to bring out of the past, out of the darkness.

So for the past three weeks Lefever had lobbied, threatened, cajoled, arm-twisted and promise-bribed harder than he had ever done before to defeat the Governor's Nullification bill that was currently before the legislature. He could not believe some of the people who were on the verge of bowing to the pressure of this rabble that followed Cummins.

There was no doubt in Lefever's mind that this bill was a hundred times more dangerous than any his State had faced in generations. Exhausted by the effort and near the end of his strength, Lefever turned to his old pal Hartwell to save the day and end this threat. How could he possibly fail? After all, Hartwell's influence was legendary, reasoned Lefever.

Hartwell himself would have been Speaker of the House long ago if a political opponent had not leaked to the press about a certain indiscretion with a secretary. And yes, the secretary had a night job as a 'gentleman's escort,' a revelation that had shocked many in the capital of Atlanta, yet Hartwell had enough friends around the State, especially in the editor's office of one of the south's most influential newspaper, the Atlanta Journal and Constitution. Ranks had closed around Hartwell in his hour of need, making sure the scandal had no legs, securing Hartwell's political survival.

Having survived, Hartwell toured the State, visiting every district and reminding every politician who had ever benefited from his vast influence, especially as he chaired the powerful Appropriations Committee, deciding where the pork-money flowed to in the State.

Even local officials at the city and county level throughout the State saw Hartwell bursting his huge bulk into their offices good-naturedly, calling each by their first name with an almost photographic recall. Over plates of award winning bar-b-cue covered in Dan's Special Swine Shine Sauce, along with pitchers of sweet tea, Hartwell kindly reminded each one of the political debt owed to him.

Though he weathered the storm, Hartwell was physically worn and had added another twenty five pounds of flesh, though politically he was more powerful than ever. The scandal was buried and mostly forgotten.

Having missed his chance to be Speaker, Hartwell handpicked Lefever for the job and made sure he got it. Yet the last election had overturned their apple-cart, and both Lefever and Hartwell knew it would take every ounce of their collected political savvy to secure victory for their side, and a quick death for Cummins' insane attempt at Nullification.

And now, at this pivotal point in the Nullification debate, Hartwell was behind the Speaker's podium. Lefever realized that everything, all that the two men and their allies had achieved over the past thirty years, now hung on the most important speech Hartwell would ever deliver. Hartwell had to win the crowd, to sway the undecided.

But, thought Lefever, there was no one better to give the ball to when a game-winning touchdown had to be scored. Hartwell could score politically when no one else could, and he had proven it time and time again. He was known as one of the finest orators in the State of Georgia. And so, with great deliberation of manner, a heavy gravity in his voice, and a light sweat on his meaty brow, Representative Hartwell began his historic address.

"Mr. Speaker,Lieutenant Governor,ladies and gentlemen of this distinguished, and until recently, very reasonable, sound and stable body of democracy: I rise to address you on the most potentially dangerous and pernicious piece of legislation to come before this body in more than one and one-half centuries. I rise to shine a spotlight on the pure evil of this bill, which is as venom-filled as the bloated head of a cane-brake rattle snake. And I testify to you all, that the man behind this bill is just as evil as his proposed legislation--a man I don't hesitate to compare to Adolf Hitler himself, this one being the so-called Governor Cummins."

A deafening roar rose from the gathered session, a convoluted mixture of cheers and laughter, boos and hisses. Shoving and pushing could be seen amongst the crowd as tempers flared. As the roar subsided, Hartwell continued.

"Yes my friends, I always call 'a spade a spade,' and I tell you that this Nullification bill is an act of sedition and rebellion! It is nothing but a veiled first step towards a mad-man's ultimate goal of Secession!"

That last statement was too much for the Cummins supporters, and they began to yell at the top of their lungs at Hartwell. Shrieks, hisses and groans of despair flew toward the podium like so many daggers, hardly rivaled now by the shouts of praise from supporters of the old guard.

For his part, Hartwell was unfazed. A grizzled veteran, he had a political hide as thick as that of a Rhinoceros. And he had a strategy, albeit a risky one. Hartwell meant to draw a line in the sand with his speech, to force the issue while his side still had a chance to kill this wild boar-hog of a bill. Lefever's gavel fell hard and fast upon the oak podium, and Hartwell was allowed to continue. And now he would go for the jugular.

"That's right," he spat at those yelling insults at him, "go ahead and get angry, you rabble. You have anger aplenty, but for all of that you have not wisdom. For you, with your so-called Nullification bill, which is nothing less than a bill of Rebellion, a legislation of Sedition, a law to destroy our Democracy and a wedge to divide this Nation. I say with it you are pushing Georgia over a cliff, you are pushing Georgia into a ruin from which we may never recover. If you manage to raise from the dead this morbid, ungodly idea of Nullification, an idea our forefathers long ago consigned to the dust-bin of history and the trash-heap of political disgrace, you will have succeeded only in turning back the clock on the good people of Georgia.

"All you are doing is throwing our State back into a stone age of fanatical division, of bitter racism, and of certain catastrophe. I am no prophet, but I tell you today that your act of disunion and betrayal of the United States of America--your act of disunion will be the first step to an economic disaster the likes of which the people of Georgia have not suffered since the Hoover Days of the Great Depression!"

That's it! Speaker Lefever celebrated to himself as he listened to his friend speak. *Hit'em in the billfold and you will win every time!*

More jeers and ugly bellowing echoed throughout the great hall, although they were not as convincing as the ones before. Hartwell's speech was finding its mark, and the big man knew it. It was causing doubt in the minds of the enemy. And it was hitting hardest in the hearts and minds of those that mattered the most, those being the handful of lawmakers representing the swing votes, the ones who had been fence-sitting throughout the debate, wavering between support for the Speakers' position and support for the Governor's Nullification bill.

These swing voters could still be brought to their senses, Hartwell and Lefever knew. It was not too late. And it was time for Cal Hartwell to pick up the lumber and knock one out of the park. The huge man raised both hands, patting downward like a quarterback trying to quiet a home-field crowd.

"The Georgia Department of Labor says that ten of the twelve largest corporations in Georgia have promised to leave the State of Georgia if this bill becomes law." Hartwell was exaggerating the numbers, but it created the fear-effect he wanted. "Now, how many of you are willing to go back to your home district and face the workers who will be put out of a job when their industry pulls out of Georgia over this bill? How many of you are willing to look into the eyes of the children of parents who are plunged into the bitter pool of joblessness and poverty by your irresponsible support of this insane man in the Governor's office, this loon--who has already alienated the leading business people in the State with his outrageous antics? How many of you want to go back on the campaign trail and face the factory owners who were forced to close their doors and lay off thousands of taxpaying citizens, all because you got caught up in the emotion of a fanatical movement?

"Your constituents will have to travel over impassable roads, for not one scent of revenues will come back to your districts if I have a say in it. This dark storm cloud of Nullification, along with the unconstitutional resistance of the federal government which it represents, will soon pass as do all foolish and seditious movements in America. No matter which way today's vote goes, this charade, this political freak show will soon be overturned--and then where will you be? Where will you be when the dust finally settles? Who will you be standing with?

"Will you stand with a rabid radical who doesn't care about the people of this State, but only about grabbing the headlines and watching himself on the television news shows as he carries out his grandstanding. Or, will you stand with those of us who are for a secure and prosperous future here in Georgia? Will you stand with me, and with Speaker Lefever, and with the men and women who made this country great, men like Georgia Washington and Abraham Lincoln, men who rightly understood that the federal government is here to help us, not to harm us.

"Will you stand with one crazed radical, or with the leaders who have the full weight of the federal government behind us?" Again, plenty of jeers and boos could be heard from the crowd of lawmakers, but the speech had stiffened the resolve of Hartwell's supporters and it was their screams of approval that were now the loudest. Hartwell's heart swelled as he realized he was winning the crowd by winning those precious swing voters that he had to have. He looked over at Lefever and the two exchanged confident smiles. Lefever nodded and Hartwell pressed on with his speech.

"Will you stand with every living former and current President of the United States, all of whom are looking to Georgia and calling on you to crush this hellacious bill of Nullification. That's right, those of you who support Cummins should know that all of America is lining up against you and your foolish so-called Governor and his foolhardy actions! He tried to turn aside our President and Air Force One--may have even tried to kill him! But the duly elected President of this country will be heard in Georgia!"

At just that moment, a massive video screen began to lower from a cylinder attached to the ceiling above the podium. The lights in the hall began to dim until all was pitch dark. A special projector located in the balcony now came to life, lighting up the screen. The official Seal of the President of the United States appeared in blue and gold colors that glowed brilliant back on the up-looking faces of the State Legislature. The room grew eerily quiet at this unexpected turn of events, Speaker Lefever and Hartwell having kept it a surprise.

Lefever knew that it was unprecedented to do such a thing as this, especially without fore-notice, but desperate times called for desperate measures. Besides, Lefever thought, this joint session would be so awe-struck that none would dare interrupt a sitting U.S. President, and after Nullification was defeated, none of this would matter.

Appearing now on the screen, live via satellite feed, sharply dressed in a black suit with stately rows of law-books lining the shelves behind him was President Abraham Soloto. Getting his cue, the President began to address the now silent gathered lawmakers.

> Greetings to the State Legislature of the Great State of Georgia. Georgia has a proud heritage of brave trailblazers and hard working people loyal to the Constitution and to their fellow Americans.
> I'm speaking to you now as one who would take my stand with those faithful Georgians who oppose the dangerous and seditious, out-dated and unnecessary idea of Nullification. Our forefathers gave us the Constitution, and inspired document that has stood the test of time, and allowed us to work out our differences according to law. America is a nation of laws, not just of men. Now, the man currently sitting in your Governor's Office, Mr. Cummins, has already made an illegal attempt to silence the President of the United States. All of you know about the deadly stunt he pulled involving my airplane, Air Force One. That event is still under investigation, but one thing we know for sure is that a fighter pilot in the U.S. Air Force died, leaving behind a grieving family. Mr. Cummins will be held responsible for his actions, that I can promise you. Because of his actions against the President, I have signed a special executive order a few moments ago that removes any authority Mr. Cummins believes he has as Governor of Georgia. Therefore, any bill he signs is automatically Null and Void, and of no legal effect whatsoever. Let me be clear: any bill signed by Mr. Cummins will not be

recognized by the United States Government.
But I want you to go ahead and carry out the
planned vote this evening; it will be a great
opportunity to show both Mr. Cummins and
those who would follow him that the people
of Georgia want no part of his destructive,
illegal and rebellious activities.

Awesome! Thought Speaker Lefever. What a brilliant speech
by the President, and what a political mind Hartwell must
posses to have asked Soloto to make it! To bring to bear the
historic power, gravitas, and authority of the President of
the United States at such a pivotal moment was a stroke of pure
genius, one that would surely do the trick and bring the swing
votes instantly over to their side. Fanatics could not be
reasoned with, but anyone with a sense of proportion would
surely be convinced to vote down Cummins' crazy idea of
Nullification.

But then something happened that neither Lefever nor
Hartwell were ready for. President Soloto, instead of closing his
address cleared his throat and added one last note to his
speech. His face took a more stern and angry demeanor as he
concluded,

And let me add this clear warning:
Those who defy the will of the American
Government are nothing but terrorists
and rogues who will be crushed under
the unbearable weight of her strong
and almighty fist! Think long on that
before you decide. I bid you Good
Night, and may God have mercy on
the enemies of this Administration, for
I will have none!

As the house lights were turned back up, a weak cheer began
to rise from Hartwell's supporters, but it seemed to lose its
punch before it could reach crescendo. People on both sides of
the debate were talking nervously to their fellow lawmakers,
trying to digest the violent threat that Soloto had just made.

Another howl, angry and dark, began to rise from the crowd,
this time from Governor Cummins' supporters, drowning out
all other voices. Lefever looked nervously at Hartwell, whose

forehead was beaded with heavy drops of perspiration. Both men realized that, having grasped victory with a perfect address, Soloto's last couple of threatening sentences would be taken as a challenge to the manhood of the legislature, and may have just ruined everything. Analysts would later compare these last phrases to the bring-it-on false-cowboy machismo of a former President named George W. Bush.

Hartwell, feeling the shift of momentum, tired to recover by finishing the last few lines of his own speech, but it was already too late. Even with the advantage of the microphone, the now rising roar of the Cummins supporters, along with the swing voters who were obviously angered by Soloto's threats, converged to drown out the sweat-stained fat man behind the podium. Lefever's eyes spotted the knot of lawmakers that contained most of the swing vote, and worry filled him as he saw the group booing lustily along with Cummins' people.

At that moment, the noise of the crowd was pierced by the crack of a solid oak door being smashed open. Lefever had had the doors to the meeting hall locked to keep out unwanted visitors, but now his most unwanted guest was making his entrance. He was bracketed about by eight big and muscular men dressed in blue Georgia State Patrol uniforms, the lead two of which still held the sledge hammers they just used to smash the doors through.

None of the patrolmen wore side arms, they simply used their mass and strength to make a way for the man they escorted into the hall. All eyes were on the group of men, and as that group now divided, the crowd of lawmakers could identify the tall, athletic, unmistakable form of Governor Jim Cummins as he made his way to the Speaker's podium.

Sporting a confident and excited smile upon his tanned and finely featured face, Cummins seemed to glide up to the steps to the podium. Lefever, jealous now for his Speaker's authority over the proceedings, tried to race back to the podium ahead of the Governor, as an evangelist would race a demon to the pulpit. Lefever made it there first, but Cummins continued to approach with a calm and even movement.

How dare this man invade the Legislature unannounced and uninvited, thought Lefever. The Cummins supporters in the crowd realized what was happening and were now ecstatic, going wild with excitement at the grand entrance of their leader.

Lefever grabbed the gavel and began to pound it wildly on the solid hardwood of the podium, but the gavel could not take such stress. As the gavel's handle splintered, its heavy head flew off, striking the nearby Hartwell dead center of his forehead as if he had been Goliath, the victim of sling-and-stone.

The huge man's eyes rolled back into his head and he fell backwards, flat on his back with a thump. Lefever felt badly for his friend but did not leave the Speaker's podium, determined to deny Cummins a chance to speak.

Lefever was short of breath and his face red as a turnip, yet he summoned the strength to shout into the microphone,

"Order, order in this body I say...the Speaker of the House DOES NOT RECOGNIZE GOVERN—" Lefever caught himself and could not bring himself to dignify Cummins with the title of Governor. "I do not recognize Mr. Cummins..." Lefever's voice trailed off, for not a word he had said had been heard by anyone. The boisterous welcome for the governor had now become a celebration in the throats and mouths and hearts of his supporters, of which the swing voters were now an indiscernible part.

They were offended by the President's threat of force against the Legislature, and coupled with his touting of an Executive Order to remove a sitting Governor, the undecided had been instantly converted to Governor Cummins.

The moment now belonged to Cummins. Lefever was brushed aside as the Governor and his blue-clad escort over-ran the podium, on which he now stood unmolested. When he raised his hands to greet the crowd, hoots and hollers and what some would later call 'rebel yells' filled the room from marble floor to domed ceiling.

Finally, after long minutes of unabated cheering, the Governor, beaming and confident, lifted his hands to ask for quiet. As the crowd became silent, a sense of gravity, and history, seemed to fill the place. Cummins began his address.

> Gentlemen, and Ladies, I bring you
> tidings of great joy—for this is the day
> when freedom is reborn in the
> Great and Sovereign State of Georgia!

The crowd went wild again. The opposition tried to compete, but their voices were now but a drop of water in a sea. Many of them found themselves, against their own will, hushing to hear what manner of things this man they considered crazy had to say. The Governor did not disappoint.

> On this historic night, you have the
> opportunity to pass a law that will once
> again establish the ideals that our
> forefathers bled and died to secure. As the
> Colonials bled at Bunker Hill, as the
> Confederates sacrificed themselves upon
> freedom's alter at Gettysburg, as your
> grandfather's died in the trenches
> of France during the Great War, as your
> fathers suffered at Pearl Harbor and on
> the Burma Road--so now you can choose to
> take your stand for LIBERTY!

Again the crowd sent up a roaring cheer, and they watched as the Governor's people began to distribute paper ballots that had been prepared for the event.

Modern voting in the Legislature was done electronically, but Cummins had dug up some old paper ballots that had been stored in the Georgia Archives, all government issued and perfectly legal.

As the ballots were being handed out, some of Lefever's people tried to grab them and tear them up, but these scrapers were quickly and efficiently corralled by the State Patrolmen that had escorted the Governor. Later, Lefever and Hartwell would call a press conference to accuse the Governor of using the State Patrol as muscle to force the legislature to vote for Nullification. But the television cameras situated in the balcony filmed everything and offered no evidence of foul play.

The ballots were quickly filled out and collected, then brought to the podium to be counted as many legislators looked on to verify the correct count. When the tally was made, Lefever was given the chance to announce the result, but he would have no part of it, stomping out indignantly over what was left of the oak doors.

Lefever having abdicated his duties, Governor Cummins took the podium to announce the vote count to the joint session, to the nation, and to the world.

> On the House and Senate bill, jointly
> considered, to here-by declare Null and
> Void the federal law, in any and every
> form, that requires Citizens of Georgia to
> contribute to the bailout of the State of

> California, or any federal law requiring
> any Citizen of Georgia to participate in
> Socialistic Programs...voting 'Nay' are one
> hundred one, and voting 'Yea' are one
> hundred and thirty six...the 'Yeas' have
> it! Bring the passed legislation to the
> Governor!

And right there on the podium, using a sweat stained pen that Hartwell had left behind, Governor Jim Cummins thumbed his nose at Washington, D.C., declaring two federal law's Null and Void within the State of Georgia.

All this action went out to the world via a live feed to cable news. Millions watched from around the world, though few had any great interest in the inner affairs of America.

But in the nation of Iran, one man watched with intense interest. In his office within the Ministry of Intelligence complex located near Tehran, a man sat in the glow of the television screen, watching events unfold within Georgia with gleeful interest. And he was taking notes.

The Presidential Palace
TEHRAN, IRAN

The Iranian Presidential Palace sits a few miles outside of the capital of Tehran. Situated on its eastern side is a small but ornately decorated room often used for official purposes by Iranian President Akmad Ahmadenna.

Presently, Ahmadeena was seated there at a four-feet by eight-feet rectangular table crafted of heavy blackened Persian Oak. With Ahmadeena at the table was the head of the Iranian Oil Ministry, along with five other men who held various positions in the Iranian government. The men were there to witness the signing of an important Presidential Order, one that might change the future of Iran forever.

The oak table was carved with writings, verses from the Koran, the Muslim holy book. Jeweled insets depicted Arab girls, young and beautiful, dancing in Heaven around their beloved. Ahmadeena looked into the seductive, oval rubies that were their eyes. He regarded those virgins depicted on the table-top as symbols of the purity and sacredness of Iran.

Although some might think of Iran as a rogue nation, even a terrorist nation because of its ties to Hamas, Ahmadeena considered his country to be a model of representative government carried out under the over-arching rule of Allah--a true Islamic Republic, the only true Islamic Republic in the world!

Saddam, in neighboring Iraq, had once pretended to call Iraq an Islamic Republic, but Ahmadeena knew that Iraq under Saddam was never more than a thug-ocracy, a Sunni dictatorship ruled by fear. Saddam ruled at and for the pleasure of himself, not to mention his two sadistic sons. He had made deals with anyone, even the hated American government, who had gladly supplied him with weapons which he used to kill fellow Muslims.

But, Ahmadeena remembered with a half-smile, the Americans turned on Saddam when his use-by date expired, and then they destroyed him. And since the Americans had returned to make war in Iraq again, Ahmadeena considered his neighbor to the west to be little more than an occupied territory. Not unlike, he also was thinking, his neighbor to the east, Afghanistan.

And what of the Taliban of Afghanistan, those other pretenders to Muslim leadership? Ahmadeena thought them backward and ignorant and as feeble as women in their attempts to institute the teachings of the Prophet. The near-perfection of the Islamic Republic, he reflected with delight, had occurred only under the steady hand of the Persian Shia!

Ahmadeena was seated at the head of the table, and the others watched patiently as he traced with his finger the lettering carved into its surface. Holy Scriptures, he thought as he moved his finger with the curvature of the lettering...*Our* Holy Scriptures. We are a People of the Book, and that makes us a Holy People, a people after Allah's own will.

He thought of the American President. The Iranian President knew that his American counterpart would also have a holy book in his office. It would not be a Koran though, but rather a Bible, the book of the Jews and the Christians. He wondered if the American leader also considered his own people a People of the Book?

But how could he! America's capital might as well be Hollywood, in all its decadence and fleshliness. Did the man sitting in what they called the Oval Office even consider himself to be a Man of God? It was said that the former President George Bush was a devout Christian and Zionist. Was that why,

Ahmadeena wondered, Bush had been so easily persuaded to attack Saddam, as his father had done before him--or was it for a more practical reason?

Ahmadeena pulled a pack of cigarettes from his coat pocket, singled one out, and put it to his lips as one of the other men quickly produced a lighter. He took a deep drag on what his wife called a 'cancer stick,' holding the smoke in his lungs a brief moment before exhaling it to float across the table.

He looked down at the small stick of tobacco, rolling it between his thumb and forefinger. 'Marlboro,' it read in tiny lettering. American tobacco, he thought, and smiled at the irony of it. Maybe the American's were already killing him, albeit very slowly.

He thought again of Bush, wondering if perhaps the man indeed had some of the religious 'Crusader' in him. But he thought it more likely that Bush had attacked Saddam because Saddam had dared to challenge American financial dominance by refusing to any longer trade Iraqi oil in U.S. Dollars. World leaders rarely act out of religious motivation, Ahmadeena knew; the really religious ones usually keep to themselves, unless their religion is money. For it was only a few years after Saddam had made that fateful move away from the petro-dollar that American bombers rained 'shock and awe,' and death from the skies above Baghdad.

And soon after, the western tanks rolled over the border, and this time they kept rolling all the way to Baghdad. Saddam and his evil sons were driven into crevices of the earth to hide like frightened spiders, then hunted down and put to death like common criminals as their enemies, both American and Shia, mocked them.

All this was done, reckoned Ahmadeena, under the guise of U.S. fears of Saddam's weapons of mass destruction, none of which were ever found. And since then, he reflected further, the American government and their lap-dog media had worked to build up another guise, fear of Iran's nuclear program. And that was what was being publicly stated in Washington and in New York City at the U.N.

All the while, through private off-the-record conversations with the Ahmadeena regime, American diplomats complained more against Iran's plan to trade its own vast oil reserves in non-dollar currencies. Don't make the same mistake Saddam made, the Americans had threat-whispered through back channels.

But would the U.S. really risk an attack on Iran for exercising its sovereign right to trade its own oil in whatever currency it chose? Certainly the value of the dollar would be damaged by non-dollar oil trades, but had the greedy westerners not brought that on themselves by over-printing their greenbacks? *Could not these Americans see the enormity of their own arrogance?*

Ahmadeena realized that his body had grown tense and his teeth had clinched in anger at the thought of it all. Were these westerners so hubris-blind that they thought the rest of the world had to honour their currency as the world-reserve forever without end, and without question?

When his administration had decided to begin construction of an oil trading center, Iran's own Oil Bourse, Ahmadeena had ordered it built on the small island of Kish, just off-shore in the Persian Gulf. He had invited all foreign media to the island so that they could verify that Kish was an island home to nothing more than a financial trade-center. That way, he reasoned, if the westerners ever decided to take out the Bourse with bombing raids, they could not credibly claim that they were targeting a nuclear reactor or weapon's factory.

But this Oil Bourse had yet to go on-line, and that was what the Iranian officials were meeting this day to decide upon.

"Sir?" This one word spoken by the head of the Oil Ministry shook President Ahmadeena out of his daydreams and back to the subject at hand. Before him on the table had been placed a document printed on his own official Presidential stationary. It was the order to open the Oil Bourse for trade, and it would mark the beginning of the end of the petro-dollar in Iran. It needed only Ahmadeena's signature to become decreed Persian law.

This document would order the full start-up of the Iranian Oil Exchange located on the island of Kish. This Oil Bourse would integrate all of the Iranian petroleum sectors into a sleek, modern computerized system of international exchange, trading in a basket of currencies that would include the dinar, the euro, the rubble and the yuan, but would purposely exclude the U.S. dollar.

It would be a stick in the eye of the Americans, and every man in the room knew it. It would be an escalation, and therefore merited much contemplation.

How would the American Government react? Ahmadeena had asked his intelligence agencies that question for months, but no definitive answer had come. Some said that the

Americans simply could not afford another war, but others countered with the recent example of Libya.

Already, Ahmadeena suspected, the Americans had perpetrated an act of sabotage against the Bourse when it had cut an undersea cable off the coast of Egypt, a cable that supplied internet service to Kish. Service had been quickly restored and the Americans had denied any malice. Yet it had been a warning in which they were saying that they could shut down the Bourse any time they chose. It was a bold but limited move by American Special Forces, Ahmadeena reasoned, but would the U.S. go all-in and actually launch a full-scale attack on Iran over the petro-dollar?

The U.S. Armed Forces were the best in the world, Ahmadeena admitted to himself, but he believed they were a mixture of volunteer and for-hire forces that had been stretched thin by operations in both Iraq and Afghanistan as well as propping up a world-wide military presence. Would these armed forces risk another war on top of the others? Would they institute a forced draft to swell their depleted ranks? Would the common people of America even allow for such?

Ahmadeena had finished the Marlboro and now balanced a ball-point pen between the fingers of his right hand, thinking it all through. While he hesitated over the order on the table, another man walked briskly into the room. He paused in deference to the man at the head of the table, then politely placed another piece of paper on the table in front of Ahmadeena.

He picked up the paper and saw that it was a flash-report from the Ministry of Intelligence. The report began with a boldly printed INTEL headline, followed by details in finer print. The headline read:

> GOVERNOR OF U.S. STATE (OR PROVINCE)
> SIGNS LAW DECLARING PRESIDENTIAL
> LAW NULL AND VOID (OF NO EFFECT)
> GOVERNOR OF 'GEORGIA' SAYS HIS
> STATE WILL NO LONGER OBEY DECREES
> FROM WASHINGTON GOVERNMENT.

Ahmadeena read the report, then looked up sternly at the intelligence officer who had delivered it. The officer knew what the stern look meant: this better be good intel or you will find yourself in a Revolutionary Guard dungeon, strapped to a wet metal chair with electrodes attached to your soaking wet body.

"This 'Nullification' threat, how serious of a challenge to Soloto and his Government would you say it is?" asked the President. The officer had anticipated just such a question and pulled from his coat pocket a map of the U.S. He took the liberty to spread out the map on the table as Ahmadeena and the other officials looked on.

"Mr. President, this nullification threat has crossed over the threshold of mere threat, and had now become the law of the local State, or Province, that is called 'Georgia.' This State is located here," said the officer, pointing to an area on the southeast portion of the U.S. map. "The leader of this land is called Governor Cummins, and he along with representatives of the people of this land have together voted for a promise not to obey certain laws handed down from the central government located here," said the officer as he pointed to a spot on the map marked 'Washington, D.C.' "This State of Georgia is located deep within a larger section of the United States that was once known as the 'Confederacy,' a section that banded together some one-hundred and fifty years ago to separate itself from the other part of the country, just as the American's had earlier effected a separation from its mother country of Britain." The officer paused now, proud of his knowledge of American history.

"And how, exactly, was that earlier dispute between this 'Confederacy and the Washington government resolved?"

"Violently," responded the officer with a grin. "It resulted in an inner struggle that claimed some 600,000 lives and the assassination of the American President called Lincoln."

"Yes, I know of this 'Lincoln,'" responded Ahmadeena, "I have visited his Temple while in Washington years ago."

"The rebellious region was forced to remain in the American super-state at the point of a gun, sir."

A grin now sat on the face of the Iranian President. This was the news he had been waiting for, a true sign from Allah saying now is the time to open the Oil Bourse. Now, it appeared, the Washington government faced trouble at home as well as abroad.

He put aside the intelligence report and found the Oil Bourse order. Taking up his pen, he bore down firmly on the line calling for the President's signature, making his name in large strokes of dark ink. Putting the pen aside, Ahmadeena took the document in both hands as if it might weigh ten pounds rather than mere grams.

"A stick in the eye of the American Government," he said loud enough for all to hear. "Well, let them remove the stick from their own eye, and then they shall see clearly to remove the splinter from mine." The men around the table chuckled together at Ahmadeena's statement, recognizing it as one from the Jewish-Christian book.

The Governor's Mansion
Atlanta, Georgia

Governor Jim Cummins leaned on the edge of a table situated near one of the massive, second story windows that look out of his personal office in the Governor's Mansion. A glass of sweet tea, swirling with ice and slices of lemon, was in his left hand.

The forty-eight year old Cummins and his wife, along with the two youngest of his six children, had enjoyed the move into the thirty-room, Greek Revival mansion.

The home was complemented with one of the finest collections of antique furnishings in the United States. The other four children had either married or away at college.

There with Cummins in his spacious office was one man, his closest confidant and seventy-year old attorney, Wilder Fields. Not only had Fields been Cummins' life-long attorney, he had been Cummins' late father's attorney as well. Fields had even been with the elder Cummins' when he had died of a heart attack while on a White-Tail Buck hunt in the South Georgia piney woods.

The two men had an old, tight bond, and Fields had watched with pride as the younger Cummins succeeded in sports as a linebacker for the University of Georgia Bulldogs football team, then later as a businessman and now, a politician. Or, as Cummins would have corrected, a 'Statesman.' Cummins had come to hate the term 'politician' as had most Georgians, and most Americans for that matter.

"Well, the ball is in their court now," said the younger man, still looking out the window and taking a sip from his glass of tea.

"Yes, I'd say that it is," replied the white haired Fields. "The only question is whether they will come with a light or a heavy hand. It'll be a good test of their wisdom, and of their resources."

"If Soloto responds lightly, with a slap on my wrist, then he takes the chance of looking weak," opined the Governor.

"And his supporters who are calling for our blood will not like that," replied Fields, taking a deep draw on a hand-rolled Havana. A wispy trail of smoke rolled off the end of the cigar, drifting out over the Governor's huge mahogany desk.

"No, his crowd will not appreciate it. Chris Matthews is already calling for a CIA hit on me."

"Coming from Tip O'Neill's' former flunky, that's rather funny," said the older man, laughing puffs of cigar smoke into the air of the Governor's office. "Maybe we'll get Zell Miller to go whip that little sissy Matthews." Both men broke out in fresh laughter at Fields' reference to the former Governor and U.S. Senator Zell Miller's challenge of Chris Matthews, live on MSNBC, to an old fashioned honour duel.

"Well shoot-fire, Zell is nearly ninety-five years old now, but I still think he could get'er done." That remark brought forth a full belly laugh from both men.

As their laughter trailed off, the conversation returned to a more serious subject. Cummins was looking out the window at the blooming magnolia trees mixed with blossoming dogwoods on the mansion lawn.

"O.K.--If Soloto responds lightly, we ramp up the pressure. This will play into our hands. But what if he responds with a heavy hand? What then?" asked the Governor of the elder Fields.

"Then you play it as an overstepping of his boundaries, as over-kill, as an attempt to crush all dissent," replied Fields. "This will hurt Soloto badly with the Right and Middle, and even undercut him with his base on the Left." Cummins nodded his head with approval of the older man's strategy, then asked, looking around at the man with the cigar,

"What about our friends in the Georgia National Guard, are they ready? Can we count of them when the time comes?"

"I talked with our principle assets yesterday. They seem to be excited to play their part," replied Fields. Cummins turned again to look at the dogwoods.

"That's good to know. Let's pray they don't lose their nerve."

"Let us pray that we don't lose ours," replied the old gentleman with raised eyebrows.

Fields got up out of his chair and walked over to where the Governor still sat looking out the window. Both men sat silently, admiring the beauty of nature for a brief and quiet moment.

Fields had cut his philosophical teeth on the old States' Righter's Thomas Jefferson, John Calhoun and John Randolph. And Fields had been the primary political influence on the man now sitting as Governor of Georgia. Cummins' had also adopted the political philosophy of a hard-edged States' Rights position as the only and final check on what he called 'the Leviathan power' of the national government.

The two men sincerely believed that if someone did not stand between their people and the feds, that serfdom would be the inevitable fate of the middle class. And they believed passionately in the Sovereignty of the States, that no State gave up its right to self-government when it joined the Union.

Their idea of a Sovereign Georgia was rooted and grounded in a blood-and-soil conservatism that would remind many of 1860 rather than modern times. The world may have changed around them, but these men and those like-minded did not believe it had changed for the better. And the current economic and cultural chaos was ready proof to back their case, and to strengthen their resolve. They considered their politics the most local kind, the closest to the people, and it was, in their minds, the very antithesis of D.C. consolidationism.

And now, with the American empire staggering under the weight of a world it had sought to change, these men believed it was time to make their move--a great and final push for liberty.

"Jim," said the older man, putting a hand on the Governor's shoulder, "I know you have set your face for this game, but be sure you understand that if you interpose yourself between the President and the people of Georgia, he must crush you just to save face."

"Yes," replied the young Governor, "and that is precisely what I want him to try. It must come to a head, Wilder, this struggle between Tyranny and Liberty. It is time to water Jefferson's tree. Why not here?" he asked the older man, "Why not now?"

Tommy Davis

Across the State of Georgia

The people of Georgia had watched the recent events unfold before their eyes, along with the rest of the country, via the television news. And more than anyone else in the world, the citizens of Georgia took very, very seriously these events involving President Soloto and their Governor, Jim Cummins.

These citizens knew that though others may or may not be affected by these events, the people of Georgia most certainly would be. Whatever federal wrath that their duly elected Governor was calling down, the weight of it would surely fall nearby. No one within the State would escape that which would surely come, for Washington, D.C. could not let its iron law be defied. Everyone was talking about it—in their homes, their classrooms, their workplaces, over coffee, over dinner, over the phone and over their computers on Facebook and Twitter.

'What do you think is going to happen next,' they would ask one another. And, when the time came, which side would the people choose?

Many argued in favor of the Governor and his actions--he was only standing up for his people, they said. But just as many, it seemed, argued for the President, saying that the Governor had gone too far. These said that Cummins would bring nothing but disruption to the lives of the people and that nothing good could come from his antics.

The major metro areas and large cities were mostly behind President Soloto, but in smaller towns and rural areas, the pro-Cummins side held sway. Only in the mountainous region above Atlanta in the northern-most part of the State, a section that had been solidly pro-union back in the 1860's, was there no consensus of opinion.

Everyone continued to talk it up, to wonder aloud if Georgia was ready for all of this drama. In 1864, General Sherman had burned much of the State to the ground, someone pointed out. But that was for our own good, someone else would counter. Another would ask, 'If Georgia burns again, what would the people do? Would they simply hide until the fire burned out, or would they have a hand in the outcome?'

Slowly but surely people began to choose sides, and to recruit.

Chapter Five

The Roosevelt Room
The White House
Washington, D.C.

Cal Limkey was a big man at ROX News. Standing six-four, and weighing 275 lbs. and with the mouth to match, Limkey could bully his way through nearly anyone at ROX. Few people dared to stand up to the man, most just avoided confrontation with him. And that is why, after the story of Air Force One and Governor Cummins broke, all the other news anchors in the ROX lineup knew that the hottest interview on the planet would be with President Soloto and the second hottest would be with Governor Jim Cummins, and they knew that Limkey would get both of them before anyone else.

And, they would admit privately, he deserved it. Limkey had led the network on its way to the top of the cable news world. His prime-time show consistently beat out all competitors. That's how Limkey liked it, not just defeating a competitor, but crushing them without mercy. And since nothing like the Soloto-Cummins story had happened in the U.S. for at least half a century, Limkey put all of his considerable weight behind leveraging the desired interviews.

Limkey, as the leading news anchor in America, had two basic means of leverage: the carrot and the club. The carrot leverage was that Limkey and his producers could promise a news worthy individual a full hour of top-rated interview air-time at precisely the time that it would help them the most. For a politician, it was nearly always just prior to an election, when a Limkey interview could guarantee the politician a bump of several points in the polls.

On the other hand, the club leverage was simply that if a news figure refused to grant an interview to Limkey, he would use his show to pummel that person weekly, if not daily, resulting in negative publicity that would cost literally millions of dollars to counter-act. With these tools at his disposal, Limkey usually got the interview that he wanted.

And so it was within hours of the story-break that Limkey had his producers place calls to the White House requesting an interview with President Soloto. Even though Soloto had already been re-elected for a second term and therefore did not need Limkey for the pre-election, poll-bumping interview, there were others in Soloto's party who would need that kind of help.

The ROX producers promised not just one but three prime-time, prime-slot interviews to either Soloto or his hand-picked successor over the next three years in trade for an exclusive with the President while the Air Force One story was still all the buzz.

When word of these offers reached the ears of Chief of Staff Brandenburg, it got the man's attention. Eli Brandenburg himself had an eye on making a future run for his party's Presidential nomination, and nothing would help him more than landing slots on Limkey's news cast.

Brandenburg began to use his powerful influence with the President and his handlers to go ahead and make the deal with the ROX producers. He knew that they needed to strike while the story was hot. If the story was allowed to cool down and lose its legs, then Limkey would soon break out his 'club' and begin to nail the President and his staff for failing to deal with the slap-in-the-face that Governor Cummins had given him during the attempted Atlanta trip. One way or another, President Soloto and Cummins would be the topic of Limkey's nightly newscast until the matter was resolved.

It took several days of cajoling fellow staff members and some face-time with the President himself to get the Limkey interview approved. The President had never felt that ROX News had given him fair coverage, but the Limkey producers had been willing to put their promises in writing and even Soloto had to admit that ROX enjoyed a wide viewership, even though much of it would never consider voting for either Soloto or his party.

When the day of the interview arrived, Limkey and his crew of camera, lighting and makeup personnel were directed to the Roosevelt Room located in the west wing of the White House where they prepped for the interview.

Though his crew was somewhat nervous, Limkey was as cool an interviewer as the news-business had seen and was not at all intimidated by either the White House or its occupant.

When Soloto arrived, he and Limkey exchanged civilities, and briefly reviewed the prior arranged parameters of the interview. The two men were then seated opposite one another, and the interview began. With his back to the door, the President did not notice that a flush-faced LeBeau had rushed through the door, only to be stopped short by a Secret Service Agent.

LeBeau had been kept out of the loop about the ROX interview, thanks to COS Brandenburg. Finding out about it at the last minute, LeBeau had literally run down the hallway of the west wing of the White House to try to stop the interview from taking place. He was sure it would be used by ROX to make the President look bad, but he had been too late to stop it.

Limkey's usual modus operandi was to at first flatter the interviewee, putting him or her at ease, only to go right for the jugular in the next instant.

With the President, Limkey got right to the point.

"Mr. President, I want to say how relieved I was to hear that you were not hurt in the recent attack on Air Force One while flying into Atlanta. And I know that all patriotic Americans agree with those sentiments, and also agree that the stunt that the Governor of Georgia pulled was insane, it was dangerous, it was illegal. And so, Mr. President, can you tell us what action you are taking to hold this Cummins person accountable?"

"Let me thank you, Cal, and I want to thank all Americans for their thoughts and prayers during this troublesome time. As you said, it was an illegal and seditious act--..that which Governor Cummins perpetrated in the skies over Georgia on July third. And we will seek justice, we will hold this man accountable for his actions. I have ordered the Attorney General to seek indictments against Governor Cummins on all counts that relate to his actions."

"Mr. President, can you tell us precisely what those indictments will charge? We know that the fighter pilot was killed in the explosion, so we expect that a murder charge will be part of the indictment."

"Well, Cal, let's start at the beginning of this whole affair. Governor Cummins and his accomplices first entered Hartsfield-Jackson Airport and subdued members of the Secret Service who were there awaiting my arrival. To do this, Cummins and his men had to take firearms into the airport, which is a serious crime. Then they subdued and held the federal agents—locking them in the men's room-- which is kidnapping."

"Mr. President, to clarify, are you saying that Cummins himself was armed when he entered the airport?"

"Well, we think he was--we have eye-witnesses that have testified to that fact. But he ordered armed men into the airport, Cal, so it doesn't make any difference if he had a weapon on his person--he is still guilty of it because he conspired with others to do so."

"But those violations pale in comparison to what happened next. Can you tell us, Mr. President, about the charges related to Air Force One, the denial of permission to land the plane, and especially about the explosion of the fighter jet?"

"What I can tell you, Cal, is that it is a violation of federal law to interfere with the movements of the President of the United States, so we've got him there on a serious federal charge."

"Right, Mr. President, you emphasis the federal nature of that charge because the breaking of a federal law allows you to use federal agents to make the actual arrest, correct?"

"Yes, Cal, it does, but allow me to say that, as President, I can enforce State law as well. For example, I can order the FBI or the NSA to apprehend violators of State law when a violation of that law was done against the President."

"Well," said Limkey with a hint of doubt in his voice, "I'm not sure about the federal/State thing. We'd have to consult some constitutional scholars on that. But let me ask you, Mr. President, about the fighter jet, the Raptor that exploded. Please tell us about that experience, and about the murder charges related to the death of the pilot."

"Well, again, Cal, allow me to reiterate that as President and head of the Executive Branch, I can enforce--we can enforce all the laws of the land, be they federal or State," said Soloto, not wanting to let Limkey's doubt of the President's statement go unchallenged. Soloto wanted to leave no doubt that he was going to get Cummins on whatever charges he could make stick, whether federal or State. Limkey did not appreciate the President's return to the subject, nor did he like it that Soloto was not following his lead in the interview.

"Well, Mr. President, I mean--its not like you can have agents of the NSA out issuing speeding tickets in Georgia. You can't really go there, can you?" Soloto now felt a bit insulted by Limkey's questioning the President's legal analysis. After all, reasoned Soloto, he had been to law school and Limkey was merely a news reporter.

"As Commander in Chief," responded the President matter-of-factly, "I can use every power at my disposal to apprehend criminals who have perpetrated war-crimes against the President."

"Mr. President, I whole-heartedly agree that this Cummins' idiot has got to be dealt with, but dealt with as a common criminal, not a war-criminal, since what he did was not done in the context of a war."

"I disagree with you Cal. I think you are mistaken, and the Attorney General agrees with me on this legal question." Cal Limkey thought the Attorney General to be an idiot himself, appointed only as a political payback to the man who had helped deliver an important State into Soloto's camp on election night. Limkey's enormous arrogance had been offended by the President, but he could not simply cut off the President's microphone, or just end the interview. This was, after all, the President of the United States that he was interviewing.

"Okay, Mr. President, we'll save that discussion for another time. Right now, could you tell us about the fighter jet. How do you think Governor Cummins was able to bring that jet down?"

"Well, what I can say is that it has been difficult to recover all the debris from the Raptor. We were flying over tree-covered mountains when the explosion took place, and that makes full recovery almost impossible. Some of the locals have taken the Governor's side down there, and have hampered our efforts also."

"Hampered the efforts? Why not just have your agents arrest those local-yokels if they interfere? You have that authority, right?"

"Cal, we're working on it--its being addressed as we speak. I'm confident that we will get all of the jet recovered, it just takes time."

"I understand, Mr. President, but that dead pilot's family needs some justice and some closure, so maybe--"

"Cal," snapped the President, cutting Limkey off mid-sentence, "don't suggest a lack of concern on my part for the pilot's family. I had to watch that man die! I could see it out of the cockpit window!"

Both men began to shift in their seats now. This was not how the interview was supposed to go. Both men now felt that the other was trying to control the interview, and both were offended. Skins were growing thin. It was at this point that LeBeau, the political advisor standing off-camera, snatched up a glass of water and rushed toward the President.

"Here, Mr. President," said LeBeau, handing Soloto the glass.

"Stop the tape!" yelled Limkey, angry that LeBeau had barged in to interrupt the interview. The President looked up at LeBeau as he accepted the glass of water.

"Hank? I did not know you were here," said Soloto, irritated.

"Mr. President," said LeBeau, whispering in the President's ear, "could I have just a minute with you before you continue this interview. I really don't trust Limkey. I wish I had been informed that this interview had been scheduled for today."

The President took several swallows of the water to cool his throat. LeBeau noticed that Limkey was watching his every move, trying to hear what he was saying in Soloto's ear.

"Not now, Hank. If you did not get the memo on this interview, take it up with Brandenburg. No, wait! Don't say anything to Eli, I don't want you two fighting again. We'll talk about this later," said Soloto. But LeBeau did not want to take "not now" for an answer.

"Mr. President, please, just a few seconds of your time--"

"Could we pick up where we left off now, please," said Cal Limkey a little too-loudly for LeBeau, who felt another wave of chest pain coming on.

"NOW LISTEN TO ME, YOU RIGHT-WING CHATTER BOX!" shouted LeBeau, as he lunged toward the still seated Limkey. Limkey, enraged at the man's outburst, reached out to push LeBeau away. LeBeau grabbed his own chest as he fell head-long into a light-stand, sending it crashing down on Limkey's head. The light-bulb hit the news anchor square on his forehead, shattering with the impact. Limkey yelped and grabbed his head with both hands. The shattered light-bulb left a nasty gash running across the forehead, along with a second-degree burn that singed the man's skin and eyebrows. He cursed a string of invectives as he fell to the floor.

All of that was bad enough, but there was more insult in store for the ROX News man. The commotion around the President caused the three Secret Service agents in the room, agents already on-edge due to recent events, to burst into action. All three rushed to surround Soloto. As they did, Limkey tried to get to his feet, still cursing. Two of the agents took this as a threat to Soloto, and bum-rushed Limkey like a double-team of fullbacks, knocking the big man backwards into a wall.

Soloto watched all of this with disbelief. *Am I surrounded by complete idiots on every side?*

Shaking loose the grip of the Service agents, Soloto marched for the door. The interview was obviously over. More Service agents had entered the room to investigate. Four of them could barely hold an enraged Limkey on the floor.

One of the agents, a rookie, came to the decisive yet unfortunate conclusion that he should employ his Tazor stun-gun, which he drew and fired directly into the chest of Limkey. The other agents backed off to watch as Limkey convulsed across the carpeted floor as if possessed. Their forlorn looks back and forth begged one question: How could this be happening?

Sorubi, Afghanistan--30 miles outside of Kabul

The hour was late, for darkness had crept over the lands of Afghanistan five hours before. These were the lands, the natives boast, where great empires come to die.

A robed figure shuffled quietly through the stone and straw structures lining the streets in the village of Sorubi. Yusef Atta had grown good at not being seen since the Americans had come. His father had done the same when the Soviets had come, though he had died at their hand, but not before giving life to a son, a future Mujahideen, a holy warrior for Allah.

Though only twenty-three, Yusef had gathered his own militia of twenty warriors and coordinated their attacks upon the hated American soldiers, with enough success to be noticed by the leaders of the Taliban hiding in the far-away mountains.

Two men were waiting patiently for Yusef's arrival. There was no need for impatience, the American usurpers had no plans to leave anytime soon, although those plans could perhaps be influenced.

Yusef stopped behind a small building, a shop that sold tanned leather goods during the day. He rapped gently on the wooden door and was allowed entry. Waiting inside were Marwan Sharrah and Benhaddad Houmani, senior representatives of Mullah Mohammed Omar, the undisputed leader of the Taliban.

The senior leadership of the Taliban had restricted their own movements and traveled often under cover of darkness ever since the Americans had devastated their ranks using airborne, rocket laden Predator drones to surgically remove them. The darkness helped give a sense of security although they knew the unmanned drones carried technology that worked as well in the dark as the daylight.

"Welcome faithful Yusef," said Houmani in a voice just above a whisper, for Houmani had often wondered if the Predator drones could hear him through walls and recognize his voice. "Our Holy Leader Mullah Omar and the faithful brethren of the Taliban want to congratulate you and your fighters for your work against the infidel occupiers of our homeland. You have bled the Americans deeply, and the Afghani people praise Allah for your success." Yusef bowed deeply to the two older men.

"Thank you for your kind words. I praise Allah and his servant the Holy Leader Mullah Omar. I live but to serve Allah and Mullah Omar. Our warriors will fight to the death to restore Allah's servants and the rightful rulers of Afghanistan, the Taliban."

"Allahu Akbar!" said Sherrah. "The Taliban is especially grateful for the entrance into paradise of Ziad al-Beridi, one of your trainees, whose sacrifice took ten American mercenaries to their deaths. He is with the holy virgins, but the Americans are roasting in the flames of Hell, praise be to Allah."

"Ziad was a true believer, brother Sherrah, and told me as I strapped the vest to him that his one regret was that he had but one life to sacrifice for Allah and the restoration of Sharia to the homeland," replied Yusef. The older men nodded respectfully.

"Yusef," continued Houmani, "we bring news, plans and resources from our Holy Leader."

Yusef had already noticed the boxes of plastic explosives on the floor nearby, a much larger quantity by far than was usually delivered at one time.

"As you may have heard, the long expected uprising within the Great Satan of America has begun, and it has begun in a place called Atlanta, in the province of Georgia. Of course, all the peoples of this heavily Christian land of Georgia deserve to die and burn in flames, and one day shall, but for now the Holy Leader sees an opportunity in this uprising. We have special friends located in this city of Atlanta, and they have promised to soon take up Jihad there."

Yusef nodded his head in approval, not mentioning that his own cousin Raffi was a member of an al-Quaeda terror cell centered in Atlanta. The Taliban probably knew of the family connection already, but why blab more information than necessary, even to fellow Mujahideen.

"The Holy Leader has plans to exploit this infighting among the Christian dogs. It will be done through escalation here, in these our lands, what we all have wanted for so long. And it will begin the moment the infidels are forced to draw down forces here to face their troubles at home," said Houmani "but we have to be prepared for that moment." Houmani paused briefly to gage the young jihadist's reaction.

"Yusef, have you heard of a place called Vietnam? Years ago, the Americans sent their armies to conquer that place, but the natives bled the invaders slowly, over time, and when the occupiers least expected it, the natives launched what they called the 'Tet' offensive. This movement drained the Americans of their resolve, and eventually they turned and went home. Yusef, for the freedom fighters of Allah here in Afghanistan, this will be our 'Tet' offensive--this will be the stone that breaks the will of the infidels."

"But Yusef," added Sherrah, "in order to be successful there are two things your warriors must accomplish. The first is that your people working inside the American compound in Kabul must be ready to strike upon an hours notice, without hesitation, and to seal their faithfulness with their own blood."

Yusef nodded gravely in understanding; his people inside the compound must become sacrificial bombers.

"And secondly, Yusef, those willing to sacrifice their lives to kill the infidels and to be ushered into paradise--their numbers must be multiplied. For every one sacrifice you have in training, you must now find nine more to go with them."

Nine more for each one! *They are asking me for ten times the carriers! Where will I recruit that number?* Yusef was set aback, but tried to keep his face kindly and obedient. Still, his alarm showed.

"Yes Yusef, we need your people to increase tenfold, for our Holy Leader has a plan to clean Kabul itself of the occupying American infidels in one fail swoop...a glorious night of blood and holy violence! So you must concentrate all your efforts upon recruiting these new sacrifices. The Holy Leader Omar is sending to your village a brother who will put together the devices for you so that you have time for reading the Holy Koran and to pray with the sacrifices. Recruit Yusef, bring in the young men that the Holy Leader needs to help win this struggle."

"The young men," added Sherrah, "the young women as well, the elderly, even the children must be recruited and trained to fill up the number of sacrifices required to satisfy the plan of the Holy Leader Omar. And it will happen sooner than you think, Yusef, it will happen soon, so we must work now, and work with all diligence. Truly, ours is the Land where Empires come to die!" said Sherrah, reaching over to gently lay his palm on a box of c-4.

No one in the little shop felt the need to remark upon the irony of the fact that the boxes were boldly lettered in the language of the infidel: PROPERTY OF THE U.S. ARMY.

Chapter Six

NSA Headquarters
Fort Meade, Maryland

The Director of the National Security Agency, Dennis Click, had called an urgent meeting of the agents of the Interior Affairs Division of the NSA.

The NSA was originally created to break enemy codes and to create unbreakable codes for use by the armed forces of America. But as Congress had ballooned its funding, the scope of the NSA had ballooned right along with it, though its operations were supposed to deal with foreign nations only.

The division labeled 'Interior Affairs' had officially come into existence after 9-11, a tragedy which many in D.C. blamed on the FBI. The Interior Affairs Division of the NSA now handled research and analysis of any security threat *within* the United States that came to its considerable attention.

The FBI was doing their own leg-work on the Atlanta matter, but the NSA had a reputation as having an elitist as well as an aggressive attitude. Hiring only the best and brightest from Ivy League schools, the NSA did not trust the Bureau to dig deeply enough, nor did they believe the FBI had the resources it would take to get the job done.

Turf battles had already erupted between the two federal agencies several times. An incident down in Miami had caused even more cross-agency suspicion when two FBI agents had disappeared in the Everglades. The Bureau learned latter that the agents had stumbled onto an arms deal that somehow involved agents working for the NSA. The two lost agents had never been found and were presumed dead, but the NSA claimed to have no knowledge of the arms deal, or of what had happened to the missing Bureau men.

The e.mail that each Interior Affairs analyst had received from the Director calling them to meet in a small conference room had also mentioned that the situation in Atlanta, Georgia would be the subject of the meeting.

The atmosphere around the super-secretive NSA had been tense of late. Nearly one third of the agents and analysts had been 'reassigned,' which was NSA-code for 'laid-off.' The layoffs were a matter of simple economics. Beginning with the economic crash of 2008, government funding had come under increasing pressure. Even with the up-turn in the economy that helped President Soloto get re-elected, most of those laid off had not yet been re-hired. Morale had suffered terribly.

What was more, a Congressional investigation had discovered that several top NSA operatives had been taking bribes from foreign intelligence services, and stashing the cash in off-shore accounts. The operatives were planning to retire early and live in wealth and luxury in some exotic location.

Having been caught up with, some had fled to other countries while others had taken their own lives rather than face prosecution. A few especially 'sensitive' operatives had simply disappeared never to be seen again, and speculation ranged from the idea that those disappeared agents had gone over to other governments, to the rumor that those agents had been dealt with 'internally.'

Still, no one around the NSA asked too many questions. Everyone wanted to know a lot of information, but no one wanted to know too much.

The meeting room the analysts were called to was a totally enclosed cube with no windows and only one door. Present at the meeting were Director Click, a Deputy Director, and six analysts. A psychological profiler had also been invited.

"Good morning," said Click to the analysts as he opened the meeting. "This meeting will not be a long one, I have a chopper waiting for me on the pad as we speak. Whatever you have been working on is now tabled. From this moment until further notice, each of you will put together a fresh file on a 'mark' named Jim Cummins, who is currently Governor of the State of Georgia. I want a complete work-up and history on the man, uncover it all. You know the drill: what his family and childhood were like, any brushes with the law, any and all organizations he has been a member of, etcetera.

"Dig deep, people. Roll over every stone and look underneath for things that grow in the dark. You know how important it is to the White House that we find out what makes this man tick. Fly down to Atlanta if you have to and do some interviews of people who have known the man--but that which you do, do quickly. Within ninety-six hours I want your reports presented to Dr. Griner here, our psych-profiler on this case.

"You will work closely with Dr. Griner to complete a full profile of this Cummins person--I want to know what motivates the man, what all he has done and why, and what he is capable of doing. That is all."

Click had turned to exit the room before the last word left his mouth. He had been called back to D.C. to meet with the President's team to discuss Governor Cummins and the situation in Georgia. Without a profile of Cummins in hand, Click felt like he was flying blind, but he had to be present at the White House meeting with or without the information he would need to advise the President.

After Click left the meeting room, the analysts talked among themselves, divided the labor on the research, deciding who would research which part of Governor Cummins past. It took about twenty minutes to divvy up the work, and the meeting broke up. Lingering behind was the Deputy Director and the psychological profiler Griner.

"So, Dr. Griner, what is your initial thoughts on this Governor Cummins character?" asked the Deputy Director.

"Well, I hesitate to draw any conclusions before I have reviewed all the information."

"Dr. Griner, relax. We are strictly off-record right now, and this room is not bugged, so just shoot from the hip for a second or two."

Dr. Griner seriously doubted that there were any of the thousands of rooms in the NSA complex that were not affixed with listening devices and cameras, but since the words 'off the record' had been openly stated, he would answer as best he could.

"Well, this Cummins, from what I have gathered on my own, came from a traditional southern home, the deep-south mind you--a two parent upbringing, the oldest of three siblings, church-going--fairly typical middle class family for that region of the country. He excelled in public schools and in college, both academically and athletically, and is likely motivated by a sense of patriotism, along with a hero-complex of some degree. Likely he feels responsible for the welfare of others, and wants to be admired by those same people whether they are his own family, or his entire native State. That, along with a probable sense of honour inherited from the medieval Christian Knight tradition latent in the male psyche down there in that part of the country--in all likelihood those types of ideals drive this man to do what he does."

"Dr. Griner, the person you are describing sounds more grounded and stable than the man who pulled that stunt with Air Force One. How can that be?"

"You must remember, Deputy Director Finch, in his mind, all that he has done is completely rational, even admirable, though risky. In fact, the risk or danger element only compliments the heroic nature of his deeds--in his mind that is. And whatever else he intends to do will also be justifiable in his psyche. That is how the mind of this type of person thinks."

"A hero and a patriot, you say--sounds like he wants to be Braveheart--William Wallace to the rescue!" The Deputy chuckled at his own joke, but Dr. Griner was not laughing.

"Sir, let me ask you a question: if the Scottish warrior William Wallace had acquired the advanced weaponry to destroy the British Crown in his day, do you think he would have hesitated to use it? If Wallace perceived that the destruction of the British was a righteous goal, would he have gone to any length to destroy them?" Deputy Director Finch sat thinking just a moment before answering.

"Well, I have not read that much about William Wallace, but according to the Mel Gibson movie, I would have to answer 'Yes.' Wallace would have used any means of ruthless violence to obtain his 'perceived righteous goal.'"

"That is correct, sir," replied the psyche profiler. "I *have* read much about the Hero of the Scotts, and I still agree with your analysis. But," he added as he stood to leave the meeting room, "just remember; to this Governor with the 'William Wallace complex,' the NSA and the federal government *are* the British."

Dr. Griner patted Finch on the shoulder as he left the room, leaving the man alone with that thought.

Communications Laboratory
Campus of Georgia Tech University
North of Downtown Atlanta

The two students had told their communications professor that they needed to work late in the computer lab to finish the assignments that were due on his desk the next day. They hoped he would not take special note of the hardware they had requisitioned for their project: circuit boards, microchips, soldering tools.

Late into the night they had labored, hovering over a work bench in one corner of the lab. One of the students, a female with blond, shoulder length hair, put a microchip in its appointed place on a small circuit board. Her compatriot, a skinny male with prematurely thinning hair and a patchy working of chin hair and pimples, deftly used a micro-soldering pen to complete the circuitry. The soldering tool sent tiny puffs of smoke into the air as he worked. When the work was done, the girl took a deep breath.

"There now," the man said, "that should do it." He took off his thick magnification glasses and sat them on the table.

"Sure hope these work as well as our first ones. They said the first batch worked well enough, so I hope these will too," said the young lady.

"I still wonder how they *know* the first ones work. They have no way of knowing if they were overheard unless..."

"Unless," she picked up the thought he did not want to voice, "unless Cummins has a mole inside the NSA who lets him know."

"A mole inside the NSA--good Lord, the NSA is mole-proof," replied the male student, "Even if they have a contact there he is probably a double agent and will rat us all out in the end."

"Don't worry Sammy, no one but Fields even knows my name, and I've never mentioned your name to him. If anyone goes down, it will be me, so chill out."

"I can't believe we're doing this Lindsy. Do you know how much it costs my parents to send me here to Tech? If I get in trouble, all that money will be down the drain. My father is a plumber for goodness sake!"

"I know Sammy, it's a big chance to take, but I for one will not be a serf to the federal government and their elitist corporate buddies. No one but Governor Cummins has the guts to stand up to the feds . He's only doing what is right, the traditional American thing to do--resist Tyranny. Besides, you had plenty of time to consider all that before agreeing to help me."

"How could I not agree to help you do anything," said the young man, looking away from her, his face blushing pink with embarrassment. "I've had a crush on you since we were in the eighth grade together." The girl smiled at the shy fellow beside her.

"Sammy, you're the sweetest thing, but I told you this had to be done for the right reasons."

"I know, I know. Besides, you would never have figured out the algorithms by yourself," he said, grinning like a tomcat.

"Ha! Who aced advanced calculus last semester?" replied the young lady. She looked down at the device they had just put together. "O.K. Lets hook this up to the mainframe and run the computer models. This has got to work properly every time. No matter how brave our Governor is he still has to communicate with his friends if he is going to organize his movement. This scrambling unit will attach to any cell phone or land line he uses. The will eventually break the codes we've installed, but by that time we will have come up with some new ones."

"We have to stay one step ahead of those guys out of D.C.," replied the goateed Sammy. "If they break the codes too soon, Cummins is toast. We know they've already tapped all his lines, and are intercepting his cell phone transmissions."

"Which is completely unconstitutional," added the young lady.

"Lindsy, you know they make up the law as they go, so save the constitutional talk."

"Hey buddy, even the government has to obey the law, or should have to anyway. Otherwise, it becomes an absolutist, tyrannical power."

"Right, right, Patricia Henry, give you liberty or give you death. Anyway, these new encryptions are based on the work of that guy from M.I.T. I was telling you about, along with some of my own modifications. These will keep the NSA dudes scratching their heads for a while I would bet. But you don't defy the President of the United States without bringing some heavy hitters down on yourself, and the boys at Langley or the NSA nerds will break it eventually. They've got computers even faster than those here."

"I know Sammy," she said, "and our professor is probably getting tired of our requests for so much extra computer and lab time. But we've got to keep trying. There's a lot of liberty loving Americans that are depending on us."

"Yea, let's just hope they don't hear about us on the six o'clock news. I'll probably end up with a black bag over my head at GITMO."

"Come on silly, let's finish this. Mr. Fields is dropping by in the morning to pick it up."

The Oval Office
The White House
Washington, D.C.

The NSA Director, along with his Deputy, were waiting in the Oval Office when the President and his COS walked in. Again, both men stood when the President entered and greeted him humbly with "Mr. President."

"Gentlemen, lets gather around my desk and take a look at Down-South Georgia," said Soloto.

The four men walked over to the huge executive desk where an enlarged map of the State of Georgia had been laid out. The major cities of Atlanta, Macon, Savannah, Agusta and Columbus were highlighted, along with a few smaller but significant population centers. The map showed major interstate highways as well as major topographical features such as rivers, lakes, mountain ranges and swamps. A separate, more detailed map of greater Atlanta was on the desk beside it.

"Director Click, show me your plan to keep track of this rogue Governor," said Soloto.

"Let's start with Atlanta itself," said the director, moving over to the smaller of the two maps. He picked up the stainless steel pointer that lie atop the map and put its sharp end on a spot in northeast Atlanta. "Here, sir, is the location of the Governor's Mansion, which is Cummins' primary residence. He has four older children who reside in various other residences that will be subject to surveillance as well. As far as the primary residence, we have local assets already in route to plant a ring of camera and other sensors on the roads leading in and out of the compound. We have also exercised authority granted under the Patriot Act to tap all of Cummins's phone lines, including interception of all cell phone traffic generated from his immediate vicinity."

The man with the pointer failed to mention to Soloto that his techno-snoops had mysteriously failed to capture the traffic of two particular cell phones registered to Cummins.

"Very well, this is all appropriate to the situation," said Soloto. "Continue."

"This Governor apparently had two extra fences erected around the property as soon as he was elected. He's been planning this stunt all along, Mr. President. But we have dispatched a separate team that will move in under cover of darkness and plant devices within the compound itself."

"How will you defeat his security?" asked Soloto, curious now.

"Sir, we have enhanced techniques of device installation specially designed to defeat such security which mostly consists of the fencing, armed guards and k-9 patrols." The director was satisfied with his evasive answer, but the look on Soloto's face told him the President was expecting more detail. "Sir, we will use drop technology to air-drop sensors from predator drones. Our drones have already made a couple of high-altitude passes over the residence," added the director.

"I don't recall ordering those passes, Director," said the President coldly.

"Uh, sir, it is our standard operating procedure to be proactive in these kinds of situations," said the deputy director smoothly.

"And just how many rogue sitting Governors have you had to deal with before?" asked Soloto, his arms folded across his chest.

"None, sir. I was referring, Mr. President, to situations of high security risk to the President and of a delicate political nature," replied the deputy, unflapped by Soloto's tone. His professionalism put Soloto more at ease.

"O.K.," said the President, "but be sure all major operations are first cleared through this office. Remember, these operations are being carried out within the United States, and one false step could spell disaster. Now, tell me about these drones. Are they the same ones we've been using in Afghanistan against the Taliban?"

"Precisely, Mr. President. Unmanned, remote controlled, ordnance-ready Predator drones. We have two working out of Fort McPherson Army Base, located southwest of Atlanta. We have another squadron of six Predators stored at Moody Air Force Base located in the southern part of the State, near a town called Valdosta."

"Valdosta," said the President, "now why does that sound familiar?" The deputy director, proud of his technological savvy, quickly tapped the buttons of his Blackberry.

"It says here that Valdosta has been known as a traditional powerhouse in high school football, sir. A small college is located in the town also, and not much else," said the deputy.

"Oh yes," said Soloto, himself an avid sports fan, "high school football at its finest. Winnersville, it has been called, because of so many football State Championships won there. Well, gentlemen, the good people of Valdosta and all of Georgia are counting on us to protect them from this nut in their Governor's Mansion. Let's be sharp, fellas. Use only your best people. Make sure those drones are in perfect working condition. We can't afford any screwups on this. Its not Iraq we are dealing with here, collateral damage is not allowed. A few dead civilians will not be so easily covered up on American soil."

"Yes sir, Mr. President," responded the NSA director, "The NSA fully appreciates the nature of this operation. In addition to the local assets we have already activated, within twenty-four hours we will have our swat teams on location in Atlanta to act as backups. Mr. President, our swat teams recruit directly from the Olympic shooting teams from countries around the world. We have the very best shooters available, many of them foreign born."

That statement was followed by a pause as no one wanted to acknowledge what the director was implying, this being that if it came to an order to eliminate this rogue Governor or his facilitators, it would be possible to achieve it using shooters who are not from America. Asking Americans to fire upon fellow Americans for political purposes was something that might become necessary, but all in the room knew it to be a risk they had rather avoid.

"O.K. It looks like you're on top of things. Keep me briefed daily, more often if needed. And remember, all operations are cleared first through me, especially orders to shoot people," stated Soloto.

"Yes, sir. Thank you sir." And the meeting was over.

Chapter Seven

Arnold Air Force Base
South-central Tennessee

Every scrap that had been found from the exploded Raptor was gathered in a hanger at Arnold Air Force Base located in Tennessee, about twenty-five miles above the border with Georgia.

Also gathered there was a team of the best crash investigators from the United States Air Force, the Federal Bureau of Investigation and the National Transportation Safety Board.

The guys from the NTSB were the recognized crème de la creme among this group of experts, and even though it was an Air Force investigation, all gave deference to those who did this sort of thing every day.

Kyle Smeltzer was the lead investigator from the NTSB and had nearly forty years experience working airplane crashes. Smeltzer and his team had been around, examining everything from JFK Jr's Piper Saratoga to Pan Am Flight 103 that exploded over Lockerbie, Scotland. Smelter had even dug parts of aircraft from the rubble of ground zero after 9-11.

Presently, Smeltzer and his team were frustrated that the ground search teams sent into Georgia had recovered only less than half of the wreckage from the downed Raptor. Even more frustrating was the fact that even though they had gone over every available piece of the fighter jet, they could find no evidence of a missile strike of any kind.

"I just can't get a handle on this one," said Smeltzer, trying to rub the fatigue from his eyes with both hands. His assistant offered him another cup of hot coffee, but he had had three cups already and refused a fourth.

The team had worked nearly around the clock, and were under heavy pressure to submit a report as to what brought the bird down. The White House COS was calling Smeltzer daily for an update, and to keep the pressure up.

It was currently 10:15 A.M., and few had gotten any real sleep in days. Nearly a whole month had passed since the Raptor had fallen burning from the sky.

"There was obviously," said Smeltzer, "an explosion that began somewhere in or near the Pratt and Whitney Turbofan that quickly engulfed the whole of the aircraft, but it cannot be proven from the partially recovered aircraft that any externally penetrating projectile caused said explosion. And we have no evidence that a catastrophic engine malfunction caused this either. I hate to say it fellas', but from what I see, our report is still inconclusive."

"Need more of the bird," said one of the Air Force investigators. "But that wreckage is scattered over miles and miles of forest and mountainous grounds. We may search forever and never find enough of that Raptor to complete this report. Plus, the locals in Georgia are playing hardball. We received another report last night of one of our search teams being turned around by a local Sheriff in a north Georgia county."

"Someone get the White House on the phone, I've got to give them the bad news. Something blew this jet away, but we can't pin this on the Governor of Georgia yet, and I'm not going to falsify documentation to prove it."

The Situation Room
The White House
Washington, D.C.

President Soloto sat at the table in the Situation Room with a worried look on his face.

He had called the Joint Chiefs to meet him there, and to the surprise of those military leaders, Chairman of the NBR Ben Rothfellow was already there when they arrived.

Having a financial official in what they considered to be a military meeting made some of the Generals and Admirals a bit apprehensive, but they knew that it was the President's call, not theirs.

"Gentlemen, thank you for coming, and I'll get right to the point," said Soloto. "I've just received word from the Israelis that Mossad operatives have confirmed that the Iranians have issued a go-ahead order for their Oil Exchange. This is a move that we did not expect the Iranians to make at this time, but Ahmadeena has proven his irrationality to the extent that nothing should surprise us now. Regardless, I cannot stress how serious a threat this is to the United States. The time has come to put into operation the plan to neutralize this economic threat from the Iranians. I'm putting 'Operation Persian Dust' on the table right now, gentlemen."

"Mr. President," said the Air Force Chief of Staff, "as you know, our Intelligence has concentrated on Iran's development of weapons' grade nuclear material. We believe Iran is close to having such material, but is still a couple of years out, thanks to the disruption caused by the Stuxnet computer worm and the ground operations associated with it. It is my understanding that 'Operation Persian Dust' was specifically designed to deal with these nuclear ambitions. Since Stuxnet bought us more time, why is now the time to launch the raids, and what does this Oil Exchange have to do with it?"

"That is why I've asked NBR Chairman Rothfellow to join us. Chairman Rothfellow, please explain to these men what Iran is trying to do to our currency, the U.S. Dollar."

"Certainly, Mr. President. Gentlemen," said Rothfellow as he pulled a crisp dollar bill from his pocket and put it on the table, sliding it forward to the middle. "This is our currency, the U.S. Dollar. In and of itself it has little intrinsic value, just a few cents worth of paper and ink. You can't go to your local bank and redeem it in gold or silver or any other precious metal. The only reason it carries any value is because the U.S. Government says that it's worth something.

"And the only way we can get by with creating money out of thin air is because the world needs our Dollars to buy the one commodity that no country can survive without: oil. Petroleum is the lifeblood of every industrial economy on earth; without it, the economy of any nation will grind to a halt overnight. And to buy oil, the world needs the U.S. Dollar," he said, holding the bill up once again for all to see before continuing.

"Because, ever since World War II, oil has been traded in Dollars. America's enemies are trying to use this fact to destroy us; they know they can destroy the value of the Dollar if they can begin to trade oil in a different currency. Saddam Hussein tried to trade his oil for other currencies back in the year 2000, but subsequent events corrected that mistake. Ditto for Gaddafi in Libya. Now Iran, which sits on an ocean of crude oil, has opened an Oil Bourse, or Exchange, through which they will trade all of their oil in non-Dollar currencies. If allowed to go forward, and if other oil producing nations follow suit, it spells nothing less than the collapse of the our currency. You mentioned weapons' grade material and nuclear bombs--well, sir, the opening of this Oil Exchange is nothing less than an economic nuclear attack against the United States! And it has the power to destroy our way of life just as effectively as if an actual nuclear bomb were used against our country."

Everyone was now clear on why this meeting had been called: the United States was about to go to war with Iran.

The Iranian Island of Kish
Off the coast of Iran

Nawaf Saladin really enjoyed his job as an accountant at the International Oil Bourse of Iran, located on the island of Kish. Even though it meant working on an island apart from his home in mainland Iran, the money was good and it enabled him to help his parents in their old age, just as they had sacrificed to put him through school in the west.

He did not get off the island very often, but he had little reason to do so--Kish was one of the top resort islands in all the Persian Gulf. Nawaf had made friends with some of the higher-ups at his office, people who could afford to visit elegant attractions like the Grand Hotel and fun spots like the Dolphin Park, all right there on the island of Kish.

Joining his friends at the exclusive clubs was not something that happened every weekend, but it happened often enough to keep Yoosuf very happy with his social life.   On Kish, the standard laws of the Islamic Repuplic are far more relaxed. And after one of *those* weekends enjoying such freedoms, Nawaf always came back to work feeling refreshed and excited. It was just another one of the perks of working at the International Oil Bourse.

Nawaf's work at the Bourse represented a good paycheque for him and was considered very important to the country he loved, his country of Iran. For it was in a specially built facility on the island of Kish that the government of the Islamic Republic of Iran had established a major hub of international oil trading.

Iran could use this Bourse, or Exchange, to further solidify their leadership position in the middle east in terms of the oil trade. Iran could also dictate what currencies would be used to trade oil at the Bourse. It had been a desire of the Iranian leadership to crowd the US Dollar out of its historic position as the petro-dollar, the reserved currency with which the world buys oil. Iran wanted a basket of various currencies to replace the dollar, and with the opening of the Bourse, an important step had been taken in that direction.

Nawaf had studied economics at The University Of Michigan in the United States. While there, Nawaf daily suffered the insults of hearing his native country of Iran being derided by the American students as a backwards, Islamo-facist country, insults launched by silly people who had never even traveled to Iran.

The American government constantly harassed Iran for its alleged Nuclear Warhead program, a program that Nawaf doubted even existed. And the American media agitated daily for more and more pressure to be placed on Iran in the form of sanctions, and even a pre-emptive military attack. His fellow students at the University of Michigan talked nonchalantly about 'bombing Iran,' never even thinking about the actual Iranian people that would be maimed and killed in such an attack.

Those were his people that the Americans talked about bombing, his kinsmen and countrymen. For a nation that prided itself on be a 'Christian' nation, Nawaf found many of the people to be quick to support wars of aggression that would sacrifice many innocent civilian lives. If that was Christianity, I thank Allah that I am not one, thought Nawaf.

And so it was with great pride that upon graduation from college Nawaf landed an accounting job at the Oil Brose on the Island of Kish. The work was intense and interesting, the money was good, and on the resort island of Kish with its many foreign visitors, females weren't afraid to wear western clothes and hairstyles. The women were indeed beautiful.

And today was Friday, the day that Nawaf had planned to take one of those beautiful young ladies out to dinner, and then for a show at the Dolphin Park.

Still working over some spreadsheets at his office in the Bourse, Nawaf checked his watch. Yes, he thought, I have plenty of time to finish here and drop by my apartment for a quick shower before meeting the girl. Only a few more numbers to calculate and the day would be through. Just as Nawaf was reaching for his last stack of reports, the door to his office burst open. It was the office manager, Khatib who rushed in to speak to Nawaf. Nawaf saw that Khatib was sweating profusely and that his face was red with stress.

"Nawaf, is your internet working? I need to see it, right now."

Nawaf had not been on-line for a few hours. He turned to his computer and made a few clicks with the mouse. His internet home-page did not appear. Nawaf clicked a screen icon once again, but all he saw on the screen was a line of script that said his computer had no connection to the internet, with instruction that he should check that the wires were properly hooked into his computer. He started to bend down to check the wires, but his boss stopped him.

"No need to check the cables Nawaf, the internet is off in the entire Bourse. They have cut the linnes out in the ocean."

"What? Who has cut the internet cables, Khatib?" Nawaf knew that the whole Bourse depended on the internet as its trading apparatus. Without it, there *was* no Iranian Oil Bourse.

"The Americans and the Israelis have cut it, they will bring this building down" said Khatib with a voice cracking with fear and frustration as he rushed out the door and down the hallway.

Nawaf arose from his desk and walked out into the corridor. He looked across the wide room that held hundreds of office cubicles, suddenly realizing that a sense of chaos infused the scene.

Some of the workers were frantically checking there internet connections, a few bent under desks making sure cables were still connected. But others, Nawaf noticed, were abandoning their cubicles and workstations. He saw female workers gathering coats and handbags to leave. Male workers, some of them hurrying for the exits, were running past the slower females in trying to escape.

But escape from what? What is this all about, Nawaf wondered. Forcing himself to remain calm, he went back to his desk and found a clock-radio, flipping a switch to turn it on. He tuned in a local station and was glad to hear a newscaster's familiar voice, though the news it brought did Nawaf little good.

"It is being reported that the Iranian power facilities at Darkhovin and Bushehr have been attacked and bombed by jet planes with American and Israeli markings. Some reports also have oil fields and tankers being bombed. Besides these power facilities, other political buildings in Tehran have been bombed and are on fire. Many people are killed and badly burned."

Nawaf sat still at his desk, hardly believing his ears. Surely Allah would not allow his people to be attacked by the hated Israelis and their American lapdogs. But if those first words from the radio newscaster had made his skin grow cold, the next words were truly chilling.

"We also have reports from shipping vessels located off the coast between the mainland and the island of Kish. These vessels report large numbers of jet bombers flying over them, leaving the mainland and heading towards Kish."

Heading towards Kish. Heading towards Kish. Nawaf heard the words repeating slowly in his mind, as if they were spoken in a slow, sodden voice. But why would they come to Kish, Nawaf asked himself. Kish is a resort. Kish has dolphins and tourists and casinoes. It certainly has no nuclear processing centers. *There's just the resorts and--and this Oil Bourse I am sitting in.*

Nawaf got up and ran to his door, looking out over the now deserted office floor. Nawaf began to feel a panic he could not control. He moved quickly into the corridor and began to run, to run as fast as if he were on a soccer field driving for a goal. He slowed down to make a corner but his feet slipped on the waxed tile floor and he fell, sliding and slamming into a cubicle wall hard enough to knock it over. Nawaf knew he needed to regain his feet and run. He could see the glass exit doors at the end of the corridor. But the corridor was long, and the distance from where Nawaf fell was some 300 feet to the exit. Clamoring to his feet, he started to run again.

Outside, those who had already escaped the Bourse building were looking for cover to hide behind. They could hear the scream of the huge Pratt and Whitney jet engines delivering thousands of pounds of thrust to the joystick held firmly in the bomber pilot's right hand.

The pilot of the lead American bomber was named Cleave Linbeck, also a graduate of the University of Michigan. He and Nawaf had actually shared a class together in college, though they never formerly met one another. Nor would they ever. For the right thumb of Lieutenant Linbeck reached up and punched a button located near the top of the jet's joystick control.

Linbeck felt his bird lighten as it was freed of the heavy ordnance of bombs. The pilot pulled the nose of his jet up and skyward as the two thousand-pound tactical bombs he had just released dropped earthward through the air over Kish, headed for the building in which Nawaf Saladin had been working in, and through which he now ran for the exit.

Nawaf was young, athletic and a fast runner. He had made it almost to the glass exit doors when first bomb hit. All that Nawaf saw was a flash of light as the bomb's tip smashed through the glass door. Then there was an explosion so loud that Nawaf's last memory was one of unbelief that the world could even hold such a noise. The compression from the bomb's blast picked Nawaf up and blew him 300 feet back up the corridor he had just ran down. Before he hit the floor, Nawaf's internal organs ruptured and liquefied from the compression blast of the bomb, and he was as good as dead when he landed on a desk, unconscious and already bleeding from his gentle mouth. The thousands of pounds of concrete that were thrown atop his body did nothing to hasten his death but served only to entomb him, to cover his face from the gawking world until his lifeless body could be dug out a few weeks later.

Many more bombers, some American and some Israeli, made runs over the Oil Bourse, unloading bomb after bomb on the facility. The last six bombs to hit the Bourse served only to rearrange the dust and debris and mangled bodies that had been torn asunder by the first twenty payloads dumped on the site.

It would be reported in the United States that the Iranians had located a secret uranium enrichment site on the island of Kish, and that is why the island was targeted. But the Iranians knew it was not true. They realized now that their greatest sin against America was not the pursuit of nuclear materials and weapons. The Iranians knew that their greatest insult to the American government was to dare to trade oil in a currency other than the Dollar. It had cost Saddam Hussein his life, and now it would cost many Iranians their lives as well.

The Press Briefing Room
The White House
Washington, D.C.

President Soloto bore a solemn expression on his face as he made his way to the rostrum fronted with the official Seal of the President of the United States. The room was full of reporters and cameras, but as Soloto began to speak the room grew perfectly quiet. The reporters had been told that a major announcement was about to be made concerning the nation of Iran.

> Good evening. I come at this time to
> the vast and diverse family of
> Americans to inform our nation that
> just hours ago I, as Commander-In-

Tommy Davis

Chief of the Armed Forces, did issue the order to begin the bombing of sites within the Nation of Iran. It is with great trepidation that I take such action, and only after years of seeking to negotiate with the Iranians an end to their Nuclear Weapon's Program. I want all Americans to understand that I and my Administration went to every conceivable length to persuade the Iranians to give up their nuclear ambitions, all to no avail. And then, two weeks ago, came the final straw. I was informed by members of our Intelligence Community that the Iranians were within weeks of manufacturing enough enriched uranium to make a nuclear weapon. We have further learned that the Revolutionary Guard, operating within the upper ranks of the Iranian government, had made a pact with the terrorist organization Hamas to hand off a nuclear device that Hamas planned to smuggle into the United States and detonate in a large American city. The city that was going to be targeted was defined by Hamas and the Iranians as a large city in the deep-southern portion of the United States. My intelligence team believes that U.S. city targeted by these terrorists to be the city of Atlanta, Georgia. As your president, I want all Americans to rest assured that I will do all in my power to keep you safe from those bent on destroying our nation through terror and the murder of our citizens. Just as I have acted to protect the people of Atlanta, Georgia from an attack that could have killed literally millions of Georgia citizens, so I will continue to take whatever actions necessary to protect American lives.

> The bombing campaign against Iran
> will continue just as long as it takes to
> ensure that Iran no longer has the
> weapons to harm either
> the U.S. or Israel, or any of our allies
> around the world. Thank you, God
> Bless You, and May God Bless
> the United States of America.

Soloto finished his remarks and retreated from the rostrum, refusing to stop for reporter's questions. Instead, the Secretary of Defense took his place at the rostrum and took questions. As he gave his answers, American's heard the names of Iranian places such as Natanz, Arak, and Bushehr, all of which were said to be sites which the Iranians were using to develop nuclear material and weaponry.

And the Secretary of Defense also took a moment to single out a place most American's had never heard of, the island of Kish. He explained how that, though the Iranians had tried to disguise Kish as a combination of resort island and business destination, US Intelligence had discovered months ago that located on this island was one of the main secret, underground nuclear research and test facilities. That explained to the press why the Island of Kish had been one of the primary targets of the bombing campaign.

News coverage of the bombing raids over Iran would continue all night and into the next news-day. ROX News, CNN, MSNBC, as well as all other major news networks would bring in countless military and political experts of every political stripe to comment on the bombing campaign. Almost all of them spoke in approving, glowing terms of the bombing of Iran, many of them adding that Soloto's only mistake was not to have taken this aggressive action months before.

Chapter Eight

An isolated hayfield in rural middle Georgia

The gathering was held in a hay field located nearly ten miles outside the little town of Fort Valley, Georgia. Fort Valley was near the geographical center of the State and that area was known as the largest production base of peaches in the Peach State.

Gathered there on this day were several hundred men, most driving four-wheel drive pickup trucks. Unofficially, the group called themselves the 'Middle Georgia Militia.'

It was an eclectic group. About half of them were heavy readers, the range of their literary taste running from daily newspapers to Shakespeare. A few of them studied the Federalist Papers, the lives of the 'Founding Fathers,' or some other document associated with the country's founding. Most of them kept a 'pocket-copy' of the Constitution of the United States in the glove-box of their pickup, usually underneath a box of rifle cartridges and a pack of chewing tobacco.

The men came from all walks of life; there were laborers, retired military men, factory workers, bankers, mechanics, pastors, farmers, teachers and businessmen. Women were not officially disallowed from attending, but few ever showed up. This militia was, more or less, a men's only club.

From time to time these men would gather in the field, collect into small groups of ten to twelve men, and have a round of target practice with their deer-rifles. Along with shooting, the men would eat bar-be-cue and discuss politics. Most of the men drank beer, but none was allowed at the meetings.

Though there was no ranking system in this self-styled militia, usually the conversations would be 'led' or 'taught' by the more well-read members of the group.

One of these leaders was Bubba McCloud. Bubba was the one who usually called around to let the guys know when a meeting was scheduled and was mostly recognized as the unofficial leader. This loose-style of organization reflected the hands-off political philosophy of the members of the Middle Georgia Militia, which could be boiled down to a basic thought that each man believed the Constitution stood for: you leave me alone and I'll leave you alone. For most of them, the multi-billion dollar bailout of California by the federal government was the straw that broke the camel's back.

As things began to heat up politically in the State, Bubba noticed that the militia's numbers had started to swell. They kept no list of names, nor were their any dues to pay to be a part of this group. Communication was done by word of mouth. The group was simply made up of whomever showed up at the next meeting.

Ever since Jim Cummins had become Governor the numbers attending had increased every month. In the first meeting the group held after the Air Force One incident, twice the usual number of men had shown. And, Bubba had noticed, the men were growing more and more fierce in their both their anger at Washington D.C., and in their defense of Governor Cummins' actions. The militia's numbers were swelling due to a combination of worry about the direction of the United States government, distrust of the Soloto administration, and anger over the decisions Soloto had made.

These men felt that Soloto was clearly a Socialist bent on destroying the old foundations of the Republic. In Governor Cummins these men found a leader that would stand up to the what they considered to be the dark and dangerous powers of the D.C. Government. None was more worried than Bubba McCloud.

Bubba figured that nearly five hundred men had presently gathered for the militia meeting. After a couple of hours of target practice and eating, in which copious amounts of pork ribs, coffee and ammunition had been consumed, Bubba called the group together in the center of the hay field. Standing on the tailgate of a pickup truck with a bullhorn in his hand, Bubba addressed the small sea of camouflage and ball caps.

"Men, I hope you have enjoyed another meeting of the Middle Georgia Militia!" A hearty cheer rose from the crowd of men. "I remind you of our purpose: to stand up for our way of life, and to defend the Constitution and the State of Georgia!" Another round of loud applause followed. "And to pray for our brave Governor, Jim Cummins!" Now the cheering grew louder than ever. "Now, it has come to our attention that even though we call ourselves a Militia, we are armed only with our deer rifles. Many of you are crack shots with these guns, but at least half of us could not hit the floor if we fell on it!" At that the crowd erupted in laughter.

"Now then, if we are going to have a Militia, we need to have, shall we say, ample supplies of persuasion." Approving grunts, sounds and some loud Amen's! went up from the group of men. "Today, we are going to take up a collection--let's call it a 'love of liberty offering.' And the collection plate is going to be the bed of this pickup truck on which I am standing. We are taking no checks or credit cards—in God we trust, all others pay cash. This 'liberty offering' will go to purchase the fire-power we need if ever called upon to defend our hearth and homes. I ask you to give generously, and to give in remembrance of all those who have sacrificed so much so that we might have freedom in this country, and in the Sovereign State of Georgia!" Another loud cheer went up from the crowd as the men began to reach for their wallets and form single-file lines that would pass on either side of the pickup truck.

One by one the men walked past the pickup and tossed their cash into the truck. After nearly a half hour the offering was complete. Bubba McCloud and three other men had been appointed to count the offering. Each of the counters sorted through the Fives, Twenties and Hundred Dollar Bills that had been tossed into the truck bed. The counting was slowly and carefully done, and after another half hour each counter had several neat stacks of greenbacks arranged on the tailgate of the truck.

Bubba began to write down the totals, and he could not believe what he was seeing. On the tailgate of the truck sat a total of $146,020.

"I'm not believing this," Bubba said to the men standing around the truck, "each man here today had to give an average of around three hundred dollars."

"That's a week's salary for many of them," replied Billy Updyke, one of Bubba most trusted 'lieutenants.' "People are worried--and afraid. They see their country being lost, and they don't trust the federal government any longer."

"Well, what are we going to do with all this money? I expected to raise enough to buy a few thousand rounds of rifle ammo, but we could get a real bang with these bucks--but I would not know who to ask. Anybody got an idea," asked Bubba of the small group of men. One of the men spoke up, though reluctantly.

"Well...I might know someone who knows someone," said Hamp Cartright. Cartright, it was known, had once had a meth problem. His brother-in-law, a career criminal that went by the name of 'Wildcat,' had tried to join their Militia but had been asked to leave for promoting the ideology of a local group of meth cookers that called themselves the 'Bulldawg Shanks.' It was a skinhead, neo-Nazi group of drug running racists that even the rawest of rednecks avoided.

"Wait a minute Hamp! We're not getting mixed up with 'Wildcat' and that bunch of scum he runs with. I think your sister could do better," replied Bubba.

"No, don't jump to conclusions," replied Cartright, "just hear me out. I don't want nothin' to do with 'Wildcat' either. You know I been clean for three years now. Them skinheads give me the creeps--like to died from what they're cookin'. But I did overhear them talkin' one night 'bout some Russians they had dealt with. Said these Russians claimed access to some serious weaponry."

"Russians?" replied Bubba. "Hamp, do you really think that anyone here is fixin' to go all the way to Russia?" That remark drew scattered laughter from the small circle of men.

"But that's my point Bubba, these here Russians ain't in Russia no more--and neither is their hardware. According to what the Shanks said, these Russians have set up shop in Florida," Cartright said with a grin.

"Florida? Well now, ya don't say?" said Bubba, his interest pricked. "Florida ain't all that far from home. But are you sure these Russians have good weapons? We ain't buying no junk-surplus."

"Well, I saw some of the AK-47s that the Shanks had bought from them. Brand new, right out of the box, and fully automatic."

"AK-47's? That does sound like something we could
use. Okay, Hamp see if you can set up a meeting for me with
these Russians. Tell 'Wildcat' that we will give him a finder's
fee to set up the meet, but make sure he knows he's still not
welcome in this Militia. I hate drug runners and I hate
skinhead race-haters. Make sure he knows that we got whites,
blacks and Hispanics, Jews and Gentiles in this militia—that'll
keep him far away!"

"Okay," agreed Cartright, "I'll try to set it up."

The other men helped Bubba put the cash offering into heavy
plastic bags. Everyone got in their trucks and left--everyone
except Bubba. He pulled his pickup to the back of the hayfield
and stopped. Taking the bag of money in one hand and a
shovel in the other, Bubba McCloud headed off into the woods
to bury the 'liberty offering.'

The Island of Kish
Off the coast of Iran

The Al Jazeera camera crew arrived at Kish a mere half hour
after the last bombing sortie had run. As the Arabic leader in
news coverage, the Qatar-based news network has contacts
throughout the middle-east and actually had someone
from Kish to call-in to one of its news shows while the bombs
were falling all around.

The network had immediately dispatched a news crew, via
speedboat, to the island. The crew transmitted live footage of
buildings all over the small island that were now little more
than burning, smoking rubble. The American bombers did
their work with utter efficiency, and every targeted
building suffered devastation.

While the footage was still coming in from Kish, a newsroom
manager at Al Jazeera had a sudden epiphany; he recalled
that the network had taken exclusive footage of Kish just after
the Iranians had completed the construction of the Oil
Exchange.

At that time, the Exchange was not fully functional, but the
basic infrastructure had been completed. The Iranians
had invested in the billions of dollars in the Exchange on Kish,
and gladly allowed Al Jazeera to film the facilities. While on the
island, the Iranian officials had told the Al Jazeera reporters

that they feared that the island might one day become a target of the Americans and the Israelis. At the time, the reporters laughed this information off as a combination of Iranian paranoia and propaganda.

Now as he watched the footage of the devastating attacks come in, to this newsroom manager at Al Jazeera, the idea seemed like neither paranoia nor propaganda, but more like prophecy. And he had an idea. He first checked to see if the old footage of Kish was readily available. Next, he assigned one of his assistants to monitor the US cable news channels to see if an official statement concerning why the island of Kish was bombed would be given.

Only a few hours had passed when the assistant came and got his boss, dragging him before a Television tuned to CNN. There at a press conference was an Air Force spokesman making statements and answering questions concerning the attack upon Iran.

The two men at Al Jazeera listened intently as the uniformed officer at the Pentagon in Washington explained to the world that the island of Kish had been secretly used for research and development of nuclear weapons.

That was the moment that the newsroom manager made his decision; he would begin to broadcast, intermittently, old footage of the facilities on Kish with the new footage of the destruction wrought by American bombs. This would make for interesting news coverage, he thought: footage of buildings when they were newly built running alongside those same buildings turned into rubble.

It would seem clear that the buildings on Kish were useful for nothing more than business and financial purposes, but the world would be free to draw its own conclusions.

The Iranians were already protesting all the bombings carried out against their country, and especially of Kish, where they swore there was nothing more going on than oil trading. Now, the Americans were on record claiming the exact opposite.

Within an hour both the old and new footage from Kish was being looped each hour over all Al Jazeera outlets, including the internet. Within two hours the American news networks were borrowing from the story while the internet was immediately abuzz with theories about what it all meant.

Tommy Davis

Palm Coast, a city on the
East Coast of Florida

It had taken six and a half hours of hard driving, but Bubba
McCloud arrived on time at the Holiday Inn in Palm
Coast, Florida.

His ride did not look like all that much, a 1989 Chevy four-
wheel drive pickup truck, but the engine still purred like a lion,
and it got Bubba where he needed to go.

Bubba had picked up Interstate 75 South just outside his
hometown of McDonough, Georgia and kept his right foot
heavy until he crossed the Florida line.

Bubba developed a sickly feeling in his stomach as he crossed
over into Florida, not because of something he had eaten, but
because lots of folks from Georgia just don't like Florida. In fact,
the Georgia-Florida rivalry spanned everything from water-
rights to college football. The annual football game between
those two universities, played out in the 'neutral' site
Jacksonville each year, was perhaps the most bitter and intense
rivalry in all of college football, if not in all of sports.

And though Bubba had no love for the State of Florida, he
was on his way to meet some people there that he thought
might help him and the cause of Georgia. After crossing
the Florida line, Bubba hung a left on Interstate 10
to Jacksonville. He skirted southward around that city, picking
up Interstate 95 which runs parallel to the east coast of the
Sunshine State.

Located about half-way between St. Augustine and Daytona
Beach, Palm Coast was a city of some seventy thousand
people. What many did not know was that a significant portion
of that population were Russian immigrants.

Most of these Russians came to Florida looking for a peaceful
life in a warmer climate. Some had left their native land, first
stopping off in a northern city such as Detroit or Chicago or
New York, but when the winters proved too much like those in
Mother Russia, they migrated south. Russian snow-birds.

But with that peaceful majority of Russian immigrants came
a minority who had come to set up criminal enterprise. These
were members of the Russkaya Mafiya, the Russian Mafia.

Organized crime had been one of the biggest beneficiaries of
the breakup of the old Soviet Union. Former KGB officers
suddenly found themselves out of work, but also discovered
that the same ruthless disciplines they learned in the secret

police fit nicely in the hard world of the black market set up by the Bratva, the 'brotherhood' of Russian gangsters.

When the socialist government could no longer supply the needs of the Russian people, the gangsters had set up a black market that brought in everything from televisions to drugs. Anything could be had for a price. Government officials and policeman living on the meagerest of salaries were easily bought off by the Bratva.

In America, the center of activity for the Bratva had been Brighton Beach in Brooklyn, New York. But as the American authorities tightened down on Brighton Beach, many of the Mafiya looked south. Of all the southern states, Florida was found to be the most fertile soil to plant new bases for their criminal organizations.

Because the Soviet Union had been one of the most militarized empires in human history, with its breakup came a flood of guns and hardware into the marketplace. And that is why Bubba McCloud had driven six and a half hard hours to a Holiday Inn in Palm Coast.

Bubba had a friend who knew some guys involved in the Aryan movement. The Aryan's were known for racial hatred and anti-Semitism, something Bubba McCloud had no stomach for. Bubba had attended school with, played sports with, even gone to church with Blacks, Jews and Hispanics throughout his whole life.

But even though he was no racist, neither could Bubba and his friends stomach any longer what he felt was the oppressive hand of the federal government tightening its grip on every facet of life in America. There was no where you could go to escape its reach.

That hand was in the schools, taking away prayer and the Bible. It was at work, stealing a large portion of ones paycheck each week. It was even in the churches now, where hate crime laws threatened to lock up preachers who spoke out against what they felt was wrong.

And now, Bubba believed, the feds had acted so irresponsibly with the nation's money that they had gutted and hollowed-out the economy.

Bubba's friend had contacted the Aryan's, who were rumored to be trading crystal meth for guns. These Aryan's mixed their racial beliefs with criminal activity, mostly involving the meth trade. It was further rumored that they had developed contacts with the Russkaya Mafiya. Bubba kept up with the news enough to know that if anyone could get their hands on weaponry it would be the Russians.

Bubba had done four years in the United States Marine Corp right out of high school, and he knew that the Soviet Union had developed weapons that were plenty lethal, if not as advanced as what the U.S. military had.

The Soviets had mass-produced their conventional weaponry in anticipation for what never took place: a massive European ground war with N.A.T.O. Now, all that hardware was floating around the world on black seas, looking for a conflict to call home. Most of those deals would be brokered by the Bratva.

The Aryans had arranged this meeting in exchange for a percentage of the total sale. That percentage would be added to the total and would come out of Bubba's pocket, not off the Russian side of the deal, the Aryans had explained to Bubba. He did not like it but felt he and his militia had little choice but to play ball with the Aryans, at least for now.

The meeting was set for six o'clock in the evening at the hotel bar. Bubba was alone and did not know how many Russians would be at the meeting. One representative of the Aryans was also supposed to be present to confirm the total of the sale.

Bubba had been entrusted by his militia friends with a very large amount of cash with which to make the deal. Not sure who he could trust, Bubba had pulled over into a rural area before he entered the city. After he was certain he was alone, he dug a hole near a tree and hid the cash there. If the Russians tried anything crooked, Bubba might not make it home, but neither would the Russians ever find the hidden money.

Presently Bubba pulled into the parking lot of the Holiday Inn. He checked his watch and smiled at being on time. Bubba was raised poor but knew to be on time for such things as supper and church, and he reckoned the same manners would apply to a meeting with the Russian Bratva.

Bubba had been given no names, no descriptions of those he was to meet. He had been instructed to come into the lounge, sit at the bar and order an Extra Large Russian Lemonade.

Making his way to the bar, Bubba noted that the place was quiet except for a black grand piano in the corner on which the player covered an old Floyd Cramer tune Bubba recognized as one called 'Last Date.' Still nervous, Bubba hoped today would not be his 'Last Date.'

After ordering the drink, Bubba sat at the bar for another half-hour. Bored because no one had approached him, Bubba downed his drink and ordered another Extra Large Russian

126

Lemonade. He sat waiting at the bar another half hour and still no one approached him. He looked around the room about every five minutes. Bubba had no idea what a Russkaya Mafiya member would look like, but everyone he saw looked like regular folk to him. Bubba went ahead and drank his second order, and ordered yet again.

He looked at his watch: Seven-Fifteen. The Russians had kept him waiting an hour and fifteen minutes. Discouraged, Bubba decided to down his last Lemonade, visit the men's room, and get back in his pickup for the long drive home.

Just as he was about the lift the last of the Lemonade to his mouth, a large meaty hand gently caught his arm, stopping the glass a few inches from his lips.

Bubba looked at the man now sitting beside him. The man had seemed to come out of nowhere. He was built like a tree trunk, with broad, full shoulders and a barrel chest tightly wrapped in a nice shirt and sport coat. The big man's jaw was as square as that of a comic book figure, his hair a mix of blond and pepper-grey.

Bubba put the glass down on the bar. The man was smiling at him but said nothing. Bubba guessed he was waiting on him to speak first.

"How y'all doin'?" Bubba said. The big Russian only grinned wider. His teeth, Bubba noticed, were pearly white and well aligned. When the man said nothing, Bubba looked away from him. He did not want to seem intimidated by the Russians' presence, so he finished off the Lemonade in one loud gulp, and added a loud burp. He heard the Russian give a deep chuckle beside him.

"Russian Lemonade very good, eh?" said the large man in a heavy Slavic accent.

"Not bad," replied Bubba, still wanting to seem unintimidated while realizing it was probably too late.

Suddenly two more big men were sitting at the bar with Bubba. Bubba had no idea what to say, and remembering that his Mama had said not to speak unless you had something good to say, Bubba remained quiet. After a moment, one of the Russians, the smallest of the three, spoke up in a voice heavy with the same accent as the larger man.

"How-dy. I am Ivan Mogilevich. And you, I think, called Bub-ba Mc-Cloud...from Jor-ja." The Russians were all grinning widely at the use of "How-dy." Bubba replied,

"Yea, I'm Bubba McCloud from McDonough, Georgia, and I ain't carryin' no money on me."

"It difficult to shop hardware no money, Bubba McCloud from Jor-ja."

"I did not say I cain't get some money--just said I ain't got none on me at the present time."

Smiling like a man who knew too much, Ivan Mogilevic asked Bubba if he would care to join him at a table where more privacy could be had. Bubba followed the men across the lounge to a dimly lit booth situated in a corner.

Not long after they were seated, another man, following a waiter, was brought to the corner booth. A chair was pulled up for him to be seated in. Bubba did not recognize the man, but cringed at the sight of him all the same. He knew it was one of the Aryan Skinheads.

The man was wearing a white wife-beater style shirt. He was small and wirey looking, bald and completely shaven but for a mustache and a goatee. Dark tattoos in a spider-web design ran up his neck and across his bald head. The black web tattoos were spotted here and there with depictions of large black-widow spiders, their hourglass abdominal markings standing out in a brilliant red. The man's facial hair could not hide the jagged yellow teeth lurking behind his lips.

The Russians seemed not to welcome this one, regarding him with harsh, cold stares. He turned out to be a representative for the Aryans who had set up the meeting between Bubba and the Russkaya Mafiya. The Aryans' were heavy into the production of meth, or hillbilly heroin, as some called it. His rotten teeth told the other men that he was using his own product, crystal meth. The Bratva had no problem with drug dealers, but trusted no one who used their own product, especially when it rotted one's teeth. The big Russian with the pearly whites seemed especially offended by this bald man.

"Ma name's Dale Rommel," stated the bald Aryan. "I'm with the Aryan Brotherhood, and no deal goes down without us getting' our ten percent! God is a white man, and we're just like him, we demand our tithe!" The Aryan pounded his fist on the table as he finished his sentence. But the Russians were not shaken, trying only not to laugh at the fact that this neo-Nazi Aryan had taken the name of Rommel, one of Hitler's Field Marshall's who had participated in an attempt on the Fuehrer's life.

But it was time to do business. Ivan said to Bubba,

"The Bratva present, and have hardware you consider—"

"We gone git our ten percent, be sure a dat!" interrupted the Aryan Dale Rommel, but Ivan turned sharply on him with a cold-furious look.

"Be quiet!" said Ivan, cutting the bald man off flatly. "We know term of sale, Field Marshall Rommel, but you interrupt again, you maybe not live to enjoy tithe!"

The Aryan sat stiffly, staring at Ivan with wild eyes, the whites of which had turned a pale, sickly yellow. Bubba began to wonder if the man had taken a meth hit before the meeting, realizing that drug use and gun running did not likely go well together.

Bubba was made nervous by the presence of the Aryan, but knew he had to tolerate him since the Skinheads had set up this meeting with these Russians. No one had all night to talk, though, and all were anxious to get down to business.

"This hardware ya got...I'd very much appreciate takin' a look at these items," Bubba said as he pulled a small piece of paper from his shirt pocket and gave it to Ivan. The Russian pulled a cigarette lighter from his coat pocket and flicked a light by which to read the list.

"Very well," Ivan said, and began to slowly read the list in a slow jagged English. "One thousand A.K. 47 rifle, fully automatic, made Russia, not Romania." Ivan smiled at the nod to Russian quality, then continued reading slowly. "One hundred thousand round 7.62 x 39 am-mu-nition. Three thousand am-mu-nition clip, forty round capacity each. Three hundred Dragunov SVD sniper rifle with infra-red scope. Nine hundred round 7.62 x 54 sniper-grade ammunition, ballistic tip." Having read the list to the last item, Ivan pulled the small piece of paper into the flame of his lighter, allowing it to catch. He dropped the burning paper into an ashtray sitting on the table, pulled a cigarette and lit it, taking a deep draw before he spoke.

"This list-- fine weaponry, Mr. Bubba, but I ask—" Ivan was cut off mid-sentence once again by the bald Aryan who was pointing his finger first at the burning piece of paper and then punching that same finger toward Ivan's face.

"We know what ever-thang on that list coss, and we gonna git our ten per—" The big hands of the beefy Russian with the pearly white teeth snatched the Aryan up and out of his chair. Two other big Russians appeared from somewhere to engulf the bald man in Russian flesh. His protests were muffled sounds as he was shuffled smoothly around the bar, past the bartender and through a curtain. Bubba felt his knees knocking together under the table as he watched.

"As I saying," continued Ivan, "This list--fine hardware. It dependable equipment for which to kill enemy--if they equally armed."

Ivan shifted in his seat, snuffing out his smoldering cigarette. "But these light armament only. If enemy come with heavy weapon, Bubba be badly beaten." Bubba took offense, thinking that he and his militia were being dissed.

"These guns won't be in the hands of women, Mr. Mogilevich. We can do fine with what-alls on that list. If it's a problem, maybe I wasted my time commin' down here."

Bubba rase as if to leave, but Ivan put a kindly, heavy hand on his shoulder, asking him to wait. Ivan seemed to like him, Bubba thought, and was not offended with Bubba as he was with the Aryan Skinhead, who was now, no doubt, being taught some Southern manners, Russian-Style, in a room behind the bar.

"Mr. Mc-Cloud, before leave, allow me ask you question. Have heard of place called Chechnya, no?"

"Reckon it's a place in your neckatha woods. Sounds Russian, anyway."

"Chechnya Islamic state on Russia border, full of crazy Muslims—not good Christian like we," Ivan said with a wide grin. "Chechnya want free of Russian Government, much like your State Jor-ja want free of U.S. Government. But Russian Boris Yeltsin, not let Chechnya go free. There was war between two, at time of war, I Red Army. We ordered put-down rebellion Chechnya.

"My brigade special brigade, much like Marine Force Recon, always first enter fight," continued Ivan. Bubba was interested when he heard the Russian mention the Marines, since he had been one.

"First to fight, first to die--Marines, Ooh-rah!" replied Bubba. Ivan nedded and smiled, lit another cigarette, and continued his story.

"We came Chechen city defended-only local men, boys--no army. Locals armed only Kalashnikov and Druganov, much like equipment on you list. But--we have tank, armored troop carrier. Also have artillery--shell city from distance for three day, before main assault. Natives fight bravely, shoot at us, resist house to house. In every building they infest like termite, we marvel at determination. But only matter of time, because we use tank and artillery for pound each building dust--fall down on brave dead bodies. True, Chechens won respect, but dead all same."

Bubba sat at the table with his mouth slightly agap as Ivan allowed the story to sink in before he finished his argument.

"Mr. Bubba, you and friends plan to resist most powerful government in world. I think you need more than light arms--fight with."

"And just what do you expect me to do Ivan, drive a Russian tank back up I-95?" asked Bubba, sarcastically.

"I have one favor ask before you return Jor-ja. We blindfold you, but have warehouse merchandise believe you find useful in you campaign."

Bubba did not like the idea of being blindfolded. But the story of the Chechen city had gotten his attention, for sure. He breathed a sigh of resignation.

"Alright, Lord hep me, but I'll trust you, Ivan. Let's do it."

"Very good. But Mr. Bubba, one question more. This resistance movement--I wonder, same as did about Chechnya: what make man hate-much his own country, enough to die fighting against?" Bubba looked Ivan coldly in the eyes.

"Hate my country? Oh no Ivan, I love my country, but I hate what its government has become."

Bubba McCloud had been blindfolded nearly two hours and his eyes were throbbing under the thick black cloth. He tried to listen for various sounds that could tell him what landmarks or places he was passing, like he had seen someone do on a late night re-run of Hawaii Five-o, but it was no use. All the sounds of the Florida night time just blended together in his head. All Bubba could deduce was the fact that the car he was in seemed to be getting on a main highway for a while, only to turn off and travel down less smooth roads. Then the car would get back on that smoother, more noisy highway and pick up speed. What could it all mean, he wondered.

Wait, Bubba thought, a long highway! They must be getting on and off interstate 95! But which way were they traveling on 95, north or south? Bubba remembered that it was still warm when they had begun the trip. He recalled the sun warming the right side of his face even though he could see nothing. That meant that they had headed South in the beginning. And I-95 South out of Palm Coast goes straight to Daytona Beach. The Russian warehouse may be near Daytona, Bubba concluded. Bubba was proud of his deduction, and would tuck that information away for future reference.

Bubba also noted that the car's tires hit many uneven types on concrete before finally coming to a halt. Uneven concrete and a warehouse usually meant an industrial area.—another mental note for the future.

After the car halted, the Russians gently helped the still-blindfolded Bubba out of the car, walking him into a building. Once inside, the blindfold was removed.

Rubbing his eyes with both hands, Bubba blinked them repeatedly, allowing his pupils to adjust to the light of what looked to be a truly massive warehouse. When finally comfortable with the light, Bubba was able to focus and look out across the long warehouse floor.

Ivan's men were walking about the floor, removing tarps that covered military equipment. Bubba was sure that he must have been on a U.S. military installation, because no one could keep this much weaponry a secret. But no, he noticed upon closer inspection, all the weapons had Russian markings and the familiar red star of the old USSR. He felt Ivan's hand rest on his shoulder.

"We walk and talk, Mr. Bubba."

Ivan and one of his Bratva walked Bubba through the maze of weaponry. They walked past crates of land mines, boxes of mortars, stack-after-stack of Rocket Propelled Grenades, crates of AK-47's, and more boxes brimming over with rifle ammunition.

Next, he saw armored vehicles with big, knobby tires. He saw attack vehicles mounted with machine guns and belt-fed ammunition.

Ivan then led Bubba through a man-door that opened into yet another huge warehouse. Now Bubba literally stopped in his tracks, because there before him was a row of five T-72 Russian tanks. Behind that row was a row of half-tracks, and behind them a row of armored personnel carriers. On they walked, Bubba wondering if he was still in the real world.

Around another dividing wall they walked until they were standing before a Russian attack helicopter, fully mounted with revolving cannons and air-to-ground missiles. Dumbfounded, Bubba followed Ivan as they circled the gunship. Now Bubba really could not believe what he knew he was seeing. There sat two genuine Russian Mig-31 fighter jets, fully armed. Bubba had no words, so Ivan spoke first.

"Well Mr. Bubba, how much this you like take home, hey?"

"Well, Mr. Mogilevich, I'm just a kid in a candy store--I want it all, of course." Ivan laughed. A kid in a candy store. Things were really going to get hot in Georgia, thought the Russian.

"But Ivan, why are you showing me all this stuff. If you can keep something like this hidden here, then you are smart enough to know that me and my friends can't afford any of this, not unless your putting on one heckuva yard sale."

"No yard for sale, Mr. Bubba. In fact, want you have all weapons, and I deliver Jor-ja, free shipping. You go back to field, dig money you bury, buy wife nice gift."

Now Bubba was ready to freak out--how in this world could Ivan know where he had buried the money?

"Allow me explain, Mr. Bubba. We track your movements, by satellite, since left Mc-Donough. We still many friend in KGB."

"No joke," said Bubba, looking at the Migs.

"In exchange this weaponry, we want no American dollars. But, when you achieve goal of separation from U.S. government, there something we require you."

No money? Bubba was thinking--he could not wait to hear what kind of payment the Russkaya Mafiya had in mind.

NSA Headquarters
Fort Meade, Maryland

Quantavious Nelson was a junior researcher within the machinery of the National Security Agency. Assigned to the Homeland desk, Nelson had been putting in extra hours on his latest assignment, researching and analyzing one Jim Cummins, current Governor of Georgia.

Nelson did not know what all he would find out about Cummins. For all he knew the man was as clean as a whistle. But if there was anything to uncover, he wanted to be the man to find it. It would be quite a feather in his cap, and Nelson planned to go far and fast in the NSA. This chance was a real God-send for him and he bent his mind to the work.

Beginning his research with Cummins's private life before the man had entered politics, Nelson sifted through reams of informationthat documented every move, purchase, and payment Cummins had made while in college and private business. He found that Cummins had been in the earth-moving and construction business at one time. Then he had been in the real estate development business, mostly along the Georgia coastline.

Cummins seemed to have been above board in his dealings, Nelson concluded. Licenses were in order. Permits had been acquired for projects undertaken. Taxes had been filed and paid on time. Hours of research passed, then days, still with no red flags appearing.

Day six of the sixteen-hour workdays he had put-in in trying to discover anything interesting about Cummins found Nelson still at his desk late in the evening when most of his co-workers had already left for the day. With bloodshot eyes, Nelson was gazing at his computer screen, looking over documents related to some development work Cummins' company had done on the coast near a place called Tybee Island, Georgia. He learned that Tybee is a barrier island just off the Georgia coast near Savannah.

Something sparked in his mind, giving the researcher pause. Nelson leaned back in his chair, rubbing the fatigue from his eyes.

"Tybee Island," he said out loud, though no one was around to hear him. "Tybee Island," he repeated, thinking. There was something about that name that troubled him.

Reaching for his computer keyboard, he pulled up the secure NSA internet search engine and typed in 'Tybee Island.' More than one million results were found, so Nelson narrowed his search to any results for 'Tybee Island' that related specifically to National Security issues.

Nelson began to skim the description of each reference. When he reached the fifth reference down, a wave of disbelief ran through his mind. It was the title of a magazine article which read,

The Tybee Bomb: Is there a Hydrogen Bomb lying under the waters off the shores of Tybee Island?

Now he remembered. For his undergraduate work he had once completed a research paper on the U.S. Nuclear Arsenal. One part of that research concerned the 'Broken Arrows.' 'Broken Arrow' was the government's old code name for a nuclear device that was lost or missing.

As an undergraduate, Nelson had been shocked to learn that the U.S. Government admitted to having lost eleven such 'broken arrows' due to air or sea mishaps. As an NSA analyst, he now knew that much of what the government admitted was just propaganda designed to either calm or alarm the public, whichever circumstances might require at the time. But this story was fact based, so Nelson continued to search.

Nelson searched all the available NSA records concerning the so-called 'Tybee Bomb.' He read that the H-bomb in question was lost in 1958 after a B-47 bomber had suffered a mid-air collision with a fighter plane not far from the coastal city of Savannah. Unable to safely land the bomber with the h-bomb aboard, the pilot had chosen to jettison the bomb in the waters off Tybee Island, Georgia.

The military had done extensive searches for the bomb, but had turned up nothing, finally declaring the device 'irretrievably lost.' The United States Air Force had assured everyone that, because it was only a training mission, the lost bomb had not been equipped with a detonation device. The bomb was therefore harmless if it remained lost in the ocean.

But what if it had not remained lost, Nelson asked himself. What if someone had discovered the lost bomb and brought it to the surface? Nelson kept reading. He next discovered that private 'treasure hunters' had taken it upon themselves to find the bomb. The trick they would use was to simply take readings of the radioactivity in the sand and waters in the area where the pilot had testified to having dropped the bomb back on that fateful night in 1958.

The government had contracted with these treasure hunters and had received copies of the radioactivity readings they had collected. With the powerful search engines available only to the NSA, Nelson quickly accessed those readings.

Going with a hunch, Nelson decided to cross-reference those readings with the development activities of Jim Cummins near the area of Tybee Island, Georgia. When the results of the cross referencing appeared on his screen, Nelson felt a light sweat pop out on his brow.

In the months prior to Cummins' development work in that area, the radioactive readings taken were highly elevated, indicating a plume of high-level radiation. But, in the months after work permits show that Cummins had finished his development work in the area, the radioactive readings had gone back to levels normal for seawater. The drop in radioactivity corresponded exactly with the time Cummins' company had pulled out of the area.

Nelson sat at his desk asking himself if it was possible. Was it possible that the current Governor of Georgia, a man who had basically declared the President of the United States to be his enemy, might be in possession of the material necessary to create a hydrogen bomb?

Quickly gathering all his cross-referenced materials and other pertinent documentation into one file, Nelson used his secure NSA email account to attach the file to an email that he immediately forwarded to Dennis Click, Director of the NSA. Nelson marked the email as 'Urgent/Gov. Cummins.'

Quantavious Nelson sat in his desk chair with completely mixed emotions. In a way, he hoped his hunch about Cummins having recovered the 'Tybee Bomb' was on the money, because such a discovery in the present political atmosphere would certainly hitch Nelson's wagon to a shooting star: he would be the researcher who made the big dicovery.

But in another way, Nelson was afraid to imagine that a man like Jim Cummins, a man that many in the government thought on the verge of insanity, might possess a weapon of such terrorizing magnitude.

Either way, Nelson knew that he might as well get comfortable in his office. Even as late as it was, there was no way he could leave, now that he had forwarded such a frightening idea to his Director. He did not know when Click would read the email, but whenever he read it, Nelson knew he had better be on hand to explain and defend his hunch.

Chapter Nine

Baghdad, Iraq

Captain Dan Kramer was in the middle of his fourth tour of duty in Iraq. As part of the original 'surge' ordered by then President Bush, Kramer's platoon had been pivotal in helping to bring a relative peace to the infamous region of Iraq called the Sunni Triangle, whose cities had seen the worst of the fighting between American G.I.s and insurgents.

Kramer had patrolled and fought in all the major cities of the Triangle. In Baqubah, a sniper's bullet had singed his scalp. In Tikrit, his Humvee had taken a direct hit from an RPG. In a suburb of Baghdad, Kramer had manned a check point that had been attacked by a car bomb. And that wasn't all.

While patrolling in Ramadi, an IED had exploded near his vehicle and overturned it, setting it on fire. He took skin grafts on both arms at a hospital in Germany before returning to the field. In Fallujah, Kramer had participated in the hottest fire-fights of the war, his unit going toe to toe with insurgents who had somehow gotten their heavy weaponry into neighborhoods that made it difficult for air support to spot and soften these targets. Kramer and his men had seen house to house fighting at its meanest and bloodiest.

Soldiers younger and newer to the job would sit for hours begging him to give the details of how he had come by each of the many scars that tracked across the skin of his back, arms, legs and face.

There was no doubt that Kramer, though educated at the Army's flagship school of West Point, had won all the street-cred he needed to impress and inspire the men under his charge. Officer or not, he had the heart of a true grunt and his men knew it. That heart, combined with a keen and well educated mind, made Dan Kramer a special kind of warrior, the kind that every Colonel in the Army would gladly slice off a finger to have under him.

Because of his outstanding record, Kramer had been allowed to spend two weeks traveling on a special assignment with General David Petraus, chief architect of the 'surge' that had been deemed by all to have successfully pacified the Sunni Triangle. Kramer had been given full access to ask any question of General Petraus that related to their duties in Iraq, and

Kramer had soaked up the Petraus doctrines as a dry sponge soaks up water.

It was all very exciting then, but that had been years ago. General Petraus had been ordered to leave Iraq for other posts, and Kramer and his unit were now back in Baghdad patrolling the streets and seeking to keep a lid on the violence. Though it went unreported in the American media, Kramer had noticed a definite change in the atmosphere in and around Baghdad over the last few weeks.

A steady up-tick in violence had been seen during the months since the United States had chosen to expand the middle-eastern war by bombing the neighboring nation of Iran. And t wasn't just the increase of car bombs and roadside IEDs that had Kramer and his men on edge. Though it sounded weird to some, it was actually the look on the faces of the Iraqi people that Kramer now found most unsettling. Especially the eyes.

Kramer could remember a time, just after the 'surge,' when most of the Iraqi faces he encountered were softened by the general acceptance of the American occupation, or perhaps by the hopes for a soon withdrawal of the U.S. troops. Now, Kramer noticed, the faces he encountered were hard, the eyes suspicious and dangerous looking.

The Captain had early been stricken by the beauty of the eyes of Iraqi women. But even their eyes were cold and unfeeling, as they hurried with clinging children through a market or down a street.

Normally, the women were only concerned with their children, leaving the Iraqi men to give the hard stares at the foreign troops. These days, even they were locking cold eyes on the Americans, and the look of bitter hatred could not be missed by a man of Kramer's experience. *Would we ever leave this place for good*, wondered Kramer. *Would we ever leave these people to build their own future?*

The soldier looked down at his watch. It told him what the sundown had already told him. Darkness had descended over Baghdad almost an hour before. What a night in Baghdad would bring could never be known for certain.

This day, Kramer thought, had been quiet. Too quiet. Something seemed amiss, though Kramer could not put his finger on it.

The eeriness bothered Kramer such that he had earlier that day placed a call to an intelligence officer who had attended West Point with him. Kramer asked if intel had picked up any chatter in the last few days that might indicate that local insurgents were planning activities, but intel had replied that nothing especially noticeable had been overheard. Kramer noticed one of his men approaching. It was Ben Cain, a sergeant in his unit. By the look on his face, Cain wanted to talk.

"Captain, I noticed that you seemed a little on edge today. Mind if I ask why?" Kramer hesitated, then looked Cain in the eye.

"Ben, have you sensed anything different lately? Anything in the atmosphere?"

"I wasn't going to mention it first, sir, but things have been so quiet today that its even got the men spooked a little. Don't get me wrong Captain, these men are fearless—they'd follow you anywhere. But I was wondering if maybe you had noticed it too?"

"Yes, I have," said Kramer, taking another look around at the darkened buildings and across the dimly lit streets. "Not many cars out today. And the children that normally play along these streets, I have not seen but four, maybe five at the most."

"Ditto for me, sir."

"Would not expect them to be out this late, but I have not noticed but a few out all day."

"What are you thinking, Captain? Do you think something is up, something being planned?" Kramer looked around the quiet neighborhood again, wondering what was being said behind the doors closed against the GIs and the cool night air.

"Maybe nothing, Ben. Maybe its just the jitters. Just to be safe, though, put the unit on alert. And tell the men not to bunch together. I don't want to create any big targets for any fools who might want to start a firefight tonight."

"Yes sir," said the Sergeant as he turned to deliver the order to his men. The Sergeant turned back to his Captain with one more question.

"Captain Kramer, what sectors do you want us to cover on tonight's' patrol? If we turn west at the end of this street, we can cover-"

Kramer saw the streaking smoke trail of the Rocket Propelled Grenade even before Sergeant Cain. Cain never finished his question as the grenade streaked past Kramer's head, barely missing him, but hitting and puncturing the Sergeant square in the gut with a tremendous thump. The point of the projectile pierced Cain's clothing, skin and stomach before it hit and stopped at his backbone. And then, silence.

Cain was bent double and knocked almost off his feat when the projectile hit him, but remained standing, dusty boots on the ground. His arms were now spread open like an evangelist inviting people down the church aisle. He looked up at his Captain, the man he had followed through countless engagements. Their eyes locked as the grenade cooked off. It was but three seconds between the impact of the projectile and the explosion, but time had slowed to a crawl and it seemed to both men as if minutes passed. Neither could help the other.

Kramer watched, disbelieving, as the grenade buried in Cain's stomach exploded, separating the body and sending legs, arms and the torso flying in different bloody directions.

A portion of small intestine slapped wet against Kramer's helmet as he stood still, stunned and covered now with parts of his Sergeant.

He saw his men scramble, wide eyed, pulling their M-16s up to firing position. They were pointing their guns at something that was happening behind him.

Partially deafened by the explosion of the grenade that had just wasted his friend, Kramer could just make out the rising sound of people yelling and screaming. He turned to face the noise and watched as hundreds of men and women emptied out of doors that opened onto the street that he and his men were patrolling.

Every Iraqi was armed, most with AK-47s, a few with RPGs. Kramer saw that a few, incredibly, rushed screaming towards him and his men with axes and clubs in their hands. Bullets flew past him as his men, taking cover to his rear, poured .223 rounds into the onrushing crowd. 7.62 caliber rounds began to zing back from the opposite direction.

Kramer felt three of those rounds burn into his flesh, piercing the scars formed in his skin by so many battles before.

Shot through, with his position being overrun before his eyes, Captain Kramer realized that his men would all die bravely, but die they would: the enemy were too many and had caught them unaware. The young man's last thought was that his instincts had been good but his intel had been lacking.

The next day, the front page headline of the New York Times, printed in bold script over a picture of the freshly killed GIs and Iraqis, boldly proclaimed:

INTIFADA BEGINS IN IRAQ
UPRISING LEAD BY CIVILIANS

GEORGIA BURNS

Diamonds, thought Captain Jade Kerrigan, *they look like diamons*. The winding concertina wire glistened as if a thousand tiny diamonds were attached to it, mounted atop the high chain-link fence surrounding his compound.

The razor wire was cold, lifeless, a thing meant to hurt. The battle-hardened soldier wondered if war in this valley had not made him as cold as the wire.

A strong breeze caused the wire to tremble just enough to play in the Afghani sunlight, and Kerrigan found beauty in the only thing that stood between him and the hundreds who haunted the surrounding mountains every night, wanting and awaiting a chance to kill him and his men.

That fence formed the perimeter of the Korengal Outpost, or KOP for short, the outpost that had been the makeshift home to his company of U.S. Army soldiers for more than a year. The firebase construction guide had called for a second interior fence, but due to supply shortages that hampered the Army's efforts, the fencing had never arrived.

Kerrigan was trying to find beauty in a place where beauty was scarce, at least for a North Carolina boy. How was he to find beauty in such a place as the Korengel Valley of Afghanistan? He knew that the beauty was there; there were trees, forests even, sweeping across the mountainsides.

And the people, the native villagers, children with soft eyes. Sometimes on his patrols through the villages he would stop to speak with the elders and would hear the children laugh in that high-pitched carefree laugh that only a child's soul can conjure.

Yes, there was beauty here, but Jade Kerrigan had day-by-day felt his own soul growing too calloused to receive the imprint of it. He was a Captain in his mid-twenties, made so by the early killing-off of the man that had been Captain before him.

Kerrigan had to keep up a brave, motivated front for his men, men who had themselves begun to lose whatever humanity they brought within them to this valley.

Though still a young man, Kerrigan admitted to himself that he felt old-old and worn and as dusty as the craggy Afghan earth. In his little hometown there was once a young boy diagnosed with progeria, the 'old person disease' that ages a

141

child to eighty by the age of thirteen. And that is how he felt inside, as if he had progeria of the soul, aging unnaturally. What would he be like if he ever made it back to North Carolina? Could he ever feel young again, after all he had had to see, and do, in this foreign valley.

Kerrigan tried not to dwell on the past, or the future for that matter, but it wasn't easy. Every time he watched one of his men die in an ambush; every time he had to help that man hold his entrails in after being gut-shot; every time a village elder smiled and embraced him in the A.M. only to lead the Taliban to where his men were patrolling in the P.M., ever time his unit had called in air strikes on Taliban hideouts only to walk in the next day and find the littered bodies of a family who were eating their supper when the ordinance exploded their home.

Each event was taking its toll on him, and he knew it. It was time to get out, he had served over two years in Afghanistan already, and it was high-time to let someone else take over.

But the Army was spread too thin. With the war raging afresh in Iraq, a new 'surge' was planned to re-pacify Baghdad, and yet another massing on the Iranian border for possible entry into Persia. Add those to the troops stationed throughout Afghanistan, not to mention the thousands of troops that the base-missions in South Korea, Japan and Germany drained from the combat zones.

The Brass had long ago instituted 'stop-loss,' a general order which extended a soldiers' stay in combat zones on a need-to-know basis. *If you need to leave, we will let you know*. Kerrigan and his men would be staying in-country much longer than they had expected.

With over half the men on Prozac or some other drug that helped them to cope, Kerrigan spent half his time in moral-boosting. He had a secret list of the men whom he thought were either suicidal or homicidal, but what good is a list you dare not share with anyone else, he wondered.

Kerrigan knew his men were good soldiers and more, yet they sat uneasy on the razor's edge. What man wouldn't? Each of them had watched combat buddies suffer and die in these mountains, and all that it would take was for one soldier to snap under pressure, and any given village in the Korengal would become the Afghani version of My Lia. It had happened to every army of occupation since the dawn of war; the fatigue of battle, the loneliness of being away from hearth and home and all you knew before, the guilt you tried to harden against

142

when the villagers lay the dead women and children out in the street for all to see. And his commanders, calling in orders from worlds away, had a name as cold grey as gun-metal to describe it--collateral damage.

What kept him here? Ah, now he remembered as he stare at the wire; duty, honour, country. Those three, and his friends about him. He wondered, had he and his friends driven out the occupiers...only to become them?

A thousand yards away an even younger man was watching Kerrigan through an old Soviet binocular. That young man was named Ahmad Qadir. Qadir had just turned twenty years of age, and was a native of one of the villages in the Korengal Valley.

Ahmad was barely into his teens when the Americans had first come through his village looking for Taliban sympathizers, though they could find none. But as the soldiers were leaving the village headed south, a patrol of insurgents was entering from the north.

When they heard that the Americans had just left the village, the patrol rushed outside to see the Americans moving up the hills to the south. Though the Americans had not hurt any villagers, the insurgents were angry that they had been there, and began shooting at the Americans from the village.

Ahmad's father begged the insurgents not to shoot from the village because it would only bring more trouble, but they would not listen.

Ahmad believes that some of the Americans were killed, because they became so enraged that they called in airplanes to drop bombs.

The bomb that hit Ahmad's home must have been very large because there was a crater left in the earth and little more. Ahmad had somehow survived, and the village elders helped to dig through the rubble to find the bodies of his mother and father and two sisters. Though just a boy, that was the night that Ahmad became an insurgent as well.

He had left the village the next day with the patrol of insurgents. They took Ahmad in as one of their own and became his family.

He traveled with them into Pakistan. There, men in uniforms of the Pakistani Army trained Ahmad and the others in how to fight the Americans.

Now, Ahmad had returned to the Korengal to make things right. Ahmad knew that the death of the Americans would satisfy his need for revenge, but it would not bring his real family back to him.

Perhaps, he thought, my own death is the answer I seek. He had always carried much guilt that he had not died with his family that fateful night.

As darkness came to the Korengal, Ahmad and his fighters crept closer to the American outpost. Ahmad had been given the most dangerous task in the planned assault; he had to plant explosives at the base of the fence that surrounded the outpost. Ahmad's explosives would open a gap through which the other Taliban fighters would enter the American compound.

Ahmad heard the first round of machine gun echo across the valley. His men had opened the battle on the far side of the American encampment, and mortar rounds began to whistle and thud into the ground in that direction. That had been the plan, that a firefight would be initiaed on the opposite side of the compound as a diversion, giving Ahmad opportunity to plant his bomb. Ahmad had to move quickly before the Americans overcame the initial shock of the attack. The Americans were very smart, and very good at defending themselves. They would have men watching all sides.

The battle was fully engaged now, and Ahmad knew that the Americans would have called for the airplanes or helicopters to help kill his friends on the mountain. He would have to work fast.

With a satchel containing C-4 explosives strapped over his back and shoulder, Ahmad broke from his hide and ran towards the fence in a slight crouch. Ahmad had girded his long tunic about his loins so he could run unimpeded to the fence, which was more than two hundred yards from where he had been hiding.

The American's called that open distance a 'field of fire' because it would give them a clear shot at anyone approaching the outpost. He singled out one of the upright steel support poles as his goal. Ahmad's task was to plant the satchel at the base of the pole so that the pole would be dislodged in the explosion and the fence would lose support and collapse.

Running now at his top speed, Ahmad had drawn no fire even though he had covered over half the distance to the fence. Long, lean and athletic, Ahmad covered ground quickly, and could hardly believe he had made it almost to the fence without being shot at. It was the blessing of Allah he had prayed for.

Almost.

The bullet smashed into the upper thigh of his right leg, snapping the bone instantly. It was a .308 round that had hit him, a large sniper's round designed to kill in one shot. Ahmad was sent tumbling and rolling headlong towards the fence. The pain in his leg was so intense he almost lost consciousness but was brought back to his senses by the high-pitched beeping noise coming from the satchel still on his back.

Ahmad realized that during his fall the bomb had been activated and would explode in under half a minute. He looked up to see the fence only a few feet away, and he tried to move but his right leg felt like it was on fire, dangling awkwardly behind him.

His friends in the trees behind him had opened fire to cover him, and he lay there in the sand with bullets whizzing in both directions over his head. Realizing that his life was about to end made him think one last time of his family that the American bomb had killed. And that made it easier to do what he must.

Seeing them in his mind, Ahmad began to pull himself forward using his hands and arms. Bullets pinged into the sand and rock around him as he crawled. One grazed his arm, ripping his sleeve open. Somehow he on one knee, falling and fighting for every inch.

Ahmad was so close now to the fence, he could almost reach out and touch it. That's when another bullet thwacked into him. The round entered his lower abdomen, spinning him in a tight circle, spilling blood and guts about. He saw a dark red gash appear on a nearby rock, and he wondered how rocks could bleed, not realizing the red gash was a piece of his liver. But he was at the fence now, and reaching out Ahmad took the steel support pole in his hand just as he collapsed.

Using the pole to lean on, the young man thought of pulling the satchel off his back to place it the pole's base, but instead his legs collapsed as he slid down and against the base of the fence support.

Face to the sky, Ahmad noticed how blue it was, with wispy clouds wind-swirling above...beautiful. The American sniper had found his range and two more rounds pierced Ahmad's body just as the bomb exploded.

Ahmad was now little more than shreds, and there would be no family to gather them. But his bomb-pack had breached the fence, and just before it had exploded a hundred Taliban had rushed forward, leaving behind heavy machine-gunners to pepper the outpost, keeping the American's heads down. The first wave of attackers threw themselves onto the now limp chain-link, their weight flattening it to the ground for their comrades to pass over.

Captain Kerrigan was on the opposite side of the outpost directing the battle there when he received the call from one of his lieutenants.

"Captain! We have a breach on the west side, sir! I repeat, we have enemy inside the wire!" Kerrigan could not believe what he was hearing but tried to keep his cool.

"Stay calm, soldier. Kill the enemy, concentrate your fire on the breach, and we will reinforce you ASAP!" But Kerrigan knew he could not spare any men from his own position until the air power arrived.

He had never seen anything like this. Several times in the past year the Taliban had sent a few fighters to creep near the base and lob a few mortar rounds at them, only to scurry like rats back up the mountains. But this was something much more serious, and he needed immediate air support.

"Base Command, this is Captain Kerrigan at the KOP. We are under attack. Several hundred hajjis are attacking from our west and eastern perimeters. I need fire support on my perimeter right now. What can you do for me?"

No response came from Base Command, located about ten miles away. That was more than odd--Base normally had people manning the radio around the clock.

The enemy continued to press the outpost, their mortar rounds dropping closer with each lob. His men were begging for support on the opposite side of the compound, and Kerrigan was angry that Base had yet to respond to his call.

"Base Command!" he yelled into his radio, "This is the KOP, and we are under assault and being pressed hard. I've got men down, and need medivac, but first I need ordinance dropped around my western perimeter now." Finally an answer came from base, but it was not what Kerrigan needed to hear.

"Negative Captain, we can not reinforce, all available birds are engaged at other outposts...you'll have to try and hold on till our gunships can reload and get over there." Kerrigan was in shock. He had never had a request for immediate air support denied. Not ever.

"We cannot wait! How many other outposts are under attack?" The answer that came back was grim.

"Looks like all of them sir. Not just here near the border--
its happening all over The Stan. Try to keep the hajjis outside
the wire so the pilot knows who to kill when he gets there!"
    And then came the young Captain's final transmission:
    "THEY'RE ALREADY INSIDE THE WIRE!"

The Pentagon
Washington, D.C.

The Pentagon is the nerve center of the United States
Military, a city unto itself though located in D.C., a powerful
reminder that the mega-state had rejected the founder's
warning against keeping 'standing armies.'
    It is a city that never sleeps, because the U.S. has troops
stationed in well over one hundred countries around the world,
and the Pentagon is the brain-box that oversees this far-flung
empire. Thousands of workers, both civilian and military, keep
the place buzzing around the clock.
    Although some element of the Military-Security complex was
constantly involved in some type of warfare, be it psy-ops
propaganda or actual shooting wars, on every Continent. Since
shortly after the attacks of 9-11 the two main theatres of hot-
war being most closely watched were Afghanistan and Iraq.
    The office of the Secretary of Defense is located in the
Pentagon, ringed by hundreds of other offices of the men and
women who work as under-secretaries, along with their
assistants, all of whom serve at the discretion of the Sec-Def.
    On this particular day, some of these workers who had been
on break and still lingered in the hallways heard almost every
phone ring simultaneously up and down the
corridors. Exchanging worried looks with one another, they all
rushed back to their desks to answer the calls.
    The calls were coming in via dedicated lines from both
occupied countries, Iraq and Afghanistan.
    With phones to their ears, workers jabbed at computer
keyboards to pull up printable versions of the messages being
relayed to them. But as soon as one call ended, another
followed it immediately.
    The calls were coming from field officers whose job it was to
keep the pentagon informed with hourly field reports of the
military situation on the ground. As the reports were
electronically recorded, a special computer program sent the
information to the main-frame computer located in the War-

Room, a large room that adjoined the office of the Sec-Def. There, technicians under the direct command of the Sec-Def and his staff loaded the information onto a large LCD screen.

This computerized, fully interactive screen could pull up and display an electronic map of any place in the world as well as displaying satellite images from any military satellite.

Symbols indicating activity could be added, subtracted, or moved by touching the screen. Technicians were taking the reports from various officers and adding the appropriate symbol as the event was reported, giving a real-time picture of what was going on.

Presently, the large screen was displaying side-by-side maps of Iraq and Afghanistan. Present in the War-Room was the Sec-Def and several of his top assistants along with other military brass. They looked at the screen with growing concern.

On the map of Iraq, the symbols representing fire-fights appeared as small images of an M-16 rifle in the midst of a flame. These symbols indicated where US troops were actively engaged with hostiles, and were at first popping up within the area known as the Sunni Triangle, causing the Sec-Def's face to tense with worry.

As the minutes passed, however, the fire-fight symbols began to spread across the country of Iraq. He felt himself shudder—and a sharp chill. What was going on in Iraq? Why was there no warning from the Military Intelligence people?

Surrounded by his assistants, the Sec-Def grew more nervous by the minute as the flaming symbols now began to spread across the map of Afghanistan as well. Something big was going on--something coordinated.

How could this be? Had not the occupying U.S. forces not broken the back of the resistance in over a decade of warfare in these countries? Did the native populations not know how to appreciate the freedom and democracy that had been hand-delivered to them at such great cost to the U.S.?

A flunky approached with a cup of coffee but the Sec-Def waved it away rudely. The Sec-Def had a serious coffee habit, but this was no time for sipping coffee. He cursed his own people, and himself, for not seeing this event coming, whatever it proved to be.

He knew that he would be the one that would have to make the call to President Soloto. He watched the LCD screen a worried moment longer, then turned to his own office where he would make the call to the White House.

The Oval Office
The White House

President Soloto had been in a meeting with his
Environmental Protection Agency Director in his office when
that meeting had been interrupted. The President, reported his
secretary, had an urgent call from the Sec-Def that he said
could not wait. The EPA Director was kindly asked to leave the
room as the President took the call at his desk.

The Sec-Def relayed the current situation to Soloto. He told
the President that though information was still sketchy it
seemed that a major event, perhaps a coordinated attack by
insurgents against U.S. troops, was now on-going across
both Iraq and Afghanistan.

"Mr. President, we are not sure yet exactly what is going on,
but it has been many years since we have seen this kind of
active engagement in these theatres," said the Sec-Def's voice
over the phone, adding, "it looks like this thing is very wide-
spread."

"Please clarify the situation," replied Soloto, "are your people
controlling this outbreak?"

"Sir, we are confident that our people will be on top of this,
but the casualties are mounting rather rapidly."

"Mounting rapidly? Wide-spread? What does that mean,
wide-spread and mounting rapidly? It doesn't sound like your
people are on top of anything. How could something like this
be happing, Mr. Secretary? We have spent millions buying off
both the Shia and the Sunni insurgents, as well as the Taliban!"

"Mr. President, as I said, information is still sketchy and I
don't want to hazard a guess as of yet."

"Well you're going to have to make a guess right now because
that's what you're paid to do!" said Soloto in a loud and
irritated voice. There was a silence on the phone long enough
to be awkward but Soloto kept waiting, indicating that he
wanted answers and wanted them immediately.

"Mr. President, we do have some reports indicating that
there may be a significant number of civilian men and women
joining with insurgents to carry out these attacks. Some reports
have the attackers armed with everything from shoulder
launched grenades to pitchforks."

Pitchforks, thought Soloto, *that can't be.*

"Pitchforks? Are you serious?"

"Yes sir, that is what the reports are telling us. Apparently
our troops have already killed many hundreds if not thousands

of these attackers, but we have lost many men as well, some killed with bullets and some others killed with axes, hoes and other small arms."

"A hoe is not a small arm, Mr. Secretary, it is a garden utensil! American soldiers are not killed with garden utensils!" Soloto realized he was yelling into the phone, and tried to calm himself. "I will meet you in the Situation Room in fifteen minutes," said Soloto as he slammed down the receiver.

Soloto felt his face grow warm as he realized that if American troops were being attacked with pitchforks and garden hoes, then this was no mere insurgent hit-and-run operation by insurgents. This was an uprising of the peoples of Iraq and Afghanistan. And if it was indeed a popular uprising, then that meant that the hearts and minds of those people had hardened against the U.S. forces within their country.

Insurgents might be cut out of a population and destroyed like so many tumors, but if the population itself was rising, those middle eastern countries were lost forever.

The Situation Room
The White House

When the Sec-Def arrived at the Situation Room he found the President already there, along with COS Brandenburg and Director Click of the NSA.

The Sec-Def reviewed the information he had shared with Soloto over the phone. More information was being sent to him via his secure Blackberry as the men spoke. U.S. casualty lists were growing rapidly, with nearly a thousand soldiers reportedly killed, injured or missing within the last two hours. These were not *Iraq-war* type numbers; these were *Vietnam* type numbers.

The men hovered around the LCD screen watching as the symbols of fire-fights continued to post on the displayed maps.

The Sec-Def stepped aside to take a call from the Pentagon. When he returned to the group, his face had taken on another shade of anxiety. Soloto glared at him, waiting for what he knew must be more bad news.

"Mr. President, we now have reports from our Shia informants in Baghdad that our old nemesis Muqtada al-Sadr has left his home in Najaf and is making appearances in the Sadr City district of Baghdad. He has held several gatherings in the last forty-eight hours, the largest of those taking place about six hours before this uprising began."

All the men in the room noted that the Sec-Def had used the word 'uprising' for the first time.

"al-Sadr is drawing large crowds of followers, including insurgents who fought for him in the Mahdi Army. This is the same Army that caused so much trouble for us back in 2004. al-Sadr apparently called on his followers to arm themselves and drive the U.S. out, even if it means fighting to the death. Our sources said that he urged all citizens to join the uprising, not just the Mahdi. He says that he is calling for a *final intifada,* a last uprising, in retaliation for the bombing of Muslim Iran. He is Shia Muslim, remember. An arrest warrant had been issued for al-Sadr under Bush, but was never enforced. As a result, the radical cleric was idolized by hundreds of thousands of Iraqi citizens who saw him as someone untouchable by the Americans."

Soloto was particularly troubled, and angered, to hear that al-Sadr might be behind the uprising. Shia or no Shia, millions upon millions of taxpayer dollars had been spent to pacify that man and his followers, secret off-the-book deals that went as far back as the Bush Administration.

"Alright," said the President, "as Secretary of Defense, what is your recommendation?"

"Mr. President, I see only two alternatives. One is that we quickly withdraw inside our major, fortified bases. The upside is that we lose no more men, the downside is that we concede the Arab Street to the insurgents, literally. The second choice is that we reinforce our troops and fully engage the insurgents. The fighting will be urban and intense. The downside is that we will lose many more soldiers, and because we must use heavy weapons such as tanks and artillery, we can expect a high degree of collateral damage. The upside is that we can regain control of the streets and the situation on the ground."

"Which of those choices would you make if in my shoes?" asked Soloto of the Sec-Def.

"Sir, I would never ask our forces to give up ground that so many of their fellow soldiers died to capture. I say we fully engage the enemy and wipe them out with overwhelming force. Employ the Powell doctrine!"

"Mr. President," injected COS Brandenburg, "you don't want to be known as the President who lost Iraq and the Middle East, and that is exactly how your political enemies will paint you if you don't retake and hold the streets of Baghdad at least!"

Soloto eyed Brandenburg coolly, knowing that the man's hard-nosed political calculations were dead on. Still, he wished that his COS would have held the political strategy close to the vest until they were alone.

"Our main concern here is not political," intoned Soloto, seeking to regain the moral footing he needed to make his decision, though all present knew he was covering for Brandenburg. "Our first concern must always be the lives of the men and women in uniform, alongside the accomplishment of our mission." But Soloto had not ordered the invasion of Iraq and Afghanistan, someone else had made those calls. Even so, Soloto was now clearly faced with a decision to either escalate or retreat in the face of this significant new threat.

Soloto thought hard for a moment, weighing his options. *How bad could it get if we retreat into our bases*, he asked himself. He recalled seeing pictures of a helicopter rescuing desperate people off the roof of the Hanoi embassy, and leaving others, as America withdrew from Vietnam just before the forces of Ho Chi Minh rode into the city.

"Alright," said Soloto conclusively, "I want us to see this thing through. We will re-engage the enemy with enough force to get the job done. The big question is, what force level and weaponry do we need to make it happen, to re-establish peace?"

"Sir," answered the Sec-Def, "we are still working those numbers up but I think I can safely say that we must begin moving an additional fifty thousand troops back to Iraq, along with thirty-five thousand more back to Afghanistan, along with full compliments of heavy armory and firepower in order to re-establish the peace, at least in the major cites, sir."

Then he added cautiously, "And we will need the divisions stationed at Fort Stewart, Georgia. Those soldiers are veterans of Iraq and Afghanistan, many of them fought in Falujah against the Mahdis. They know this enemy's strategy and tactics. Those troops are indispensable, they will be the tip of the spear for the whole operation!"

Soloto and Brandenburg traded nervous looks. They were counting on those crack troops at Fort Steward as Home-guard in case they were needed to quell the trouble with Governor

Cummins. Seeing the dilemma, Director Click of the NSA spoke up.

"Mr. President, If I may?"

"Of course Dennis, tell us what you think."

"I know a way that we can meet the manpower needs of both our forces in the Middle East as well as that which may very well be needed in Georgia to deal with Cummins. That answer is Private Military Contractors like DarkSky. We use the privateers to fill the void here at home and free up the regular troops to deal with the Mahdis in Iraq."

That remark drew a cold look from the Sec-Def. He could not believe Click was suggesting the use of mercenaries, especially the rent-a-Rambo thugs of DarkSky, to put down a potential rebellion within the United States. DarkSky security contractors had been deployed to the Middle-East by the thousands and had been accused of atrocities against the civilian population.

The President felt the tension level rise and moved quickly to end the meeting.

"We'll worry about the thing in Georgia latter," Soloto said dismissively. "Right now we must concentrate on the Middle East. Mr. Secretary, I'm issuing the command to reactivate the soldiers at Fort Stewart, Georgia, for immediate duty in Iraq and Afghanistan. Now, if you will excuse us, I need to go over some unrelated matters with Director Click."

"Yes, sir. I'll begin the implementation of your orders immediately," said the Sec-Def curtly as he rose to leave the room. He did not like the direction that the meeting had taken, but he could do nothing but follow the orders of the Commander-In-Chief.

After he left the room the President had questions for NSA Director Click.

"Dennis, are you sure about using a private army like DarkSky to handle things in Georgia? I'm not sure that is even legal."

"Mr. President, we have little to worry about in that regard. Private security firms have long been employed within the United States, and this arrangement merely expands their use. Besides, if things go south in Georgia, there will be such confusion that no one will bother to notice whether our shooters are wearing Army uniforms or 'company' uniforms. The uniforms very much resemble one another, by the way." Soloto still seemed a bit unconvinced.

"Dennis is right, Mr. President," chimed in COS Brandenburg, "any private security contractor that is attached to or working with any part of our regular armed forces will legally be considered as part of federal security."

"One other thing, Mr. President," said Click, "I will need your authorization for these security contractors to arm themselves up to the force required to meet any threat that may arise."

"Explain further," said Soloto.

"Well, we know that the Governor of Georgia has command of the State National Guard--that is, until you federalize them as JFK did back in Alabama. There is something also called the Georgia Defense Force tht is under the Governor's office, but it is a small unit. Even so, we must account for any rogue activity, and those Guard Units do have access to artillery and tanks. I'm just asking that the contractors be able to secure heavy weapons if necessary."

"Alright then, I'll give my okay to that, but it must be understood that all private contractor activity within our borders, and especially in Georgia, must be approved through me," said Soloto. "Now, let's get to work on this. We've got to meet all security challenges, whether in Iraq or right here at home."

Chapter Ten

US Army Outpost
Korengal Valley

It was several hours after the last radio transmission had been received from the outpost in the Korengal that three Blackhawk helicopters swept into the valley from the west. The choppers carried an Army Ranger Unit that knew they were coming late to the party, and the scene below them told them all they needed to know before their birds even touched down.

The Rangers had been prepared to fast-rope into the compound, but the compound was now just burning wreckage of what had once been a secure outpost.

"Just put the choppers on the dirt," ordered the Unit Commander to the pilots, "No need to hurry things now."

Heavy rotors beat the thick air against the earth as the Blackhawks touched down, reflecting the heavy, depressed mood of the grim soldiers as they began to search for any survivors in the now destroyed camp.

The body of Captain Jade Kerrigan was found near the main entrance of the compound's central building. The bodies of Taliban fighters littered the ground all about the dead Captain.

"This Captain took some Hajjis with him before he fell," said one of the Rangers to his Commander as the two looked upon the scene.

"Brave man, wish we coulda made it sooner," said the officer as yet another Ranger came up at a trot.

"Sir, it's the same all around the outpost. Each one of our guys must've taken out at least twenty Hajjis before they died. But one thing stands out as strange, sir."

"What's that, Ranger?"

"The Hajjis left their dead here. Usually they take the bodies with them." The officer paced about, thinking it through.

"Well, either these Taliban were too few to handle this many of their own dead, or they were in a hurry to leave, probably to join another unit for more attacks on other outposts. This marks a change in tactics."

"Sir, what do we do with the bodies?"

"Bag all our guys," said the officer. Then he pointed to a small wood-plank building. "Pile all the dead Hajjis in that building there. Cover it with diesel and gasoline and light it up. If the Taliban is changing tactics--so am I."

Tommy Davis

The Apalachicola-Flint River

The Bratva had developed 'friendships' throughout Florida, meaning that they had spread enough of their money around, that certain people knew how well the Bratva rewarded their 'friends' who were able to help them in a time of need. The worse the economy, the easier to make 'friends.'

And they had made a few of these friendships at Apalachicola Bay, an inlet of the Gulf of Mexico, formed by a river of the same name. This Apalachicola River runs wide and navigable through the panhandle of Florida, backing up into the southwest corner of Georgia. Cargo ships use this river to move goods in and out of Georgia.

In Georgia, the river splits in two. The split that runs deeper into Georgia's old cotton-belt is called the Flint, which also runs near a small town called Bainbridge, where a small port is located. This port handles river cargo that is mostly agricultural bulk goods.

The Bratva had been forward-looking enough to make some friends at the small port-city also, where a few thousand dollars in a man's pocket can mean the difference between bare survival and comfortable living.

When needed, the Russians greased all the right wheels along the way up the river so that they could move their merchandise in relative peace. Many of those West Georgia locals lived near poverty levels, which made the pickings easy for the Bratva.

Bubba McCloud had agreed to have fifteen tractor-trailer rigs waiting near the port in Bainbridge on a certain night. That was the number of rigs that the Russians said it would take to off-load the crates of weaponry that Bubba had selected on his recent trip to Florida's Palm Coast.

On the appointed night Bubba rolled up and parked his pickup atop a bluff that overlooked the port located on the Flint River. Not far behind him, coming in from different locations and directions, were the fifteen 18-wheelers, big tractor-trailer rigs, driven by militia members.

Everyone was nervous. His fellow militiamen had grilled Bubba as to the trustworthiness of the Bratva. Would they really show up with that much weaponry? And would it be real, workable product or would the Bratva try to pull a fast one on the good ole boys of Georgia?

Bubba had no way of knowing whether the Russians could actually get the goods to them via the river. It seemed far fetched, but he had seen the weaponry with his own eyes in the warehouse the night they had taken him blindfolded.

And the Russians asked for no money upfront. They wanted to make money, lots of money, but that would come later, Ivan had said. Still, the weaponry was highly illegal and this deal would involve trust on both sides. That is what nagged at Bubba and his friends the most, having to trust men likely to be some of the world's most ruthless mobsters.

Bubba had been forward looking also, and had sent a handful of militia down-river in small fishing boats to see if the Russians were really coming. This river-watch was under strict instructions not to try to make contact with the Russians—their boats were to anchor down river, keep quiet and keep all lights off.

It was about an hour before midnight when Bubba got a call on his cell phone from the watch informing him that they had spotted a couple of large river-barges, heavily loaded, moving steadily up-river. Men had been seen on deck, their cigarette fires orange in the still, humid-thick night, their voices carrying over the gurgling river water. Their words were unrecognizable, said the watchmen, spoken with thick foreign accents.

It looked like the Russians were coming after all.

Bubba waited in the darkness, nervous as a Bishop in Hades. So much could still go wrong. *What if the Law shows up*? He had no desire to hurt anyone, and other than getting married, this was the biggest risk Bubba had ever taken. Perspiration ran in rivulets down his neck and back, soaking his shirt to stick wet to his skin.

Finally, Bubba's cell phone rang with a number he did not recognize. He looked at the time; it was 12:31 A.M. He answered his phone to hear the husky, gravelly laughing voice of Ivan.

"Is this Mr. Bubba? This Ivan, I hope you well this fine evening!"

"This here is Bubba. I got the trucks ready, are you close to the port yet, 'cause we don't have all night."

"Yes, can see port light now. As reach dock, loading crane be turned over our men, that agreement made with friends. We have 4:30 A.M. to off-load. Must work fast, Mr. Bubba."

"Okay. I'm sending the first trailer in now. Let's get this right the first time." Bubba mashed the 'end' button on his phone, then dialed up one of the truck drives.

"Stanley, bring your rig to the north entry gate of the port. Don't stop at the gate, someone will open it for you as you arrive. Now, come on!" Bubba heard the big diesel engine roar to life in the background.

Two minutes later, the first of the rigs pulled up and aimed their truck for the entry gate. The gate swung open just as the truck approached, so that the truck driver never had to touch his brakes.

As soon as the rig pulled to a stop in the on-loading area, the 6-ton crane went into action, moving crates marked as 'gypsum' or 'cottonseed' off the barge and onto the waiting trailer. Militia members were busy strapping the crates down, and when the first trailer was loaded to capacity, Bubba ordered it away as another rig pulled through the gate to take its place to be loaded in the same fashion.

Bubba was keeping a close eye on his watch, noting that it was taking about twenty minutes to load each trailer. At that rate, they would be pushed to load all fifteen trailers by the 4:30 deadline, making Bubba very nervous.

But the loading process continued at a steady pace. He could see Ivan and a few of the Russians he had met in Florida. They were down by the dock helping direct the process.

By the time the thirteenth trailer was being loaded, Bubba's watch read 4:01. Bubba thought they might get the fourteenth truck loaded, but saw no way fifteen would be loaded by4:30. He took out his cell phone and dialed the number Ivan had called from. Bubba watched from a distance as Ivan pulled his own cell phone out of his coat pocket and flipped it open, putting it to his ear.

Yes, what Mr. Bubba, I very busy now."

"Ivan, I don't think we can get it all loaded in time. We may have to call it quits after this trailer is loaded."

"No Mr. Bubba, I no take cargo back down river. You must take or I dump in water." Bubba had heard how the Russians had polluted and ruined the rivers of their Mother Russia, and he wanted no such thing to happen in Georgia.

"No Ivan, I don't want anything dumped in the river."

"Yes Mr. Bubba, we keep—" Ivan had stopped talking mid-sentence, then said, "Mr. Bubba, we have problem." About that time the headlights of a car caught Bubba's eye.

He looked over to see the patrol car of the local Sheriff's department pulling up to the gate of the port. He watched as the deputy got out of his cruiser and walked up to the gate. The deputy had a shoulder mounted radio mic but made no move to use it, yet. Ivan said,

"My men handle this visitor," But Bubba knew a death sentence when he heard one, and he realized that this deputy who was just doing his job was about to die.

"No Ivan, let my men handle this!" Bubba, phone still in hand, took off running down the bluff towards the gate. But Ivan and two of his men were already approaching the deputy.

The deputy seemed interested but not alarmed.

"Did'nt know y'all was running a night-shift at the port now. I worked out here back in the eighties, and we never worked no night shift," said the unsuspecting deputy as he and Ivan's men drew closer to each other. Ivan, who had also moved towards the deputy, just smiled back at the man as two other Bratva kept approaching the local lawman, one to either side.

One of the men spoke in Russian to the poorly trained deputy, attracting his attention. As the deputy turned to look at the one who spoke, the other Russian was slipping a .45 handgun out from under his jacket. The gun had a long black cylander attached to the end of its barrel which would suppress the report of the shots as the slugs were pumped into the deputy.

Just before the Russian fired his weapon, Ivan sensed something zip past his ear. He turned to see one of the militia men pointing some kind of weapon at the deputy, who at that very second let out a blood-curdling yelp.

Ivan looked back around to see the deputy on the ground, writhing and shaking as if the victim of epilepsy. The militia man ran past the Russians to where the deputy writhed, pulling a roll of duct tape from his pocket. Another militia man ran up and helped to hold the stricken man, and together they began to tape his mouth, wrists and ankles together.

Bubba was breathing heavily as he ran up to the group of men. Ivan now realized what had happened.

"Mr. Bubba, Tazor man o.k., but Tazor soon wear off. Why not silence completely"

"No Ivan, this man is just doing his job. We've got to have those weapons, but if I can spare a life, I will." Ivan began to laugh.

"I see now; Mr. Bubba wants take on whole U.S. Government, but is, how say, squeamish to kill one man! I think, Mr. Bubba, you need get used to killing. Much killing be required to reach goal." Bubba looked up at Ivan sternly.

"Maybe so, Ivan, but I'll put it off as long as I can. I can't take this man with me, but I want him kept safe." Ivan laughed again.

"Very well, Mr. Bubba, I take man, he live, but be hard journey on him."

"Hard journey is fine, just let him live. Look at his left hand, that's a wedding ring. He's got family," said Bubba, pointing to the deputy's ring finger.

Ivan bent over to regard the man's wedding band. He grunted and said,

"Young widow easy find new husband. I three wives," said the big Russian, holding up three fingers. "All find new husbands, I not even dead yet." The other two Bratva laughed loudly at Ivan. Ivan merely jerked his head towards the barge and his two men scooped up the deputy like he was a sack of feed, carrying him towards the dock.

"I keep him alive, Mr. Bubba, no worry. But why care for this man? Is he friend?" Bubba looked up at the star filled heavens, then back to Ivan.

"Baptized when I was eleven years old." Ivan looked puzzled, then looked to the heavens and understood.

"**богобоязненный,**" Ivan said, then shrugged as he translated his own Russian. "God fearing." He then pulled an envelope from his coat pocket, extending it to Bubba McCloud.

"Here is, what you call, Invoice." Bubba took the envelope and stuck it in his back jeans pocket.

"Let's finish loading," Bubba replied.

In another thirty minutes all the trucks were loaded and gone. The barges were completely empty now except for one deputy's cruiser, which the militia had wrapped in camouflage tarp. Ivan would wait till he was back in salty water to slip the cruiser over the side of the barge.

The Russians quickly mixed a thick black liquid and forced the deputy to drink it. Swallowing it was the last thing the Georgia lawman remembered until, six days later, he was found at the bottom of an empty, dry oil-cargo tanker that had just arrived at a dock--in Saudi Arabia. Though badly dehydrated and covered in grimy filth, the fortunate man would live to see his family again.

After all of the Russian weaponry was safely hidden away at various spots near his home base, Bubba sat down with a cup of coffee and opened Ivan's envelope. He was anxious to learn what price the Bratva would demand for the weapons shipment.

The envelope contained one folded piece of paper. Unfolding it, Bubba noticed a picture of a group of running horses. Each had a jockey on his back with a large number attached. It was a picture of a horse race, and under the picture in bold print was one simple sentence:

When this comes to your New Georgia, we would like to control it.

A SECURE LOCATION
25 MILES OUTSIDE TEHRAN, IRAN

The secure bunker where the President of Iran took refuge during the U.S. attack was located deep under the hardened earth and had been designed to withstand a direct hit. Ahmadenna had personally overseen the construction of the bunker, watching as layer upon layer of concrete reinforced with steel was poured. A tunnel beneath those layers led to the President's personal command center.

The sly Ahmadenna wanted a hiding place so secure that not even a nuclear bomb, from either the Israelis or the Americans, could destroy it. The government engineers, under pressure to perform, assured their President that the bunker could withstand such a hit, though they were by no means sure that it could. Better to tell Ahmadenna what he wanted to hear than to risk losing their jobs. Besides, they reasoned, if a nuke did take out Ahmadenna they would likely die in the attack as well, which greatly minimized the risk of their lie.

Huddled now deep within the bunker with his advisers close at hand, Ahmadeena and his staff had to decide what their next move would be.

Ahmadeena sat grim faced at the head of a conference table in the bunker's war room. His advisors, which included military leaders as well as the head of the Iranian secret police, were standing about the table, none too quick to speak or to take a seat. These men knew that in times like these, when their country had been successfully attacked, it was likely that heads would roll as blame for the disaster was assigned.

He certainly could not afford to take the blame upon himself, and no one failed to notice that the Ahmadeena himself was wearing a sidearm. Neither did they fail to notice the three members of Ahmadeena's personal escort stationed around the perimeter of the room, each armed with HK MP7 automatic rifles. Finally, the head of the small Iranian navy ventured to make a suggestion.

"Mr. President, if I may speak?" Ahmadeena slowly turned his gaze upon the man.

"Certainly, Admiral Mohtaj."

"Sir, perhaps it is time to launch our wave of destruction in the Strait of Hormuz. We have a fleet of thirty-three catamarans armed with the latest anti-ship missiles. They are stationed at Bandar-e-Lengeh and are on full alert as we speak. Even with the presence of the American submarines and battle ships, these attack craft are so fast that we can sink hundreds of oil tankers before the Americans can react." Ahmadeena had looked away but now looked the Admiral in the eyes again.

"Hundreds, Admiral? Hundreds of tankers?" Admiral Mohtaj hung his head, suddenly realizing how ridiculous his exaggeration had sounded. He tried to recover his lost ground.

"Many tankers, sir, if not hundreds then many...as many as the American puppets dare to put in the Strait!" The Admiral, now red in the face, strained to seem confident of his assertions. But it was the President's top economic advisor that saved face for the Admiral.

"Sir," injected Hosni Abjil, the head of Ahmadenna's economic panel, "if the Admiral is successful in sinking one-third of the hundred tankers he hopes to attack, those alone would be more than enough to choke the flow of oil to the West. Fuel prices in the land of our enemy the Americans will triple overnight!"

The President considered what his economic advisor had said. Pushing himself away from the table, Ahmadeena rose and folded his hands behind his back. He began to pace towards the other end of the table, his subordinates parting to make way for him as subordinates are expected to do.

Pausing at the other end of the table, Ahmadeena turned to face the other men in the room. He looked directly at the Admiral.

"Many tankers, Admiral Mohtaj, you will indeed sink many, many tankers by utilizing the ninety catamarans at your disposal." The Admiral now looked confused, he had mentioned only thirty-three attack craft.

"Sir, the number of attack catamarans stands at thirty-three, all ready for service upon your order!"

"Thirty-three is the number that you have at Bandar-e-Lengeh, Admiral. But I have an additional fifty-seven catamarans that I purchased from the Chinese government, and all are armed with the best anti-ship weapons that the Chinese can produce. You see, Admiral, the Chinese have made a lot of money selling goods to the American Wal-Marts--enough money that they can afford to drive cars. And to drive cars, Admiral, the Chinese need Iranian oil." Ahmadeena pulled a piece of paper from his inside coat pocket.

"Here, Admiral Mohtaj," said the President as he handed the Admiral the piece of paper. "Here are the locations of the catamarans. All are based near Hormuz, with trained members of the Revolutionary Guards for crew. You will also find listed here my personal codes that will be recognized by the crew commanders. You may contact them from this bunker using my secure frequencies."

Ahmadeena put his hand on the shoulder of the still amazed Admiral.

"Ninety lightning fast attack vessels at your command, Admiral--good hunting." And then to all in the room he said, "Let us see how well the U.S. economy runs without oil."

The attack runs against the huge, lumbering oil tankers began almost immediately. The US Navy had fully expected such an attack and had been ready in intercept the missile boats, and this was done with ruthless efficiency. With both air and sea power the Americans let loose on anything the Iranians put into the water as soon as it was spotted.

Much of the time it was like shooting ducks in a barrel. But the Iranian catamarans were also equipped with floating mines that they scattered in their path, making it more difficult for their American pursuers. And for every three Iranian missile boats the Americans sank, one escaped into the wide Persian Gulf, or into the narrow Strait, to prey upon the monstrous super-tankers, the largest of all ocean-going ships, full to the brim with that dark liquid cargo for which the industrial world so thirsted.

The hull length of such a ship is over one thousand feet, and with the Chinese-made missiles it was impossible to miss such a target.

Within an hour of the launch of the Iranian missile boats, three super-tankers suffered direct, broad-side hits just below the water line. It took less than half an hour, from the time they were hit, for these leviathan vessels to be swallowed whole by the merciless sea which so quickly and efficiently disposed of the mega-ships, the only trace that they ever existed being an ever widening oil slick bubbling to the surface.

When two more hours had passed, ten tankers were at rest on the ocean bottom. Within eleven hours the Iranian Admiral, though he had lost nearly all the catamarans as well as the majority of his other naval vessels to American guns, had managed to sink over fifty oil tankers, the cargo value of each equal to the GDP of a small country.

The Oval Office
The White House
Washington, D.C.

President Soloto was at his desk when the calls began to come in from the Pentagon concerning Iran's attacks on oil tankers in the Gulf. It had not been unexpected, though Iran had been much more successful in sinking tankers than anyone had projected.

Soloto was glad that he had been proactive in regards to the expected disruption in the oil supply that would be caused by the bombing raids in Iran. His counter-weight was to release massive quantities of oil from the strategic reserves that the federal government held in case of emergency.

Before he gave the go-ahead for the bombing of Iran, Soloto had issued an executive order releasing millions of barrels of oil from the reserves, which he believed would soften the impact of the disruption of supply.

And, if that did not work, Soloto had another Ace up his sleeve. Americans had long known about the ocean of crude oil hiding deep under the frozen earth of Alaska. But to allow the drilling of the pristine Alaskan wilderness for oil was, for the environmentalist crowd, akin to taking away abortion rights from feminists: it was the worst environmental blasphemy possible. And it was an unthinkable crime for a member of Soloto's party.

But Soloto was in his second term, and by law there could not be a third. That meant that for Soloto, all bets were off in terms of pleasing his political base, which included the most radical of the environmentalists. In a sense, Soloto's second term in office would last as long as he lived, he would always be addressed as "Mr. President," and that would be true whether the environmental crowd loved or loathed him.

So, reasoned Soloto, if worse came to worst, he could always play the Alaskan Oil Card. He knew that within days of a Presidential order opening up the Arctic National Wildlife Refuge, major oil companies would race to get the oil out of the ground, and even speculation of a major new domestic source of crude oil would drive oil and gas prices down.

Environmentalists would surely curse his name for such a move, but there were no higher offices to pursue, and being in his second term, he did not need their votes anymore.

Administration estimates of light damage to the U.S. air fleet and moderate collateral damage to Iranian civilians proved to be fairly close. Only six planes were shot down, and fewer than three thousand civilians on the ground were killed, all numbers well within the 'acceptable margin' range of those planning the raids.

Sadly, government spokesmen added, some American pilots that ejected from damaged aircraft were captured by the Iranians and were most likely being tortured. Iran even posted on Youtube scenes of downed American pilots being water-boarded for days before being beheaded. Still, the results were acceptable to the American central government. War was war, and bad things happened.

Over the course of the next three days, Soloto continued to receive updates from both the military and his own State Department informing him of continued retaliatory strikes against the oil supply by the Iranians.

The American press had been covering that story, as well as the uprisings going on across Iraq and Afghanistan. These intifada were being interpreted as retaliation for the bombing of Iran, even though the President's spokespeople were quick to point out that such uprisings had to have been in the planning for weeks before the bombing of Iran.

Soloto and his advisors watched the network and cable coverage of the events, and noticed that attention began to turn to the quickly jumping prices at the gas pump. The administration had expected as much, but also expected it to be short-lived.

The White House grew more tense as they heard reports of gasoline prices doubling, then tripling, all within a week of the bombing of Iran. Surely the prices would stabilize and begin to creep back down as the reserves were released into the market and drivers chose to stay off the roads, Soloto and his team reasoned. Things would be tense for a while but would surely soon calm down.

But the expected stabilization did not occur. It seemed, the President's advisors told him, that American's had reacted to the Iran bombing and retaliations with an almost apocalyptic fear. Instead of curtailing their use of gasoline, American's began to horde supplies. Runs on gas-stations were occurring all over the country. People began to fill up any and every container they could get their hands on with the precious fuel that enabled them to get to work, to school and to the grocery store.

When CNN reported that the average per-gallon gas price had reached $7.50 within the continental U.S., Soloto called an emergency meeting to address the crisis.

That meeting was held in the Oval Office, and when the President floated his idea about an executive order to open ANWR in Alaska to the oil drillers, jaws dropped all across the room.

Many members of the President's cabinet were present, including the Director of the EPA. She locked eyes with Soloto and tried to stand up and leave the room but fainted before she could make it to the door. Moaning something about 'the ultimate betrayal,' she was strapped to a gurney by White House paramedics and carted away.

Meanwhile, the rush continued by the American public to secure as much gasoline as possible before the price doubled again. Soloto marveled at the stupidity of the masses; did not they know that it was just this sort of panic that drove prices even higher?

And, day after day, the price of fuel continued to climb.

GEORGIA BURNS

Two Days Later
The Oval Office

Even though the gas-price crisis was on-going and showed little sign of relenting, Soloto was almost enjoying his day. He had just hung up the phone with the Prime Minister of the Nation of Israel, a nation thought by many to be one of America's most important allies in the world, and especially in the Middle East. The Israeli leader had lavished praise on Soloto as the only US President that had proven himself man enough to deal, once and for all, with the Iranian threat.

And that had not been the only call Soloto had received. Leaders from all around the United States, leaders from Soloto's own political party as well as those representing the opposition party, had called the President to congratulate him on his decisive and courageous action in neutralizing the threat posed by an Iran armed with nuclear weapons.

Even Faron Y. Huxtable, the opponent Soloto had defeated to win his second term, called to congratulate the President and to pledge his support of Soloto's actions. Huxtable had assured Soloto that even if gas prices went to $10.00 per gallon, he still had done the right thing in defending America and her allies from Iranian aggression and terror.

Soloto realized what this all meant. The opposition party was going to provide him with the political cover he needed to come out of this crisis looking fine. And that would go a long way in promoting and protecting his legacy as a great leader and President.

The President took several more congratulatory calls before he was interrupted by his office secretary. It seemed that Treasury Secretary Tag Tower was in the outer office asking to speak with the President in an unscheduled meeting. And, she added, Secretary Tower seemed to be suffering some kind of panic attack.

Soloto said he would receive the Treasury Secretary, though he wondered why the man had not thought to call ahead and ask for the face-time.

When Tower entered the room, he was patting his blood-red face with a damp cloth. Tower's appearance gave Soloto immediate alarm. His hair was unkempt and his tie loose, a poisonous look of deep distress seemed to drag his whole face downward.

167

"Tag, come in. What's this all about?" Tower's only response was to make a line for the beverage table.

"Gotta have a drink...nerves..." is all he said to Soloto. This worried Soloto even more, for though Tower was not religious, he was known as a total abstainer from alcohol. After swigging down his drink, Tower turned to the President, pausing as if to summon the courage to speak.

"What is it Tag? What's going on?" Tower looked away from the President now, taking yet another drink from his glass. Soloto quickly grew annoyed with having to pry an answer from his Treasury Secretary. Soloto was the kind of man who wanted news quickly, especially if it was bad news.

"Tag, this is the Oval Office. Either tell me what's on your mind or leave me to my work." Tower looked now at his boss but turned away again quickly, as if he could not bear to look the man in the eye. Soloto walked over and snatched the drink from his hand, forcing the man to look him in the eye.

"I'm sorry Mr. President, I'm a little flustered. It's...it's China sir--the Chinese have made a major move on currency, a move against the dollar," said Tower, his face breaking out in fresh sweat. "The Chinese have started dumping their dollar reserves. Our people in Beijing said it started with no warning about six hours ago." Soloto paused for a moment, trying to digest the news.

"Who is buying their dollars?" asked the President.

"Several governments, some private interests, sovereign wealth funds...but mostly the Iranians."

"Iran is buying dollars? Why would they help us?"

"I don't know for sure sir, but they may want to hold the greenbacks as assurance against another attack from us. But it is the Chinese that most concern me, Mr. President. They've taken other actions as well, sir, moves to keep their own markets stable. They've kicked in their stock market controls which will shut down trading if their markets over-react to this dollar-dump."

"What about the Russians? The Saudis?" Soloto asked, beginning to look very worried now himself.

"The Russians are staying out of it, they're not buying dollars but they're not selling their own dollars either. I've already put in a call to the Saudis, but their finance minister won't take my calls. I don't know why they won't, but I need the Saudis to counter this move by the Chinese. I need," Tower said, sweating profusely now, remembering then to whom he was talking. "Sir, *we* need the Saudis to back us on this. They are the only ones with the reserves to buoy the dollar verses the Chinese and Iranians. We need for you to call them, Mr. President. They *cannot* refuse your call."

Reserves. Soloto was not sure if Tower was referring to the Saudis' vast dollar reserves or vast oil reserves, though in this situation, one was as important as the other. Saudi banks were stuffed with US dollars, meaning that any play against that currency could hurt the House of Saud badly, and it was in their interest to support the dollar, though they could not do it indefinitely.

All of that meant that the value of the currency of the United States was more or less in the hands of a Muslim country in which both Mecca and Medina were located.

Allowing western troops onto that Islamic Holy Ground country had caused widespread hatred of the Saudi Royal Family, threatening their regime.

And though the House of Saud was officially Muslim, their princes had come to so enjoy oil profits and the pleasures it afforded that they would gladly dump Allah and all his promised virgins for a few more million barrels of sweet black crude. In their minds, oil drives the modern world, not religion.

So, reasoned Soloto, the Saudi Princes were more businessmen than anything else. They could be counted on, Soloto and Tower both hoped, to make decisions based on money and oil, not religion.

The Saudi government had reluctantly acquiesced to having American troops in the Middle East permanently since the first Gulf War, as a business decision that would help them maintain control over their population, lands and oil.

All these thoughts were running through Soloto's mind as he made his way to his desk to ask his secretary to place the call to the head of the Saudi Royal Family.

In a short moment, the secretary told the President that the connection had been made over a secure line. Picking up his phone receiver, Soloto asked to speak to His Highness King Abdullah of the House of Saud. A Saudi female who spoke clear English, though with a strong accent, responded to Soloto. Her words were offered with a professional coolness that took Soloto aback immediately.

"Mr. President, His Highness King Abdullah regrets that he is unable to take your call at the present time. His Highness, in begging your forgiveness, wants to assure you that only an emergency of the most personal kind would keep him from talking to you. An illness to a member of the Royal Family has caused this delay in conversation, but His Highness King Abdullah assures you, Mr. President, that he will return your call as soon as humanly possible."

Soloto hung up the phone and sat there stunned. He had never even heard of another head of state failing to take the call of the President of the United States. This was not Andrew Cuomo putting Bill Clinton on cold hold...this was serious business. Perhaps the Soviets had done it at the height of the cold war, but that was an enemy with a calculated snub, not an ally holding the value of your currency in their palm! The look on his face was a mixture of fear and humiliation, and it told Tag Tower all he needed to know.

"He would not take the call? He just snubbed the Leader of the Free World? The President of the United States?" sputtered Tower incredulously. Soloto looked up at Tower, embarrassed and angry now.

"Shut up Tag, I need time to think."

Tower walked over to the sofa situated in the middle of the Oval Office and collapsed there, holding his face in both hands. Then he reached for his Blackberry, dialing up an operative based in the Saudi capital. When the connection was made, he told the operative to try to find out what moves the Saudis were making on the open markets.

Next, he made similar calls to Beijing, Tokyo, Moscow, Frankfurt and three other capital cities across the globe. Though it was unknown to the public and most of Congress, the U.S. Treasury Department maintained operatives within the financial apparatuses of at least ten foreign countries. Money spooks, financial information gatherers who reported directly to the Treasury Secretary.

The U.S. Treasury had these agents all over the world, and now was the time Tower needed them to provide the real-time information that was hidden from the general public so he could figure out what was going on.

Whatever it was, it looked like a major orbital realignment was about to take place in the financial universe, and it looked like America's favorite loan officers, the Chinese, were the ones pulling down the stars.

Chapter Eleven

The Saint Marys River, on the Georgia coast, not far from
Kings Bay Nuclear Submarine Base

Kenny St. John had been a shrimp boat worker his whole life,
as had his father before him. When Kenny was young, he had
fished with his father, learning the trade directly from the older
man.

Those had been good days. The shrimp were running thick
and regulations were low. It was the time before
environmentalists were able to get passed rules and limitations
on shrimping activity along the Georgia coast. The money had
been plentiful, which made the hours aboard the boat with his
dad all that much sweeter.

Things had not stayed the same. New regulations had
sprung up that hindered local shrimping. The fishing season
was shortened. New netting had to be purchased that were
more friendly to turtles and dolphins. New equipment meant
more expenses. Competition from abroad was importing
shrimp by the thousands of pounds, driving down the market
prices. The federal government would offer no protection from
the foreign competitors; it would only pour on more
regulations that made it even more expensive to operate.

Kenny St. John had watched his father age under these
growing threats to their livelihood. The older man had
developed lung cancer, which proceeded rapidly, and Kenny
had watched his father many a night, bent double in pain,
coughing up saucers full of an awful mix of tissue and
blood. When his father had died, Kenny used a small life
insurance policy the bury the older man. The few thousand
dollars that was left over he paid to the bank against money
owed on what was now his shrimp boat.

The boat had been a good one for many years, but the sea
and age had taken its toll. The outdated motor was in need of
an overhaul, if not complete replacement. The deck had places
where the wood had rotted through. The shrimp nets had holes
in them that were large enough to make other shrimpers stare
in wonder as to how Kenny even kept his catch within it long
enough to haul them aboard.

His father had been dead for three years now, and Kenny had
taken to drinking heavily on the night of his father's
funeral. He had married his high school sweetheart years

before, but she had never really gotten used to being a fisherman's wife. Never knowing when Kenny would be home, or if he would even bring home a paycheck from week to week, had been hard of his wife. The drinking, coupled with the depression, had overpowered her love and she left Kenny two years after his father had died. Kenny had been alone now for a year. He had no sons with which to share his dying trade.

Alone and lonely, Kenny was falling ever deeper into the cave of darkness, dreaming dark dreams, and looking for someone to blame. He had lost his father, his wife, and was losing his profession. His world was passing away, and he could find only one entity to blame, the federal government. Those pukes who sat in Washington, D.C., handing down their fine little laws and regulations, with no concern for the lives they destroyed, he reasoned.

And who was the symbol of the ever-expanding, ever-taking federal government, for men like Kenny St. John? President Abraham Soloto. And now, finally, someone was standing up to the President and his federal thugs. And it happened to be coming to a head in his very own State of Georgia.

Kenny St. John, sitting in his dark, dank apartment, took another swig from the almost empty bottle of whisky, and decided that he was going to help strike a blow against the government that had taken from him all he had ever loved. His shrimp boat was old, but it still had enough pluck to carry an extra heavy load out of the mouth of the St. Marys river, down the coast and into forbidden waters. Kenny would need some help to pull it off, but he knew a few good ole boys that were in about the same shape and attitude he was in. They would be more than glad to lend a hand.

Arnold Air Force Base
Tennessee

Kyle Smeltzer sped over the Tennessee roads well above the speed limit as he headed to Arnold Air Force Base. The federal government was putting him up in a Holiday Inn in nearby Manchester. Smeltzer had been leading the examination of the downed fighter escort that had disintegrated over the neighboring State of Georgia.

Frustration had mounted when the recovery team had failed to recover most of the airplane, and when Smeltzer and his team could not isolate a cause of the plane's explosion.

That the plane had exploded while the Governor of Georgia denied landing privileges of Air Force One was not in question. But that fact only put more pressure on the investigation, and the investigators.

Smeltzer's entire career was built on his methodical, tedious examination of the remains of a downed airplanes 'carcass.' He would accept nothing other than fact-based conclusions. Over the years, many an assistant investigator had been fired on the spot by Smeltzer for sloppy work or, even worse, for manufacturing evidence to fit an assumed or desired conclusion.

And in this particular case, Smeltzer had felt pressure to come up with a conclusion that would dovetail nicely with the White House's version of events. White House Chief of Staff Brandenburg had called Smeltzer daily, pushing for a wanted conclusion. According to Brandenburg, it was obvious that the Governor of Georgia had somehow had the fighter escort shot down. Brandenburg made it clear that he would accept no other explanation, but he obviously did not know Kyle Smeltzer.

Now Smeltzer was on his way back to the central hanger at the Air Force Base. A few minutes before, he had received a text that a recovery team working in the mountains of Georgia had recovered a large chunk of the jet engine that powered the Raptor. Smeltzer could only hope that this section of the plane would give him the clues he needed to solve the puzzle. And, he had determined, he would follow the facts to whatever conclusion they led him to, regardless of what Brandenburg and the White House wanted.

After passing through security and arriving at the hanger, Smeltzer entered the building where his research team was already waiting. No one had touched the recovered engine parts as of yet, they knew that Smeltzer would not allow anyone else to have the first look.

Donning a pair of white cotton gloves, Smeltzer approached the wreckage that had been set atop a stainless steel workbench. Cameras recording the mechanical postmortem were turned on. He noticed that it was the top part of the Pratt and Whitney Turbofan Engine casing, along with part of the main shaft, the combustion chamber, the turbines and the exhaust nozzle. The fan itself was missing, as were the compressors, but Smeltzer was clearly excited about what he had to work with.

Walking around the table a few times to size things up, he began to reach within the engine parts and feel about. Someone asked him what he was looking for but Smeltzer worked on in silence, and no one asked anymore questions until he was done with his examination.

After about twenty minutes of meticulously rubbing down every surface area that he could reach within the engine, Smeltzer pulled out his gloved hands. Both gloves were covered in smut, but his left glove also had significant traces of a whitish chalky substance. Smeltzer looked at that left glove for a long moment before speaking.

"Well boys, this is the engine that failed, and it failed catastrophically. That catastrophic failure caused the explosion of the aircraft," Smeltzer said matter-of-factly, almost as if he had expected this conclusion, which he clearly had not.

"Well," asked one of the NSA investigators who was observing the research, "what do you think caused the failure? Is there evidence of a penetrating missile or rocket?" Smeltzer looked up at the FBI agent soberly.

"No, I see no evidence of any penetrating device. What I see is an explosion that began inside this turbofan engine. You see this chalky substance on my left glove? That's the remains of part of the fan. The fan failed first, sending debris into the compressor, the combustion chamber, and the turbines."

"Well," continued the agent, "can we not conclude that some projectile hit the fan, causing it to disintegrate back into the engine itself?"

"No," Smeltzer said, "we cannot conclude that. The few parts of the fan that we have recovered, bits and pieces really, were not blown apart, but rather melted apart." Smeltzer walked over to another workbench where small metal pieces had been laid out. The others present followed him as students following a master.

"See here," Smeltzer said, holding up a few shards of metal, "these are pieces of the fan. Notice along the edges here that the metal is melted in-two. Something melted the fan blades and sent them flying into the rear of the engine. And these engines don't make for good trash compactors."

"Wow," said the FBI agent, "what in the world could have melted the blades?"

"Very few substances on earth could have achieved such cuts so cleanly. One comes to mind, that being a type of thermite. Thermite is the substance often used to cut the steel beams out from under a building during a controlled demolition. There is no missile or rocket that uses thermite," Smeltzer said as he pulled off his gloves. "The destruction of this aircraft was done by sabotage, and that saboteur had to place the thermite on these engine blades sometime before the aircraft took off."

"Wait a minute, are you saying that the Governor of Georgia would have had to have someone working on or around that Raptor to sabotage the engine before it ever took off? How could that be possible?" asked the agent, incredulous.

"I did not say any of the things you just mentioned. You are drawing conclusions based on other information or theories that you have arrived at independent of my findings. What I am saying is that this engine failed catastrophically, and that failure was caused by an act of sabotage prior to takeoff. That is what I'm saying and that is all I'm saying--and that is what I'm about the report to the White House right now."

Smeltzer walked away to call D.C. in private, leaving the others there gawking at the engine and at each other.

The Grand Concourse
The Bronx, New York

As the fuel crisis worsened across America, the food supply chain began to suffer breakdowns, and the Soloto administration was not ready for it. One of those early breakdowns took place in the trucking sector that serviced grocers in The Bronx, northeast of Manhattan in New York City.

The public panic over fuel prices led people in New York, rather than shunning the high priced fuel, to quickly buy up all they could before the price doubled to over sixteen dollars a gallon, as internet rumors said that it surely would.

Every car and truck tank along with every spare container was being filled as a hedge against the coming price increase. This led to an immediate shortage of available fuel.

When several trucking companies could not get the needed fuel, their grocery carrying trucks sat idle for nearly two weeks while management tried to secure the needed petroleum. As it turned out, one of the tankers that the Iranians sank had been scheduled to service refineries that in-turn serviced gas stations in the northern boroughs of New York City. Fresh produce rotted on docks, grocery shelves emptied, and local officials were caught off-guard by what happened next.

The first riot began as just a protest march down the Grand Concourse thoroughfare in The Bronx, New York. City officials had heard rumors that a march was being organized, but were sure that whatever crowd showed up would be small and manageable.

These officials did not realize that news of the protest march went viral on the internet in the last twelve hours before it was scheduled to begin, effectively quadrupling the number that actually showed up.

With their cupboards bear of food and many of them without fuel for running their homes or cars, there was little reason to stay home and the angry residents of The Bronx emptied into the streets as if going to a free Yankees game.

Extra police had been called up just in case, but a full third of them were no-shows because they themselves had no gasoline for their personal vehicles to drive to work. All these factors resulted in over sixty thousand citizens showing up in an angry mood with an inadequate police presence to keep them 'in line.'

The march began around noon, filling the wide Concourse with hungry protestors. Most just chanted and yelled insults at the powers that be. Some held up signs blaming the government for the food and fuel shortages. Ominously, several firearms were spotted amongst the crowd. That had officers growing nervous, speaking into their walkie-talkies. Still, things went relatively well until about 5:00 P.M. Even that late in the day, very few protestors had gone home, the presence of T.V. cameras encouraging them to hang around.

That's when the police decided that the crowd had to disperse, and in a show of force formed a line of officers in full riot gear across the Concourse. A solid line of helmeted men in black padded uniforms carrying thick plexiglas shields on one arm and steel batons in the opposite hand marched towards the crowd.

The crowd grew defiant when they saw that they would be dispelled by force. Bottles, rocks, and pieces of pavement were thrown from the crowd towards the on-marching police line, much of the debris hitting its intended policeman target. The crowd of protestors had become a mob.

This angered the police even more, but the closer they moved to the mob, the more defiant the mob became. The line of police was within forty yards of them now but they had moved not an inch, growing louder every second. When the line of black-clad riot police stopped, the crowd gave out a victorious cheer. But when the line of police parted at two different points, the people realized that the line had only paused to allow two huge vehicles to come through.

The black vehicles were high-top trucks with large knobby tires. Mounted atop the trucks were round black disc-like devices known as Long Range Acoustic Devices. These devices emit a directed tone so loud that it causes intense pain to the ears of humans, so intense that it can cause permanent hearing loss.

Both LRAD's were turned on the crowd simultaneously. People in the crowd were seen grabbing their ears, or else trying to wrap their arms or jackets over their ears to stop the pain as they scrambled about. The police were happy with the initial results as the crowd was clearly intimidated by the directed noise and began to fall back. But the crowd was too large to be driven off by only two LRAD's, and the use of them on the crowds served mostly to enfuriate.

Someone with a gun in the crowd took aim at the black discs emitting the noise.

Gunshots in such a situation are the last thing the police want to hear because it means that at least someone in the crowd was willing to risk killing the police in order to carry out their protest. It was an escalation of violence that the police were not ready for.

The shooter had aimed for the LRAD but missed it with his first shot. Instead, the bullet slammed into the officer atop the vehicle who was manning the noise making device. The shot hit the officer in the head, jolting his head and body backwards. Sprawling over the edge of the truck top, the instantly dead officer careened off the side of the vehicle head first, smashing to the pavement below.

The sound of the gunfire, combined with the sight of their fellow officer being treated so meanly, pushed the other riot policemen into a new gear of aggression.

The front line of cops was purposely not armed with guns so as to present a non-lethal though threatening presence to the crowd.

But now, enraged by the murder of their brother-at-arms, they reformed their riot-line of shields and batons. The men in black then double-timed their pace while maintaining a disciplined line, yelling and cursing the crowd of protestors. They meant business and would prove it.

"Push! Push!" yelled the leaders in the police line as their shields slammed into the closest of the rioters.

"Strike! Strike!" came another order, as shields were lowered to allow for the arching whirl of batons through the air.

The blond hair of a protestor became a smeared cap of blood-crimson as a police baton crashed into it, parting the scalp and fracturing the skull beneath. His rage not satisfied, the officer swung again and again, beating the blond man down all the way to the pavement before moving on to his next victim.

Rioters raised arms in defense of the batons, only to feel and hear the cracking of radius and ulna. Baton strike after baton strike was answered with shrieks of pain, and fractured bones split through arm-skin in jagged edges.

After a few moments of this the Concourse began to grow slick underfoot with blood and gray brain matter. The riot police proved that you did not need a gun to kill, a baton would do just fine if used with enough skill and authority.

Even so, the rioters were in no mood to be bullied by the authorities whom they blamed for the shortage of food and fuel. Someone in the crowd sang out a rally cry, and a group of young people, both men and women, first threw a volley of bottles at the riot-line and then rushed them.

That part of the police riot-line was initially overwhelmed by the concentrated onrush of rioters, with some officers pushed to the ground and trampled. A few had their shields kicked from their hands and their batons ripped away, and were then beaten with the steel objects.

But the police were well trained, and other parts of the riot line converged on the overwhelmed portion to confront the charging rioters. The rioters were now pushed back by the re-formed solid wall of shields, and the rioters took many a bash from the batons as they were beaten into a bloody retreat, back into the main body of the protestors.

Some of the older members of the crowd, seeing now that the entire thing was turning dangerously violent, were looking to get out of harms way. But most of the crowd was made up of younger people, many of them harboring bitterness from years of jobless poverty, with that bitterness now exacerbated by the recent shortage of necessities.

This crowd was no rabble, as many of them held college degrees that had done them no good in a jobless economy. The police tended to view all protesters as rabble, and rabble is easily dispersed by a show of force. But this crowd was different and would not be so easily cowed.

Having witnessed the initial success of the last rally, other groups within the crowd now tried the same thing, attacking various portions of the police line, trying to punch a permanent hole in it. Back and forth the rioters battled the police. A second line of police now came up behind the first, but because of the manpower shortage it was too thin and far spread.

This second line was armed though, both with guns and teargas. The clunk of gas canisters being launched into the crowd was heard again and again. But again and again the rioters picked up the canisters and hurled them back over the heads of the first line of police while fighting that line more or less to a stale mate.

Those who had emerged as leaders in the mob had secured bullhorns and, sensing a victory over the authorities, began to use the bullhorns to urge the crowd to summon courage and direct the attack to the right or left or middle en masse in order to overwhelm the hated police. The march had now taken on the characteristics of a pitched battle.

Just then a new sound was heard across this asphalt urban battlefield. It was a low, thunderous roll of noise that had the rioters frozen still and the riot-police backing cautiously away from the mob.

Almost dusk now, there was still light enough for the rioters to make out what was clearly a long line of mounted policeman riding atop tall, thickly muscled horses.

There were nearly two hundred of the horses, and they came up the Concourse in a single-file at a steady lope that spoke of discipline and fine training. Here were the police reinforcements, their ace in the hole.

The horseman made their way across the pavement with something akin to ceremony, and at the last moment fanned out into one solid line of horse-and-man flesh across the Concourse.

As many a foot-borne army in the middle ages had found, there is nothing as exactly terrifying as to be ridden down upon by a line of charging, heavy horse. Even the extra-brave had, over the centuries, found it difficult to stand up to a well delivered cavalry charge.

As both the first and second line of riot police faded back through and behind the line of horseman, both sides knew that this would be the authorities' last attempt at a non-lethal solution to the rioting mob which had failed to disperse upon orders to do so. A few were dead or dying on both sides, but the situation had not yet gotten fully out of hand.

An order rang out from the ranking horseman situated in the middle of the line, and as one, the line surged forward, towards the waiting crowd, in a high-stepping semi-trot that made some hearts proud and others fearful. The horseman had a handful of leather reigns in one fist and a long club in the other which was held perpendicular to the ground, tip pointing skyward.

The moment of truth had arrived, and as the line of horse drew nearer the mob, many in the mob began to back away. When he saw the mob begin to waver, the horse-captain shouted out another command, and the line increased their pace, coming on now in a full trot. That action caused the crowd of rioters to waver even more, and in a few more seconds the crowd was backing quickly away, many turning their backs to run.

That is when reinforcements arrived for the mob. These were reinforcements no one had asked for and none of the march organizers had invited. Yet they were there, of their own accord and with one purpose; to defend the crowd by whatever means necessary. They arrived at the rear of the protest march in ten pickup trucks, the beds of which were filled with men dressed in camouflage fatigues.

At first glance they looked like regular army troops. The way they exited the pickups and formed quickly to face the authorities, one could tell that they had trained for battle. They were dressed in camo-fatigues and on their shirt sleeves they wore patches that read in bright red letters the word 'Oathsworn.'

And in the days that followed, as the public waited for the smoke from this battle to clear and the facts to come out, people would learn that these Oathsworn were members of a group of army veterans who had banded together to swear allegiance to the Constitution, and in defense of the people upon whom the heavy hand of government was falling.

Oathsworn literature would later be found that stated a belief that they were living in the 'last days of the republic,' and that the group had been called to 'defend the people' as they tried to 'recover that which was lost.'

Having had enough of politics, polling and elections, the Oathsworn believed the present government was so far gone as to have surrendered any legitimacy. Maintaining that they were the 'tip of the spear' for those who would no longer obey a government from which the 'consent of the governed' had been effectively withdrawn, each man and woman of the Oathsworn had pledged their 'lives, fortunes and sacred honour' to defend what they considered the freedoms of the people.

Armed with assault rifles, the Oathsworn numbered about fifty men, with a sprinkling of women as well. They formed neatly in front of the crowd, a crowd which had been on the verge of full flight but now stopped and turned to watch what would happen when the horsemen of the police met these Oathsworn who were armed with deadly weapons.

The horse-line was facing west, into a sun almost set but which still gave just enough light to make colors and objects hard to distinguish. The ranking member of the horse-police, a Captain and twenty year veteran of the force, therefore did not realize the new threat he faced until he was almost upon the Oathsworn.

His horse was still moving at a brisk pace when his eyes finally made out the line of soldiers, all in the kneeling positions, with automatic weapons pointing at his line. His mind said 'reign up' but the 223. rounds entered his neck and chest before his hands could obey the orders of his brain. As his head and torso fell backwards, pulling him out of the saddle, his horse bolted at the report of the rifle, jumping to the left.

The dying Captain's limp body was thrown to the right, his left boot dislodging from its stirrup but his right boot holding fast. His head and shoulders hit the pavement with a hard thump, hard enough to kill him if the bullets had not already accomplished it.

But his right boot did not dislodge from the stirrup, a fallen riders' worse nightmare when alive, a shockingly violent scene still, even when the rider was as good as dead, as this Captain surely was now. All fifty of the Oathsworn fired at near pointblank range into the line of charging horse-cavalry. Spinning, tumbling bullets popped heads like old gourds, like ripe melons. Blood and brain matter flew into the air, splattering onto the clothing of fellow horseman.

Normally the police would have had their own armed spotters dressed in plain clothes, melded within the crowd to warn of just such possible escalations. But, again, the shortage of officers due to the shortage of fuel meant that today the regular crowd-spotters had not been available and no one thought to order others to the task.

It was a fatal mistake for all two hundred of the horseman. Charging as they were, right up onto the fifty Oathsworn armed with automatic weapons, it was an awful and hellish slaughter that awaited the proud police cavalrymen. A few managed to turn their mounts for a retreat, but the Oathsworn's blood was up, and few held qualms about dispatching the government's enforcers with shots to the back.

The horses themselves fared little better, most of them being shot as well. When struck by bullets, the horses pulled sharply away from the rifle's report, crashing into the horse next to them, knocking the rider off to be trampled under hoof.

Just as there is nothing as terrifying as be ridden down by a charging horse, there is equally nothing that equals the feeling of being atop a terrified, out of control, fear-crazed charger that weighs over a thousand pounds.

Those not trampled to death lay helplessly on the pavement to be dispatched from this present life either by point-blank rifle shots from the Oathsworn, which moved up quickly for the gruesome work, or worse, by members of the mob who had picked up fallen batons so recently stained with their own mob-blood. The surviving horsemen learned in agony of the mercilessness of a mob whose blood is boiling hot for revenge.

Even though it was the Oathsworn who had fired on the police and not the locals, the authorities saw no difference between the two and felt they had no choice but to answer in kind.

Held in reserve by The Bronx Police Department were two Humvees mounted with M-60 machine guns. On loan from the New York National Guard, these militarized vehicles were fully armored and mounted with the machine guns as well as grenade launchers.

These were rolled in immediately after the horse-line had been decimated and, along with thirty shock-troops carrying M-16 assault rifles, they all opened fire on the mass of flesh that was the gathered crowd.

When automatic fire is laid down on a crowd of people, there is little discrimination between militants and bystanders. The largest massacre of police in recent American history had just occurred, mostly at the hands of the shadowy Oathsworn, but in the mass confusion that the riot had become, there was but one target for the police: the crowd. The police unloaded everything they had, pouring fire into the riot, knocking it down and driving it back. Bodies and body parts soon littered the Concourse, and puddles of blood quickly formed, some of it running off into the street gutters.

Twenty of the Oathsworn were down, the others having retreated to safety. This overwhelming police firepower soon dispersed the crowd now running for its collective life.

By the time a cease-fire was ordered, hundreds lay dead, thousands lay injured or dying. People were running, screaming, crying. It had happened near New York City, and though the police tried to drive off the ever present reporters and cameramen, the wide Concourse and surrounding buildings provided ample places from which to film.

Americans awoke the next morning to television images that they were certain had been filmed in a third-world country far away from the United States. The scenes that were recorded could only be described as horrific, looped time and again on CNN, ROX News, MSNBC and all the network news shows which cancelled regular programming to show the startling footage.

Youtube and other internet sites were flooded with scenes filmed from within the crowd using cell phone cameras. A collapse of order in a major city like this, in the age of cell phone cameras, streaming video and easy access to the internet was so traumatic that the FCC sought to limit the broadcast and transmission of such images, bringing loud charges of press censorship and violation of First Amendment rights.

Survivors from the crowd were interviewed, blaming the escalation on the police. The police in turn blamed the escalation of violence on members of the crowd, and on this group calling themselves the 'Oathsworn.'

Because many of the injured rioters were Black or Hispanic, charges of racial homicide and even racial cleansing flew wildly. The Reverends Jessie Jackson and Al Sharpton arrived on site the day following the massacre, competing for face-time before the T.V. cameras to call for a federal investigation. Daniel Ortega, head of the National Council of La Raza (The Race), arrived to add his voice to the call for an investigation, and to seek equal footing with public figures like Jackson and Sharpton.

News anchor Keith Olberman brought in Rodney King from Los Angeles for expert, strike-by-baton-strike analysis. Bill O'Reilly countered by sending Geraldo Rivera to the crime scene.

Authorities in other major American cities like Los Angeles and Chicago scrambled to make sure that shortages did not occur there, and to beef up their police units just in case.

The pressure to 'do something' was felt by officials at all levels, but nowhere was it felt so strongly as at the top, by the office of the President, and the man in the Oval Office.

Soloto, so fresh from his electoral victory, was now suddenly under intense pressure because of these events at home as well as those abroad. His reaction to what was quickly dubbed The Massacre in The Bronx was predictable: he flew over the Concourse in his helicopter, Marine One. He then held a press conference to witness his signing of an executive order for a special investigation into the incident.

The president promised to bring to justice any and all who caused the massacre, including rioters and police. Soloto denounced the Oathsworn organization, branding them as terrorists no better than Al Queada, and appointed a special task force to hunt down all its members. Spokesman for that group countered by posting their own internet video, filmed at the riot scene and then at undisclosed locations, spinning their involvement in the Bronx riot as that of defender of unarmed and helpless citizens who were wrongfully attacked by authorities who would gladly leave the people locked in their houses to starve, with no fuel for heating or transportation.

The Oathsworn made loud threats of what would result if and when Soloto declared Marshall Law. They urged all citizens and 'lovers of freedom' to actively and manfully resist any attempt by the government to enforce Marshall Law.

Those videos received over ten million hits within forty-eight hours of posting, so much that Youtube servers were overloaded and crashed. Rumor immediately spread over the internet that Soloto had ordered the CIA or some other government agency to sabotage Youtube. This was not true, but in a time of widespread panic, truth is the first casualty.

By any measure, President Soloto was left looking weak and out-of-touch. At the first meeting of his advisors, he asked for suggestions if in fact the civil unrest began to spread. The opinion of those gathered around the President was almost unanimous: declare Marshall Law.

GEORGIA BURNS

Governor's Mansion
Near Atlanta, Georgia

On the night of the riot in the Bronx, Governor Jim Cummins watched on television as the events unfolded, sitting with his wife on the sofa in his den at the Governor's Mansion.

Never had he seen anything resembling such chaotic violence on an American street. It was a scene, he was thinking, one might expect to see in a South American or African country, but never within the United States. What had happened to the America he had once known?

Cummins watched in disbelief as the TV cameras captured the images of Americans being shot and killed by other Americans in large numbers, the injured left to bleed-out, prostrate on the cold, red-puddled pavement.

The Governor felt badly for those hurt in the riot, sending up a prayer for them, though he figured something akin to this would happen sooner or latter when the shortages got bad enough. He knew that nothing stirred up trouble quiet like families with empty stomachs, and hungry children asking to be fed. People will not watch their children starve, he told his wife.

And though he did not wish for what was happening in New York, Jim Cummins realized that these events would play a part in his over-all plan to resist what he called the Leviathan on the Potomac, which he considered a monstrous and out of control government that no longer honoured the Rule of Law embedded in the Constitution.

Governor Cummins discerned that it was time to put the next part of his plan into motion. He reached for the phone parked on the sofa's end table and dialed the number of his closest friend and advisor Wilder Fields.

"Wilder, hello...are you watching the news? Incredible, isn't it? Yes, awful, but no more than we expected--still a shock to watch it. Are you thinking what I'm thinking? Yes, in light of these events, I think we need to move immediately on part two of the plan. Yes, I'll start calling in favors tonight, and you call the guys on your list. With a little luck, the Sovereign State of Georgia will be the first State in modern American history to successfully resist the power of the Federal Government."

"That is what we're hoping for, Jim," replied Fields. "In the meantime, I will be arranging for you to deliver a major speech to address all these issues and bring clarity to the situation. I have friends already working on the event, and your own staff can help with the planning. I think Macon would be the best place to deliver the speech. It's centrally located in the State, you enjoy heavy support in that region, and it is far enough from Atlanta to give us some breathing room from all that is happening here. We can get good press there. What do you say?"

"You're the genius here Wilder, don't you remember? Yes, of course, Macon will be just right for the speech. Set it up. If I live long enough I'll deliver it, that is. And after that Macon speech, I'm heading to my lake house over in Cobb County for some R and R."

"Well deserved, no doubt."

The Governor hung up the phone as his wife walked back into the room with two cups of coffee in her hands. Cummins turned the volume up on the television as he took the coffee cup, his wife sitting close at his side to watch with a mixture of shock and sadness as events unfolded in the Bronx.

They watched reporter Shepherd Smart of ROX News, who announced that he was already live on the scene in The Bronx. A few hundred yards away from the worst of the riot, Smart was trying to stop terrified people who were running past him on the street. He was having a hard time of it, most were too afraid to stop and talk with him on camera.

The couple watched as Smart in frustration reached out and grabbed a woman by the arm in an attempt to stop her to ask her a question.

But the Bronx woman did not want to be grabbed and she turned quickly and slugged Smart square on the nose with a hard-fisted atraight right.

All of this happened with the camera rolling. Smart was caught off guard and off balance, and his head jerked violently back as the Bronx woman's fist tagged him solidly. The veteran news anchor landed hard on the pavement on the seat of his pants, a bewildered and confused look on his face, and trickle of blood at his left nostril.

"Mississippi boys never fare well in the Bronx," Cummins said to his wife, shaking his head in mockery of Smart's now almost comical plight.

And Governor Cummins of Georgia knew that the Bronx Riot had marked a new and dangerous chapter in American History.

GEORGIA BURNS

Mouth of the St. Mary's River,
Not far from King's Bay Nuclear Submarine Base

It had been dark for two hours already when down-on-his-luck shrimp boat operator Kenny St. John pulled up to the dock in his old truck where his boat was moored. The dock was an older one in a secluded area near the mouth of the St. Mary's River, where the woods grew nearly up to the rivers' edge.

It was situated only a few miles south of the Atlantic homeport for United States ballistic missile submarines, King's Bay Nuclear Submarine Base.

The base covers sixteen thousand acres and is home base of the jewel of American military might, the most powerful killing weapons-entity ever produced by Adam's race, the Trident Nuclear Submarine.

The Trident is a true water Behemoth, and carries a complement of twenty-four ballistic missiles, each one outfitted with several nuclear warhead vehicles that are independently targetable upon reentry. Any third-world country in the world that were to acquire only one Trident would instantly become one of the top ten nuclear powers on the globe, with the destructive power of nearly five hundred Hiroshimas at its beck and call. The United States Federal Government admits to owning fourteen such Ohio-class submarines, though many suspect it has a few more hiding under the world's seas.

Like most of Kenny's possessions, his pickup truck had belonged to his father and had been mostly worn out when Kenny inherited it. The driver's side door creaked on a rusty hinge as he pushed it shut. Two other men, both driving heavy duty flatbed trucks, were waiting when Kenny got down. Kenny smiled at the old friends.

"Boys, good to see y'all. Did ya get the chain?" The two men looked over their shoulders at their trucks. Each truck had a large tarp-covered mound in the middle of the flat beds.

"We got it Kenny," said one, "had to call in some favors for that much, but we managed it. We're not real sure what you could possibly want with that much log chain on a shrimp boat, but we got what you asked for."

"We owe you more'n this for all you've done for our family," added the other man, "Many a night our folks woulda gone hungry if you and your Pa had not brought fish or shrimp to the house. We ain't forgot."

"Thanks fellas. I'll need some help getting it all aboard." The three men slipped their hands into their leather gloves for the

187

work. Loading that much chain was hard, back breaking work. Hours passed as the men made pass after pass from the flatbeds over the wooden dock and onto the shrimp boat, though the coolness of the night helped a lot.

Finally, the last link of chain was loaded. Kenny made one more trip to his own pickup, from which he brought out a welding tank and torch, loading it aboard the boat beside the chain. All three men sat down on the mound of chain and popped the top of a cold coke.

"Dang, Kenny, you got enough chain here to make the biggest fishing net on the east coast," joked one of the friends, "only problem is, chain don't float so well in water." But Kenny wasn't laughing.

"Chain don't normally float, old friend," replied Kenny with a knowing smile. A slight moon had come out, and the other two men looked at one another. They looked at the welding unit Kenny had brought aboard, then looked out across the water. Then one of them said,

"Kenny, whatever you're planning to do with all this chain, I'm thinkin' I wanna be there when it goes down."

Chapter Twelve

Office Building of
The Interior Proceeds Service (IPS)
Downtown Atlanta Georgia

The month of April springs warm, sunny and green in the State of Georgia. For the citizens of that State, April means the Easter Celebration is here: Sermons about the Resurrection on Sunday morning, egg hunts with the children in the afternoon. But April also brings something else to mind; Tax Day. The fifth day of the month, being the last day to legally file Interior Proceeds Taxes, perhaps the most hated of all taxes because it was imposed on a person's labor. That date on the April calendar had become a symbol of an intrusive, heavy handed government that taxes folks when they make, spend, save or invest money. And that date had naturally become the day when more tax protests were held than on any other day of the year. The agency that enforced the tax that many in Georgia and across the country called the 'slave' tax was the IPS. No three letters, when strung together and pronounced separately, were more insidious to Americans than those three: IPS. Wailing against the IPS had become as American as apple pie. Not all Americans had forgotten their history, and they knew that America began as a tax protest against the King and Parliament of England.

None of this was lost on the new Governor of Georgia, Jim Cummins. Cummins had read the polls that said Americans feared an IPS audit more than a shark attack. Cummins was raised at the knee of his white haired grandpa, and his grandpa had long been an opponent of the IPS. He recalled his grandfather once saying,

"I'd rather my son bring home a boyfriend than go to work for the Revenuers!" That's what the old timers called the agents of the IPS, 'Revenuers,' especially old timers like Papa Cummins who was known to supplement his income as a corn farmer with a corn-liquor still tucked away in the woods. The new Governor had no moonshine stills, but his Papa's disdain for the IPS burned as strongly in his mind as it had in his grandfather's. He simply felt it was immoral to tax a man or woman's labor. And as Governor of the Sovereign State of

Georgia, Cummins felt duty bound to 'brush back' those who intruded into the daily lives of the citizens of Georgia. Cummins knew that it would be a bold stroke, as well as a huge political risk, but if it worked right, what he had planned for the IPS on Tax Day could be a huge step towards a fairer and freer life for his people. He knew that he could not shut the IPS down by himself in a day, but he could certainly rattle their cage. He had never heard of another Governor making such a challenge to federal power, but he had run for Governor to be a game changer, and that is what he intended to be.

Cummins knew that a large tax protest was planned to take place outside the Interior Proceeds Service building in downtown Atlanta. Small protests could be seen there every April 5th, but this year the "Rev. Party" crowd was sponsoring the event and it promised to draw thousands of angry protestors. The marchers planned to hold up signs denouncing the Proceeds Tax, and listen to speakers on bullhorns do the same. But Cummins planned to give them something they never expected, and would never forget.

The morning of the fifth burst bright with blue-clear skies over the city of Atlanta. Atlanta had been called many things; the Heart of Dixie, the Soul of the South, and the City Too Busy Too Hate. Today it was the city where one authority would challenge another on behalf of the people. Having gathered a contingent of nearly one hundred armed officers from the Georgia State Patrol and the Georgia Bureau of Investigation, as well as from the Georgia National Guard, Cummins had also organized a support militia of armed men gleaned from various Police and Sheriff's Departments across Georgia. All these men were trained in the use of weapons as well as in the science of making arrests of those who resisted officers of the law. No yahoos or untrained individuals would be used in this raid in the hope of avoiding accidental or uncalled-for violence. Cummins, who had donned a flack vest and armed himself with an M-16 from the National Guard, gathered with half of his men in the parking lot of the Atlanta Visitor's Center just a few blocks north of the IPS building located on Pinetree Street. The other half of his raiding party had gathered at the Marta-Pinetree Center located south of the target building where John Brown International Boulevard crosses Pinetree Street. At exactly 10:30 A.M. on the morning of the 5th, both groups struck out on foot to make the short trip to the offices of the IPS to enter the building at previously assigned entry points. The Governor had arranged for the electric power to be cut to the building just before his men made their entry. Cummins led his party, while his longtime friend and compatriot Del Castronous, a Colonel in the Georgia National Guard, would lead the group approaching from the south. Another friend of Cummins, this one a State Court Judge, had given the Governor strong legal cover by issuing a search warrant for the property of the IPS. The warrant stated that evidence had been presented to the signing Judge that crimes of theft by taxation and/or theft by intimidation were being carried out from the premises.

The leaders of each raiding party carried a copy of the warrant to be presented to anyone questioning their legal authority to carry out the raid. Of course, to those relying on federal authority, the warrant issued by a State Court Judge would be meaningless unless a federal court judge, carrying the authority of the Government of the United States, also signed the warrant. Cummins did not have the signature of a federal judge on his warrant, but then again, that was the very point of the entire exercise, to challenge the authority of the feds to dictate to the people of Georgia in all matters. For Cummins, it was all a matter of States' Rights.

As he and his men neared the target building, Cummins called for a double-quick pace, and all fifty men broke into a semi-run that caught the tax protestors who had gathered outside the building completely by surprise. Some of the protesters had half expected to see Government agents filing *out of* the IPS building to make arrests, but absolutely none of them dreamed they would see armed authorities filing *into* the building as well.

The protest which had been noisy and boisterous in an instant grew deathly quiet when they realized that an armed raiding party was entering the IPS building. Mouths fell open and jaws hung slack among the protesters as they realized that a second armed party, this one approaching from the south, had rushed forward and entered the building.

Unconsciously and without being asked to do so, the protesters began to take steps backwards, away from the building. None of them knew what was going to happen, but whatever it was, instinct and common sense told them they needed to put some room between themselves and the building.

Hushed now, and somewhat confused, they were clearly taken aback, yet not one of them was going to leave until they found out just what was going on.

At least one of the protesters thought he recognized Governor Cummins at the head of one of the raiding parties. That rumor circulated quickly through the crowd of nearly a thousand protesters as the people began to whisper among themselves their own private theories of what was taking place before their eyes.

Governor Cummins and his men filled abreast the corridor leading from the front door of the building through which they entered. There were armed security guards standing at the end of the corridor and in the lobby, but the sight of fifty men armed with assault rifles bearing quickly down on them caused the guards confusion. They put their hands to their side arms, but never pulled the guns from their holsters. Approaching quickly, Cummins spoke in a voice that boomed across the lobby.

"I am Governor Jim Cummins, and I have a warrant to search this building for evidence of high crimes and misdemeanors committed against the people of Georgia." With that Cummins waved a copy of the warrant in the faces of the startled and confused security personnel. Cummins' men immediately moved forward and removed the side arms from the holsters of each security guard, as well as confiscating any radios and cell phones.

A similar scene was being played out in the corridors on the other side of the building where Colonel Castronous was leading his contingent through. As a double-sided wave, the two raiding parties swept through the building, barely halting when encountering security, sweeping all before them as they made their way up the stairwells located on either side of the building. Their goal was to reach the top two floors of the building, leaving a few men to hold the stairwells and keep an eye on the disarmed security guards so that an exit could be made as cleanly as the entrance was made.

Rushing up the stairwell, Cummins was the first one through the door of the top floor of the building where the IPS bosses had their offices. Cummins had researched enough to know that the head of the Atlanta Division of the IPS was a tall, slender man with thin hair and black, wide rimmed glasses. The man's name was Reginald Nardly, and he was known to deal harshly with anyone who crossed him, be they IPS employees or taxpayers.

Cummins and his men quickly made their way through a gauntlet of office cubicles, swallowing up a couple of security guards who had been caught lingering near the coffee machine with some female employees. A hush had fallen over the entire floor as the armed party filled the room. As one of Cummins men announced their warranted presence, Jim Cummins singled out the largest office on the floor, the office of the Director of the Atlanta Division, Mr. Reginald Nardly.

The Governor saw no need for niceties, kicking the office door in without ceremony. Behind a large desk with granite top sat Director Nardly. Standing to his feet, Nardly managed to say only the words "What the heck are you-" Cummins feet never stopped as he entered Nardly's office. Marching straight towards the Director, the Governor pulled back a fisted glove and punched Nardly square in the teeth. Nardly was knocked backwards into his leather chair, blood already gushing from his smashed pie-hole. His black rimmed glasses were askew across his face as Nardly regained his feet, aghast at what had just happened. Cummins allowed Nardly a few seconds to let things play out in his mind.

"Cummins! You worthless piece of-- " Thump! Another straight right from Cummins dropped Nardly again, this time knocking him across his chair and onto the tile floor. One of Cummins' men went around and behind the desk, pushed the rolling leather chair out of the way, and collected Nardly by the rear of his shirt collar, hauling him off the floor.

Nardly's skin was pale white and clammy, his upper lip split nearly to his nose. Blood gushed from his wounds and his mouth was filling with blood from his broken teeth. To his credit, Cummins noticed, Nardly refused to cry, break down or even wince at the pain he surely was feeling. His hands stayed at his sides as he defiantly looked into the face of the Governor who had punched him twice. Clearly, his anger outweighed the considerable pain he must have felt.

"Mr. Nardly, here is a search warrant authorizing me to search these premises for evidence of all the stealing and intimidation you and your cronies have carried out against the good people of the State of Georgia."

Cummins offered the warrant to Nardly but the bleeding man refused to even acknowledge it had been offered. "Suit yourself," said the Governor, tossing the warrant onto Nardly's desktop. "This warrant further authorizes the arrest of the person or persons responsible for the crimes committed from within this building," continued Cummins. Three of Cummins men now made their way past him, pushing two-wheeled appliance dollies toward a row of filing cabinets that lined a wall near Nardly's desk. The men began to pull the heavy metal, fireproof filing cabinets away from the wall so as to get the dollies under them for removal from the office. Another of Cummins' men moved behind the large desk and found Nardly's computer. He began to remove wires from the CPU, then picked it up and headed out of the office.

"We will be taking your files with us, as well as your computer, as evidence of course" said Cummins. Nardly's face had turned several shades of red, and the red coloring had crept all the way down his neck. His anger was so intense that the man now began to shake. His hands clenched into tight fists, yet for all that Nardly retained enough composure to speak.

"Well, Governor, you have what you came for, so you can get out of my office now. But before you go, I want you to know that you and these Timothy McVeighs with you have committed serious crimes against the United States Government. You will be prosecuted for this, I promise you. You will pay for this little stunt until your last breath! Assault, burglary, disruption and prevention of the duties of a federal agent...the list goes on and on, not to mention Treason against your own country!"

"Would you like to add kidnapping to that laundry list," asked the Governor, producing a pair of hand cuffs. Nardly's face turned an impossible shade of red now as his brow burst forth with heavy beads of sweat. Cummins worried for a moment that the man would suffer a coronary on the spot. A man dressed in camouflage made his way through Cummins' men. It was Colonel Castronous. He took the handcuffs dangling from the Governor's finger and walked around the desk to where Nardly stood. Taking the Director by the wrist, Castronous roughly jerked the man's arm behind him, slapping a cuff on it in the process. Taking the other arm, he pulled it behind Nardly and squeezed the cuff around that wrist as well. Then he took both cuffs in his two hands and squeezed them until they cut into the skin on the Director's lower arms and wrists. As Nardly winced at the pain, Castronous whispered in his ear,

"That's for the six month audit you put me through last year." Through clenched, bloody teeth Nardly addressed both men.

"You people can't imagine the trouble you are in! The President will burn you and your precious State to the ground. Sherman's march to the sea was nothing compared to what you have coming to you!" Cummins only smiled, and replied,

"This ain't payback for Sherman's march. We paid y'all back for that when we sent Jimmy Carter to D.C. to torture you for four years." Cummins men, who filled the office now, burst out in laughter at the joke.

"Come on, Nardly," said Castronous, jerking the Director by the cuffs and causing the man more discomfort. "You are under arrest for crimes against the people of the Sovereign State of Georgia." And then, as either a joke or just from force of habit, someone began to read Miranda to the man in the handcuffs.

Cummins and his men quickly made their way back down the stairs. The filing cabinets had been brought down in the elevators and were already being loaded onto a bus that had pulled into the parking lot as the raiding party made its way outside. When Cummins was sure that all his men were loaded on the bus, he stepped up and closed the door. Before he closed the door, Cummins took a bullhorn and made a quick address to the crowd.

"My fellow Georgians; I have on this day taken steps to hold accountable the people that have tormented you for years with oppressive taxation. This is just the first step, there will be many more to follow. I can only promise you that I will continue to fight for your liberties until we have drained the swamp and run all these minions out of the State of Georgia."

The people, having recognized their hero Governor Cummins, broke forth in a cheer that could be heard for blocks in both directions. But as Cummins' bus pulled out, the crowd quickly broke up and moved purposely toward their waiting vehicles. None of the protesters wanted to be around when more federal agents arrived at the scene of the crime. Just who the criminal was, Cummins or Nardly, was going to be decided, though no one was at all sure as to how that judgment would be made.

Tommy Davis

Across the State of Georgia

The changing of the flags was noticed by the media first in the suburbs of Atlanta. The trend then seemed to spread to the mountainous region north of Atlanta, then stretched across and through the piedmont plains and on down through the sticky southern portion where the State butted up to Florida.

And though it was marked by a change of coloured, flapping cloth, most understood that it represented a hardening of opinion. Many who had been undecided as to whether they could defend the actions of the Governor of Georgia were now declaring their open support of the man, and they declared that support with a flag.

Georgians had always considered themselves an exuberant flag-waving people. On many of their homes, businesses and properties they had always flown a flag of some kind, be it the Star and Stripes of the U.S. Flag, or the official Georgia State Flag adopted in 2004, or even the Black Liberation Flag with its three bold stripes of red, black and green. Or, it was just as often a flag celebrating their favorite football team.

But now, it was noticed, many of these flags were being taken down. In their place rose a bold and familiar banner, one that had been by far the most controversial in the history of the State.

It was known as the 'old Georgia Flag,' also called the 1956 State Flag, due to the fact that its design had been adopted by the State Legislature that same year.

This 1956 flag was dominated by a Saltire; or large, X-shaped cross historically known as the Saint Andrews' Cross. Saint Andrew is said to have been crucified on such a cross, but the star-filled cross was chosen by Georgia in 1956 because it was identical to the Confederate Battle Flag.

Promoters of this flag said that it was chosen in '56 by a Legislature standing up for State's Rights. Opponents said it was chosen by people determined to keep segregation alive in Georgia.

Whatever the reason in '56, the Battle Flag had not been prominent on the official Flag of Georgia since changed by Governor Roy Barnes in 2001. For his trouble, Barnes earned a trip to Massachusetts to rub shoulders with the Kennedy's, although back in Georgia he was rudely dismissed as Governor by the voters in the following election.

Now, as one rising from the dead, the '56 Georgia Flag was taking back its place at the top of flagpoles, brick chimney's, attached to car antennas and affixed to bumpers--everywhere one could imagine a flag to be flown, the Georgia-Battle Flag was turning up there. In many cases, on poles where the Stars and Stripes had flown atop the old Georgia flag, the positions were simply reversed. And the flag on top was understood to represent the superior power, and to be afforded a higher allegiance.

In neighborhood after neighborhood, the sea of '56 Georgia Flags with its proud Confederate Battle symbol, was flying high. It could not be denied that something major was happening, and it was something President Soloto and his friends feared most: he was beginning to lose the battle for the hearts and minds of the people of Georgia.

Meeting Room at the U.S. Capital Building
Washington, D.C.

News of Governor Cummins' unprecedented raid on the IPS building in Atlanta and the arrest of a high ranking agent of the federal government swept across the whole nation in just a few hours. The story dominated the news cycle for days, with all the talking heads of the chattering class asking 'just how far is this Governor Cummins willing to go?'

Washington, D.C. was also abuzz with the news, and reaction was strong and emotional. In the House of Representatives, everyone was talking about what had happened in downtown Atlanta, and none were more excited, or divided, than those Congressmen who were sent to D.C. by the Rev. Party.

One of every three sitting Congressmen had been put in office by the Rev. Party. Some of these newly elected representatives had run on a third-party ticket, while others had run on the ticket of one of the established parties.

Either way, there was no doubt that they were there to change things. These newly elected Representatives had already formed a caucus of their own they simply called the Patriot Caucus.

Presently, this caucus consisting of a third of Congress was meeting in an anteroom within the Capital Building. As soon as word had spread about Cummins' raid on the IPS in Atlanta, leading members of this caucus sent out word to all members that the caucus would meet to discuss this event the following morning at 9:00 A.M.

Members of the caucus began filing into the meeting room around 8:00, and by 8:45 every member was present and one could barely hear oneself think for all the noise.

At precisely 9:00, Representative F. Trent Ragsdale mounted a podium and banged a gavel, calling the meeting to order. Ragsdale hailed from California, one of five Rev. Party types from the Golden State. An outspoken critic of over-reaching, intrusive government, Ragsdale had been elected as chairman of the caucus at its second official meeting.

"Can we please come to order at this time?" The room grew quiet and Ragsdale continued. "Ladies and Gentlemen, as you have no doubt heard, Governor Jim Cummins of Georgia has conducted a raid of the IPS buildingin downtown Atlanta. Though I have met the Governor on several occasions and call him a friend, I have not been able to talk with him about his actions on yesterday. I did talk with one of his assistants and gained some information from him." The crowd was still and quiet, everyone wanting to here the scoop about Cummins.

"From that conversation I can tell you this: Governor Cummins did have a legal warrant for the raid of the IPS offices. The warrant was issued by a judge in the State Court System."

Now everyone was ooing and ahhing, some clapping and some complaining at the news of a warrant, which seemed to cover the Governor's action with legality.

"This was a State warrant, not a federal warrant," continued Ragsdale, "Cummins and a large party of sworn officers carried out the raid. He and his men were armed with rifles and side arms. No one was seriously injured in the raid. Evidence was collected, and a certain Mr. Nardly, a Director with the IPS, was taken into custody and booked on charges of theft against the taxpayers of Georgia."

Oos and Ahhs along with some cheers erupted from the Rev. Party Caucus, though some held their peace. There were some in the caucus, maybe a good many, who were wary of praising a raid that everyone knew the feds would have to denounce as illegal, and would be forced to prosecute.

Still, the cheers were growing loud and boisterous. Clearly, there were many there who had been hoping for the arrest of unlawful federal agents by a State authority. Such an event would help, they believed, to clarify the fact the power of the federal government does have a limit, and that limit can and must be enforced by a State in the Union.

Though it was certain to call down federal wrath, it would help to clarify the difference of opinion between the powers that be and the Rev. Party. The average person needed to see the difference, the Rev. Party believed, especially as it related to the hated IPS.

Carolyn Bingham, a newly elected Congresswoman from Missouri and a leading member of the Rev. Party Caucus, stepped forward and asked to address the gathering. Taking a mic in hand, Bingham addressed the crowd:

"My friends and compatriots, every one of us hear probably feels strongly that the IPS is a nuisance to our constituents and the American people in general." That line was received with cheers and hurrahs. "All of us are in agreement on that. However, I believe that this raid conducted by Governor Cummins has gone too far. I believe Cummins has stepped over the line and into lawlessness himself." The caucus grew quieter, a few jeers breaking the silence here and there.

"We are the Rev. Party--we believe in the Rule of Law and in the Constitution. If we are demanding that our government in Washington act within the bounds of the Law, how can we support a Governor when he is clearly breaking the law by raiding and arresting an agent of the federal government, just for doing his job? We as a movement will lose all credibility if we go on record supporting this action taken in Atlanta by the Governor of Georgia. We all know that the feds will retaliate, and then things could get out of hand in a hurry. I think we as a caucus need to use moderation here and refuse to go along with this. I hear-by make the motion that we as a caucus condemn the Governor of Georgia for this action. We did not act when he refused President Soloto landing privileges in Atlanta, and now we can make up for that by condemning this raid. We must distance ourselves, our caucus, and our movement from all acts of violence!"

A few scattered claps of approval were heard across the room, but very few in the crowd were eager to support what Bingham had said, which would be to denounce Cummins. At that same time, very few seemed eager to totally dismiss the points that Bingham had made. As rowdy a crowd as the Rev. Party was, they were still hesitant to be labeled as rebels or extremists, or as radicals prone to violence.

One man, however, was ready to take the side of Governor Cummins. Representative Kevin Crowder of South

Carolina stood and asked to address the caucus. Crowder took the microphone offered to him while everyone tried to figure out which side he would take.

"Friends and fellow patriots, I rise to oppose the motion offered by Mrs. Bingham. I agree that none of us have a desire to be labeled an 'extremist' or a 'radical,' and all of us hope that the problem of big government can be solved without any violence or bloodshed, though look at the blood already shed in The Bronx! But let me say this; for too long have our leaders held themselves aloof from the actions necessary to reign in big government." Scattered yelps of approval went up from the crowd as Crowder continued.

"For too long have those members of Congress who say they oppose big government been reluctant to support bold actions taken in the name of liberty, and for too long have we hesitated to take our stand against the Leviathan state that daily tramples upon our rights as a free people, all because we are so careful that our reputations never be soiled with the label of 'radical.'

"But as our great forefather Patrick Henry asked even as the British guns were firing upon American Colonists, is life so dear or peace so sweet as to be purchased at the price of chains and slavery? Forbid it, Almighty God! I know not what course others may take, but as for me, give me liberty or give me death!" Now the meeting room was overcome with cheers, hollers and yelps of support for what Crowder had said.

Bingham breathed a sigh of resignation. She knew that, not only would her motion fail to pass, but a motion of support for "Governor Cummins' courageous action to protect his people from abusive government" would pass the caucus with votes to spare.

Though it would have zero force of law, being only a caucus action, it would send a powerful message to the whole country that a sizable portion of Congress was on record supporting a State Governor in his arrest of a federal agent of the IPS, and in support of that Governor's defiance. As Crowder reminded everyone that day, at a Rev. Party, no one messes with Patrick Henry.

The Oval Office
The White House
Washington, D.C.

President Soloto was seated behind his executive desk when NSA Director Dennis Click and his deputy director, along with FBI director Rodney Bound, were personally escorted into the Oval Office by COS Brandenburg. As the four men approached the president's executive desk, Soloto spoke first.

"Gentlemen, everyone here knows about the latest stunt pulled by this madman in Georgia, raiding our IPS office in Atlanta. And we all agree that he is openly and recklessly challenging the power of the federal government. Now, this man must be stopped and stopped immediately!" Soloto then looked to the NSA Director and said, "I understand you have finalized a plan to serve the federal arrest warrant on this rogue."

"Yes, Mr. President, we have," said director Click. The FBI Director said nothing, keeping his expression blank. Soloto caught a glimpse of it and knew something was amiss, but let the meeting go forward. The President moved to the edge of his seat and asked,

"O.K. So where in Atlanta are we going to take this guy down?"

"Nowhere in Atlanta, sir," responded Click, clearly taking the initiative in the meeting. "We have developed a plan to take Cummins down outside of Atlanta, no where near the Governor's Mansion. We have learned through surveillance that in four days Cummins will be visiting his lake house located in a very secluded, rural setting in Cobb County, Georgia. This is the perfect site to take him, Mr. President. It's far away from the city. No media, no public crowds to deal with, and very low expectations of collateral damage."

Soloto felt a chill run down his spine at the mention of the words 'collateral damage' associated with an operation within the borders of the United States, though he was glad to hear that the plan would be carried out away from the crowded city.

"Director, show me how you will proceed."

"Sir, I've prepared a high resolution satellite photo of Cummins' lake property, if I may, sir," said Click as he spread the photo magnification sheet on the President's desk. "Here, sir, is Cummins' lake house. He enters and exits his property by this access road, which is an unpaved dirt road. Since the house sits almost on a peninsula jutting out into the lake, our strike teams will utilize the water as an approach to the house. Cummins is known to take family with him to the property at times, and if he has a couple of body guards, they would likely be watching the road. My two strike teams will come across the water using stealth approach tactics, while a third team provided by the FBI will come up this access road and through the gate, but only after the house itself has been breached."

Soloto looked up at Click, then over to director Bound, whose Bureau had just been assigned second fiddle in the planned raid.

"Director Bound, we have not heard from you yet. Are you on board with this plan?" the President asked sternly, not sure he would like any answer Bound would give.

"No, sir, not entirely. I like the idea of taking him in a secluded area. But coming across the water with only the cover of darkness seems nonsensical to me. I've shown the plan to my tactical people, the best we have, and they don't like that aspect of it either. They have registered strong objections to it, as I do now, Mr. President."

"Mr. President," interrupted Click somewhat frantically, "I've considered the Bureau's concerns, but sir, our NSA strike teams train constantly for just such a scenario. Our guys will be fine coming across that lake. It is a very small lake, Mr. President, more of a pond in fact. We have access to stealth technology that will play an important role here. It is the best that money can buy." The FBI director's face had not changed. It was now even more stone-grim, if that be possible.

Bound had raised strong objections when Soloto had sent him an e.mail memo ordering the FBI to cooperate with the NSA on serving the warrant. Since Soloto had authorized the NSA to conduct the surveillance on the Governor's mansion, the President felt it necessary to include that agency in the actual serving of the domestic warrant. Bound and the FBI had not hesitated to remind the President that it was the duty of the Bureau alone to serve the warrant, but the President had over-ruled his objections.

Bound felt offended for himself and his agency, but, in the end, for a career guy so close to retirement, it just wasn't worth resigning over. But that did not mean he had to like it, or to keep his mouth shut when he had legitimate objections. Bound wondered if the President's decision had anything to do with the fact that his agency, the FBI, had a file on Soloto's now dead father, a Nigerian national who made frequent trips to and from the United States back during the fifties and sixties and had been a known associate of the Communist underground.

Bound, of course, was not even around when the Bureau spied on the elder Soloto, but news of the investigation had leaked during Soloto's campaign for a second term as President. It had to have been leaked by someone inside the Bureau, someone who wanted to hurt Soloto's campaign by casting a cloud of suspicion over his family.

"Proceed, director Click," said the President somewhat irritably.

"Of course, Mr. President. As I stated, two teams will come in across the water, a third will block the road and act as a backup team at the gate. Once across the water, team one will neutralize the guard dogs while team two will disable the electricity and the phone landlines. A Predator drone overhead will circle and scramble all cell phone activity within a mile of the target. This Georgia thug, Cummins, will be totally isolated and helpless. Once the house is breached, everyone inside will be restrained. In this situation, we plan to use stun grenades along with Tazors to secure the occupants and render them helpless." Click fell silent, satisfied with his presentation. But Soloto had more questions.

"These strike teams, how many men are assigned to each? It sounds like you're going after this guy with only twenty or thirty guys," asked Soloto.

"The strike teams are relatively small, sir, but here is the beautiful thing about our contract with BlackSky. We have at our access five hundred shooters, all well trained, many of them former black op. military guys, as part of our BlackSky contingent. Sir, these five hundred are already assigned to the NSA for this mission. With those five hundred men we can totally surround the entire lake perimeter! And we don't even have to cross any imaginary lines of using regular military within our borders," said Click, proud of his preparedness.

"What say you, Director Bound?" asked the President.

"I say it borders on lunacy to take five hundred trigger happy mercenaries to serve this warrant!" replied the FBI Director cynically.

"Mercenaries!" replied Click angrily, "BlackSky is a professional organization. They pay their people well because they only want the best, most well-trained men. The owner of the company is a personal friend of mine, and I'll not hear his men degraded as mercenaries!" But Bound did not back up an inch.

"Well trained? Tell that to the dead civilians in Iraq. Tell that to the tortured prisoners at Abu-Ghraib!" replied Bound, his voice a razor. Click and Bound stood there before the President's desk, eye-balling one another angrily, their bodies tense. Soloto moved to change the subject off of BlackSky.

"Gentlemen, please! Now listen, BlackSky will be used on this mission, but only as a backup plan. They won't actually make the assault on the lake house. But Dennis, you mentioned that Cummins might have watchdogs. What did you say about those?" he asked.

"Cummins keeps dogs on the property, sir. They may be well trained watch dogs, or even attack dogs. The dogs could compromise our efforts if not neutralized."

"Neutralized how?" inquired Soloto suspiciously.

"Well, sir," said Click with a bit less confidence, "usually we use either an instant-acting poison or else we shoot them with suppressed weapons, sir. We don't like to do it but it is often unavoidable." The President had a concerned look on his face.

"I'll have to clear this with PETA, director Click. You know my administration is committed to the ethical treatment of animals," said Soloto firmly. Click was not sure if the President was serious, and made no reply at first, though he wanted to yell out that a strike team had no time to worry about animal ethics during a hostile raid. Instead, he only replied,

"We'll look into non-lethal means of dealing with the dogs, sir, if possible." The statement was made with little enthusiasm, but Soloto nodded his head in approval, then said,

"Alright, in that case I can authorize you to carry out your plan. No mistakes, gentlemen. I don't have to remind you of how precarious this situation can become, politically speaking. This country is a powder keg, and we must defuse it, not blow it sky high. But powder keg or not, no rogue Governor is going to defy the power of the Presidency and get by with it."

Chapter Thirteen

Convention of the Confederate Sons United
Macon Coliseum in Macon, Georgia

The Macon Coliseum is located in Macon, Georgia, a city of some 100,000 people located about eighty miles south of Atlanta.

This Coliseum will hold nearly 10,000 convention goers, and on this day, every seat was filled and there was little room left in the aisles where men were standing elbow to elbow. Each was present for the annual convention of the CSU, the Confederate Sons United, a fellowship of the descendents of the Army of the old southern Confederacy, which fought against invading United States Troops in the Civil War of 1860-1865. Or, as the men gathered here preferred to call it, The War of Northern Aggression.

To a man, every member of the CSU believed that their forefathers fought in the War Between the States, not to preserve the peculiar institution of Slavery, but rather to preserve the Constitutional principles of State's Rights, federal restraint and ultimately, secession. To say that this was a conservative group of white men was to understate the fact by a light-year at least. Almost all of them were members of the NRA, Gun Owners of America, or some other gun-rights group. And most of them were still upset about how the Civil War turned out.

If the Governor of Georgia could find support anywhere for his resistance to federal authority, one might think he could surely find it blooming in this fertile soil.

Groups like the Southern Lawyers Against Poverty had branded the CSU a racist group that bore a close resemblance to the KKK, using the guise of 'heritage preservation' to push what SLAP labeled Neo-Confederate ideas.

The CSU countered that it was traditionally a heritage preservation group, not a group hell-bent on a return to secession or even Jim Crow. Being proud of one's southern heritage did not necessarily translate into being in favor of secession today, or even in favor of resistance to a federal government seen by many as too big to fail.

The CSU *did* have many members who were for more than just preserving old Confederate gravesites, and the rise of Governor Cummins had given hope to these fire-eaters that their long hoped for resurrection of the Old Confederacy was at hand. But even in an organization as conservative, male and white as this one, the fire-eaters were in the minority. Year after year the fire-eaters had offered politically oriented, State's rights resolutions, placing them before the convention goers and urging them to go on record in favor of modern-day resistance to the federal government. And year after year, the cool-headed leadership of the CSU had beaten back these attempts, branding them as attempts to radicalize the group and change its basic tenet from heritage preservation to political activism.

State's Rights *was* a legitimate issue in 1860, they argued, but that issue was settled on the battle-field where the Federals in Blue had defeated the Men in Grey. It's fine to dress up as a Confederate soldier and reenact a Civil War battle scene, but the guns of the re-enactors were loaded with blanks, and few had a desire to be shot at with live ammunition from actual U.S. soldiers.

Sure, power had been consolidated in D.C. and that was regrettable, but the world was already that way when we were born, said they, just as the sky was blue when we were born. Trying to change the one was like trying to change the other, a hopeless endeavor that could bring nothing but trouble and waste.

But the fire-eaters would not be reconciled to modern realities, and this split in the CSU had continued to grow. The collapse of the economy only added fuel to the flames for the discontents.

What worried the heritage traditionalists now was that Governor Cummins' challenge to President Soloto had started a prairie fire of secessionism amidst the CSU membership, and the rumor was that the radicals felt that they had enough votes this year to put the CSU on record as supporting Governor Cummins and political secession for Georgia.

Rumor further had it that they might even try to pass a resolution binding members to commit acts of violence against the federal authorities. The leadership realized that such a resolution could well mean the end of the CSU. A radicalized version of the CSU would not last five years, and the traditionalists were not going to let it happen.

Name calling had already begun at the local meetings. The fire-eaters had dubbed the traditionalists with the effeminate name of 'Granny's,' while the traditionalists had countered by branding their opponents simply as 'Lunatics.' And now the Coliseum was packed with men who knew where the lines had been drawn, and most had chosen their side already. It was only when the voting began that they would know if the fire-eaters had gained enough support to take over the organization. Either way, the split had become so deep that it was likely that one group would withdraw and go a separate direction if their side did not prevail.

A very important election was going to be held on this the first day of the convention, an election that would determine the direction of the CSU, perhaps forever. In the opinion of some, it would be either the direction of sane, level headed heritage defense, or else towards an agenda of radicalized political activity.

The first step was to elect a new president of the CSU. Placed in nomination by the heritage side was one R. E. Lee Chancey, a known traditionalist who had spent thousands of his own dollars to help preserve Civil War battlefields and erect marble monuments to various Civil War generals.

Placed in nomination for the Presidency by the secessionists was one Nathan Forrest Kalwaskie, a man who could trace his family directly back to Confederate General Nathan Bedford Forrest, arguably the greatest cavalry warrior produced by either side in the War Between the States.

Kalwaskie was known as a man who did not back down. Though a successful businessman, Kalwaskie had had several brushes with the law. He had once pulled a gun on an IPS agent who tried to enter his place of business. The agent left but returned later with the local Sheriff, at which point Kalwaskie stepped aside and allowed the agent to conduct an audit of his records.

Later, Kalwaskie explained to a local newspaper reporter that he did not know the IPS agent, and therefore did not recognize the man's authority when he arrived at his place of business. On the other hand, he knew the local Sheriff well and recognized *his* authority as legitimate. Kalwaskie explained that he allowed the audit to be administered because the IPS agent came with and under the authority of the local Sheriff, and that was the only reason. The audit was conducted and Kalwaskie's records were found to be in impeccable order. The

IPS brought charges against Kalwaskie for pulling the gun, but a judge threw the charges out for lack of evidence.

Kalwaskie was also known to be active in the Council for European Citizens, a group dubbed as 'white supremacist' by leftist watchdog groups such as the National Advocacy Association for People of Color and the Southern Lawyers Against Poverty. Kalwaskie countered that the NAAPC and the SLAP were themselves race-baiting agitators and money grubbing charlatans, accusations that did not sit well with either group.

On the convention floor, the time for the election of the convention President had arrived. The Coliseum was alive with activity; everyone was talking to their neighbor and many were racing back and forth across the floor, pushing their way through the mass of flesh, taking messages back and forth.

The convention parliamentarian had disallowed the use of cell phones within the Coliseum, so pages were being used as communication between various leaders of each faction. The leadership of the Heritage faction was nervous; they were no longer sure that they had the votes to beat back the fire-eaters faction. Yet it was time to call for a vote.

It was the duty of out-going President Lawrence 'Kansas' Lockaby, a Heritage man, to present the candidates and call for the vote. He strode to the microphone on the huge hardwood stage.

"Members of the Confederate Sons United, it is time to elect the man who will carry the torch for the CSU for the next 12 months; the man who will conduct himself with respect and integrity, bringing honour to our great CSU!"

Lockaby paused while a mighty roar lifted from the gathered crowd of men. The union of uplifted male voices would have sounded wonderful to him if Lockaby had not known that at least half of the cheering men had a totally different view of what he meant by bringing 'honour' to their organization. He soldiered on anyway.

"Members of the CSU, I call on you to prayerfully consider two names that have been placed in nomination before this body as candidates for the Presidency of the Confederate Sons United for the next term. So that none of you accuse me of favoritism, I will present the names in alphabetical order." This caused a wave of laughter to roll across the large crowd of men. At least, thought Lockaby, these guys have retained their sense of humor, which ought to count for something.

"The first candidate I submit to you is Mr. Robert Edward Lee Chancey. Mr. Chancey is a third generation member of the Confederate Sons United, as both his father and grandfather were members of our organization. A business man whose success had earned him a seat on the Board of the Atlanta Chamber of Commerce, he is also a family man and a man of faith. Mr. Chancey has led the fight for the preservation of three different War battlefields within the State of Georgia. I hereby place in nomination for the Presidency of the CSU Mr. R. E. Lee Chancey!"

About half the men in the crowd let out a boisterous cheer, while the balance of the crowd issued a low murmur of boos.

Lockaby smiled brightly and clapped loudly into the microphone as Chancey, who had been seated on the stage behind him, made his way to the microphone. Taking Chancey by the hand with both of his hands, Lockaby shook the hand vigorously, beaming brightly all the while. Hearing some jeers from some fire-eaters standing close to the stage, Lockaby turned and gave them a hard, cold look as he gave way to Chancey, who now stepped to the microphone. Shorter than average, Chancey had a narrow face, thinning hair, and wore wire-rimmed glasses.

"Members of the Confederate Sons United; I am a lifelong member of the CSU, proud to be in the business of honouring those who Wore the Grey, and if elected President I promise that the case for Heritage preservation will never find a champion more diligent, able, or honourable than myself. I will work tirelessly to preserve and protect our Southern heritage, and to promote the cause of the Confederate Sons United!"

Again there was a chorus of loud cheering by Chancey supporters, while the fire-eaters groaned and mocked what they considered a watered down version of leadership they saw in Chancey.

Lockaby now returned to the microphone, hardly waiting for the noise to subside before beginning the second nomination, prepared beforehand by the candidate himself.

"I now place before this convention a second nomination for President of the CSU. I submit the name of Mr. Nathan Forrest Kalwaskie. Mr. Kalwaskie is a native of the State of Georgia, and can trace his family back to the Wizard of the Saddle himself, General Nathan Bedford Forrest."

Lockaby had to pause at this point, as any mention of N. B. Forrest brought forth wild cheering from any gathering of the CSU. Even many of the Chancey supporters could not help themselves but to cheer at the mention of that genius of war. But Lockaby failed to wait for the cheering to subside before moving on with the nomination, a move that further angered the fire-eaters.

"Mr. Kalwaskie is a fifth generation member of the Confederate Sons United, his ancestor having been a charter member of this great organization." These were awesome claims made on Kalwaskie's behalf, though clearly Lockaby was delivering them with as little gusto as he could manage. "Mr. Kalwaskie is a businessman who has consistently stood for State and Individual Rights against an ever encroaching federal government. He is also a family man and a man of faith. I hereby place in nomination for President Mr. Nathan Forrest Kalwaskie."

A great roar was unleashed by the Kalwaskie supporters, who clearly felt they needed to out-rebel-yell the other side. The Coliseum echoed now with reverberations of a modern version of that blood-curdling yell that many a Bluecoat heard just before tasting southern shot and steel. Somehow, someone had snuck an electric guitar into the building and began to play Skynard's 'Sweet Home ,' which had become a kind of anthem for southerners.

This, of course, was highly out of order, but it had the fire-eaters rocking and dancing as well as a group of white men could manage. The guitarist was well into his second verse before security guards escorted him and his instrument outside.

On the stage, Lockaby traded worried looks with Chancey. This was getting out of hand, and they still had to endure Kalwaskie's speech. All the traditionalists could do was to hope Kalwaskie would fail to influence the swing voters in the crowd who had not made up their minds about whom to vote for.

Kalwaskie, cutting a strong figure at six-two with wide shoulders, was laughing and grinning, waving to his supporters as he approached the microphone. His voice was powerful and deep as he spoke.

"Well, I did not ask that guy to play that guitar, but it sounded like 'Sweet Home Down In Georgia' to me!" In a high mood now, the fire-eaters went berserk as the anthem was acknowledged from the stage. Kalwaskie was clearly enjoying himself, shooting glances at Lockaby and Chancey, both former friends of his who had become his bitter enemies over the past months of struggle within the CSU.

Suddenly, Kalwaskie's face was washed over with a serious demeanor, his eyes flashing fire.

"My name is Nathan Forrest Kalwaskie, and I am a direct descendent of a man of unbending courage, of uncompromising valor, General Nathan Bedford Forrest!" Kalwaskie paused for what he knew would come, an uproarious, rising yell/shriek of raw, throaty approval. As the yelling subsided, Kalwaskie continued.

"Now, just because I have that great General's blood running through my veins doesn't make me a great man like he was. It is doubtful that we will see his like again. However, if you want a man who will charge forth, upholding the same ideals of manly resistance to the federal D.C. monstrosity now gorging itself on the fruits of our labor, hell-bent on destroying the country handed down to us by great Southerners like Washington, Jefferson, Madison, Lee, Forrest and Stonewall Jackson, then say 'no' to the limp-wristed whiners who are in the pocket of the Atlanta big-money boys, say 'no' to those who hate the Real Georgia Flag and hate our great Governor Jim Cummins, and say 'yes' to the man who loves and supports all these great things, say 'yes' to N. F. Kalwaskie as the next President of the Confederate Sons United!"

Wild cheering, yelling and laughter boomed across the Coliseum. The traditionalists tried to mount a decibel challenge with boos and jeers, but were drowned out and quickly gave up trying.

Lockaby made his way to the podium, took a gavel in hand, and pounded it until the cheering finally ceased. He then called for ballots to be cast.

Every delegate had a ballot with the two names listed on it. It was a punch-out ballot, and each urged his neighbor to punch his ballot thoroughly so that no 'hanging chads' would ruin their vote. Designated collectors carried official ballot boxes down the aisles of the Coliseum, stopping at the end of each row of seating while the completed ballots were passed down. The boxes filled quickly as each side grew nervous about which way the vote would go.

There would be a few moments of downtime as the ballot boxes were carried to the counting room to be computed. Nothing was scheduled to be said from the podium during this downtime, but everyone watched as Kalwaskie rose from his chair on the podium and began to belt out a slow, almost mournful version of 'Dixie.' His supporters near the podium immediately stood and joined in.

211

Lockaby and Chancey again traded worried looks, and Lockaby briefly considered using his gavel to silence the fire-eaters, but interrupting a version of a tune considered almost as sacred to these men as 'Amazing Grace' would not be a wise move. Instead, Lockaby and Chancey simply stood and joined in as the slow acapella version of the old anthem 'Dixie,' a favorite of both Lee and Lincoln, swept across the wide hall with irresistible grace.

> Oh I wish I was in the land of cot-ton
> Old times there are not for-gotten
> Look away, look away…

Eyes began to swell with tears as every emotion familiar to men began to flow through the crowd. *Is this what it felt like, just a little perhaps, in the grey-clad crowds of men who charged the blue lines at Manassas, at Sharpsburg, at Gettysburg?* Who could say, but the singing went on and on, from one verse to a chorus, and then another verse.

> In Dix-ie land where I was bornin
> Ear-ly on a fros-ty mornin
> Look away, look away…

The men sang on until they noticed the official parliamentarian mount the podium to reveal the results of the vote. The parliamentarian, a man of slight build and monotone voice with a to-the-point attitude, pounded the gavel and was given the hall's full and quiet attention.

"I have received the vote count from the Secretary of this convention of the Confederate Sons United. The vote was counted four times due to the fact that it is the closest vote ever recorded in the history of the CSU."

The low rumble of serious discussion echoed across the huge room but subsided quickly as the Parliamentarian continued.

"The vote totals are as follows: Mr. Robert E. Lee Chancey received five thousand, three hundred and twenty one votes. Mr. Nathan Forrest Kalwaskie received Five thousand, three hundred and thirty votes. The new President of the CSU is Mr. Kalwaskie."

Those last few words were spoken by the Parliamentarian but few heard them because the roof of the Coliseum was virtually trembling at the uproar created by the supporters of Kalwaskie.

Lockaby and Chancey were visibly shaken. The swing voters had swung to the fire-eaters, and lunatics were now in charge of an old and sacred organization. With heads hanging low and grim, the losers made their way off the podium as Kalwaskie strode a victory lap, with his hands lifted high and wide, from one end of the stage to the other. The cheering from his supporters went on minute after minute until finally Kalwaskie stopped at the microphone in the middle of the stage.

"Free at last, free at last, thank God Almighty we are free at last!" boomed Kalwaskie's baritone voice across the hall. Those words were all-too familiar to this crowd, but never had they cheered them until now. "Let us join together tonight as brothers in the cause for which our forefathers died. Let us join in arms those men whose bones lay under the cold earth at Sharpsburg, Gettysburg and The Wilderness...those who bled the ground red at Chickamauga, right here in the Sovereign State of Georgia! Let us press on now from a heritage of freedom to the reality of freedom that our Fathers bequeathed us with their last breath and ounce of strength!"

The roaring cheers were almost a constant river of sound flowing through the Coliseum now, but rose to an even higher level when five young men came out of the wings of the stage, each holding high on flag poles the 'old Georgia flag,' the version of the State Flag that flew over Georgia from 1956 to 2001 when it was changed amidst great controversy. For its supporters, this flag tied together forever the State of Georgia and the historic Confederate States of America.

Lockaby and Chancey had almost made it out of a side exit when the renewed burst of cheering caused them to stop and look back to the podium. They saw the five young men leaping across the stage, then leaping down into the aisles and running up them as men cleared the way for the sacred banners that waved atop the poles. They knew that many of the men who had supported their side just moments before were being converted to what they considered the lunacy of Kalwaskie at that very moment. And Kalwaskie wasn't finished yet.

"And, my brothers, let us on this historic night, as did our forefathers of old, pledge our lives, our fortunes, and our sacred honour in the struggle that our great Governor, Jim Cummins; Jim, who has himself picked up the mantle of State's Rights. Our great Governor is leading the charge, risking life and limb to make us free, but he needs our help, he needs men who will shed blood and treasure to see a rebirth of freedom in our land. Will you join me in that pledge tonight?!"

Tommy Davis

The crowd went wild one more time, feeling rebellion and defiance palpable in the air.

GEORGIA BURNS

Mouth of the St. Marys River,
Not far from Kings' Bay Nuclear Submarine Base

All day and deep into the night Kenny St. John
worked. What drove him to such life-spent madness? Was it
revenge? Despair? Patriotism? A concoction of these? Kenny
did not know for sure and had no time to think about it. He just
worked and welded, weaving and tacking together an obscene
menagerie of regular shrimp netting, log chain, and floatation
devices. He would stop for a moment now and then to take a
drink and smoke a cigarette, then the work would begin anew,
with a new ferocity.

The large mound of steel chain was patiently moved until it
wa all on the boat-deck. Kenny pulled chain and netting
together, weaving and welding. Late in the hours of the first
night of work he dozed for a bit, and that was all the sleep he
took in nearly forty-eight.

Anyone looking from a distance would have seen the orange
light and spray of sparks from the welding. If anyone asked,
Kenny was simply making repairs on his old boat. For the first
time in a long time, since his last outing with his now dead
father, Kenny St. John felt he had a purpose in life. He labored
on.

Twenty hours later, with a Herculean effort of sweat, twisted
pride, and patience, Kenny had finished his creation. He was
resting on deck when he saw the two old shrimp boats of his
two good friends moving through the water toward his
boat. He felt his heart thumping within his chest, that
thumping only, along with attendant hate, being the only two
things telling him he still lived. Yet, even in such a state, his
manners remained intact.

"Howdy fellers, how y'all doin'?" he said as his two friends
stepped off the dock and onto his boat, both carrying great
heavy sacks over their backs.

"We doin' fine, but you...you look like somethin' they
scrapped off a floatin-dead tuna."

"Thanks," replied Kenny with a slight smile. "Got it all
done," he said, waving an exhausted hand towards the chain-
netting he had made. "Any news from your ex-brother-in-law?"
asked Kenny.

One of his buddies had an ex-wife whose brother worked as a
civilian computer contractor on the sub-base
at Kings Bay. Disgruntled from having been laid off, the ex-

brother-in-law had managed to smuggle off the base two things that Kenny would find very useful.

The first was information regarding when the next Trident Nuclear Sub was going to be departing the base to head out into the Atlantic. This information was highly classified since the Russians, and now the Chinese, were known to station smaller, fast moving attack subs just off the coast in an attempt to pick up a sound signature of a Big Boomer so that they might shadow the sub on its route under the seas. It was a game played by super-powers as far back as WWII. But in the age of Wikileaks, classified info like this was getting harder to protect.

"The news is this: you got no time to rest cause the next Big Boomer is scheduled to move out tonight." Kenny regarded his friend with a blank face. "Kenny, we're guessing that you're gonna try to spread this here chain-net across the channel leading out of the base harbor, and snag yaself a Boomer...that about right?"

"That's about right, Einstein," replied St. John. "Gonna spread it across the channel, and its weight will pull it to the channel bottom, but the floats will keep it suspended midway down. I used heavier chain on the bottom of the net and lighter on the top. When the heavy chain hits the channel bottom and comes to rest there, that will lighten the load enough that the buoys will keep the lighter chain floating at mid-depth."

"Okay, we figured that much, which brings us to the second part of the good news. My ex-brother-in-law was also able to sneak these babies off the base. Don't ask me how, but here it is."

Kenny's two friends dumped the contents of the large sacks out onto the boat-deck. Metal discs about as big around as a hubcap and eight inches thick lay before them.

"Those look dangerous," noted Kenny St. John.

"They are dangerous, cause these here are gen-u-ine Navy issued harbor mines. I figure if these babies are attached to your chain-net, it might make for a more excitin' evenin' for some of them Navy boys who so enjoy harassin' us Shrimpers. None of these are big enough to breach the hull of a Boomer, but it ought to at least serenade that big fish a bit."

"You boys beat all, I tell ya," said Kenny. "Okay then, let's use the large hook-clips to attach the mines to the chain net before we pull it across the channel.

A few hours later that night, three Shrimp boats neared the mouth of the channel of water that the Trident Subs used to enter the Atlantic. Kenny called his two friends on his ship-radio.

"Okay, this is it. After this, there ain't no turnin' back. Anyone needin' to turn back now, then go ahead, no hard feelin's."

"Got nowhere to go, nor anyone to go home to," said one of them.

"Same here," replied the other man, "let's do this guys, show the gub-ment what these Shrimpers can do."

"Alrighty then," said Kenny, "we just passed the first sensors. That means gun-boats will be coming around that bend in the channel within a few seconds."

And just as he spoke the words, Kenny and his friends could see the powerful spotlights of patrol boats moving quickly around the bend. But the three made no movement, because ten minutes before, they had already cast a large spread of the harbor-mines across the channel.

The first of the patrol boats would have been safe if it had kept more distance from the Shrimpers, but it closed too fast and much. The harbor mines were magnetized, and Kenny thought he heard a metallic clink when the first mine magnetically grabbed the metal hull of the patrol boat. The resulting explosion sent fire and sparks into the air above the channel waters, blowing a hole the size of a claw-foot tub in the hull of the patrol boat. The mine wasn't powerful enough to split the boat in two, but plenty large enough to sink it. Kenny and his friends watched as the sailors aboard the patrol boat jumped safely into the water and swam for the shore as their boat quickly sank to the bottom.

"That boat is stuck in river mud for sure! Best duck down boys," yelled Kenny into the radio mic, as two other patrol boats immediately opened fire on the Shrimpers with the large caliber machine guns mounted to their decks.

Kenny and his friends had mounted upright steel plates on their boats to hide behind. Some of the bullets banged against the steel plates as each man took cover. The barrage of machine-gun fire was not long lasting though, because within a few seconds the two patrol boats had also run too close to the floating, magnetized harbor mines, resulting in two more tremendous explosions.

All three of the patrol boats were now either burning or sinking, or both. Kenny knew that many, many more boats were already on the way, and that his time on earth was short.

"Okay guys, been a privilege knowin' y'all. Hope to see ya on the other side of the watery grave, if there is one. So long!"

"So long guys," came back replies from Kenny's friends.

All three Shrimp boats now spread out across the water channel, each pulling a section of the chain-net with them. The second that the chain-net was fully spread across the channel and sunk below the surface, the three Shrimpers turned and headed full speed back towards the open seas of the Atlantic. They made only a couple hundred yards before they began taking fire from behind them, more patrol boats having arrived on the scene.

But the harbor mines were plentiful and the speedy patrol boats were going off like Roman Candles across the surface of the channel. Kenny and his friends hooped and hollered as the mines went off, bringing the patrol boats to a quick halt and making swimmers out of their sailors.

Kenny and his friends knew the victory was short lived though, for in seconds they heard the wind-beating sounds of helicopter gunships, and the three Shrimpers barely had time to reflect upon the lives they had lived when the choppers opened fire on all three. Depleted uranium rounds ripped through wood, steel, flesh, man, engines and the hulls of the three boats, exploding their fuel tanks and killing their Captains within seconds.

As Kenny St. John and his two friends died and sank beneath the channel waves, the chopper pilots called-in the kills.

It took only a few hours for the proficient Navy tugs to sweep the channel clean of the debris. Counting the Shrimp-boats, eight vessels had sunk within a few minutes that night. But the ex-brother-in-law's info had been correct, and a Boomer was indeed making its way through the channel.

The Channel Security Commander on the scene determined that the threat had been neutralized, and, under pressure to green-light the Boomer, gave the go-ahead, never imagining that Kenny St. John's chain-net still lurked several yards below the channel surface.

As the Trident behemoth moved through the channel, the Navy Ensign manning the listening devices that were used, along with on-board radar, to steer the ship safely along now detected a scraping sound, as if something were being pulled along the under-surface of the sub.

The junior officer called the Captain, asking him to listen to the strange noise. The Captain had run Boomers through this channel a hundred times and never had a problem. He put his set of head-phones on to listen to the problem.

"Sounds like we're scraping rocks on the channel bottom, sir," said the Ensign.

"There are no rocks on the bottom of this channel, son!" replied the CO, "Surface! Surface now!" he ordered, too late.

St. John's chain-net had worked to perfection as the Trident had moved across and then over it. The chain-net had dragged along the bottom of the Boomer and, just as the Captain had issued the order to surface, the chain-net had gathered about the sub's massive propeller, harbor mines and all, drawn by the powerful vortex. The shaft of the propeller was in an instant wrapped in the chain-net, and at that moment the mines attached to the chain-net exploded, twelve of them detonating almost simultaneously.

The Ensign and the Captain threw their earphones off as the sound of the explosion nearly deafened them, the shock of the blast rocking the massive sub. The Trident's propeller shaft was pinched by the blast, such that the screw separated from the vessel and fell away, coming to rest in the muck of the channel floor.

The Trident sub, now propeller-less, came to rest on the channel floor as well, with no means to move forward or backwards. But the hull of the ship was never in any danger of a breach, just as the Shrimpers had figured. The CO simply ordered that high-pressure air be blown into the ballast tanks, causing the submarine to surface where the crew could be safely off-loaded. The crippled but otherwise unharmed Boomer would be towed back up the channel to port.

It would be weeks before a Naval Investigation Unit could put together the puzzle of Kenny St. John. That unit included in its official report the fact that Kenny St. John and his two cohorts had died for nothing; they took no lives but their own, having undertaken a suicide mission succeeding only in making some kind of twisted, anti-government statement by destroying Naval and Government property valued in the millions of dollars. It fell to some of the local Shrimpers who knew the dead men to speak up and say that, knowing strange Kenny and his friends, that is just what they had likely intended.

Chapter Fourteen

Interstate 75 South
Near Macon, Georgia

Although no one in the Middle Georgia Militia had ever met or even talked to Governor of Georgia Jim Cummins, most of the men admired the man. They were the types of men who wanted someone to standup against the 'big guy' on behalf of the 'little guys.'

So, when word spread that Governor Cummins was going to be visiting Macon to make a speech, many of the members of the MGM decided that they would all go to meet their hero.

Macon, Georgia, famous for being the home of Otis Redding and the Allman Brothers, is a city located nearly dead-center of the State, so it was close by the home-base of the MGM. Even though Governor Cummins had never called for the formation of local militias, the men of the MGM chose not to hold that against him. They firmly believed in his message of resistance to the federal government, even though the Governor had never called upon any to join his personal struggle. 'We can't let the good Governor fight the fight alone' was the prevailing sentiment among the militia members.

On the day the Governor was to speak, nearly half the militia membership loaded themselves into a caravan of cars, trucks and vans, all heading out to Macon, Georgia. The other half of the militia would gladly have gone with them had not work, family and other responsibilities kept them at home. To a man, they were in energetic sympathy with their Governor.

The groups' leader Bubba McCloud was in the lead car of the caravan, his own black seventy-five model Chevy El Camino SS. I-75 South would lead them directly to Macon, so Bubba got on the Interstate and pointed the el Camino in that direction.

As he led the caravan down the Interstate, Bubba and friends soon noticed another caravan pulling up to run beside them on the highway. This other caravan was no rag-tag mix of old pickups and muscle cars, though. Rather, it was a one-hundred-vehicle-long line of sleek new black-and-metalic silver Humvees.

These Humvees were not the scaled-down versions created for the American consumer market. These were full-size military Humvees that had been delivered fresh to the headquarters of BlackSky Security, a special factory order with custom two-tone paint-jobs and chrome mags.

Using money from their generous government security contracts, BlackSky had militarized the Humvees with both large caliber machine guns and TOW wire-guided missiles, though on this day the weaponry was not installed because it was illegal to take such a weaponized vehicle on a public road or interstate.

The pure-chance meeting of these two groups, militia and soldiers-for-hire, while rolling down an interstate, was at once a volatile situation.

No one can say which side it was, the militia or BlackSky, that first rolled down a window to yell a question or perhaps an insult at those in the lane parallel to them. Either way it was not long before someone on each side figured out who the others were. A sense of rivalry and hostility was born in an instant, perhaps for no other reason than 'boys will be boys.'

The BlackSky men used their satellite phones to run this news down their caravan, the news that they were in the presence of a 'hick-militia' on its way to cheer on the madman Governor as he made a speech in Macon, Georgia.

The militia used their CB radios to inform their caravan that the long line of shiny Hummers belonged to BlackSky 'mercenary rent-a-murderers.'

In the cross talk, some of the more loose-lipped militia put out the idea that the mercenaries might be headed for Macon also, to interfere with or even bring harm to Governor Cummins, though in truth the BlackSky men were headed to a company golf tournament.

"Hi there," shouted one of the BlackSky operatives out of a passenger side Humvee window, "where you Bubba's going? Can't be a family reunion, since your family tree has no forks in it. Don't you in-breds know that your father and grandfather don't have to be the same guy?" The other men in the vehicle with the jokester hooted and hollered with laughter at the incest reference. But the MGM was not to be outdone.

"Hey," replied a militiaman, "did I not see you in those pictures from that Iraqi prison for queer Muslims? Wasn't that one of your friends that the insurgents burned to a crisp and hung from the bridge in Baghdad? That's how we like our chicken down here, battered and fried!" Now it was the militiamen's turn to hoot and holler.

Though the militiaman could not have known, the BlackSky man he yelled the insult at *did* have a best friend who was one of the men captured, burned and hung from a Baghdad bridge in retaliation for the torture at Abu Ghraib prison in Iraq.

Still, these insults shouted back and forth, though cuttingly personal, would have led to nothing had not the BlackSky men used their sat phones to find the CB channel that the MGM were tuned to. Suddenly, every CB radio could hear every insulting word spoken over the BlackSky sat phones, and vice versa.

Each and every vehicle in both caravans was packed with men feeling their testosterone and ready to prove it by taking a turn on the radio to cast an insult more offensive than the last one. In no time every man in both southbound lanes of I-75 was slinging every manner of verbal abuse at their new found rivals.

It was just a matter of which side would escalate the situation--then someone in a militia truck found a paintball gun.

The militia had trained with paintball guns as a way to carry out military-like training with non-lethal weapons. As one of the BlackSky operatives stuck his head out of a window to shout something, a militiaman popped off a ten-ball burst at the man's face. While a few of the paintballs splattered red paint across the man's face, some of the balls passed through the open window and into the vehicle to burst and splatter there. The paintballs were non-lethal but at that range were hard enough to break facial skin and draw terrible red welts all about the man's face and head.

In retaliation, someone in a BlackSky Hummer pulled out a bean-bag gun, also considered a non-lethal weapon, though some people have died after being hit in the head with a bean-bag projectile shot from one of these weapons.

The man with the bean-bag gun caught a militiaman with his head hanging out of a pickup truck window, and he unloaded a three-bag burst on him. Two bean-bags hit him on the cheek and jaw, breaking both bones underneath. The third bag flew wide and hit the driver of the militia pickup, knocking him unconscious and causing his vehicle to swerve off the roadway and into a ditch.

Now the hostilities between the two groups escalated quickly. Though neither side was carrying rifles, many did carry sidearms, and now, anyone with a real gun pulled it out and shots were traded up and down the lines of vehicles.

Still in the lead militia vehicle, Bubba McCloud realized what was happening. Spotting an exit off the Interstate, McCloud swerved his vehicle into the exit lane and called on his CB for all his people to follow him off the Interstate. Shots were still being traded between the caravans.

The militia caravan made the exit quickly, but the vehicles bringing up the rear caught the worst abuse from BlackSky. Having the heavy Hummers on their side, some of the BlackSky drivers moved up behind the last of the militia vehicles to bump them hard in the rear, causing the lighter vehicles to swerve, the drivers fighting to maintain control. With a few more hard bumps several militia cars and trucks found themselves wrecked in the ditch as well. All the while, BlackSky continued to pour mocking laughter upon the wrecked militiamen via their sat phones.

Content with the few blows they had dealt the 'hicks,' the BlackSky caravan of Hummers stayed on the Interstate heading south.

To pour just a little more salt in the wound, one of the BlackSky men yelled into his phone,

"Hey hicks, get back to the sticks, we're off to Macon to pop a cap in your crazy Governor!" Although it was an empty dig, for BlackSky had no intention of stopping in Macon where the Governor was to speak, the militia had their blood up and took the threat as real.

Bubba McCloud was able to gather his caravan at a truck stop just off the exit. After making sure everyone was safe, he sent one truck to take to the hospital the man hit by the bean-bag, the man's head already swollen to the size of a basketball. Others went back to help recover the vehicles that had been forced into the ditch by the Humvees.

Having regrouped, Bubba McCloud assured his men that the insults by BlackSky would not go unanswered. He further assured the men that he knew the back roads of the area and if they hurried they could catch BlackSky in a bind. The MGM was game as they cranked their rides, revving the engines.

Before they left the truck stop, Bubba made a call back to his home base. Believing the Governor's life to be in danger, he called on the balance of the Middle Georgia Militia to come to Macon, and to bring as much of the Russian weaponry with them as they could haul.

Still laughing and celebrating about how they had abused the hick-militia, the BlackSky caravan continued down the

Interstate. Thinking they had seen the last of their new-found bumbling enemies, BlackSky had no worries as they rode along until they rounded a curve and watched dumbfounded as nearly a hundred militia vehicles emerged from an acre of sparse woods at high speed.

The Humvees had no time to react as almost every BlackSky Hummer was solidly rammed, T-Boned so hard from the side that many of them were flipped over and onto the grass median.

Confusion reigned in the BlackSky caravan as smoke, dust, broken glass and debris filled the interior of the wrecked Hummers.

The softest spot on a Hummer being the doors, many of the passengers suffered broken bones from the collisions and subsequent rollovers. A few operatives who had not buckled seatbelts were ejected onto the highway or grass median.

A few of the militia vehicles were now too damaged to drive. These were simply left where they sat on the side of the Interstate, their passengers hitching rides with their militia friends. The militia again formed a caravan and sped quickly away, leaving in their wake a chorus of hoots and hollers that stung BlackSky like a swarm of Red Wasps. *No way this thing is over*, the BlackSky Commander was thinking, enraged.

Taking his sat phone in hand, that Commander called up his reserves at the BlackSky base near Atlanta. His message was simple:

"BlackSky is under attack by a local militia tied to the Governor--bring all the men and muscle you can load, use the choppers, the trucks--use everything, and meet us near Macon, Georgia. I'm uploading the GPS info now. And one more thing" said the Commander. The Commander had guessed wrong as to the Governor being tied to the Middle Georgia Militia, but by that time it mattered little.

"What else, sir?" the man at the base compound replied dutifully.

"Use our contact at the NSA to tie into their network—I'm e.mailing my personal codes now. Use my codes to download all their latest satellite streams for middle Georgia into our mainframe, then forward it to my field laptop. Specifically, I need to track a caravan of light vehicles that just left my current position on Interstate 75. They were headed south when they left here and I want them located, now!"

Bubba McCloud and his men made their way down I-75 until they found the exit Bubba had been looking for. Taking that exit, the caravan drove another ten miles into the flatlands of middle Georgia known as the old Cotton Belt. Bubba had a close friend that lived on a farm nearby.

Bubba had a strong sense that another confrontation, this time fully armed, was coming with BlackSky. He called up some of the MGM that had not made the trip. His orders were to bring as many as possible of the semi trucks and trailers that held their heavy weaponry. They were to converge at the farm where Bubba and his men were holed up. They could use the GPS on their cell phones to get there, he said.

Arriving at the farm, Bubba and his men refreshed themselves with cold drinks as they talked over the day's excitement.

Bubba gathered his men around and informed them that the entire militia was on the way to that very spot and would arrive in about two hours, so there was no time to be scarred, or to waste. The others were bringing as much of the weaponry as possible with them, Bubba said.

"Now, this field will be our staging area. I want each of you to strip your vehicles of anything you can use, then park them all in those woods over there, all except the four-wheel drives. We need those to mount weaponry on," said McCloud, pointing to a head of pines to the west.

"If you've read anything about these BlackSky characters, you know how dangerous they are--dangerous and well financed. Well financed means well armed and well informed. In other words, they know how to find us. They have probably already tracked us to this very spot."

"No way, how could they have tracked us already? We rolled em' good back on I-75," said one of the younger men.

"Ever hear of satellites, Junior Samples?" quipped an older man to scattered laughter.

"Okay," said Bubba McCloud, "we need to be rested and ready when our weapons arrive. I want each of you to divide yourselves into teams of ten men. Each team will be responsible for unloading and preparing one piece of heavy weaponry and three heavy machine guns. I want all ammunition and ordinance stacked and ready. After we unload, I want every man who hunts deer with the bow to assemble in those woods to the south. Have your bows and quivers in hand. If you did not have a tree climber in your truck, ask a buddy or find some rope."

The men were looking at one another, confused by the order but ready to trust Bubba's command. After all, he was the man who had secured all those weapons from the Russians.

When the big trucks loaded with Russian weaponry arrived at the farm, Bubba's men went into action. Artillery was limbered, RPG's loaded, machine guns mounted. All the big trucks except two were then driven down an old logging road that led through the south woods and into another hundred-acre cotton field.

The two remaining trucks were parked in the middle of the staging field. Bubba ordered that each truck have its' rear doors left open, with unloading ramps pulled out and one end resting on the ground. He ordered that two of the older pieces of artillery be pushed halfway up those ramps and chain-locked in that position so that it would appear that the pieces were in the process of being off-loaded.

"What you cookin' up for them mercs?" asked one of the men of Bubba.

"Thinks he's Bedford Forrest, I reckon," joked another man.

"Well, I don't know if we can be the 'firstest with the mostest,' but we better be the cleverest if we want to live to see-est tomorrow," said Bubba McCloud, "and we dadgum better shoot the straightest. Hey, somebody borrow that tractor over there and bring around five of the big round-bales of hay. Grab an axe and a pitchfork too."

A half hour later, the distant rumble of helicopters rolled across the fields and woods of the farm. Most of the militiamen had never even been near a battlefield, the fear and grim looks on their faces telling the story. But McCloud reminded them that they were standing on their native soil and had no need to fear. If they died with their friends today, he said, they would fall on Georgia soil that would gladly receive a native son. Though nervous and jittery, none of the men ran away.

BlackSky had arrived. Three Blackhawk choppers, fully armed, swept over the farm from the northwest. The three pilots, going by the handles Eagle, Falcon and Hawk, had the Commander on line. He was close by in a Hummer but was proceeding to the farm with caution, fearing an ambush.

The Commander ordered the choppers to sweep the area and tell him what resistance the hick militia might have in store, but all that the chopper pilots could see in the large cotton field were the two large trucks with artillery pieces on their loading ramps in the middle of the field. There was no movement and the trucks looked abandoned.

"Looks like the hick-chicks heard us coming Commander, and have flown the coop," said Eagle. "All I see are a few big round bales of hay on the near side of a large field, and what looks like a couple semi-trucks in the middle of the field. The hicks ran away in such a hurry that they left their two tractor-trailers behind. And get this, sir--the trucks have artillery pieces being off-loaded."

"Artillery? You've got to be joking. Those red-necks don't know how to handle artillery. Where would they even get it? Are you sure of what you're seeing, pilot?"

"Hold on, sir, let me take a closer look," said Eagle, pushing his Blackhawk on across the field to hover near the big trucks as Falcon and Hawk stayed to hover at the edge of the field, near the hay bales.

"Sir, I can definitely confirm that there are two artillery pieces being off-loaded in this field. And get this Commander, I'm almost certain that these are Russian hardware, looks like 122 millimeter field pieces, sir," said Eagle.

"Okay pilot, any idea which way the scum went?"

"Hold on sir, I see something emerging from a dirt road on the west side of the cotton field."

What Eagle was seeing was a pickup truck pulling to the edge of the field. The truck quickly came to a stop. A man had been lying down in the bed of the truck. That man was Bubba McCloud, and he rose instantly, popping up from behind the cab with a shoulder-launched missile perched on his right shoulder.

"Missile targeting me!" yelled Eagle from where his aircraft still hovered near the two trucks. Working the choppers' joystick control, the pilot went to turn his bird, but it was too late. McCloud had already popped off a projectile, not towards the chopper but towards the big trucks. The big trucks were not empty but had been fully loaded down with barrels of diesel fuel and ammonium nitrate stored on the farm.

When Bubba's projectile hit the first truck, the explosion ignited the chemicals in both trucks, creating a chain reaction explosion of such force that the resulting fireball, rising with both intense heat and speed, engulfed the Blackhawk in a spit second. The explosion of the BlackSky chopper added its own fire and force to the deafening blast.

"Bird down," yelled one of the other pilots into his radio, "I repeat, Eagle is on fire and going down!"

"Falcon and Hawk, get out of there, it's a trap!" yelled the Commander at the two remaining choppers. But again it was too late, at least for Hawk.

Hawk looked at his video screen that showed, via an underside camera system, what was going on directly underneath the aircraft. He watched as the top flew off of one of the six-foot high round hay bales. Hawk realized in an instant that the hay bale had been hollowed out and a man was concealed inside it. That militiaman had another shoulder-launcher, and the weapon was now pointing straight up at the underbelly of the Blackhawk. Smoke belched and the projectile flew upward and into the chopper's gut.

The BlackSky commander rolled up to the farm just in time to see the second Blackhawk explosion of the afternoon. He watched, incredulous, as fresh rage rolled over him.

"Kill that man in the hay! Kill him now!" yelled the commander into the mouthpiece of his headset. Two Humvees had rolled up with alongside him, both mounted now with .50 caliber machine guns. Both guns erupted with sustained fire directly at the bale of hay, the bullets cutting the militia man to bloody ribbons. He had taken out a chopper but paid for it now with his life.

"Bring everyone up!" yelled the Commander. "Form line-of-battle along this field and sweep it clean of this vermin! Find them where they hide and destroy them all! They just killed good men and a million dollars worth of choppers."

Over a hundred Humvee's sped quickly onto the farm, spreading out across the edge of the field. Some had the mounted .50's while others had mounted missile launchers. Still others pulled artillery pieces behind them, and with efficient movements the BlackSky ops quickly had them loaded, aimed and prepared to fire. But the only aiming point of reference BlackSky had was the logging road from which Bubba McCloud had fired at the truck-bombs, though Bubba had by then disappeared out of view, back down the road that descended into a depression.

The BlackSky Commander was still enraged at having lost two choppers but now regained enough composure to realize he had to protect his last bird . He said to the remaining pilot,

"Falcon, you're the only eyes I have left in the sky. I want you to get your bird to a higher altitude and stay there, I can't afford to lose another chopper."

"Roger that, Commander, but at that altitude I can't lay down precise ground cover."

"I know that Falcon, don't lecture me, just obey the order! And one more thing, move to the south and tell me what's behind those woods to our left--but stay up high until I call you down!"

"Roger that, sir."

As the BlackSky Commander waited for Hawk's report on where the militia had run to, the rest of his men arrived at the farm. The men and their armaments were spread out to form one long line across the edge of the hundred acre farm field.

An eerie silence now descended over the land, the kind that only exists when nerve-racked men wait for battle. No sound was heard except for the still burning choppers and the occasional metallic click of a gun being locked and loaded.

The BlackSky line of battle was impressive. It now contained over four hundred operatives and looked disciplined, complete, and without gaps. The line was curved back on each end to prevent a flanking movement by the enemy.

The line was formed by artillery-piece crews, mortar crews, Humvees mounted with machine guns, others mounted with missile launchers and still other Hummers filled with shooters, each man armed with fully automatic M-16's and as many loaded ammo clips as he could physically carry.

Those military style Hummers were stoutly built with massive support springs underneath. Still, some of them were so loaded down with weaponry, reserve ordinance and ammo that the rear suspension of the vehicles sagged from the weight. If Bubba and his crew allowed themselves to be hit with even a third of what BlackSky had waiting for them, the MGM would be little more than a black spot on scorched earth. And the BlackSky Commander knew that it was his job to put his men in the position to accomplish that very thing.

"Commander," said the voice of the chopper pilot Hawk, "I can see another large open field behind the woods to the south. That's where they are sir, to the left of your line. There are about forty vehicles and artillery pieces waiting there, sir. They look to be sighted in on the logging road that moves west then circles south from where you are located. They are waiting on you to come up that road Commander, but you'll have to cross that field in front of you to get to it."

"What is their posture in relations to the dirt road?" asked the Commander.

"They are facing the road entrance. They are facing west, just as your line is, sir. The woods on your left form their right flank, sir." And that was the piece of intel the BlackSky

Commander needed. He grabbed a mic and issued a general command to his line-of-battle.

"All BlackSky operatives: The enemy is to our left, behind those woods there to the south. I want the line-of-battle to pivot to face those woods to the south. Our left flank will anchor and the rest of the line will swing around to face due south. EXECUTE NOW!"

Every driver of a Humvee cranked his vehicle immediately. As the entire line began to move, the Commander was struck by the beauty of the maneuver. If the whole line-of-battle were one long gate, then the extreme left was the hinge that the gate swing on.

It is no small thing to swing around a line of men and arms that long, but BlackSky nailed the movement almost to perfection. It took no more than fifteen minutes. One portion of the swinging line had to go around the burning trucks and chopper in the middle of the field, causing a temporary gap to form. But that gap was quickly closed up again as the disciplined line kept the gate swinging across the wide field until the line faced due south, directly facing the woods.

No sooner had the line reached its new position than the Commander was on the radio again.

"Move our line to the woods. If the woods are too thick for your Hummers to navigate, I want half the men in each vehicle to dismount and enter the woods with assault rifles, heavy machine guns and grenade launchers. EXECUTE NOW!"

Again the long line lunged forward across the field, its goal the tree line. The Hummers picked up speed now, the men eager to engage the enemy that had already killed some of their friends. It was blood-for-blood time.

But as the line closed within thirty yards of the tree line, six explosions were seen and heard in rapid succession across the lin. Six Hummers exploded, the vehicles blown backwards or sideways in fiery cartwheels, shedding men and metal as they spun.

For any who had done time in Iraq, the sound of an Improvised Explosive Device is one they never forget. Formed by a live, buried artillery round and a detonator, several of these IEDs can be wired together to attack a convoy or a line of battle.

"Daisy Chain! Daisy Chain!" yelled an veteran operative who recognized instantly what had happened.

"Mine Field! Mine Field!" yelled another operative as the line of battle came to a dusty halt. Acrid smoke drifted across the field, hanging low. The vehicles were stuck there and could risk going no further. The soft, oft plowed dirt of the farm field had been perfect ground in which to plant the devices, and the BlackSky line was fortunate that they had lost only six vehicles.

"Dismount!" ordered the Commander, "All operatives dismount and walk into the woods. Leave the vehicles behind. Take all weaponry, and watch the ground and step lightly." He could have saved that last order, thought some of the men, for it is impossible to step lightly carrying a .50 caliber machine gun or a TOW missile launcher on one's shoulder.

But the BlackSky operatives were nothing if not well disciplined, and in a moment four hundred men were marching towards the woods, heavy laden with weapons. As they marched the men watched the ground intensely for any signs of disturbance.

Most of those men were city-raised and easily mistook a gopher hole or the rooting of an armadillo for a bomb site. These they dodged around. But just as the line of shooters was about the enter the tree line one of the men, stepping around a gopher hole, planted his boot directly on a buried Claymore type mine. The explosion drew the attention of the entire line and they watched as their comrade's body soared into the air, landing in separate pieces with sickening thuds that kicked up bloody dust.

The line had no choice now but to try to make it into the woods. Once there, they realized that there was no guarantee that the woods had not also been mined and booby trapped. And so it was that nearly four hundred men walked gingerly into the trees, serching the ground with every step.

It was now that the iron discipline of the line-of-battle began to break. The men were already growing fatigued in the merciless Georgia heat and humidity, coupled with the raw nerves of walking through mine fields. The men picked their way through the brush and trees, trying to avoid anything that looked like a beaten path. Rabbit and deer trails looked to them like death traps. Some of the men tried to hop from tree root to tree stump and back to tree root again, anything to avoid soft ground.

Each man had his own headset-communicator, but despite their Commanders harsh order to keep the line straight and tight, the line became disjointed as each man picked his way along.

One of the BlackSky operatives stopped for a rest, risking the ire of his Commander. Pulling a handkerchief from his pocket the operative removed his cap and wiped at the sweat pouring from his head and running down his neck. As he wiped, he happened to look up into the trees. The razor tipped arrow was already on its way before he realized that there was a man clinging to the top of one of the pine trees. The militiaman who had released the arrow had been a bow-hunter since his father first took him bow hunting at the age of ten. At a range of seventy-five yards he could scarce miss. The broadhead arrow tip took the victim through the chin at a downward angle. The point of the arrow sliced through the man's chin and lodged deep in his throat, pulling his jaw down and pinning it against the man's Adam's Apple.

Appalled, the operative stood stiffly in his tracks a moment, unable to speak or move further or understand why his life was ending in these Georgia woods. He was from Ohio, and had figured on dying old and grey at home. Nearby shooters looked up to see their comrade standing open mouthed with an arrow through his lower face and throat. From the tops of a hundred pines, heavily camouflaged men now released their arrows at a distance of seventy-five to a hundred yards. Almost every arrow found its mark, and BlackSky began to cry out as the arrows took them high and low through chests, ribs, groins, legs and heads.

As soon as they had released the first volley, the archers had knocked new arrows and, drawing back the string in fluid, confident motion, they released a second volley. Their targets were moving faster by that time and only about sixty of the arrows of the second volley found their marks. The bow-hunters were shimmying down the pine trunks by the time that the BlackSky men began to fire their M-16's into the tree tops. A few of the militiamen were hit, but most were able to reach the ground and take cover behind tree trunks, palmetto mounds or fallen pine logs. Each archer had a partner waiting to hand him his hot-iron, to go from Indian back to Cowboy.

In seconds there was brisk rifle fire which soon became a serious firefight raging in the piney woods as hundreds on both sides engaged. Pine bark and tar, ripped from the trees by spinning bullets, filled the air with debris and the pungent scent of turpentine.

The militia had earlier had time only to dig depressions behind logs they piled and covered with palmettos and brush. This was their cover for the firefight they knew would follow their bow-and-arrow volleys.

Far from ideal cover, still it was better than what BlackSky enjoyed.

Enjoying their advantage in cover, the MGM directed their AK-47 fire at the pines that the operatives were hiding behind, using their bullets as the teeth of a rip-saw to try to cut enough of the soft pine-meat away to allow a round to punch through and hit the man hiding behind it.

That technique would take time and lots of ammo considering the relatively low power of the 7.62 rounds used by the AK's. Bubba had kept the higher powered machine guns further south, about a quarter-mile deeper in the woods in fear that they might be captured in the initial surge of the BlackSky lines. That feared initial surge had not happened, and now his militiamen were calling for the heavy machine guns to be brought up so that they could use them to decimate both the pine forest and the hated mercenaries hiding in it.

The BlackSky Commander received a bad report from the piney woods firefight. His men were pinned down with small arms fire and could not move, the stressed voice on the radio told him. His men had no cover from which to set up their own heavy machine guns, and if the enemy brought their .50s up, BlackSky would be annihilated.

The Commander knew his men had only minutes to live if something was not done, and his proud men would die before they ever surrendered to a hick militia.

Just then, the Commander heard what was at that moment the sweetest sound in the world. Two Boeing AH-6 Little Bird helicopter gunships belonging to BlackSky Security had arrived over the farm, fully armed with dual Gatling-style Miniguns, along with Hydra rockets and Hellfire missiles. These choppers were much smaller than the Blackhawks, but also much faster and more agile.

"BlackSky Commander, this is 'Phoenix' gunship. The other Little Bird with me goes by 'Firebird.' The boss sent us to help. What can we do for you today, sir?"

"Phoenix and Firebird, my men are engaged with the enemy in those woods to the south. My men only penetrated the woods about three hundred yards max. I need you to lay down fire just beyond that point, and I need it now or I'm going to lose my men!"

"Roger that, Commander. Firebird, you take the left quadrant of the woods and I'll take the right. Drop your first round three hundred and fifty yards from edge of the woods."

"Roger that, Phoenix. Miniguns or rockets?"

"Mix it up, Firebird, our guys are in trouble down there."

"Roger that, Phoenix."

The two Little Birds zipped quickly across the cotton field, slowing as they reached the edge of the woods. They moved over the woods several hundred yards before the rotating barrels of their Miniguns began to spin, raining death from above.

In the forest below, the tops of the pines began to fall as if sliced with a razor. Underneath the canopy, bullets were penetrating, ripping and tearing at tree trunks, bushes, dirt and man-flesh. Within seconds, ten militiamen were cut down while the rest tried to figure out where the fire was coming from. These had to stop firing at their enemies on the ground to seek cover from the chopper fire.

Emboldened, the BlackSky shooters, who had been forced to keep their heads down before, now began to return heavy fire at the militia positions.

"Move up, move up!" yelled one of the BlackSky unit leaders, trying to get his men to press the new advantage. At the same time many of the militiamen realized that the only ground safe now from the strafing runs of the Little Birds was the woods-ground *to their front* occupied by BlackSky. These militia called for a charge of their own, forward onto that ground, thinking their chances better against the ground shooters than those gunships flying above.

The result was that the two bodies of enemy in the woods moved almost on top of each other. Men were firing at enemies no more than twenty yards from them, at times even closer. Men were screaming out in pain, some calling for their mothers as people died on both sides in heavy numbers.

The Little Birds continued to strafe the woods, capping off rockets here and there, tearing great holes in both the tree tops and the forest floor. Fires began to burn and spread quickly across the drought-stricken ground thick with dry red pine needles, pine cones and other dry brush.

There was no chance now for Bubba McCloud to get his heavy machine guns to the front of his lines, and he knew he had made a major mistake in not having them there in the beginning. A rookie error, he knew, but it would not be his last.

In the woods men continued to shoot at one another, but now the air was so thick with smoke from the fires that visibility was quickly reduced to ten feet at the most. At that point the militiamen stopped shooting and tried to escape the woods before they were surrounded by the fires. Men on either side were collapsing due to smoke inhalation, their buddies trying to drag them out of the kill zone.

The BlackSky commander called on his lines to surge forward, but the smoke and fire made it impossible, and they also had to withdraw to the edge of the woods. The Little Birds had saved them from certain annihilation, but neither could they penetrate further into the woods to punish the MGM.

When he saw his men streaming back out of the forest, the BlackSky Commander ordered the unit leaders to regroup the men. If they could make it back to the line of Hummers they could backtrack and get away from the land mines and IED's.

His men proved tough as well as game, and made their way back to their Humvees, only a couple of them stepping on the weight-activated land mines as they went. The BlackSky Commander had to watch those explosions, the force blowing his men into the air. He cursed himself for not thinking the rebels would use landmines, they had been doing so since Confederate General Rains had improvised them back at Yorktown where he battled Union General McClellan.

He looked down at his watch, only to jerk his head up at the sound of another explosion. A ball of smoke and fire rolled up over the top of the trees.

"Come in Phoenix, come in Firebird! What is going on?" A frantic voice answered the Commander.

"A Little Bird is down, sir, a Little Bird just got hit." It was Falcon, the Blackhawk pilot, making the call.

"FireBird is down! I repeat, Firebird is down and burning!" yelled Phoenix into his mic. "They were waiting for us at the other end of the forest Commander. These hicks have got Heat Seekers? Why did you not tell us that Commander? We are sitting ducks flying this low!"

"What kind of missile took down Firebird?" asked the Commander.

"It was shoulder-launched," responded Phoenix, almost in a panic. "I swear I saw a barefoot hick in overalls in a treetop pop off the round that took FireBird down! Not a Stinger though, had the signature of a Russian model. I got hit by a Russian Strelet in Bosnia once, had a proximity fuse. Only has to get close to you. You should have warned us!"

"Phoenix, calm down and do your job. Don't lose your head now!"

Checking his watch, the BlackSky Commander realized there was only a couple hours of daylight left. If he was going to destroy his enemy he had to do it soon. Though the Governor had no connection to the Militia, the Commander did not know that and thought the Governor might be planning to reinforce the enemy.

"Okay, Phoenix, you and Falcon listen up. I want you to cover our movements. I'm taking my line of Hummers down that dirt road that heads west and curls back around on the militia's position. It's my only way to get to them and they know it. Strafe the road first to neutralize any IED's, then strafe the rebel position. Keep their heads down until I can bring my line up! Now do your job and avenge the BlackSky dead!"

"Roger that," said both chopper pilots, their blood up for the killing. Both choppers, the one remaining Blackhawk and the one remaining Little Bird, positioned themselves to move ahead of the Hummer line, which now formed itself into a column and headed across the cotton field towards the logging road from which Bubba had fired the shot into the truck bombs.

The unit leaders reported the numbers to the Commander; he had lost about a hundred and fifty men. That left him about two hundred and fifty to finish off the militia, whose numbers he was not sure of. The militia had somehow secured good weaponry, but the BlackSky gunships were the key to the battle. If they could stay in the air and unharmed, he knew that he could devastate his enemy, an enemy he now hated with all his soul, be they Americans or not.

At the Commander's signal, both gunships began to lay down gunfire on the ground directly in the path of the Hummer column. The choppers were in effect acting like mine sweepers, cutting a safe path for the column to move across. Several tell-tale explosions of smoke and dust proved they were doing their job, their bullets striking land mines planted by the Militia.

As the column of Hummers neared the entrance of the dirt road, the gunships strafed both the road and the roadside. More explosions testified that the MGM had prepared IED's alongside the dirt road, but BlackSky had outsmarted them and were moving at a steady pace now down the dirt road toward the militia position. If he could make it there with no more losses, the Commander knew he could crush the militia; he had air support and they did not.

Bubba McCloud had left a few snipers in the woods on either side of the dirt road. These now were taking shots at the column, but the shooters in the BlackSky column were well trained and their returning fire kept the militia from doing any real damage.

When the BlackSky column arrived at the end of the dirt road they could see the open field awaiting. They had lost only one man on the two miles of dirt road and no IED's had survived the gunship strafing to harm the column.

As the column emerged it quickly formed another line of battle, covered by Falcon and Phoenix, both gunships immediately engaging the militia.

BlackSky artillery pieces began firing on McCloud's line as soon as they were in position. The fire was precise and the Commander watched through a spotter's scope as his artillery began to tear huge gashes in the rebel line. He smiled, sensing a route.

On the other side of the wide field, Bubba McCloud had arrayed his line behind a double line of large round hay bales, using the bales as cover. The bales proved to be good cover against bullets but could not withstand the pounding from the artillery.

Bubba called on those of his men with the Russian anti-aircraft missiles to bring down the chopper gunships that kept a constant fire on his line. Several missiles had been fired, but had missed the choppers completely, their ordnance dropping harmlessly behind the BlackSky line. Bubba knew that if he did not think of something soon, he and his men were doomed. The dirt road now behind the enemy line was the only road out and he and his men had no retreat but through more woods that surrounded the field.

An F-16 Eagle Fighter Jet makes a terrible scream when it flies in low on a battlefield. When Bubba McCloud heard that scream, he was sure that it meant the end for him and his men. The screaming Eagle came in from the south, behind the militia line. Bubba did not even bother to take cover, there would be no use.

Shocked at what he felt would be the violent end of his life, Bubba McCloud held his face up boldly to face the incoming fighter jet; he would die like a man.

But the waited explosions detonated, not on his position, but across the field, within the BlackSky line.

Bubba watched the Eagle soar overhead, following it with wide, upturned eyes. The Blackhawk gunship was now the target of the F-16's rotating cannons, and the chopper exploded suddenly in a brilliant ball of orange flame. The Eagle had also dropped two of its five hundred pound bombs, both of which struck near the BlackSky lines.

Bubba McCloud watched through dust and smoke as the F-16 Eagle continued on its path; it was not turning for another pass. Bubba heard other sounds and knew that other jets were in the sky, though he did not see them. He had no idea why it had happened, but he knew it was his only chance to live to see his wife and kids again.

"Artillery, begin firing!" he ordered. "Everyone move up and attack!" He was ordering a full frontal charge on the BlackSky line-of-battle, something that would have been sure suicide only a minute before.

"Take out that chopper !" ordered Bubba, referring to the one remaining chopper gunship, the Little Bird piloted by Phoenix, and painted solid black.

The F-16 had come in low and Bubba had caught a glimpse of the emblem painted on the bird near the cockpit; it was the emblem of a colonial rifleman against a blue background, the symbol of the Georgia Air National Guard. And underneath that symbol was the post-1956 Georgia Flag with its familiar star-filled X.

But McCloud had no time to ponder what that meant. His life would last a few more minutes, or maybe thirty more years, all depending on what happened in the next few seconds.

Two four-wheel-drive pickup trucks, both carrying men armed with the Russian Anti-Aircraft shoulder launched missiles, had dug out in response to his last order to take down the Little Bird. The chopper had been sent into a spin when the Blackhawk had exploded, but it looked like the pilot had regained control.

The two militia trucks had made a bee-line for the gunship and the pilot had apparently been warned by a spotter because he now turned his Little Bird to face the oncoming pickups. The gunship's side-mounted miniguns unleashed on the trucks, the bullets churning up the ground as they moved on a collision course with the vehicles. Just as the rounds tore into the pickups, an anti-aircraft round streaked from each truck bed. At that short range, neither the gunship nor the Russian Strelet could miss. The two pickups both exploded and flipped over in the field just as the missiles took the Little Bird on each side. The resulting explosions first compressed the gunship inward, upon itself, and was then thrown back outwards violently, completely obliterating the chopper. Other than the rotors, not a piece of the chopper would be found that measured bigger than a cake dish.

Bubba and his men were all charging forward now, some in pickups, some on foot. At the same time the BlackSky commander, also baffled by the appearance of the F-16, now ordered what was left of his men to charge forward, which they did, some in Humvees, some on foot.

What was left of the two small armies met in the middle of the hayfield. Men killed and were killed by rifle fire, grenades thrown at the last second and, finally, in hand-to-hand combat.

Bubba McCloud was at the center of his charging line, as the BlackSky commander was at his own. The two leaders were both now on foot, having had their vehicles blown from under them. Spotting one another, both brave men fired the last bullets in the clips of the assault rifles, each missing the other in the smoke and dust. Both charged screaming, but only Bubba McCloud had thought to fix his bayonet.

The cold steel of the bayonet entered the gut of the BlackSky Commander, slicing through skin and organs till it stuck in the intestines. Bubba rammed it again, harder, looking his enemy in his eyes the whole time. The point of the bayonet went all the way through, emerging out of the Commander's back, its blood grooves running with a thick redness.

Those on both sides who lived would limp away and try to make it back home. Both sides would claim to have won what came to be known as the "Battle of Macon," though both the Middle Georgia Militia and BlackSky were shredded and bloodied as they withdrew from the field. All wondered, was this to be a climatic battle that ended hostilities, or would it be just the first of many such battles fought on American soil...fought by Americans, against Americans?

Whatever ending one put on it, that battle insured that both the Militia and BlackSky were too shattered and broken to participate in whatever it was that Washington had planned for Governor Jim Cummins.

Chapter Fifteen

Governor Cummins' rural Lake House
Cobb County, Georgia

The two NSA strike teams along with one from the FBI had arrived on the scene of the upcoming raid within twentyfour hours of the President giving the green-light. They were immediately busy conducting reconnaissance and surveillance of the target. The 'go' order had come down on a Saturday, and the actual raid would take place on the following Wednesday morning at 3:00 A.M. At that hour the subjects would most likely be asleep within the lake house, and there would likely be no activity on the lake itself such as fishing or boating.

Members of the strike team had rented nondescript fishing boats and dressed as fishermen in order to make some rounds on the water to get a closer look at the Cummins property. Pictures from satellites and drones were fine, but the agents knew there was nothing like putting your own eyes on a target to orient yourself to the topography and distance-spatial relationships of the property.

Having those images stored in one's memory would be invaluable, especially in a night raid. Well hidden cameras aboard the fishing boats captured images of the property as well.

As their boat passed slowly by the Governor's property, the agents noticed a man standing on the wooden dock that jutted out into the water. He looked to be about six feet tall, with an uncovered head shaved bald. He was broad of shoulder and chest, yet narrow at the waist, all supported by a foundation of thick, muscular thighs. The man held a cane pole in his hand, its monofilament line hanging down into the water. The agents recognized the Governor of Georgia, Jim Cummins.

As the boat passed, Cummins lifted a hand to give a friendly wave. For whatever reason, it made the agents nervous and they just looked the other way. Not being from around those parts, the agents did not realize that folks in rural Georgia always waved when passing one another. Cummins just smiled as the boat passed on by. He knew that the men on the boat had failed to notice the shingle-covered camera lens mounted on the roof of the lake house as it took pictures of the operatives in the fishing boats.

Neither could these operatives have known that these zoom-focus, high resolution images of their faces were automatically downloaded to a computer, and that the computer was sending the digital images via a wireless sat-phone to another computer located somewhere on the campus of Georgia Tech University in Atlanta. That was on the Monday before the raid. Later Monday night, two Tech students would retrieve the images and run them through a program that would use the latest in facial identification-recognition technology to seek matches with facial images from personnel files hacked from federal government databases.

If any positive matches were found, Lindsey and Sammy would forward that information circuitously to the Blackberry of Governor Jim Cummins, who had been looking to relax for a few days at the lake. This would not be a peaceful respite for the Governor.

On the night of the raid, the agent in charge of strike team A checked his watch: Strait up twelve midnight. The raid was scheduled to launch in three hours.

Despite the loss of the BlackSky shooters, NSA Director Click determined to proceed with the raid on the Governor's lakehouse. His intel told him that Cummins was there and no large body of men had been seen on the premises. They had caught the Governor off-guard and had to seize the opportunity.

The NSA had rented a small lake-side cabin for the week. The cabin was on the opposite side of the thirty-acre lake, as far away from the Cummins property as possible. That cabin would act as the staging ground for the raid.

Discarding their fishing boats, each strike team would mount inflatable military style rafts powered by Honda 60-horse outboard motors specially modified to hum at an extremely low decibel rate. Despite running quietly, the outboard motors had plenty of power to push the water craft and its sizable load across the water at high speed, though in this case stealth was more important.

As the strike teams inflated their rafts and set up the quick-mount motors, the team leaders went over their plan one last time.

At the same time across the lake, Governor Jim Cummins sat on his comfortable leather sofa watching an old Clint Eastwood film. Cummins had seen 'The Outlaw Josey Wales' more times than he could remember and could almost quote the lines before the actors said them.

His wife and children were staying at her mother's house for the week, but the Governor had not come alone. And beside him on the sofa sat his personal Blackberry.

"It is good that warriors such as we meet in the struggle of life, or death," said the Governor. And the Blackberry began to ring. The Governor paused the movie and picked up the device and read the message. It began, 'Governor, the fishing must be really good there, even shooters from the NSA are trying their luck.' Cummins grinned, and hit the 'play' button on his remote control.

"It is good that warriors such as we meet in the struggle of life, or death," said Ten Bears in a deep base voice.

On yet another piece of lake-front that night, a 15-foot long wooden john-boat was slipping silently into the water. Thirteen year old Billy Joe Merritt was supposed to be in bed asleep, and his father had no idea that his son and his son's best friend Bob Weldon had conspired to sneak out of the bedroom window to retrieve their rods and reels for some night fishing.

Billy Joe's dad was an indoors guy and had never known the excitement of night fishing, of casting and dragging across bass infested waters a 3/8's ounce Arbogast Jitterbug top-water lure armed with double treble-hooks. But his son Billy Joe knew all about it from an article he had read in the *Georgia Angler* magazine.

The boy had read that when a ten-pound largemouth bass rose and broke the water to attack the wobbling gurgle of the Jitterbug, it would hit the lure with such aggression that the water would boil and spray, and a loud popping noise would echo across the surface of the otherwise smooth surface. There was no experience quite like it in the fishing life, and Billy Joe and Bob meant to have some fun on the water that night.

The two teens snickered quietly as they took their seats in the boat and began to paddle silently away from the shore. The young boys would have to pull those paddles through the water with many long strokes to bring the heavy wooden boat across the lake, but the night was young and they had brought along a cooler full of Pepsi. Billy Joe had the perfect spot in mind, right in the middle of the lake.

At 2:30 in the morning, the television was still on in the Governor's lake house though no one was watching it. The interior of the house was dark except for the glow of the TV. One outside security light shone brightly from atop a tall wooden light pole standing some forty feet from the corner of the house. That light was photo-cell activated and turned itself on as darkness covered the land each night. That light illuminated the yard between the lakehouse and the water, as well as casting a faint light on the fishing dock at the water's edge.

They would most likely shoot that light out if they approached from the water, thought the Governor. He had brought four men with him, close friends who were loyal to both the Governor and his cause. None of them had military experience, but they had all been close friends of Jim Cummins from childhood, and had honour-bound themselves to him. They would give their lives in a fight with anyone who threatened the Governor, and he knew that that kind of loyalty could make up for the lack of experience, at least to a certain extent.

Cummins had stationed each of his men at various points on the property. Each was armed with a Benelli 12-gauge semi-automatic shotgun loaded alternately with buckshot and slugs. NSA body armor would offer little resistance to such penetrating loads at close range, and tonight's work would be close-up work, with targets most likely being within the seventy-yard kill range. Cummins noticed that the signal of his second, decoy Blackberry had been scrambled twenty minutes before, which reassured him that this *was* the night they would come for him.

The leader of the strike team A gave a flashlight signal to his counterpart with the strike team B. It was time to move out. He and his team were jacked up for the raid, ready for whatever might be waiting on the other side of the lake. He and his men secretly used diet pills to get hyped for a mission. He added to that a stiff swig of alcohol just before he stepped into the raft. He screwed the top back on the bottle and stuffed the bottle into a tactical bag sitting at his feet in the bottom of the raft.

"Push us off," he ordered, "let's take this scumbag down."

The plan was to move out quietly a few hundred yards, then pick up speed at that point. They wanted to be at full speed by the time they made it to the middle of the lake. No running lights would be used, total darkness had to be maintained. The target must be given no prior warning.

GPS was aboard to steer by and lights would only serve to give warning to their target. All were equipped with the best set of night vision goggles that money could buy, so not even a flashlight was allowed on board, other than that held by the team leader. The rafts were not to slow down until they neared the Governor's lakeshore property, and that's where the real fun would begin.

Each strike team consisted of eight men. When the rafts were near the target and in four feet of water, some of the men from each strike team would slip from their rafts silently into the water. Those men would then wade to the shore and move in attack formation towards the house. The first agent ashore was to neutralize the dogs, taking them out with their suppressor-equipped assault riffles. When the yard was secure, half the shooters would take the front door and half the rear door. The house would be breached and cleared. The completed operation would take little more than half an hour.

The two NSA military-style rafts were moving now through the water, keeping about one hundred and fifty yards distance between them. The night air over the water was cool and exhilarating to the men on the rafts. All were 'crunk,' and ready for action.

When the rafts were about a quarter of the way across the lake, the leader of strike team A gave the order to increase to full speed. The Honda motors were amazingly quiet even as the rafts approached their top speed of fifty miles-per-hour. At that rate of speed it would not take long to cross the lake. As his raft neared the middle of the lake, the strike team leader thought he could already see the security light shining brightly in the Governor's yard, though the waters between his raft and the shore were as dark as outer space. He turned in his seat to speak to the agent operating the motor. He gave the order to cut the motors back to half speed, but before the order could be carried out he turned back to face the target and his eyes caught the briefest glimpse of a large object in the water just ahead.

Billy Joe and Bob had rowed hard to get to the middle of the lake but had finally made it. Billy Joe wasted no time, picking up his favorite rod and reel and slinging the Jitterbug as far as he could cast it. He smiled as he listened to the gurgle-gurgle sound of the top-water lure plowing its way through the water back towards the boat.

It was Bob's job to drop anchor, and he had reached for a concrete block that had a twenty foot rope tied to it. The block was what the boys used for an anchor, and just as Bob had picked it up to drop it over the side, his ears picked up the faint hum of the Honda outboard.

Neither the boys nor the agents had time to react. The nose of the NSA raft hit Billy Joe's heavy wooden boat at full speed, T-Boneing it dead center of portside. Billy Joe had cast his line to starboard, and felt his boat lifting up from behind him, flipping up and back over on him.

The walls of the government raft were made of a thick polymer and wrapped in a ballistic material and, though inflated, it crashed as hard as a boulder into the wooden john-boat. Its heft jacked Billy Joe's boat up and into the air as if a toy. Billy Joe's friend Bob had been holding the concrete block-anchor in hand when the attack-raft struck. When the boat was snatched out from under him, the block flew into the air, along with rods, reels, tackle boxes and two life-vests that the boys had not bothered to put on. Their bodies would be recovered, though the grieving souls of their parents never would.

The glimpse of something in the water ahead of his raft had been so slight as to offer the strike team leader no time to prepare for the collision. When his raft T-Boned the boys' boat, the nose of the raft was crushed inward, collapsing back in upon itself, bringing the raft to an instant halt. Inertia carried the strike team leader and his men forward, making them projectiles moving at nearly the same speed that the boat had been traveling.

The team leader flew head-first through the thick night air and into the underside of Billy Joe's boat, which had been flipped so that the bottom that had just been on water was now upturned to face the agents in the raft. The NSA agent's skull was crushed upon impact with the boat bottom and, mercifully, his spinal cord snapped like a twig. The strike team leader would feel neither pain nor any other sensation ever again as his lifeless and broken body splashed into the water and sank to rest on the lake bottom with the hungry, curious bottom-feeding catfish looking on.

Three of the other agents on the raft were thrown into the up-turned wooden boat, while three more were thrown into the water. None were wearing floatation vests; they had not planned on being in the rafts very long and found the vests cumbersome.

The eighth member of the team, the one that had been manning the outboard motor, had been sitting low in rear of the raft with his hand gripping the engine throttle. Somehow, almost miraculously, he had stayed on the raft, though flung about as it a rag-doll. But when Billy Joe's boat had flipped, the concrete block Bob had planned to drop as an anchor had been thrown into the air. The rope tied to the block was attached at its other end to the boys' boat itself, and the flipping boat whipped the concrete block up in the air and then back downward towards the raft.

In a circumstance indicative of the strike teams' luck that night, the rope snapped and the concrete block had slammed down into the raft precisely where the eighth team member had been flung. The corner of the block hit the agent on his right hip, just above the thigh, crushing the hipbone and cracking the pelvis all the way across. The broken pelvis pinched the thumb-sized sciatic nerve so hard it nearly severed, shooting a torrent of flame through the lower half of the agent's body. He would have screamed out, but the pain came in waves of flame that were too much for his mind to bear and he passed out, his body resting in the bottom of the raft. The other seven team members were either dead, unconscious and drowning, or trying to swim for their lives, the weight of their guns and gear working to drag them under.

The night was so dark and the members of the other strike team, Strike Team B, so focused on the target that the collision was not visible to them. They had heard a brief noise from the collision, but sound carries strangely at night on water and they had no idea what had just happened to the other team and had received no calls on their radios. As far as they knew, the mission was going as planned.

Their leader brought his raft silently into the shallows near the Governor's lakehouse where six of the men, including the leader himself, slipped immediately into the water and began to wade to shore with no idea that the NSA mission-force was now at half strength.

The two agents who first made it near the shoreline found themselves in a bank of reeds that grew along lakeshore. The reed-bank was thick underneath the water-line and extended several feet above the water on that part of the lake. Both men also detected a strange odor in the air, a combination of decaying organic matter and a strong musky scent they did not recognize.

Each had been well trained in every terrain but were city-born and raised far away and far in the Northeast of the U.S. They did not know that Georgia was the home of the Okefenokee Swamp, a 350,000 acre swamp so thick with alligators one could almost cross its streams by walking across their backs. That swamp was far south of the small lake they were in, but despite the best efforts of wildlife managers, some of those gators had migrated northward.

Those agents also had no idea that a few of these gators had settled in that particular lake and had grown long and huge feeding on the local wildlife, pets and table scraps thrown out by lakeside dwellers.

The agents probably did know the fact that humans feeding gators made the gators less afraid of people, and therefore tens times as dangerous. But they could not have known that a nine-hundred pound, fourteen foot long bull-gator lurked near them and had mated sometime back with a female of nearly the same size, and that she had nested in those same reeds and laid her eggs, covering them with decaying reeds to keep them warm.

And so it was really no fault of his own when one member of the strike team crept through those reeds on that dark and cloudy night with his M-4 rifle, a shorter and lighter version of the M-16, held high to keep it out of the water, and was almost on top of the mama-gator before he ever saw her two huge eyes, crimson-red against the blackness of the water .

Neither was it the mama-gator's fault when, sensing a threat to her nested young, she bore without hesitation into the terrified agent, her huge, vice-like jaws engulfing and clamping down on his head, popping his skull like a brain-ripe melon. His finger instinctively pulled against his rifle's trigger, but he had kept the safety switch on and the trigger did not engage. His horrified yelp had mostly smothered itself in the gullet of the female, but enough sound escaped to reach the ears of another agent not far away in what seemed in the darkness a sea of reeds.

Hearing the muffled yelp and the splashing of a brief struggle made that agent flip the safety switch of his M-4 to the 'off' position.

But the bull-gator, the male, had been floating close by just off-shore, and had felt the vibrations of his mate's attack, and the reptile's massive tail had propelled his pound bulk with frightening speed through the water and into the first threat he sensed.

The jaws of the bull were even stronger than that of the female and the man's ribcage could not resist the compression, nor could his sternum stop the penetration of three inch incisors as they pierced to his heart. He screamed and pulled the trigger of his weapon just before the gator death-rolled him under the water. His safety switch was 'off,' so the gun did fire, though it would have been better for his friends if he had died in silence. He was close enough to Cummins' house that, with his wasted shots, he alerted the target. The element of surprise had just evaporated.

Cummins and his men heard the shots that told them the attack had started and that at least one prong of it was coming from the shoreline. Since the Governor had only four men with him, this would prove to be a key piece of information. And the battle would turn on that very fact.

The four remaining members of strike team B that had also exited the raft recognized the gunshots as made by their team weapon, the M-4. The two members that had stayed on the raft were just as confused as the rest. Who had fired their weapon and why? Now the whole mission was in jeopardy and everyone knew it, stealth having been the very key to success.

But the leader of strike team A had command-control and no one could raise him on the radio and no one knew he was already dead at the bottom of the lake on account of the wreck with Billy Joe's wooden boat. The leader of strike team B was second in command, but he was one of the men in the reeds and the bull gator had already propelled the dead body fifty yards along the shore to stuff it under a sunken log for a later feeding.

Leaderless now, there was but two things for the remaining members of strike team B to do: proceed with the raid or abort immediately. The two agents on the raft quickly conferred. They concluded that since the exact location of strike team A was now unknown, added to the fact that shots had been fired that would have alerted the target, the only professional decision was to abort. The target had yet to fire upon them, which gave them an 'out.'

The ranking officer aboard the raft, a Lieutenant, touched his mic switch and gave the order to abort, repeating it several times. The shooters in the water heard the command in their earpieces, their radios seemingly the only thing working right that night.

Each man in the water had to now turn and wade back through nearly chest-deep water to the raft, but the raft had not anchored and had drifted in the night breeze and the shooters were not sure where to find it. They had no choice but to break radio silence.

"Who fired theose shots? I can not see the raft, where are you team leader?" Still in the water but with no mission to complete, these shooters would be sitting ducks, at the mercy of the target if he should happen to spot them and mean them harm. The Lieutenant in the raft had no choice but to dig out an emergency handheld flare for the others to see.

"Come to the flare. I repeat, come to the flare," the Lieutenant commanded into his mouthpiece. Popping the end off the flare, he held the sparkler high for his men to see. It was all he knew to do, but it was also the worst, and last, mistake of his young career.

On the shoreline one of Governor Cummins' men suddenly stepped out from behind some cover, a tubular shaped weapon perched on his shoulder and aimed at the flare-lit raft. The rear end of the shoulder mounted weapon belted fire and smoke as a projectile exploded from its front end, trailing a plume of blue smoke as it sped towards the raft. The men on the raft saw the weapon fire but had no time to react because it took only one second for the projectile to cross the water and slam into the raft. The projectile was an incendiary round and the resulting explosion turned the raft into a fiery hell of shrapnel and death.

Both the Lieutenant and his comrade were blown to bloody rags of scorched flesh and charred bone. The raft was punctured and ripped, and quickly took on enough water to sink it to the bottom.

Just before that rocket propelled grenade had been fired from the shoreline, the four NSA shooters still alive in the water had turned and started to wade back to the flare-lit raft. They had watched in disbelief as the grenade zoomed a trail over their heads and towards the raft. *It was not supposed to go like this.*

The agents had then turned to face the shoreline in order to return fire, but by that time the man who fired the RPG was gone from sight.

Now those men were in a terrible position, standing in near chest-deep water, with a capable, well armed and hostile enemy on land close by, and their rescue raft on the lake bottom. There was still no answer from the other NSA strike team. Nothing was left for them to do now but try to make it to the shore alive.

The four began to struggle through the water but found that the lake bottom was thick with soft clay as they neared the shore, creating a powerful suction around their boots. This made any movement very difficult and quick movement impossible.

As they struggled shoreward, one of them saw a figure moving across the yard. He pointed his M-4 at the figure, and before one of his fellow agents could stop him, he let off two three-round bursts of fire.

This was another serious error, for no soldier struggling in open water with zero cover wants to draw fire from an enemy, but that is precisely what he had accomplished.

The fishing dock was only thirty yards away from the four men, who now compounded their error by beginning to cluster together as a group as they struggled for the lakeshore.

The security light cast its glow on the boardwalk dock itself, but it had been a dry year and the low water level of the lake created a three-foot space between the water level and the dock's boardwalk. That space was completely hidden in shadow, but the agent who had just fired his rifle now caught a glimpse of a shotgun barrel emerge from the darkness under the dock. The agent pulled the muzzle of his M-4 quickly around, but the shotgun was already vomiting fire and hot lead in his direction.

The first round that smacked into him was double-ought buckshot; twelve steel balls, each .25 inches in diameter, flying toward him in an expanding formation at a speed of 1225 feet per second. Four of the balls pierced his neck and throat, and they alone did enough damage to kill him, but the other eight hit him in the chest and shoulders as well. The trauma plate of his protective vest, a quarter-inch thick plate of steel mounted over the heart area, stopped three of the steel balls, but the others all penetrated flesh, ripping nasty tissue cavities through skin, blood vessels, muscle and bone.

That agent was not dead before he hit the water, but the pain was such that he was hating his life all the same. The second round that hit him just before he went under was a Remington Buckhammer slug shot; one large solid, spinning chunk of lead, .73 inches in diameter, moving at a much faster rate of speed than the buckshot. The slug met the man center-torso, slamming into him with a sickening thud heard clearly by his three fellow agents. The Buckhammer slug entered and took a downward path, fairly gutting the agent and punched him down into the miry clay of the lake bottom.

The agent nearest him tried to move towards his teammate to offer aide, though it would be of no use to the buck-shot man. The other two shooters opened fire at the space underneath the dock. They saw sparks flying in the darkness underneath the dock and at first thought it was muzzle blast as someone returned fire. But then they recognized the sound of their .223 rounds pounding against metal, as if someone were hammering on a metal drum.

They then realized that the man with the shotgun under the dock had some type of iron-plated hide mounted there and the sparks they were seeing were made by their own bullets striking the metal. It seemed that the Governor had planned for this assault at least as well as the NSA had. And now the advantage belonged to Cummins.

At the dirt road on the other side of the lake house, the FBI strike team had been waiting anxiously to get in on the action. The NSA-designed mission plan had called for them to wait until the house was breached before they rolled through the gate and to the target. The FBI had no idea that one of the rafts had collided with young Billy Joe's fishing boat, nor could they imagine that two NSA shooters had been half devoured by gators.

A simmering bitterness over the President's decision to give the NSA the lead on the mission had caused them to sit on their haunches for longer than they normally would have, but when they saw the first RPG light up the night, they knew it was on.

Sixteen S.W.A.T. grade agents, mounted in four armored Humvee's, cranked up and tore out towards the security gate blocking the Cummins' property access road. The lead vehicle was a 'rammer' and had extra steel plating mounted to the front of its chassis, frame-welded, in order to burst through the gate.

But Cummins had planned, and before that ram-vehicle ever made it to the gate, an RPG launched from somewhere behind the gate slammed into the front windshield of the Hummer. The explosion carried all the windshield glass back into the seating area along with hundreds of pieces of steel shrapnel. The driver and the agent in the passenger seat were killed instantly, half decapitated by the force of the exploding grenade. The other four men in the vehicle were all hit multiple times by glass and shrapnel. Those four would survive but were now out of the game.

Their Hummer swerved hard into the ditch running alongside the dirt road, jumping it and smashing into a thick Georgia pine. The Hummer first ignited, and then the pine, as the wounded men helped one another escape the death trap.

The three trailing Hummer's all came to an abrupt halt when the lead vehicle was attacked. The shooters quickly jumped out and sought cover from which to return fire. As they did, three more RPG's zoomed over their heads and into their vehicles.

One of the agents was a former Army Ranger who had served in Somalia during the infamous 'Black Hawk Down' incident which took place when Bill Clinton was in the White House. That agent had been in Mogadishu that awful day when his Ranger squad had been torn to ribbons in the streets of that foreign capital, when a savage mob armed with A.K. 47's and RPG's trapped the soldiers in the city where they could fire at the soldiers like fish in a barrel. Now, that former Ranger could not believe he was experiencing something similar to that within the once-safe confines of his own country.

The Bureau agents looked for specific targets to fire at, but the Governor's friends must have prepared their hides well, for no ready target presented itself and the dark night was lit only by the burning vehicles. They would have fired on the lake house itself, but a bend in the road ahead coupled with the surrounding woods and tall brush served to cover the house from view.

The agents knew they were pinned down. They also knew that if the Governor had more men he could bring up, the fight was going to be fierce.

Cursing the NSA for trying to use the mercenary BlackSky shooters as backup, a backup that had failed to even show, seemed pointless now but they cursed them anyway. There was no way to know if the Governor already had men in the surrounding woods for an ambush. If so, the agents knew that none of them would survive. They now had wounded men to care for and all their vehicles were on fire. When the fire reached the gas tanks, more explosions could be expected not forty feet from where they had taken cover in the ditches and at the edge of the woods.

The FBI team leader was still alive and spoke into his radio mic, trying to call his Director, Rodney Bound, to ask for more shooters as well as medical attention for the wounded. How, he wondered, could an attempt to serve an arrest warrant become a war zone within minutes? And how could the U.S. Government find itself on the losing end of an engagement within its own borders? Was this a sign of things to come in America? He certainly hoped not.

Jim Cummins had not yet exited the lake house. This Governor held a Benelli 12-Gague pump shotgun in his hands. Over his back was slung a Browning Automatic Riffle with a full forty-round clip loaded alternately with .30-06 hollow-point and ballistic penetrating rounds. Extra clips were stuffed in the leg pockets of his tactical pants. Two bandoliers full of 12-gague loads were wrapped criss-cross around his chest, and underneath all that he wore a Modgear Black Armor Vest loaded with armor plates.

The guns had been bought from private dealers; the bandolier, ammo and vest had been purchased online by the Governor from gandermountain.com. About his head was a headset equipped with microphone and earpiece. Cummins and his friends could communicate and had been prepared, though it was the two gators that had actually given them a chance in this fight.

When the first shots had been fired near the shoreline, Cummins was looking out one of his rear windows at the access road. He had hurried to the other side of the greatroom to peer out of a front window facing the lake. Watching intensely, he expected full scale assault which he knew he might not live through.

Cummins' was fully aware that he could not survive against the heavy hand of federal power. Many of his die-hard supporters talked big, but were not ready to shed blood for the man. They were the kind that would wait to see how the fight was going before they joined. But he was in it now and could not turn back. He wanted only loyal men alongside him, whether in life or death.

That is why he had only four other men with him, yet they were four that he could count on. Initially, he had two stationed near the access road to watch the gate, and two stationed near the shoreline, including the man under the dock, to keep watch there.

Their orders were to fire only when fired upon, or when unauthorized, armed persons crossed onto the Governor's property. Besides the shotguns, three of the men were armed with RPG's.

The first RPG to hit the raft, the Governor would later learn, was fired when the man armed with it saw the flare being set off on the raft. That flare he had mistaken for muzzle blast, and believing his friends were taking fire caused him to cap off a flying grenade at the raft. It was a mistake, but one caused by the NSA and there was no way to take it back now. Yet it was that mistake, along with the gator attacks, that had given the Governor the advantage.

The federal agents in the reeds had actually fired first, and that might be an 'out' the Governor would need later. The fog of war, indeed, clouded things on all sides.

When the raft was hit, Cummins had been watching. He saw no other rafts or flares and knew that any attackers who remained in the water alive would have no choice but to try to make it to shore. He hoped they would throw down their weapons and surrender, and live, but doubted that they would. The situation was too charged with pride and emotion to admit of such compromise or surrender.

This fight might well become a fight to the death, until all on one side or the other, or both, were dead. Turning his attention back to the access road to the rear of the house, Cummins made it to the rear window in time to see one of his men set loose an RPG. He heard the resulting explosion, but could not tell exactly what happened because the woods also obscured his view of the access road. His man transmitted over the radio that a Hummer had been hit and was burning, and that three more vehicles were behind it.

"Burn them all," was the Governor's order in reply. It was on, and there was no need to hold back now. Cummins felt justified now in taking the fight to those who would make themselves his enemy.

How dare they try to bring fire and death into a man's home! For all the feds knew his wife and children were in the house with him. That callous disregard for his family hardened the Governor and suddenly he wanted to rush from the house and kill them all, every agent arrayed against him in this unholy raid. But instead he took a deep breath and repeated to himself a proverb that had kept him level headed in the past: 'Moderation in all things.'

Though he could not let himself become an animal, Cummins still knew he had to, as a matter of principle, defend his life and property. If he could do that with no additional loss of life, he would be satisfied with the night's work. The feds had obviously failed in their first attempt to take him, so they already had a bloody nose. Now it was time to make them slink away with their tails tucked between their legs.

There in his lake house, Governor Cummins came to a decision. He reached for a bullhorn he had kept handy and ducked out of a side door. The Governor ran in a crouched position, staying low, towards the lake. He found cover near the shoreline beside one of his men, the one who had taken the raft out with the RPG.

"How many of those flying grenades you got left?" he asked.

"Got four more Jim, including the one locked and loaded."

"O.K. How many shooters left in the water?"

"We count three left alive."

"Alright, I'm gonna give'em one chance and one only to surrender. If they surrender, we let'em up easy. If they refuse, I want all three floating. Understand?"

"Yea, I got it," said the man, glad that *he* wasn't one of Jim Cummins' enemies. The Governor cupped his hands around the mouth of the bullhorn for more sound projection.

"Agents of the NSA; this is Governor Jim Cummins of the Sovereign State of Georgia. Throw down your weapons and you will be spared. You will live to return unharmed to your families and homes. This raid is over, and there is no need to waste your life here. You have ten seconds to throw down your weapons and come out. You will not be mistreated."

In the water, the three remaining agents had crouched as low as they could, still trying to keep their weapons dry. Two of the agents heard the wisdom of Governor Cummins' words. They both had families to go home to and for whatever reason, they believed the man with the bullhorn was telling them the truth. Besides, the Governor was holding all the cards it seemed. Apparently they could not count on the FBI raiding party for help.

But the third NSA shooter thought differently. He had no one at home, and had no inclination to listen to reason. He had just watched his friend get his throat ripped apart by buckshot, and now would demand a blood payment in return.

"Go to hell you scum!" he yelled and opened fie in the direction from which the Governor's voice had boomed. His two teammates were tempted to shoot him down, for they knew he had sealed their doom with his recklessness. Trying to live, they struggled now against the muck sucking at their boots, but the shot-gunner under the dock opened up on them again, sending buckshot and slugs flying towards the three targets in the water. Cummins opened up with his shotgun as well.

The three agents would have done better to stay still, for every time they moved, the water about them splashed, catching what light there was, giving away their exact positions in the water.

The distance was too close to miss with a 12-gague. One man fell spinning bloody, his arm nearly severed at the shoulder by a slug. One took a load to the head and was dead before his face hit water. The last agent threw away his gun and vest and tried to swim out of the kill zone, but as he did buckshot raked across his back, turning him over, and he floated for a moment in that position, face up-looking blank-eyed into the cloudy night sky before sinking.

That finished off the visible threat from the lake, and there would be likely be no more trouble from off the water tonight, the Governor judged. He left one man under the dock just to be sure.

Cummins and his man with the RPG now turned and ran towards the other side of the property where the Hummer had exploded on the access road. Having used all their grenades, Cummins' two men stationed there were now in a firefight with what remained of the FBI team.

Cummins' men were firing A.K. 47 assault rifles, trading rounds with the feds who were firing back with M-4s and M-16s. The M-16's were equipped with under-mounted grenade launchers and had dropped several explosive projectiles dangerously close, but thankfully for Cummins, his men had yet to take a direct hit and their prepared hides were hardened against such ordinance.

"Kevin," said the Governor to the man he brought with him from the lakeside, "see if you can work your way into those woods to our right to get a shot at their position with your RPG. I'll go the other way and try to flank from that direction."

"Yes sir, Governor," said the man enthusiastically, sensing a complete route was at hand. And a complete route was indeed now within the Governor's grasp. If he could get a man in position to flank the FBI strike team with the RPG, it would be over in minutes. Up to this point, Cummins thought all the attackers were from the NSA, but then one of his men gave him some new information.

"Jim, I saw one of those guys running for cover. He had a jacket on that said 'FBI' on the back. I don't know who the guys on the lake were, but these may not be NSA spooks we're facing now."

Cummins was bothered by this information. He had no respect for the shadowy, spooky NSA that to him had become little more than professional eavesdroppers who hated their own people enough to spy on them. It was like something out of Orwell's *1984*. The NSA had long been involved in monitoring telephone and cyberspace traffic inside and outside the United States, with or without legal authority.

Though Cummins had no inhibitions in fighting off an armed attack from the NSA, the FBI was somewhat different. That organization had a proud heritage, and Cummins had old friends who were employed in its ranks. Hopefully, none of those friends were here tonight, yet he had to defend himself and his property, no matter who it was out there. There would be regrets, he reasoned, but all men die regretting something.

Cummins made his move towards the far woods, moving with a fleetness of foot that was not bad for a man in his forties. If he could get in those woods he could move up and bring flanking fire into the attackers dug in behind the burning Hummers.

Encountering no resistance in the woods, the Governor made his way through a couple hundred yards of brush and standing pine. He took up a position which concealed him behind some palmetto bushes growing atop a mound of dirt.

On one knee behind the palmettos, Cummins put down his shotgun and pulled the Browning Automatic Rifle from off his back. The BAR would serve the purpose of rousting the dug-in agents from there hides, and its .30-06 rounds would do the job from a much longer range than any shotgun scatter-load could do. Cummins had brought along his night vision goggles, which he found cumbersome, but they had come in handy when traversing the woods. He needed to get a little closer to the access road to get a clear line of sight on his target, but just before he started to move closer he heard one of his men call to him through his headset.

"Governor, we've got company. A chopper is circling over the lake and may be headed our way."

A chopper. That was bad news. A gunship overhead could be a devastating tool for the feds, and could prevent Cummins from achieving the route so close at hand. The Governor took a gun in each hand and turned to run back through the woods, backtracking over his own footsteps, until he reached the clearing where his men were. At about that time the whipping noise from the helicopters' rotors roared in their ears as the chopper swept in quickly.

Before the Governor could react, a blistering fire from a belt-fed machine gun mounted on the chopper ate into the ground all around him. Cummins heard bullets popping into the dirt and flying off the steel plates they had used to harden their hides. Hundreds of rounds of ammunition were being loosed on his position, and Cummins could do nothing but dive to the ground.

When there was a pause in the barrage, Cummins raised his head. He was not hit, but the man with him was not so lucky. He had taken two rounds to the upper torso area. One must have found his heart and killed him instantly, for he lay there eerily supine and blank in a way only the fresh-dead can lay.

This was the first Georgia man, the first Cummins' man, that would be lost in this struggle, but something told Cummins that it would be the first of many. But he had no time to ponder the loss, for the gunship now opened its second barrage. Just then, Cummins' man with the RPG emerged from the woods, his weapon perched on his shoulder as he ran. Planting his feet in a parallel stance, he pointed the weapon at the low hovering chopper and loosed ordnance in its direction.

As soon as the man had fired the grenade, the launcher dropped from his shoulder as his hands reached for his right thigh that a .223 round had just ripped through. Blood spurted from the fresh wound as the man went down clutching his leg.

Cummins looked up in time to see the flying grenade smash into the underbelly of the chopper to explode there. The chopper was bounced through the air by the force of the grenade and began to spin about, but the grenade was not potent enough to crack the bird open. As elated as he was by the direct hit, for a moment the Governor feared the chopper would crash into his house. But both the helicopter and its pilot must have been of the highest quality, for the pilot was able to somehow keep the bird airborne.

Wasting no time, Cummins ran towards the downed man. He took the man's blood covered hand, singled out one finger, and pushed it into the bullet hole, ordering the man to keep the hole plugged.

"Oh Dear Lord!" the man cried out in pain.

"No, it's only Jim Cummins, but praying is probably a good idea about now," replied the Governor. Somehow the injured man managed a grim laugh despite the fact that his leg felt like it was under a torch-flame. Cummins then pulled a fresh grenade from the injured man's backpack with his right hand while reaching for the launcher with his left. Pulling the front end of the tubular weapon around, he quickly shoved the projectile's tale-end into the launcher until he felt it click home. Throwing the weapon on his shoulder, Cummins turned to face the security gate guarding the access road.

Five agents were now either climbing the gate or had their M-16's propped on it ready to fire. The Governor burned off the

RPG round towards the gate as he heard the agents open fire on him. He dropped to the ground, rolling and crawling towards his hide. He did not see it, but heard the explosion as the RPG hit the fence and detonated.

The explosion brought the gunfire to a stop. Cummins looked up to see a smoky haze hovering over the destroyed gate, the smoke canopy being lit up by the pieces of the shattered gate that lie burning all about.

When Cummins realized that the gunship was going to re-enter the fray, he touched his mic switch on his headset and commanded his men to regroup at the lake house. His RPG strike on the gate drove the enemy back for a moment, but he knew they would come on strong again once the gunship resumed its strafe runs.

The Governor motioned for help with the wounded man. He and the other each grabbed one of the wounded man's arms, heaved the man upon his feet, and headed for the house as quickly as they could. When they got to the back door of the lake house, the man who had been stationed under the boat dock was waiting for them. He had the door opened and had his 12-gague up and ready to cover their retreat, but none of the FBI strike team emerged from the area near the still-burning gate. The door slammed behind them and was bolted with a cross-board as they got the injured man to the sofa so that they might bandage the bullet wound. As Cummins wrapped the wound he said,

"We lost a good man out there, Gerald Claymore. The chopper gun took him out, four or five rounds hit him. Gerald was a good man, faithful to the end, wasn't afraid to make a stand."

"We'll missim'," replied Reggie Carroway, the man who had been under the dock with the shotgun, "but just now we've got to get ready for the assault on this house. They'll use the gunship to keep our head's down, launch grenades through the windows, then try to gain entry. We must use our shotguns to deny entry until we can knock that chopper down."

But the feared assault did not come as they expected. In the chopper that hovered above sat FBI Director Bound himself. Bound had taken off his headset, trying to get a hold on himself and the situation. He was thinking of his old friend Jim Cummins, Governor of Georgia. In the dark he could not tell which of the men was hit by fire from his chopper. He hoped it wasn't his friend. The last thing he wanted to do was to kill Jim Cummins, yet Bound had ordered his gunner to open fire in order to protect his strike-team on the ground.

Bound cared for his friend Jim Cummins, had even broken bread with Cummins' family in their home before. But Cummins had gone way over the line with his stunt at the airport and with Air Force One. Bound despised the NSA as much as he did the spooks at the CIA. If anything, the NSA guys were even more creepy, what with their constant spying within the US, spying on US citizens who had no ties to terrorists, with little to no oversight from Congress or the courts. Turf wars had continued between the agencies, had even increased after 9-11 and the formation of the umbrella Homeland Security Mega-Agency. The additional layers of bureaucracy had only made matters worse, not better. It was nothing more than politicians trying to look competent, to do something to deflect attention away from the massive failure to protect the country on 9-11. But the posturing of politicians always got in the way of people actually doing their jobs.

Whether he respected the NSA or not wasn't the issue. Even with a federal government as corrupt and inept as this one could at times be, Director Bound believed that it was still the highest authority in the land. He knew Jim Cummins well enough to know Jim believed every bit as passionately in States' Rights as others believed in federal authority. But the supremacy of the federal government over the individual states was an issue settled already by the Civil War. And Bound was determined that he wasn't going to let even a good man like Jim Cummins use that dead issue to tear the country apart.

As for the President, Bound had not voted for him, nor did he really trust him. Yet Soloto was still the President and Cummins had to respect that office just like everyone else. These thoughts had been heavy on Bound's mind for weeks, but now, in the chopper above Cummins's lake house, watching people starting to die, such thoughts were becoming painful indeed.

"Sir," interrupted the pilot, "the strike team reports multiple dead and injured, but the survivors are game, sir. They want to finish the raid and attack the dwelling." The pilot was asking permission to give the strike team a green light on assaulting the lake house, but now that it had been confirmed that some of his men had died, Cummins realized just how badly the raid had gone.

Bound did not know how many survived from the NSA team that had come across the lake. And he did not know how many men Cummins had down there, or what kind of firepower the Governor had at his disposal. He knew it was taking great risk to order the go ahead for the final assault. Bound realized that Governor Cummins was deadly serious about defending his property, and that he would use everything he had to make his stand. When a man like Cummins felt his honour attacked, nothing but death would stop him.

Bound made his decision. Cummins would have this round, but the next time things would be different.

"Jim, what have you done?" the pilot heard Director Bound say to no one.

"Sir!" said the pilot, "Sir, what are your orders?"

"Abort."

"Sir?!" asked the pilot, not believing his ears.

"Abort, I said. Abort this raid. It's over. Tell them to high-tail-it out of there. Between Cummins and the NSA, they're going to get all of us killed!"

Chapter Sixteen

Downtown Atlanta, Georgia
New Bithynia African Baptist Church

Darrell Nudley and his brother Donley had been driving by the New Bithynia African Baptist Church in Atlanta in a rickety old pickup truck every day for a week. They wanted to be sure that they knew the layout of the buildings, and had several routes from which to escape the area. Neither of the men had finished high school; they had learned about the historic black church at their local Klan meeting.

The brothers were from a little town in middle-Georgia where a scarce job market and a white-trash childhood left idle men with little else to do but grow dope, grow bitter, and look for someone to blame for their problems. Though neither would mention it in public, both of them were jobless and, if not for the monthly welfare checks they drew, would be homeless and without cigarettes as well.

It was at the local Klan meetings that they learned to hate the memory of New Bithynia's one-time pastor and civil rights leader, the Reverend Marrion Sing, holding him personally responsible for what they considered the abomination of race-mixing in the schools and the pollution of white society some called the Civil Rights Movement.

"The spooks has brought us down, we ain't brought them up even a notch," Darrell was often heard to say. The men saw nothing extreme about their racial beliefs, it was what they were taught from childhood. Their mother had told the boys she had been raped by a black gang while assuring them that neither of them was a result of that forced union, though they felt tainted by it nonetheless. That grinding hatred, nurtured as a babe at its mother's breast, had separated the brothers from society, most of which had long-since moved on.

Their lives had gone precisely nowhere and nothing seemed to go well for the Nudley's. Once, the two brothers carried a Confederate Flag to a local Civil War reenactment. When the burley white Confederate Soldier Reenactors were marching past with their muskets in hand, the Nudleys began to shout 'kill the blacks, kill the blacks." The two of them were completely aghast when five of the Confederates turned on them, snatched the flag from their hands and beat them both bloody. It was the worst whipping the two had ever had. The Confederates did not even return the flag.

Feeling alienated, lonely and outcast, the brothers fed off one another's hate. Their only friends were their fellow haters in the Klan, so the two brothers sought to out-do the other Klansmen in anti-black atrocity. On the wall of their small living room hung a large framed photo of Timothy McVeigh.

At first, it was enough for them to just harass the occasional black pedestrian who was unlucky enough to be walking alone on the same road the Nudleys had taken on a given day. That harassment had grown steadily, finally exploding in violent attacks on lone blacks, beatings that had left several black men and women lying in blood, left for dead along a lonely strip of highway. The brothers had been picked up by the law in a couple of cases, but no charges had stuck and the brothers remained free. Yet each attack, like the next drug fix for an addict, had failed to satisfy their hate-lust.

Nudged on by their brothers-in-hate within the local Klan, the Nudleys had grown bold enough to carry out what they thought was sure to spark the thing that all virulent race-haters wanted the most, a race war.

And what better target, they thought, than the heart and soul of the civil rights movement, the place where the arch-enemy got his start, New Bithynia African Baptist Church. 'Strike at the heart,' became their rally cry. And so they had carefully planned, with the patience only true evil can acquire, the bomb they needed and the time it must be delivered and detonated to have the most effect. With hearts fueled by a mixture of ignorance, self-loathing, and bitter racial strife, the Nudley brothers began to work through the preliminary stages of building their bomb.

Though never able to hold down a regular job, the two actually worked hard, with a purpose fired by hate, preparing and pouring up the diesel fuel and ammonium nitrate. Ten 50-gallon barrels of lethal bomb-mix they prepared and loaded into the bed of a stolen florist delivery van that had a picture of flowers and a business name painted all over it. The van was just the type the two figured would not seem so out of place near a church on a Sunday morning.

The plan was to carefully load the barrels, wiring them all together along with a detonator. Affixed to the detonator was a cell phone which, when called, would set off the detonator. This was a technique which had been perfected by the Al Queada terrorist network as well as Iraqi insurgents, and the knowledge of how to rig such a device had made its way through various hate networks via the internet.

The attack was planned for a Sunday morning. The Nudley brothers planned to pull out of the driveway of the single-wide mobile home they shared no later than 8:00 A.M on the morning of the planned attack, headed for Atlanta, so that they could arrive at their target in time to catch the large Sunday crowd.

Donley would drive the stolen florist van with the bomb-load. They planned to steal the van from a local florist shop on the previous Friday night and take all day Saturday loading the bomb. Hopefully no one at the flower shop would miss the van until Monday morning, and by then it would be too late. Darrell planned to trail the florist van to Atlanta in the old pickup.

The rest of the plan was simple: claiming to have a flower delivery they would drive the bomb-laden truck right up to the steps of the targeted church at about 11:30, just when the church was full of black worshipers. The doors of the truck would be locked, the emergency brake applied, and the keys taken from the ignition.

The two then planned to get in the old pickup and drive a block away, still in view of the church, where they would then detonate the bomb via cell phone. Darrell would load a few handguns, a rifle and a shotgun into the pickup in case they were interfered with in any way.

The Nudleys planned to visit as much death and destruction on the hated 'darkies' as possible and be safely back at home by the time the smoke and dust settled over the bombsite. Their

GEORGIA BURNS

home was only two hours south of Atlanta, and so the two
believed that their plan would work. After the bombing, it
would take only minutes for the news to spread across Atlanta,
and in only an hour or so the television newscasts would spread
it all across the country. The race-riots would start
in Atlanta within hours, the two believed.

The brothers figured that whites would be targeted in the
reprisals that would follow the bombing. This would be
unfortunate, but necessary sacrifices would have to be
made. But as whites moved to defend themselves against gangs
of marauding blacks, the brushfire of racial war would be set,
and once set, the Nudleys hoped, it could not be stopped. The
violence would spread to every major city with a significant
black population, probably to smaller cities as well. And then
the Klan types would have what they had always wanted, an
opportunity at ethnic cleansing in an atmosphere so chaotic
that few Klansmen would ever be law-caught for what they did.

Though not very smart, the two brothers at least knew that
the fewer people involved in a conspiracy, the less chance of
someone leaking it to the authorities. So they agreed not to tell
any of the local Klan about the bombing, and the only other
person they shared their plan with was one who could be
trusted above all others; Dean Camper, Grand Dragon of the
Georgia Knights of the Ku Klux Klan.

The two brothers had only met Grand Dragon Camper twice
before, but they knew the man to be a certified legend among
race-haters. Dean Camper had been active in the Klan
in Georgia for over thirty years and his hate-credentials were
impeccable: twice the FBI had arrested him for the murder of
homeless blacks, and twice he had beaten the rap. It was well
known in Klan circles that Camper had been investigated in the
Atlanta Child Murders case back in 1981, an investigation that
ceased only when a black man, Wayne Williams, was charged
and convicted for *some* of the murders.

Camper had responded enthusiastically when the Nudleys
had shared their plan with him. He had even funneled
thousands of dollars to the men to buy the bomb making
materials. The Nudleys certainly could not afford it on their
relief checks from the government.

In return, Camper had asked only that the two keep him
updated on their progress with the bomb, as well as when they
planned to use it. He said that he needed to know the exact
date because he had kin living in the Atlanta area and he would
need to evacuate them before the racial firestorm hit.

The two brothers felt especially honored to be in a 'conspiracy' with such a revered leader as Camper. However, there was one clash with the law that the Camper family had purposely not publicized.

Years earlier, long before Dean Camper had risen to Grand Dragon, Camper's sixteen year old son Carroll had taken a tire tool to the head of one of the neighborhood blacks in a violent, unprovoked attack. The local authorities were going to handle it, but the FBI got wind of the case and saw an opportunity. The Bureau had already fingered the older Camper as a rising star in the Klan network, one who would be in positions of influence for years.

Now the Bureau had found a way to take away what Dean Camper loved the most, his teenaged son. Quietly but effectively, the feds came down hard on the Camper youth, charging him as an adult with attempted murder. They promised the older Camper that his son was about to be convicted and would do hard time in a super-max prison where he would be immensely popular among the large black inmates with life sentences and nothing to lose.

The older Camper was left with no good option and he folded to the pressure, agreeing to become an inside-the-Klan informer. In return, the case against his son was dropped. Ever since then Dean Camper had been in secret but regular contact with his FBI handler, feeding him information on Klan activities.

Over the years, many people in Georgia had wondered how the Klan had been kept from preying on the large concentration of poor blacks in Atlanta. The answer was Dean Camper.

The information he provided to the FBI had foiled at least eight planned murders and two major bombings. In return for such riches, the FBI went to all pains to build Camper's credentials, hence the two separate murder trials and the Atlanta Child Murders investigation, all of which were total fabrications of the Bureau, farces carried out with the cooperation of judges and prosecutors in order to build Camper's hate-resume. The Klansmen wanted a hero and the Bureau was only too happy to build them one. Dean Camper moved steadily up in the Klan leadership and would prove to be one of the most valuable informants in the history of the Bureau.

But the feds could not keep Camper under threat forever with just his son's legal problems. So they began to put cash into Camper's hands, large amounts that financed a lifestyle

Camper could never have otherwise known. Once he and his family grew accustomed to the fine-life of a two-story brick home, Cadillacs, ATVs, boats and plenty of cash to spend, Camper *really* belonged to the feds. Dean Camper was twice bought and knew it.

Of course, Camper's handler also hinted that if he stopped informing, he would be outted to the Klan as a Narc and face a certain and torturous death at the hands of his fellow Klansmen. Camper therefore had no intention of ever turning on the Bureau. At times he had even marveled that it was the FBI that had given him his greatest life-lesson in love by asking him to prove what he would risk to save his only son.

And now Camper was informing on the Nudley brothers. He forwarded every detail of the plan to his handler. The handler even asked Camper to secure and turn in receipts for the farm chemicals that the Nudleys were purchasing for the bomb. They would need those receipts to build an air-tight case against the Nudleys, they told Camper, although the Special Agent in charge of the case had no intention of the Nudleys ever seeing the inside of a court room.

If the brothers lived to talk, they and other Klansmen would eventually figure out that Camper was a mole for the Bureau. That was a chance the Special Agent was unwilling to take. After all, Dean Camper's inside information over the years had *made* careers in the Bureau. So, at some point after the arrest but before being arraigned, the Nudley brothers could be 'accidentally exposed' to the general prison population, and the black inmates would take care of the problem. A little prison riot was a small price to pay for the preservation of Camper as an asset.

Camper's FBI handler assured him that the Bureau was all over the case and had the Nudleys under close surveillance. Although the Bureau needed to allow the Nudleys time to make the bomb and actually get on the highway with it in order to nail them for terrorism, they assured Camper that the Nudleys would get nowhere near Atlanta with the bomb. Camper had no concern for the black church targeted, but the relationship with the Bureau had proven very lucrative for a man with only a sixth grade education.

As the day of the planned attack drew near, Camper began to grow nervous. The truth was, he felt that the Bureau was taking too much risk by allowing the Nudley brothers time to build the bomb and even get it on the road. His handler had assured him that once on the road, the brothers would be stopped along a lonely stretch of highway and arrested, but the agent in charge was playing his own game, keeping the FBI Director in the dark. The agent had to play it so that *he*, not the brasshats at the Hoover building in D.C., got the credit for stoping a major racial attack. He had been passed up for promotion long enough.

As for the Bureau, they would benefit by having television news cameras on hand to dramatize the biggest, most talked about bust of racial terrorists in the history of the FBI. Any talk of FBI budget cuts in Congress would be instantly quashed, regardless of the economy or National Debt. Jobs would be saved, and the agency could recover some of the ground it had lost. Later, the Director would bemoan the fact that he had not kept a tighter grip on the Dean Camper situation. Decisions were being made that he knew nothing about.

The FBI handler thought his own plan smooth, but it turned out to be a little too smooth.

While Darrell Nudley was in town to cash his welfare cheque for beer and cigarettes on the Friday before the Sunday target date, on a whim he picked up a copy of the Atlanta Journal-Constitution. Darrell was barely literate and was not a heavy reader, and certainly not a regular reader of the Atlanta paper. But thumbing through the Metro section of the paper he recognized a picture of the New Bithynia African Baptist Church. It seemed that the Church was planning a major rally for Civil Rights on the evening of Saturday, the 14th. Darrell Nudley looked at his watch. The Civil Rights event was to begin some thirty hours from that moment. Reading further, Darrell noted that the following Sunday morning there would be a short prayer service only.

It now looked to Darrell like there would be few people expected to attend the Sunday morning service, while the big crowd would come in on Saturday night for the Civil Rights rally. Arriving back at the mobile home, Darrell showed the paper to his brother Donley.

"Take a look at this," he said. Donley looked at the article, trying to make out what it said and why it was important. Finally it dawned on him that Sunday morning would be a bad time to detonate the bomb; few would be in the church building. The opportune time would obviously be Saturday evening during the rally when a large crowd was expected.

The two brothers looked at one another, realizing what must be done. Instantly they went into action, pouring up the diesel/fertilizer mix and putting the final touches on the device they would later load in the back of the florist delivery van. The plan had changed, and now the brothers planned to head out for Atlanta and their target on the very next day, on Saturday afternoon instead of Sunday morning. There was no time to waste.

In the rush, one of the brothers mentioned that someone should give Grand Dragon Camper a call to let him know of the change in plans. But Darrell thought Donley was supposed to make the call, while Donley assumed Darrell would make it. In the confusion, neither of the brothers called Camper, and their hurried preparations continued.

The easy part was stealing the florist's van. Darrell's niece worked at the local florist. She always left her keys in her purse and when Darrell dropped by the flower shop pretending to order some flowers for the funeral of a friend, he simply waited until his former niece went to fix the flowers. Spotting her purse, Darrell quickly found a set of keys in it and identified the flower shop key. He removed it from the keychain and replaced the set of keys in the purse.

Darrell had paid for the flowers with cash up front, which so shocked his former niece that she never suspected the bum had been in her purse. Later, the store owner came in and gave her the rest of the day off, saying that he would lock up the shop. So the girl did not notice her shop key was missing until later when the FBI had traced the van back to the flower shop.

Having secured the large van, the two men worked silently and steadily to get everything loaded into the back. Several hours later they had everything loaded and ready. They would drive the next day towards Atlanta and into the Klan hall of heroes.

Following a restless night in which the two men fought off the last faint resistance of their consciences, they rose, dressed and chain-smoked cigarettes until the early afternoon. They then cranked up the two trucks. Donley pulled out first in the big van, with Darrell following closely behind in the old pickup.

It was at this point that the FBI surveillance broke down. The surveillance team was watching the dirt road that led to and from the Nudley's mobile home site. But the brothers had inexplicably taken a different route to the highway, a two-path logging road that cut through the woods behind their mobile home. They had never taken that route before, and the surveillance team didn't even realize the two had gone.

Soon enough the two trucks were running North up I-75 headed towards Atlanta, having slipped passed the FBI without even realizing they had been under surveillance.

The two were nervous and time passed quickly as their trek of hate took them up the Interstate, off which they could exit within a few blocks of the historic church. But as they neared that exit, the Nudley's two trucks passed an unmarked car, traveling on the Interstate but in the opposite direction heading South, in which two junior FBI agents were riding. Those agents were actually heading south to join the team that would apprehend the Nudleys before they could set off any explosives.

But the FBI was still under the impression that the terror-bombing was being planned for Sunday morning, and it was only Saturday afternoon. The Nudleys had failed to let Camper know of the change in plans, therefore the informant was left just as much in the dark as the Bureau. The Bureau had over-relied on Camper's heretofore flawless information.

There had been a team assigned to watch the Nudleys home so that, if the Nudleys moved sooner rather than later, the Bureau would not be caught off guard. Unfortunately for the Bureau, that watch-team had failed to detect the Nudley's movement through the woods and had let the men escape undetected. And that was a mistake that would haunt the FBI for decades.

Even though the Bureau had dropped the ball in letting the Nudley's leave town unnoticed, the FBI had now been given a reprieve, another opportunity to intercept and foil the plans of the would-be killers. The alert junior agents, recognizing the Nudley's vehicles from surveillance photos, suddenly realized that their 'mark' had come to Atlanta early. There was now a weapon of mass destruction loose in the city of Atlanta.

Rushing to the next off-ramp while calling for reinforcements, the agent driving made the exit and was turning onto the ramp that would allow them to get back on I-75 heading North, to try to catch the Nudley's from behind. There was no time to lose and the agents realized that even if they could catch up to the bomb-van, they would likely have to ram the van with their car in order to keep it from getting near the targeted church. It was at that moment when the agent in the passenger seat reached into the back seat for his pump shotgun. He had to be ready to attack the bomb-van at the earliest possible moment, so he went ahead and worked the gun's action, pumping a shell into the firing chamber. The agent forgot that with pump shotguns, sometimes just working the pump action is enough to set off the firing pin. When the firing pin struck the shell in the gun's chamber, a violent mixture of fire, smoke, lead and noise erupted from the barrel of the gun.

When it went off, the muzzle of the shotgun had been pointing across the face of the agent driving the car. The shot flew over the driver's arms which were holding the wheel, and blew out the driver's side window. The shock of having a 12-gauge shotgun blast-off so near one's head caused the driver to jerk the wheel of the car. The car swerved down the off-ramp out of control, its momentum jerking it about as if it were a toy. The driver jerked the wheel again, trying to correct the vehicle, but this only added to the problem. The car's tires left the pavement as the vehicle went airborne, turning cartwheels as it picked up speed tumbling down the cement off-ramp.

The thoroughly demolished car finally came to rest at the bottom of the off-ramp, but the passing motorists saw no movement from the two men inside the vehicle.

Before the blast, the two agents had made the call for other agents to converge on the Nudley vehicles. That backup included a Bureau helicopter gunship that had been assigned fly-over duty over Atlanta for just such a contingency. As soon as the pilot received the call he had made for the target area, but as he arrived, what the pilot and gunners saw filled their guts with nausea.

There, pulled right up to the front steps of the church, was a big van with a floral scene painted across it. Hovering over the scene, the pilot and other agents aboard the chopper saw that several men, probably church parking lot attendants, were mulling about the van trying to figure out why it was parked and locked down in front of the church.

"Oh no," said the chopper pilot into his radio mouthpiece, "the mark has already locked the vehicle down. EVERYONE LOOK AROUND FOR THE OTHER TRUCK! FIND IT NOW!" As he shouted these orders into his mouthpiece, the pilot dropped his chopper lower, hovering even closer to the church building and the parked van, hoping to get a line of sight on the Nudley brothers' pickup. It was at that moment that one of the agents aboard, holding a pair of binoculars to his face, yelled out.

"There, one block to the east," the agent yelled as he pointed his finger. The gunner then shouted to the pilot,

"Turn the chopper clockwise. Pull me around to the east for line-of-fire." With perfect precision the pilot pivoted the chopper so that the gunner now had a direct line-of-fire on the Nudley's old pickup. As soon as the pickup came into his fire-field, the gunner compressed the trigger as his .50 caliber machine gun belched and rattled bullets and tracer rounds toward the target. Within seconds the rickety old truck was punctured and pounded with huge chunks of lead that tore the vehicle, along with the Nudley's, to shreds.

But it was the bloody finger of Darrell Nudley, in its last earthly act, that mashed the 'send' button on his the cell-phone. In the back of the flower delivery van, a ring tone sounded briefly. The cell-phone set off an electronic pulse that in turn set off a blasting cap. The hundreds of gallons of bomb mix ignited. The Bureau chopper had no time to move out of harm's way and, hovering over the van they felt a uprushing wave of hot gas move through their aircraft but felt nothing more as they and their chopper disintegrated under the pressure of the blast and heat.

The blast wave attacked the front of the church edifice, obliterating it, sending brick and mortar flying as shrapnel into the sanctuary behind it. The entire front half of the sanctuary collapsed as the supporting columns and walls were blown away. Screams and cries for help echoed across the neighborhood.

Four hours later, Dean Camper sat on the comfortable leather sofa in his living room, watching dumbfounded as ROX News reported the bombing of the church in Atlanta. News cameras were kept several hundred yards from the scene but were still able to capture footage of the carnage.

The whole church complex was surrounded by fire trucks which pumped long streams of water into the still smoking ruin. A huge crowd had already gathered, some of them folks from the neighborhood whose windows were shattered as the truck bomb was set off.

Women were crying, kids were running, and men stomped angrily though the dark water now running along the street gutters.

The next morning, the television news channels continued their round-the-clock coverage of the bombing. Camper sat on his sofa, his wife now beside him, as they watched the coverage. The two of them and their adult son were the only ones in the house.

Camper's wife had known for years that her husband was an informant for the FBI, though he never shared with her all the information he forwarded to the Bureau. But as they sat together on their sofa, Camper explained to her the fact that he had known of the plan to bomb the historic black church in Atlanta. Although his wife had at one time shared her husbands' racial prejudices, both she and Camper had, over the years, felt their hatred cool towards other races of people. Slowly, their hate had melted to an almost bored indifference, helped along by the moneyed-life provided by the Bureau. The Camper's found that the rich-life gave them less to be bitter about.

Judy Camper also knew that the game her husband played was a dangerous one, akin to taking a rattlesnake in your arms.

She was from the hills of Tennessee and had, as a child, watched her own preacher-grandfather 'take up the serpent' in a little clapboard-sided hillbilly church. She remembered watching from a church pew in suspended horror as the white haired old man, the same old man who often crept into her bedroom on very cold nights to have his way with her, pulled the snakes from a wooden box. The creaky rusted hinges on the snake-box made the same creak that her bedroom door-hinges made when the old man would make his night-visits.

There, before the congregation, he would pick up the big rattlers and wave them around as he danced about the pulpit spouting gibberish words as bubbling streams of thick white foam run from the side-creases of his mouth.

It was not long after that she had met her future husband Dean. And it was on her thirteenth birthday that Dean asked her to run away and marry him, and that was the same day she had, in a child-like effort of full disclosure, confided in Dean that her only carnal dealings with a man were the unwanted ones her grandfather-preacher had forced upon her on those awful hill-country winter nights.

Even at thirteen and in-love, Judy knew that Dean had enough meanness in him to hurt folks, though she never intended for him to hurt her grandfather. Still, she felt a pang of guilt when, just before they ran away together, Dean had taken her grandfather by the throat, drug him to the nearby cemetery and threw the old man into a wooden coffin where the old preacher's collection of some twenty Diamondbacks were already waiting. Dean made Judy wait in his truck as he drove the twelve penny nails through the coffin's pine lid, muffling the cries of the old man.

Dean and Judy were long gone when searchers had found the coffin, the body within so swelled with snake venom that it threatened to pop the nailed lid back off the coffin. It appeared that the old man's faith had failed him.

Judy forgave Dean, knowing he was pushed to do it only when, having confronted the old preacher about his abuse of the girl, the old man claimed the visits were just to 'pray with a misguided gurl-child.'

And now, on the sofa watching the unfolding carnage, neither of them took any special joy in what had been done. The camera also showed the nearby burnt-out blackened shell of a pickup truck. The reporters on the scene could only speculate as to what part the old pickup containing two charred bodies had played in the horrible drama, but Dean Camper knew exactly. His wife wondered out loud that, if her husband had informed the FBI ahead of time, then why had the bombing been allowed to take place?

"I still don't know how the feds could have messed this thing up. I gave them the Nudley's on a cake-platter."

"But did you not say the bombing was planned for today, on Sunday-meetin' day? Why did it happen yesterday, on a Saturday?"

"Don't matter none which day it happened. The Bureau was supposed to watch them two at all times. Something reeks to high heaven 'bout this whole thing." Dean sat quietly, thinking it through. In a moment he said, "A couple thoughts do come to mind; one is that the feds might have let the bombing take place on purpose for some political reason, but that seems far-fetched. The other is that the Bureau got caught off guard by the Nudley brothers goin' ahead with their plan a day earlier than they had told me about. Either way, somebody is gonna take a big fall for this one."

His wife started to say something but Camper held up a hand, asking for silence. He heard the sound of a vehicle pulling up in front of their house. From his seat on the sofa Camper looked out the living room window to see a man dressed in a brown uniform getting out of a UPS delivery truck, a large box in his arms. A second man dressed identically to the first also stepped out of the truck, also holding a box, but Camper found it odd that the second man's arms were covered with tattoos.

"UPS truck?" he said to his wife.

"On a Sunday? They never run on Sunday before," replied Judy Camper. The two delivery men were almost at his front steps before it occurred to Dean Camper that, since the Nudley brothers were both dead, he was the only man outside the Bureau who could prove that the feds had prior knowledge of the black church bombing--a church bombing that had, for whatever reason, been allowed to take place.

Judy Camper had already got up to answer the door. She had ordered new draperies and was excited about opening the package.

As Judy put her hand on the dead-bolt to unlock the door, her husband, still seated on the sofa, began to push against the hardwood floor with his bare feet, forcing the sofa to slide backwards across the floor.

Dean then stomped hard, straight down on one of the floor boards that had been covered by the sofa. As he stomped down on the board, a metallic click sounded and the spring-loaded floor board sprang upward and was kicked to one side, revealing a hollow in the floor. Camper was instantly on one knee, reaching into the hollow to pull out a long gun that had a rounded ammunition drum attached to its underside. Just before she opened the door Judy Camper looked back to see her husband charging at full speed towards her with a Thompson Machine Gun held at chest level.

"MOVE!" he shouted, but his wife had already darted out of the way and was running into the kitchen when she heard the .45 caliber rounds of the Thompson explode from the muzzle in a quick burst of fire.

Camper spread his first volley across the door and window area. The hollow pointed rounds tore through the oak door and the glass of the window, their deadly mushroom shapes having already opened as they penetrated the brown uniforms. The two men yelped cursing in pain as the bullets tore large chunks of flesh and bone from their bodies. The one who had been standing in front of the window was now writhing in his own pooling blood at the edge of the porch. The slugs had taken him low, and both his legs were nearly cut from his torso by the Thompson.

His partner had been standing directly in front of the door when Camper had fired, and the force of the four slugs that hit him in the chest had sent him across the porch and back down the brick steps. He lay their on his back looking into the cloudless sky, his two heels propped up on the bottom step. He had dropped the package he was holding and now busied his hands in a vain attempt to push his large intestines back into the dark tear from which they were oozing.

Tommy Davis

Dean Camper kicked open what was left of his front door and looked out. A Thompson Machine Gun is no easy gun to master, and Camper was rightly proud of his handling of it. Both men in brown uniforms lay supine, the light of life already fleeing from their eyes. From his stance their in his front doorway Dean saw that both men had had automatic weapons strapped behind their backs, but he had never given them a chance to use them.

But Camper's pride was short lived, for the blast of yet another weapon, this one a 12-Gauge hotgun loaded with buckshot, reminded Dean Camper of just how desperate someone at the FBI was to keep their job. The buckshot pellets ripped into Camper's back and ribcage, blowing him off his feet and across the porch, face first. He tumbled down the steps and landed atop one of the assasins he had just shot with his Thompson. His spine clipped in two, Camper felt little pain but neither couldhe lift the Thompson to return fire at the third assassin, the one who had come through his back door to shoot Dean Camper from behind.

This third man, also dressed in brown uniform, was now walking through the living room towards the front door that Dean had been standing in. He had the shotgun in his hands and was in no hurry, and he laughed as he walked sadistically across the hardwood floor.

"Well, well, well...What Can Brown Do For You?" he said to himself in a sadistic tone.

As a member of a freelance hit squad sometimes used by troubled elements of the federal government, he and his team had had very little time to be briefed on the target. They had been told that only the target and his wife lived in the house. He had cut the target nearly in half with the buckshot, the wife was cowering in the kitchen and would be dealt with after he walked outside to snap a quick confirmation photo of the target.

Confirming the death of Camper, the third assassin took a few seconds to look at his two dead squad mates, whom he regarded with indifference. No real friends in this business, he thought.

But as he turned to re-enter the house and finish the job, there in the doorway stood another man, younger than the target but bearing a striking resemblance. He too held a Thompson in his hands, and Daddy had taught him how to use it. A split second before the 12 gauge could aim and fire, five .45 caliber rounds pounded into the chest-flesh of the third assassin. The rounds were so thick, dense and heavy that they punctured flesh, broke through bone and ripped organs, yet still had enough energy to punch massive exit wounds as they passed out of the body. The hitman's body flew backwards and onto the freshly mown grass of the lawn. He lay crumpled and lifeless there, as if his corpse were bereft of a skeleton.

Carroll Camper called to his mother and she came, quivering, her hands drawn to her mouth in terror. They walked over and knelt at Dean Camper's side. There they wept together for a moment, neither speaking. The young man's voice broke the silent mourning.

"Mama...Daddy loved us both, and did the best he could for us. Just now he done saved both our lives." He put his hand on his mother's trembling shoulder. "Mama, we gotta go now. We gotta leave Daddy. The gov-ment'ill give him a burial. We'll find the grave one day and visit, I swear. Now we gotta go, Mama...its what Daddy would want."

The distraught mother looked up at her son, her face a blur of eyes swelling red with hot tears. "You finish your goodbyes Mama...I'll be right around."

Carroll Camper rose from his parents' side. With the Thompson still at hand, he made his way back into the house and over to the sofa. Reaching deep into the hollow in the floor from which his father had pulled his own weapon, the younger Camper pulled out a black leather satchel and sat it on the floor. He unzipped the bag and pulled back the flaps.

Inside the bag were bundles of crisp one hundred dollar bills bound with rubber bands along with several large plastic freezer bags full of gold and silver coins. Camper dug deeper in the satchel and pulled out two more Thompson ammo drum-magazines. By their weight he could tell that the drums were fully loaded.

He quickly put the ammunition drums back into the Satchel along with the cash and coins and pulled the zipper shut. Taking the satchel in hand, the younger Camper trotted out the back door and into the garage. He walked right past a brand new Cadillac Escalade, and instead threw the satchel into a rusty old Ford pickup truck.

Judy Camper was still at her husbands' side when she felt her son's hand again on her shoulder. She kissed her husband on the forehead, rose and turned to walk to the pickup truck.

Dean Camper had told his son years before about his mother's people up in the Tennessee hills, and about the awkward leaving they had experienced forty years before. Carroll Camper had no idea if there would be any kind of welcome awaiting him and his mother in that hill-country, but he pointed the old Ford in that direction all the same. They had nowhere else to go.

The Situation Room
The White House
Washington, D.C.

Everyone stood to respectful attention as the President entered the room. They seated themselves as he took his seat at the head of the table. Soloto went right to the business at hand.

"Everyone listen closely. As you know, there has been a major racial incident—an attack--in Atlanta. A black church has been bombed, and we know it was elements of the KKK who carried out the act. As President, I must act decisively to keep the situation under control. With all the pent-up racial hostilities in this country, and especially in Georgia because of the actions of the rogue Governor down there, what we have is a real powder keg about to go off. I have therefore decided that, in order to avoid major bloodshed in this country, as well as the fact that this Governor Cummins has flaunted the laws of this land, which I believe has encouraged these racists in the KKK to bomb this black church--my decision is to order the go-ahead on an operation to take out the Governor Jim Cummins."

The room was errily silent. The President continued.

"I will have the complete cooperation of all of your respective departments. We don't know what all the fallout will be. People, we are on the verge of major chaos in this country! Desperate times call for bold measures, and I will not shrink from this task. I've also ordered the National Guard of five States in which our major cities are located to deploy under my command to deal with any racial strife caused by this bombing." Soloto paused a moment, then added, "Are there any questions?"

Several members of his cabinet and security team offered words of approval and encouragement, and the meeting ended abruptly as the President stood to walk out, then added,

"Oh, and one more thing: Hank LeBeau was rushed to the hospital about an hour ago with severe chest pains. Doctor's said he may not make it." Soloto glared at COS Brandenburg as he exited the room, hoping to see no glee in the man's face at the news of his rival's heart attack.

He had just warned them all that chaos was on the verge of a breakout in the country, but none in that room had any idea that one young man, lately 'awakened' in New York City, was about to unleash his own part of the gathering perfect storm.

Chapter Seventeen

A Residential Neighborhood
New York City

For his fourteenth birthday, Ramsi Nijeer got the thing he knew would make his life complete. His mother had lovingly wrapped the little box in silver wrapping paper, finished off with a golden bow. She thought of using a bigger box so as not to give away the size of the gift, but had decided against it.

Ramsi had been begging for an iPod for a year, ever since his last birthday. Ramsi ripped the package open, gave his parents a quick hug of thanks and ran to his computer, a trail of his friends following behind him. For the next two hours, Ramsi Nijeer and his friends surfed the net, downloading all the latest hit songs from Jay-Z, Mariah, Beyonce, Britney and the like.

His parents had emigrated from Egypt before Ramsi was born. They had not completely abandoned the Islamic faith of their native lands, but more every year the Nijeers had adopted Western ways and mores, finding these much less restrictive and more open minded. They had raised their only child Ramsi to be no different than his American friends.

They loved their son so very much, and were ever fearful that because of his Eastern heritage he might not fit in with his peers, and as a result he might be driven into some dark corner of hate-belief. His parents wanted Ramsi to *know* about his Arab and Islamic heritage, but unlike some other Arab immigrants to New York City, they did not fear Western culture.

The parents believed that in order to fit in and find success in New York, Ramsi needed to drink deeply of and come to appreciate the culture he was born into and in which he would live out his life. There would be no need for him to ever return to Egypt.

By his thirteenth birthday, Ramsi had made his high school soccer team. At sixteen, he scored a date to the Prom with one of the prettiest girls in school. His parents were so proud as they took many pictures of the happy couple, even if the girl *was* Irish.

It did not matter. The Nijeers were Americans now, not Egyptians. They were not Christians, but neither did they have a problem intermixing with the white Anglo Saxon Protestants and Catholics. They had taken note that most Americans never let religion get in the way of the things they wanted to do anyway.

Both Nijeer parents had good jobs along with a nice home in the city. The icing on the cake was that their son Ramsi seemed well adjusted and accepted by his American friends.

And so, when *the thing* began to happen to Ramsi that the Nijeers, under interrogation, would later refer to asl 'the change,' the parental couple could not for the sake of Allah figure out what they had done wrong. They tried to think back, to remember what could have triggered the change in the son they loved so much. Was it all left to blind fate anyway, as Islam had taught them?

Perhaps it began on one of the rare trips the family made to their local Mosque. The parents remembered one trip in particular, a few months before Ramsi turned seventeen. After the service was over, Ramsi's parents made their way to their car but noticed that Ramsi was not with them. They waited for ten, then fifteen minutes, and still he did not show.

His father went back into the Mosque to find his son. He found the young man sitting quietly near the feet of the Revered Imam, the leader of the Mosque, as he gave further explanation of his sermon to a small group that had stayed behind. Ramsi's father found his son's behavior strange, but when he called for Ramsi, the boy joined him without any fuss and they went home.

Nothing more was said of the matter for some weeks. But in the weeks after that incident, the parents did notice that Ramsi started bringing home books from his school library that covered the history of the Middle East and of Islam. Still, considering his heritage, this was no cause for alarm. But the *growth* that would end in so much heartache, they later realized, had by then already taken root in Ramsi's heart.

When Ramsi no longer asked for money to buy the latest C.D. or gadget, his mother did not ask why, but was actually thankful she did not have to ask her husband's permission for spending the funds. Yet it was his mother who first broached the subject of why Ramsi was making the trip to the local Mosque, even when his parents chose to stay home.

Ramsi's trips to the Mosque became more and more frequent, and by his eighteenth birthday, Ramsi was a regular at Mosque. Wondering about this, his father asked one of his own friends who had immigrated from Egypt at about the same time as he had if this was normal behavior. His friend told the Father to stop worrying, and that this was a good and positive thing and that he wished his own son showed more religious interest. Ramsi might even develop into a teacher or scholar of some sort, said the friend. *My son, a scholar*, thought Ramsi's father, and decided that that would be something to be proud of if it happened. His parents stopped worrying about Ramsi's visits to the Mosque, putting their minds to rest.

But by the time Ramsi was nineteen, his time was ripe, and the men at his local Mosque realized it, even if Ramsi's own family overlooked it. A few months earlier Ramsi had enrolled at a local community college. He would spend countless hours in the college library reading about the rise of Muhammad at Mecca and Medina, and of Islam's struggle with the Jews and Christians.

Ramsi read books about the Crusades in which, said the books, the infidel Christians slaughtered Islamic families so that they could steal the land and water of the Muslims. Ramsi read books that taught that the Jews of the early 1900's had taken Palestine by force, using terrorism and murder. He read about Irgun and the Stern Gang.

Some books taught that the Jewish Holocaust had never taken place, that it had been invented by the Zionists as a political ploy, and Ramsi wanted to believe these writers were telling the truth. Slowly, but certainly, the change had taken place. He who had so recently been a carefree, jovial American teenager who was always inviting his friends over to play video games was now a quiet, introverted, and solemn young man, so serious that he had neither time for nor interest in his old friends and their childish games.

More every day, the young man Ramsi Nijeer ceased to be Ramsi Nijeer, and took on the personage of Ramsi Jihad....a holy warrior. The leading men at his local Mosque, most of whom were ten to fifteen years his senior, had by then become Ramsi's mentors and primary peer group.

Ramsi's parents knew of these men, they seemed to be young scholars interested only in Islam, always seen with a Koran or other scholarly books in hand. Surely their son would benefit by learning from these fellows. He was a normal boy who had enjoyed a normal childhood, they had made sure of it, they had sacrificed to give it to him. Ramsi could not be radicalized, they were certain.

Perhaps, like most parents, Ramsi's mother and father chose not to look into the situation more closely, partly because they were afraid of what they might find, and partly because both of them worked sixty hours a week to provide the lifestyle they wanted for themselves and their son. It was expensive to live in New York, and life was just so busy.

Ramsi continued to grow in his 'faith.' Though he and each of his parents had their own prayer mats, while his parents' mats sat in a hallway closet gathering dust, Ramsi kept his in his bedroom or carried it with him to his classes. Each morning he would rise and in reverent silence he would unroll the mat on the floor.

The young Muslim had utilized the internet to determine the *qibla*, the precise direction that a true Muslim must face when praying, from New York City. If one's prayers were to be heard by Allah, when praying one must face the *Kaaba*, the holy of holies for Muslims located at Mecca, Saudi Arabia. Ramsi's prayers were earnest, often with tears. More and more his prayers were for the relief of his stricken Islamic brothers who suffered indignity and death in their own homelands of Palestine, Iraq and Afghanistan at the hands of the Zionists and Euro-American crusaders.

The men at the Mosque never failed to emphasis the sufferings of their kinsmen in the homelands of Arabia. At each meeting they would bring out glossy photographs of Arab bodies, adults and children, maimed and disfigured by US and Israeli bombings. The wars in Gaza and Iraq combined with the availability of such images over the internet ensured that there was no shortage of such training materials.

The parents never once suspected that the group of men that came to have the primary influence in the life of their only son was actually a home-grown Al-Queada cell who had been instructed and supplied to carry out an attack somewhere in New York City.

While other cells had been sniffed out by the FBI, this one was completely independent of those and, more importantly, was only contacted once or twice a year by the higher-ups in Al-Queada. The fewer the contacts, the fewer the chances of being intercepted and caught.

But the thing that worked to remove them farthest from suspicion, to keep them off the radar screen of the authorities, was that they were all native to American soil. Every one in the group had been born in the United States. They were all American citizens—true home grown terrorists.

Yet, in each one grew a common nerve. It was as if some vine, native only to those lives torn by the turmoil and seething hatred of the Middle East, had generated itself within each man. And feeding off one another's zeal, the vine grew within them until it strangled out all else, until all moderation was devoured. In the end, it was if they had never been anything other than Islamic Holy Warriors. Indeed, an 'American' seemed now to them something completely alien. That any of them could ever have been one, regardless of what piece of dirt they landed on when birthed, was a scandalous thought, a mere beguilement of the great Satan himself.

And they were ready, each of them, to answer the call of Allah, believing that sometimes Allah calls one to an early death. Even so, the group was shocked and even a bit suspicious when Ramsi walked into their meeting an announced that he was ready to die for the cause--a true believer. Was this young man, whose own family was often absent from Mosque for weeks at the time, somehow being used by the American snoops to infiltrate their cell?

The men questioned Ramsi for hours on end, even secretly following him around to make sure he was not a government plant. After months of watching him, the group came to the solid conclusion that Ramsi Nijeer was indeed a true believer, as true as any Palestinian youth who had taken the deadly stroll into a crowded market place in Holy Jerusalem and pulled the cord on a belt of explosives.

Yes, young Ramsi would measure up well against any of those martyrs, his mentors thought, proud of their influence upon him. He should be given the chance to prove his quality.

The target was determined, a very public setting, yet a contained space, big enough to hold much American flesh yet with enclosed walls that could catch the blast and bounce it back through the crowd: a New York City Bus.

The belt of explosives was prepared, and the day came at last. All the cell members wondered if the American spies would stop them before they could strike. The spies could listen through walls, and, they admitted begrudgingly, were very good at what they did. No, they decided, it was too late to stop them. The authorities had looked at their Mosque and their cell, and they had been written off as a threat.

Ramsi prayed for hours the night before his glorification. Yes, he was afraid, but Allah would help him strap on the belt, would strengthen his feet to mount the American bus, would surround him with glory in the midst of the throng, and when it was done, Allah would receive Ramsi Nijeer into Paradise forever! The older cell-members reminded Ramsi of this daily.

One of his mentors at the Mosque had a home nearby. It was in the basement of that home that Ramsi was fitted with the vest formed of wire and plastic explosives. Ramsi met the bomb maker on the day the bomb was strapped to his body, and he was surprised to find that it was one of the professors at the community college he attended, though Ramsi and the professor had never talked either religion or politics before that day. The bomb maker was of Arab heritage, but Ramsi had never heard from any of the other students that the professor held strong beliefs about anything. His was a very disciplined cell, Ramsi concluded with pride.

But this was Ramsi's day, the professor reminded him. After this day, New Yorkers and their fellow Americans, who already knew the names of Osama Bin Laden and Mohammad Atta, would now have the name Ramsi Nijeer emblazoned in their infidel minds. A video camera was set up to film the men outfitting Ramsi with the bomb, and to record Ramsi's last words. Though he loved his parents and had left a note in his bedroom explaining his actions to them, he did not address them on the video.

This video would go out to all Americans, though Ramsi conveniently chose not to remember that, though his parents were nominally Islamic, they considered themselves as American as anyone else in New York.

This video was for the Americans who would be watching CNN and ROX News tonight and see that the terror they were supporting against Islam in far-away lands could indeed be brought right back home and into their living rooms. 9-11 had done that, but that seemed so long ago, and its danger restricted to the elite who worked at the World Trade Center.

But to bring the terror onto a bus, a bus not unlike the bus any American might take to work or school tomorrow morning--this would bring the fear and dread down to the level of the average person.

One of the men drove Ramsi from the house near the Mosque into downtown New York, dropping him off at a bus stop on Broadway Street. The man made sure Ramsi had a few dollars for bus fair. As he put the money into his hand, he caught a glimpse of doubt in Ramsi's face. He grasped Ramsi's hand and held it firmly but kindly, looking the younger man in the eyes. His words were not harsh, but encouraging.

"Be strong, Ramsi, be strong. Show no weakness. There is no turning back now. You have committed, you have crossed over, you cannot die on the bus because you are already

dead. All men have doubts, but you will be
made *tamaam*....perfect. Now, go in the strength of
Allah. *Salam*."

"*Salam*. Peace to you, my brother," replied Ramsi, and he
got out of the car and walked towards the bus stop.

As he walked, Ramsi looked no different than any other
young man walking the streets of New York. If he could have,
he would have donned a red-checkered turban and holy shroud,
but that would only serve to draw attention, and ruin the
dream. So, dressed in American fashion, he strolled easily in
his Nike Air-Jordan sneakers and denim jeans. Concealing the
vest of explosives was a light-weight jacket. The jacket had
been borrowed from the man who drove him there. It was
several sizes too big for Ramsi, loose enough to conceal the
prize bulging underneath.

Ramsi's heart raced as he looked through the traffic and
spied City Bus #8423 easing towards the stop. Would he see
this through? All doubt vanished as he quickened his pace to
get to the bus before a rushing crowd could deny him his place.

As he joined the line of people boarding the bus, his eyes
caught the face of a lady just ahead of him. He could not help
but notice that her hand held that of her little girl. Ramsi
turned his eyes away. His mentors had explicitly warned him
not to make eye-contact with any of the passengers, or to think
of anything other than of Allah, and his people, and his cause.

Empathy for these Americans could lead only to emotional
doubt, clouding the path to Paradise. One of his handlers had
assured Ramsi that even those unbelievers who would die with
him on the bus that day were serving the cause, in their own
way. Had they not been on the bus that day, Ramsi was assured,
the desired effect would have been impossible.

He stepped up and onto the bus, making his way towards the
center. It was Friday and the bus was very crowded, and Ramsi
had to force his way between several commuters as he moved
through. He bumped into one man a little to hard, bringing a
nasty reproach from the man's mouth. Of all the things the
hateful New Yorker could think to say, he chose 'don't push me
you little sand-nigger' as his racial insult of the moment. It was,
considering the situation, an especially stupid choice of words,
though by that time it would not have changed Ramsi's mind
even if the man had been courteous. The course was set and
there was no turning back.

The angry man, pressed close to Ramsi by the tightly packed
crowd of commuters, felt an odd bulge under Ramsi's

jacket. The man watched incredulously as Ramsi peacefully lowered the zipper of his jacket and embraced the pull-cord. The angry man could now clearly see packets of explosive charges and red colored wire. Ramsi turned his face upward to the man and met the angry eyes with his own. Ramsi Nijeer smiled contentedly back at the man. All the passengers had boarded and the doors were closed tight.

The man, looking now into the glowing, ragingly peaceful dark eyes of the Jihadist Ramsi Nijeer, tried to back away and began to scream 'No...Hey...he's got a—' The words were never really heard though, not even by Ramsi who stood so close to the angry man. A time warping explosion of force and hot gas had sucked the words right out of the air before they even reached the ears of the bus driver.

Every window in the bus was shut and locked, as were its two boarding doors and one emergency door. It was inside this compact and enclosed structure, packed with human flesh, that Ramsi Nijeer unleashed the deadly chaos of the energy of C-4 Plastic.

C-4 has the detonation velocity of 18,000 miles per hour, and is 1.3 times more powerful than TNT. The professor/bomb maker had studied his craft in Gaza, and knew it well. When Ramsi pulled the lanyard, the device's battery pack released an electronic current that raced through the wires that led to blasting caps, igniting the C-4.

Ramsi had tried not to wonder what he would feel at detonation in terms of pain. He had concluded that he would feel nothing at all, and for the most part he was right. The explosion sliced him in two at the belly, pushing his torso up and away from his lower body and legs, rupturing his eardrums so immediately that he heard nothing.

His head remained intact and he might have even remained conscious for a few seconds if not for the bus's roof. At detonation, Ramsi's head had snapped back but held to the shoulders at the neck so that, face-up, his up-rushing torso forced his head to pop through the roof's thin insulation, indenting the sheet metal above it.

In the aftermath, if one had known what he was looking at, he could have looked from above, down on the now disfigured roof of the bus and could have made out the forehead-shaped bulge near the center of what had been City Bus #8423.

The angry man standing so near Ramsi was likewise severed in two by the blast. From there, the force of the blast spread so as to di-sect all those within a ten foot radius of Ramsi

Nijeer. It was this group of commuters that absorbed the brunt of the blast.

The driver of the bus, in his seat some twenty feet away was found covered in blood and brain matter, though none of it was his own. He was killed by the shock of the spreading wave of force but his skin was not severed. The shock wave had merely jelled most of his internal organs into a single mass.

The wave had rushed from Ramsi through the passengers on either side of him until it hit the metal of the bus's structure and was thrown back through the passengers to finish its destruction. Part of the blast spilt out of the windows it shattered, spraying fragments of glass into people on the sidewalks near the bus. There had been thirty-nine men, women and children aboard when Ramsi made good his pledge to be a martyr for Islam and Allah. Not one of them survived the blast.

Perhaps a few might have made it if not for the ingenious idea that the bomb maker had learned from his Palestinian teachers. Along with nails, bolts and other shrapnel he had loaded the explosive belt with, he added a heavy sprinkling of aspirin and rat poison.

The paramedics that arrived at the scene were barely able to overcome their repulsion at the type of carnage that had been seen only on the evening news reports out of the middle-east, but now was being witnessed on a downtown American street.

Even the scenes of 9-11 did not compare to this, most of that carnage being covered by debris from the collapsed World Trade Center. In fact, although they were stunningly happy with 9-11 attacks, the terrorists had been disappointed in the darkest of ways with the lack of blood-and-guts photo-ops that 9-11 had afforded.

Shock Them! Shock the Americans is what the Jihadists had preached to their followers. Nothing else would get the attention of the comfortable, spoiled Americans like the shock of ripped and dismembered bodies. It would only be images of the purest, ugliest carnage that would cause the realities of death to crawl into bed with Americans each night, that would have mothers in genuine fear for the safety of their children. In bus-bombing the Jihadists had found their *Tamaam*, perfection, the perfect medium to fulfill their darkest terrorist desires.

There in New York, in the grim and professional fulfillment of their duties, the first responders picked their way through what was left of the bus and waded through the bodies looking for one un-punctured enough to still hold life.

One veteran paramedic found a person still moving under a pile of limbs. It was the little girl that Ramsi had noticed but refused to think about as he had boarded. The girl was vaguely conscious, with a serious wound where shrapnel had ripped through the flesh of her neck and side. Her small hand still grasped that of her mother, though the woman's hand had no armed attached to it.

A spark of hope rose in the medic's mind as he found that no major artery had been severed. But no matter how hard he pressed cloth against her wounds, they would not stop bleeding. The miracle drug of aspirin worked its blood thinning wonders so consistently well that she bled out right there in his arms.

Some news reports called it a Suicide Bombing, others a Homicide Bombing. But to a terrified public watching the scenes of gore played out on an American city street, the difference in what you named it seemed less than empty semantics.

President Soloto, huddled with advisers around his desk, looked over the digital photos of the scene that were handed him within ninety minutes of the bus bombing.

To those around him, the President looked to be nearly in shock. Whatever optimism he had regained seemed to be knocked out of him, as if he had felt the concussion of the blast itself. In the days that followed, the talking heads of network and cable television analyzed the bombing from every angle. And though only the most blatant partisan had dared to blame President Soloto for allowing this to happen on American soil, that fact seemed of little comfort to him. With no major attacks on the homeland since 9-11, Soloto had hoped that the War on Terror was being won.

And now, this. His bubble burst, Soloto felt alone and helpless. He pulled himself together long enough to make a public address assuring the American public that authorities were doing everything in their control to protect them from further bombings.

He tried to put on a confident air, but most could see that this President, so fresh from re-election, was thoroughly whipped by the tragic events. Even his most bitter political enemies felt almost sorry for him as he ended his address with the obligatory "God Bless America." Well, Soloto thought to himself, on this the day of the New York City bus bombing, whatever God had done, He had not blessed America.

For days after the bombing and the short speech, Soloto kept his advisors and cabinet members out of his office as he drift into a state of despair. He had almost kicked his smoking habit but now had two fresh cartons of Marlboro's delivered. Soloto sat alone, on the floor in a corner of the Oval Office under a cloud of smoke, lighting the next cigarette with the stub of the last.

Finally, Soloto's wife convinced him to leave his office, get cleaned up and get some bed-rest. The public expected to see him taking some kind of action, she reminded him. He realized afresh how much he needed his wife, what a help she was to him, and how much she cared for him.

It was a week after the bus bombing that Soloto made another address to the nation, this one in prime time. He still looked weak, but at least spoke with some authority.

He ran down a list of the actions that he was taking to secure the country. One of those actions was to sign an Executive Order extending the federalization of National Guard troops to all 50 States so that they might be 'deployed as necessary in order to fight terror.'

His next step, he said, was to order Homeland Security and the TSA to set up check-points in all public bus terminals in the U.S., with full pat-down or body-scanners used on every bus passenger. This would require a massive expansion of the security apparatus, with required spending to support it, but in a time of terror few in congress were bold enough to challenge it, although more money would have to be borrowed to finance it in the midst of an economic collapse that grew worse by the day.

Thirdly, Soloto warned that, although all safety and security measures were being expedited with a lazar-like focus, intelligence raids conducted over the past forty-eight hours had suggested that other terrorist cells were likely present within major metropolitan areas of the country. Soloto was careful to mention one major city by name, the city of Atlanta, Georgia, as a place of special focus for Homeland Security. The President stressed that, in Atlanta, both foreign and home-grown terrorist might be at work.

Martial law had come to America.

Watching the speech from his office, Governor Cummins realized that Soloto was preparing the public for a major move in Georgia, most likely directed at the Governor himself. Soloto was, in effect, seeking to identify Cummins as a home-grown terrorist, lumping him in with the Jihadists. *Never waste a crisis*. And if Soloto could lump Cummins in with the real terrorists, he could issue the same kill-orders for both. The stakes were indeed getting high for the Governor of Georgia.

The Governor picked up his phone and dialed Wilder Fields' secure cell-phone.

"Wilder, can you meet me at my home in forty-five minutes? We need to talk."

"Thirty minutes, my boy, thirty minutes," came the reply, "I had four tires burning rubber on Georgia 400 five minutes before you even dialed."

The Governor's Mansion
Outside of Atlanta, Georgia

Cummins and his old friend Wilder Fields sat in Cummins' office at the Governor's Mansion. The two were meeting to talk over the situation and decide on their next plan of action.

No one had counted on a terrorist act in New York City. Even though this act paled in comparison to 9-11 in terms of lives lost, the media seemed determined to give as much coverage to this bus bombing as to the loss of three sky scrappers, along with thousands of citizens, on that awful September day.

Cummins and Wilder agreed that Soloto and the feds were using that event, in line with their vow to never waste a crisis, to brand the Governor and his followers as terrorists like Ramsi Nijeer, lumping the Islamist radicals with the States' Righter's. A way must be found to counter such a move by the feds, they further agreed. But how?

"Jim, this thing in New York--a real act of terror, a major event for sure. While we must pray for the families of the victims, we must also wonder just how Soloto will use this against us. They never waste a crisis, you know. Remember Oklahoma City, the Murrah building? That nutcase atheist McVeigh killed all those people like some mad bomber? Remember how Bill Clinton used that event to demonize his political opponents?"

"Yes...yes I do. Clinton tried to lump all of the right wing, including Rush and the talk-radio guys, together with McVeigh. It did not work, but he and his media surrogates tried to make that connection."

"You're right Jim, it did not work for Clinton. But you can be sure Soloto will play the same hand with this bus-bomber andyou, Jim Cummins. It's the only play he can make right now. Sure, he wants to get you for July 4th as well as for April 5th, the lake-house raid being only his first attempt. But I don't think he will move on you again until this New York thing cools down some. If he moves on you now, his opponents will say that he is focusing on the wrong event, and that he is neglecting the fight against Islamic terrorism. He knows he can't afford to risk another bus-bombing--I guarantee you he already has every available federal agent on the streets and buses of New York and other major cities, maybe L.A. and Chicago. It's happening in downtown Atlanta as we speak. He can't afford to focus any resources on you right now. Soon, perhaps, but not now."

"I follow your logic, but if we let him out-maneuver us and lump us with this nut-case in New York, he could justify hitting me sooner rather than later. We can't let him corner us...we can't let him get to Checkmate position."

"Of course we can't, but how do we show both compassion and brotherhood with the people of New York, and at the same time show-up Soloto for the socialist radical that he is?"

"I know of only one way. We've got to bust up an Islamic terrorist cell right here in Georgia."

"What? What makes you think we've even got a terrorist cell growing in this State?"

"Wilder, I don't tell you everything," said the Governor as he took a folder from his desk drawer and tossed it into his old friends' lap.

"What do we have here?"

"That," said Cummins, "is a dossier on a group known as the Moorish Nation. They are an Islamic group with possible ties to Al Quaeda and they are located in Atlanta."

Cummins let that sink in as Wilder looked down at the file and then back to the Governor.

"The Georgia Bureau of Investigation has had their eye on these cats for many months, but it is a tightly run organization and a hard nut to crack. We were able to get one guy to infiltrate the organization. He was a former Black Panther who had converted to a Freewill Baptist and was recruited by the GBI to help investigate this radical Islamic extremist group-- these Moorish Nation guys."

"Well, thanks for telling me about this sooner," said Wilder, a little piqued that Cummins had kept this information from his old friend.

"Wilder, you know a lot of this stuff is classified. It wasn't necessary to let you in on this before now. Besides, it was never relevant to our plans until this New York tragedy. The GBI was planning to bust these Moorish dudes before the end of the year anyway. But I think we might need to force an action right now." Wilder continued to survey the dossier.

"I think your plan might have merit. If these guys are up to what this file says they are up to, and we can show ample proof of it, then busting them would serve a dual purpose; getting dangerous people off the streets, and also showing that you as Governor will not wait for the feds to bumble their way to another bus bombing, this time in downtown Atlanta, Georgia. Soloto will be forced to either take your side, which he cannot do because you are now his sworn enemy, or else take the side of these Islamists, which he also can not do. He can't take the chance of looking sympathetic, not in the least, to Muslim terrorists. If he does, the entire nation will turn on him. No, he cannot take their side, and he cannot possibly take your side. He'll have to condemn these Moorish Nation guys and continue to condemn you as well. That'll be a tough fence to straddle."

"That will be a barbed-wire fence to straddle, while wearing nothing but a pair of boxer shorts," replied the Governor, enjoying the picture in his mind of Soloto in boxers sitting astride a barbed-wire fence. "And just to be sure that Soloto can't praise the police who make the arrests while at the same time condemning me, I'm going to lead this raid myself," said Cummins. But Fields looked worried.

"Jim, raiding the hated IPS in broad daylight is one thing. But this file says that these Moorish guys are armed to the teeth. There is a high probability of bloodshed here. The leader of this bunch has vowed to never be apprehended alive. And then there's the racial aspect of all this. The bus bomber in New York was of Arab decent. This Moorish group is an African American group. If something goes wrong, there will be a lot more sympathy on the left for this group as compared with the group in New York."

Wilder put down the file and looked seriously at the Governor.

"One more thing Jim, let me remind you that if something happens to you, all that we have worked for, for so long, will go up in smoke. If the Shepherd is stricken, the sheep will scatter in a hurry."

"I know Wilder, but it's a chance I'm willing to take. If I lead this raid, there is no way Soloto can condemn me, but if I sit this one out, as we just said, he will praise the 'police' and still condemn me for not being a part of it. And as far as the racial element is concerned, after what happened in New York, most Americans won't care about skin color if terrorism is involved." Wilder looked back to the dossier, realizing again that Cummins was right.

Chapter Eighteen

Compound of the Moorish Nation
Outside of Atlanta, Georgia

The Moorish Nation was an organization that grew out of the prison system of the United States. Since a disproportionate number of those incarcerated in the U.S. are black as compared with the total population, what goes on in prison can impact the black community in a disproportionate way. Black ministers in Georgia were troubled to find that much of the lyrics for 'gangster rap' come from the prison population.

It is among the black prison population that the religion of Islam had seen its fastest growth rate in America. Most of these converts are peaceful and respectful. Most prison Wardens are grateful for any influence that increases the level of peace and decreases the level of hatred and violence among the prison population.

But among the Islamic prison converts there is an element that is sympathetic to the teachings of leaders like the Jihadists who encourage all converts to Islam to conduct violence against the people of the United States in retaliation for U.S. actions in the Middle East. As these radicals are released from prison, they seek out others who have adopted similar views and beliefs.

The Moorish Nation was headed up by a man calling himself Abdul Shariq Fazaz. His given name, or what he called his 'white Christian slave name,' was Jefferson Davis. Davis was in prison for five years before he learned to read. He had dropped out of school in the ninth grade, living on the mean streets of Memphis Tennessee until arrested for a gang related double murder at age seventeen. Following his conviction, Davis found himself in a high security prison located near Atlanta.

A fellow inmate had encouraged him to learn to read in order to pass the time he had to do. He was given a Bible but disdained it because of the Televangelists. But the next book Davis was given to read was a copy of the Koran, the Islamic Holy Book. Then he found a book on liberation theology by a Muslim Imam. The book taught that dark skinned Muslims had been victimized by light skinned religions for ages and that the oppressed could never hope for deliverance until they threw off the yoke of white oppression. Any and all means, including violence and terrorism, were acceptable to Allah when one was seeking liberation.

In the course of his reading, Davis discovered that his given name was identical to that of the man who had been a slave-holder as well as the President of the Southern Confederacy. Immediately, Davis had his name changed to reflect his new belief system.

Now calling himself Fazaz, he served the balance of his time, another twenty years, studying Islam, liberation theology and putting together the organization that would become the Moorish Nation.

Upon release, Fazaz found an abandoned building on Auburn Street near downtown Atlanta. Using that building as a base of operations, Fazaz and a handful of other black Muslims, all former prisoners, began to recruit young black men off the streets of Atlanta.

Fazaz especially found success in converting those who had tried the gang-life but for whatever reason were unsuccessful at it. If a young man was making money and moving up the ladder of a criminal gang, he was next to impossible to reach, Fazaz found. But for those with no money but plenty of pent-up rage and bitterness, Fazaz and his organization seemed like a natural fit.

Christian ministries also reached out to these bitter and dangerous young men. Though these more traditional ministries had some success, many of the young men had been convinced by the Islamists that Christianity was the 'white man's religion,' and only Islam could really speak to an oppressed people with dark skin.

And, just as importantly, Fazaz and his brand of Islam taught that an apocalyptic uprising was planned by Allah, to be preceded by a campaign of Jihad, Holy War, in the name of Allah. This teaching enabled Fazaz to offer converts the strong element of revenge against oppressors that the Christian ministers, who preached forgiveness and non-violence, did not offer. Appealing to the bitterness inherent in young, poor and angry men, Fazaz saw the numbers of his Moorish Nation double every year. His brand of Islam kept the discipline of religion but added the promise of violence, a combination that proved both seductive and dangerous.

A new doctrine that Fazaz himself invented was that criminal activity such as drug dealing and prostitution was acceptable to Allah as long as the proceeds from such street business was funneled into the effort to free one's people from oppression. Therefore, Fazaz was able to justify and profit from his own special brand of Black Islam that used disciplined street troops to carry out high-profit activities that the white power structure labeled 'criminal.'

So successful was he that within ten years his group had collected enough money to purchase a three hundred acre tract of land outside of Atlanta just off Interstate 85 near Hartsfield-Jackson airport.

While Fazaz continued to use the Auburn Avenue center for recruitment, he and his followers began building a compound at the I-85 site including an 8-foot fence all the way around the property, and block buildings on the center of the property in which large quantities of guns, ammunition, flack jackets and emergency food supplies were stored.

It was this location, the Georgia Bureau of Investigation had learned through wire-taps, that would be the staging ground for terror attacks that would be launched against Downtown Atlanta. It was at this compound that the Governor and his team planned to take Fazaz down. Jim Cummins was thankful for his friends in the upper echelons of the GBI.

Cummins knew that the raid had to be carefully planned and carried out. The IPS raid was a walk in the park compared to this one. He wanted to avoid bloodshed if possible, though he knew that it was highly unlikely.

But if blood were shed, it should be the blood of the criminals and terrorists. This raid had to be hard hitting, carried out quickly and decisively, with no long and drawn-out gun battles. Cummins knew that if he got involved in a day-long, protracted gun battle, the media would converge on the compound and the whole world would watch events unfold. Then Soloto and the feds would swoop down upon the compound, using the opportunity to engage and arrest Cummins and his men, and using their supporters in the media to spin the situation for Soloto's benefit.

Each member of the raiding team would be armed with an assault rifle outfitted with a grenade launcher. Some would be armed with mortars. Cummins had well-studied the warfare doctrine made famous by Colin Powell in the Gulf War of 91: bring overwhelming force to the point of attack on any battlefield. One hundred and thirty years before that, General Nathan Bedford Forrest had taught the same doctrine, though he put it in vernacular terms: Be the first with the most.

Tommy Davis

The date for the raid on the Moorish Nation compound, 6 June, arrived with sweltering heat. A Georgia June can be a little taste of Hell: roasting heat, boiling humidity, and swarms of mosquitoes that will feast on any exposed skin. Thunderstorms can sweep in on you in minutes as the warm coastal air blowing off the Atlantic clashes with cold air rolling down from the North. These storms can spawn multiple tornadoes with almost no warning, causing the loss of more mobile homes than the best divorce attorney in Georgia.

Cummins hated to conduct the raid in the heat of the summer, but he could not wait. The planning of the raid was shrouded in secrecy, even those participating would be given only a short notice.

That notice had gone out hours before and now, in an abandoned sewing factory not far from the Moorish compound, Cummins' team was gathering gear, ammo clips and courage.

This would be no walk-about raid as at the IPS Headquarters, where nary a shot had been fired. There was sure to be killing in this one, and it was hard for the Governor not to wonder whose funeral one might be attending in a couple of days-- perhaps his own.

Someone in the raiding party had brought a bottle of whiskey, which was being passed around in secret. The men knew that Cummins and the other leaders of the posse would disapprove of the men drinking, but those men felt that part of surviving was calming one's nerves. For millennia, men have used some form of alcohol to help either blunt their fears or gather their nerves before battle, so these men were not alone in history.

This posse had trained together since Cummins' was elected and had grown into a tight unit where each man trusted the other. Although they did not yet know it, they would eventually become the core of the Governor's own personal guard that would grow to number almost five hundred men, serving and protecting Cummins for years in the struggle with Tyranny that he and his people had entered. Eventually, events would dictate that all these men would be called to leave their regular jobs and stay with and around their Governor, prepared to act as his personal protectors as well as his shock troops in raids or even pitched battles. As for now, they were not a permanent guard, but only came to the Governor's side when called upon.

Presently, the men had all their weaponry and gear squared away. Cummins had been in a small side office gathering last minute intel from sources that the GBI had developed inside the Moorish community. The men put down their gear and guns as they saw the Governor walk up, gathering them all around so he could speak to them one last time before the operation began.

"Men, the time has come for us to take down this terrorist cell." Cummins was standing near a whiteboard that had been nailed to the wall. A rough outline-drawing of the Moorish compound had been made on the board, and the Governor took a marker and began to draw arrows showing the directions from which each of three teams would enter the compound.

"This is how the raid will proceed: a small detachment of seven men will attack the front entrance gate and guardhouse of the compound with concussion grenades and incendiaries as a diversion. The Stonewall Brigade will hit the perimeter fence here," said Cummins to the squad named after the famous General, using a wooden dow rod to point out a spot on the drawing.

"The Critter Company will cut the fence at this point on the west side of the compound and enter." The Critter Company was named after another, less famous Confederate General, Nathan Bedford Forrest, whose cavalry who rode 'critters,' as horses were once referred to in the old south. "Jeb's Boys will bust through the rear gate located on the northeast corner of the property."

Jeb's Boys were not led by anyone named Jeb. They were named after another Confederate Cavalryman, J.E.B. Stewart. "Upon entry, all units will proceed towards the main building which is located here, at the approximate center of the compound. Rules of engagement are that you will not fire until fired upon. But I assure you that you will be fired upon early and often, and you will return fire immediately and with devastating impact. Use whatever firepower you must in order to penetrate this main building. We cannot afford to get pinned down out in the open. Once your team breaks through the outer fence, don't let anything stop you from reaching and breaching the main building. That building is where the fight will be won or lost." Cummins paused to let his men absorb his words of encouragement and warning.

"Gentlemen, this will likely be the most violent law enforcement confrontation you have ever participated in. These are not IPS suits we assault, but motivated and trained terrorists and gunmen. I cannot promise you that you will come out of this unscathed--or even with your life. Anyone who wishes not to participate is free to go at this time, with no hard feelings against you."

Cummins again paused to see if any of the men wanted out, but not a man moved. A few considered backing out, but the masculine pressure not to bail out was palpable in the room of motivated men, and so no one moved. The Governor smiled grimly, and then continued his address to the men.

"Gentlemen, if we don't stop these Muslim terrorists today, they will be free to carry out their plans to kill innocent people in the streets of any city in Georgia. The feds aren't going to help us, their politics won't allow it. We have no one to look to but ourselves. If the battle gets hot out there, remember, we're here for a higher purpose; to protect the people. God protect you as you move to the target."

The men were glad that their leader, Governor Cummins, was man-enough to enter the fray of battle with them, as well as to give them a good, motivating speech beforehand. They knew that these were the marks of a real leader, though a few of them did have a question about his last statement, "God protect you as you move to the target." One of the men, a deputy from a local Sheriff's office, asked a friend to explain.

"Hey, the Governor said he hopes God will protect if we move towards the target. What did he mean by that?" asked the deputy, a little concerned. But his friend looked him blankly in the eye and replied,

"Well, it means that Governor Cummins will be praying for your safety and that Providence will protect you as you attack. And if by chance you decide to turn-tale and run from the fight, then he prays that God Himself will take you out."

"Oh yea, that's what I thought he might have meant," said the deputy, concern still dancing in his eyes.

The sounds of large-block four wheel drive pickups and SUV's cranking up and pulling out echoed eerily off the block walls of the abandoned factory as each division of the posse moved to the secondary positions from which each would approach and attack the Moorish compound as the plan dictated. Every stomach was churning, every mouth pasty and dry with fear. No one knew what awaited them at the compound, and not everyone knew if their courage would hold up under the pressure of a firefight.

Several of the men in Cummins' raiding party were military veterans, having survived tours of duty in the wars in Iraq and/or Afghanistan, and had been in several close-quarter firefights. These men were warriors, having felt what it is like to have hot lead whizzing and zinging about one's head, or to feel a bullet smash hot and burning into one's flesh. It was a feeling that could not be imagined; one had to experience it for themselves. Most of the men were green though, many never even having drawn their service revolver with intention to use it. Today, theirs would be a baptism of fire.

Once each team was in place, the Governor gave the order to proceed. Cummins was in the lead vehicle of the team that would breach the front gate. Six other men were with him in a white Ford Excursion that the Governor had modified for military use, welding plates of steel and bullet-resistant glass at various points to protect the engine as well as the passengers. On the front of the vehicle, a ramming device had been welded to the frame. A large radio antenna was mounted atop the vehicles' roof, a flag attached to the antenna and flapping in the hot Georgia wind. As the front gate of the Moorish Nation compound came into his view, Cummins knew that there was no backing out now. It was on.

"Fifteen seconds until impact," the Governor spoke into his hand-held radio, letting the other teams know his status.

Cummins was sitting in the front passenger seat, a trusted lieutenant at the wheel. As the big Excursion turned off the main road that ran parallel to the entrance gate, they were headed now directly towards the entrance gate and picking up speed.

Cummins noticed some activity in the guard house located at the entrance. The gate itself was made of welded steel and was built in the shape of the letters M and N, for Moorish Nation, and stood eight feet tall. When the guards at the gate saw that the SUV was picking up speed and that it was flying an old, pre-56 Georgia flag, with its large Saint Andrews' Cross, the guards immediately opened fire on the vehicle. The bullets found no purchase on the Excursion, bouncing harmlessly away.

"They know we're here," said the Governor into his radio, "hit it!" Out of the corner of his eye Cummins watched as a patch of grass rose off the ground. The clod of grass was being pushed skyward by the man underneath it, a man holding a tubular weapon that was pointed at the entrance gate. He was one of the Governor's men who had crept up close to the gate the night before and dug out a hide on a small, grass covered embankment near the compound entrance gate. His weapon was an old Korean War era Bazooka that Cummins had bought and restored to working condition.

The Bazooka belched fire and the guard house exploded in a ball of orange fire. Two burning men rushed out of the fire-engulfed ruins of the small building, their green uniforms bearing large MN letters on the front. Two other guards were standing at the gate itself, firing their weapons at the big Ford that was now barreling down on them at 60 mph. Both guards dove to the sides as the SUV hit the gate, smashing it to scrap iron. Gunners sitting in the rear of the vehicle dropped the rear window and opened fire on the guards with the mounted .60 caliber. Both guards were killed instantly. The gunner saw the other guards who had been set on fire by the Bazooka blast. They were still moving, so he raked them with fire, a mercy killing. The Ford raced on down the road that ran from the front entry to the central complex.

On the other side of the compound, the other teams had all attacked simultaneously. Stonewall, Critter and Jeb had hit the perimeter fence with momentum, knocking the chain-link fencing down and making way for their team-mates to gain entry in their own trucks and SUV's.

Each team had breached the gate cleanly and was headed for the central buildings except for Critter. Its ramming vehicle had been a pickup truck. Though it was able to knock down the fence, as the truck rolled over the fence, the chain-link fence wrapped itself around the vehicle's rear wheels, tires and axle. Refusing to snap in two, the fence was pulled inward by the momentum of the truck, but now act as a rubber band, slowing and finally dragging the truck to a halt.

The other two pickups carrying the Critter Company had to stop and begin cutting through the fence so that their vehicles could get through it without also becoming entangled. What was more, the now tangled vehicle was loaded with important weapons and gear, and would have to be transferred to the other vehicles. The team leader called to give Cummins the bad news.

"Governor, this is Bell. Critter Company is delayed at the point of entry. Lead vehicle is ensnared in the fence. Fifteen minutes to get through at least, and that is if we draw no fire. Over." Cummins' voice responded,

"Roger that, Bell. Salvage all you can off the lead vehicle and get that fence cut. We need those mortars for the final assault. Hurry as fast as you can, and let us know if you start taking fire. Out."

The Governor's voice had been urgent but still sounded confident. He knew that his men needed to hear that confidence. Yet inside, doubts were creeping into his mind. He knew that Critter Company was carrying the mortar rounds that he was counting on to pin the Moorish fighters down at the main building. His sources had told him that there were as many as a hundred men within the compound at any given time. At night those numbers swelled to near one hundred fifty, and that is why the Governor chose to mount a day-time raid. With one team delayed and temporarily out of the game, that would put more pressure on the other teams to overcome whatever resistance was awaiting them.

Cummins spotted the main compound complex of buildings about three hundred yards distant. Both the other teams, Stonewall and Jeb, had reported clean entry and were heading towards the main complex. Suddenly Cummins saw a burst of fire and dust erupt from one of the buildings. A hole had been blown in the roof of one of the buildings, but the explosion had come from inside. *Yes!* The Governor clenched a fist in celebration. His inside-man had been able to set off an explosion within one of the buildings.

The plan was for the Governor's mole, who had secured a job with the Moors in their kitchen, to sneak into the kitchen when no one else was around. The large stoves and ovens worked off of natural gas, and the mole was to cut all the copper lines leading to each stove or oven. As the gas quickly filled the kitchen area, the saboteur was to, just before shutting the room off, pull the pin on a grenade that had been fixed with a ten minute delayed timing device. That would allow an extra ten minutes time for the gas to build up in the kitchen. As the Governor watched the smoke pour from the hole in the roof, he knew that his man had pulled off the trick. This explosion would also act as a diversion and draw Moorish manpower to the kitchen area to contain the fire, drawing them away from the fight.

Then he saw it; a plume of smoke heading toward his SUV. One of his men was yelling a warning as the projectile, an RPG, made impact on the left front tire of the vehicle. Cummins felt his seat belt tighten around him as the SUV jolted rightward and was sent tumbling off the road in a roll-over motion. As the vehicle came to a rest, the Governor knew he had to get out in a hurry because whoever had capped the RPG at his vehicle would be on them in seconds to finish the job.

Sand, dirt and dust filled the air inside the SUV, which had come to a stop resting on what was left of its wheels. Cummins, still in his passenger seat, chanced a quick look in the rear seating of the vehicle.

Tommy Davis

He could see that at least two of his men looked to be okay. Another had been thrown from the vehicle and lay dead in the dust, his neck snapped. The driver's face lay against the steering wheel, his face covered in blood from a gash that ran horizontal across his forehead. Cummins reached over to check the driver's pulse, and he was surprised to find it strong. The man would live, but was out of the fight for the moment.

Cummins shouted the order to find cover, unbuckled his seat belt and got out of the vehicle, as did the other men who were conscious. They were able to unbuckle and drag the unconscious driver out of the SUV and behind the destroyed vehicle as the first shots ripped across the side of the Ford Excursion. Luckily, each of them had had their assault rifles locked and loaded, and strapped to their bodies, allowing them to hold on to the weapons even as their vehicle had taken the shock of the grenade and the subsequent roll-over.

He peeked over the hood of the SUV, able now to identify their attackers, which was a group of four Moors mounted atop four-wheel ATV's. He realized that another direct hit from an RPG would finish he and his men, but the attackers failed to cap it off. Instead, the Moors had been so over-joyed at the first grenade hit that they mounted their four-wheelers and charged full-throttle at the damaged SUV. A more disciplined attack would likely have finished the Governor and his team, but now the Moors were actually at a disadvantage, charging openly at men who could fire at them from behind cover.

"Pour it into them!" yelled the Governor, at which he and his remaining men opened fire on the on-rushing ATVs with their automatic weapons.

The effect was devastating. Two of the riders were hit almost instantly, the bullets knocking them off their four-wheelers. One of the other riders, seeing his comrades ripped bloody by the machine gun fire, swerved his ATV to his right to make a quick retreat. But the Governor's men had skill with their rifles and three bullets ripped into the left rib-cage of the ATV rider, flipping him and the four-wheeler into bloody summersaults. Only one of the riders chose to pull up, stopping his ATV and turning it broadside towards the SUV from behind which the Governor and his team were firing.

Using his ATV as cover, the Moorish defender began to lay down fire on the SUV position with his own automatic weapon. Covering the vehicle with fire, he was forcing the Governor and his men to keep their heads down. This was a good maneuver if he had had other men to move on the Governor's position, but his comrades were all dead by then.

Behind the SUV, the Governor counted off a quick but deliberate 'One, Two, Three.' At 'three,' he and his men simultaneously poked their rifle's up over the hood or around the rear of their SUV and capped off rounds in the general direction of the Moorish defender. None of the bullets hit the man, but they whistled close enough to him that he ducked low behind the four-wheeler and ceased fire for a few seconds. That was enough time for Cummins and his men to peek over or around their SUV, get a visual of the four-wheeler and the man hiding behind it, and train their fire on him. About thirty rounds banged into the ATV within five seconds. Cummins hoped the defender would simply throw down his weapon and surrender, but sadly the Moorish gunman chose to make a run for it.

Shooting a man down from behind was no pleasure, but neither could Cummins allow him to escape. Cummins and all his men opened automatic fire on the running man, the bullets ripping into his back and neck, sending him sprawling head-over-heals. The man was unconscious but his lungs fought death off a few seconds longer, sucking a last, dust filled breath as Cummins and his men mounted the three undamaged ATVs and sped past him towards the main complex.

Up ahead, Cummins could see that two of the other teams had made it to the main complex and had initiated their assault. He knew the defenders would be taking automatic rifle fire as well as RPG attacks from his men. He also knew that teams Jeb and Stonewall did not have enough fire power to overwhelm the Moorish defenders.

If the firefight became a protracted battle, the Moors would be able to call up reinforcements from the inner city of Atlanta, reinforcements that could speed up I-10. And then Cummins would have enemy to his front and rear and would be cut to blood and guts. He hoped that the fire in the kitchen area would spread quickly enough through the compound that it would disrupt the efforts of the Moorish defenders, but that was far from a sure thing.

Cummins could see smoke rising from the building where the gas-explosion had taken place, but he did not know if the fire was spreading or not.

One thing he did know was that men riding in the open on ATVs would create a duck-shoot for the Moorish Nation defenders if he and his men did not find cover near the complex.

Cummins spotted a short, block wall to his right, not far from the main building. The wall looked to be the part of a new building that was under construction. It was about three feet high and would make good cover if he and his men could get to it. Cummins turned his four-wheeler towards the wall and motioned for his men to follow.

They were about thirty yards from the wall when they began to take small-arms fire from the defenders in the building. Cummins looked at the building and saw rifle barrels sticking out, the ends of which were belching steady, smoky discharge. He had the thumb-throttle of the ATV pushed as far as it would go. He heard a yelp behind him and knew one of his men had been hit. But Cummins and the other men did not stop until they had reached the block wall.

Leaping off the ATVs, he and his men took cover quickly. They looked back to see that their comrade who had just been hit lying motionless on the ground. Cummins wanted to help the injured man, but he knew that if they did not break the defense of the building soon, then all his men would end up dead.

The block wall was about seventy-five yards away from the building from which the Moors were firing at them. Cummins tried to rise and return fire but so much fire was now being poured on his position that he had to keep his head down. More shooters had come to the windows to direct fire on the Governor and his team.

Why was the fire started in the kitchen area not distracting the Moors? Cummins did not know; maybe they were letting it burn, concentrating on defeating his raid. Or maybe the Moors had enough men to fight both him and the fire. Whatever the reason, Cummins knew his team was pinned down and in real trouble. He needed support from the other teams.

Thumbing his radio, he called teams Jeb and Stonewall. Neither team responded, and Cummins could not be sure if those teams had yet to open fire on the opposite sides of the complex.

At that moment a tremendous explosion shook the block wall. The wall had taken a direct hit from an RPG round and Cummins could feel blood trickle down his face. The wall was not hollow, it had been poured full of concrete, and pulverized bits of the concrete and rebar had been blasted at he and his men when the RPG round hit, tearing small gashes in their flesh. A stiff warm breeze blew in at just that moment and cleared the air enough that the Governor could see the hole, about one foot in diameter, that the RPG round had left near the base of the wall. Belly crawling to the hole, Cummins chanced a look through and saw Fazaz, the founder and leader of the Moorish Nation, directing the counter attack.

Fazaz was standing in a doorway wearing a military beret on his head, and sunglasses. His Moors were now filing out of the door to press Cummins' position, their movement being covered by those still firing from the windows. As the Moorish Nation members exited, Fazaz was pushing them this way and that, spreading them out so that they would not bunch together. It was a smart move, and Cummins knew that his men were not the only ones who had trained and prepared for fighting.

Sensing a lull in the gunfire, the Governor seized the opportunity to legitimize his raid. Pulling a mini-bullhorn from his pack, Cummins announced loudly,

"Fazaz, this is Governor Cummins, and I have a warrant for your arrest for conspiracy to commit terrorism with weapons of mass-"

Cummins announcement was cut short by another grenade explosion against the block wall. Fazaz and his men were in no mood for legalities. This grenade took out a chunk of the wall, cutting a rugged V shaped crater in the block wall from top to bottom. The explosion was followed by more automatic rifle fire.

He looked over to where his men were crouched, bullets whistling over the wall, just above their heads. He saw that one of his men had salvaged an RPG from the wreck of the Ford they had arrived in. Cummins gave hand signals ordering the RPG be fired, and that followed up with rifle fire. His man dutifully shouldered the weapon and, quickly popping up over the wall, capped off the grenade. Drawing fire, the man quickly dropped back down behind the safety of the wall, discarding the RPG for his AK-47.

Peeking through the small hole, the Governor saw the projectile slam into the building near the doorway where Fazaz was standing. The exploding round shook the building and part of the building's outer wall collapsed. This diverted the Moors' attention just long enough for Cummins and his men to rise and return fire. But the Moors had good cover and there were about twenty of them now directing fire at the block wall. Cummins tried his radio again but still no answer came.

Fazaz had his men moving and firing, working around to flank the block wall. Once they flanked his position, Cummins knew he and his team would be chewed to raw meat by Moorish rounds. Two more RPG rounds slammed into the block wall, and Cummins knew that they would be flanked in another minute at the most. It was do-or-die time.

Cummins looked through the hole in the wall, searching for Fazaz. Fazaz had moved out of the doorway when the building wall had started to collapse. Though Fazaz had taken cover, Cummins saw his military beret sticking up over the hood of a Caprice that was parked outside the building.

The Governor took the RPG, loaded the last projectile, and told his men he was going to take Fazaz out. Once they heard the explosion, they were to throw the few hand grenades they had and then follow Cummins towards the building while firing their rifles on full automatic. One man would stay behind the wall and lay down cover fire.

Taking a deep breath, he steeled himself for the task, and with a yell he leapt up and over the wall, heading for Fazaz. But he had taken no more than two steps when a bullet slammed into his shoulder, knocking him back into the low block wall. He felt the hands of his men grab him and drag him back over the wall. His shoulder hurt like Hades, and the pain was made worse by the fact that he had dropped the RPG launcher on the other side of the wall. The weapon was lost, and Cummins was pretty sure he and his men would die now, behind the short wall.

Suddenly, bullets began to smack the wall on their side, and Cummins knew they had been flanked. His men tried to find the Moors flanking them and return fire. Another RPG round was fired from the direction of the building and it slammed into the wall as dust and debris filled the air. Cummins yelled out that they should all die like men, to get up and die attacking. There would be no white-flag surrender. Better to die in battle than face the wrath of Fazaz and his men as hostages, with their blood hot from the fight.

Loud whistling sounds suddenly cut trhough the noise, followed by three thunderous explosions. All rifle fire at their position ceased, but the whistling sounds of the mortar rounds dropping to earth continued, followed by more loud explosions. Critter Company had arrived! And they were placing their mortar rounds perfectly between the building and the block wall. The Caprice behind which Fazaz had taken cover had been hit in the first volley of mortars. Fazaz had been blown twenty feet in the air, his body smashing into the building behind him. His men had seen their leader die, and were confused and dazed by the sudden turn of events.

Cummins' men wasted no time. One of them jumped over the block wall, scooped up the RPG that Cummins had dropped, and turned the weapon on the Moors who had flanked their position. The RPG round sped towards the Moors, exploding near them and injuring or killing the flankers.

More mortar rounds were falling all around. With the threat to their flank eliminated, Cummins and his men simply had to wait behind the block wall. Critter Company rotated their mortar fire back onto the building itself. All the defenders scattered or fled when the mortar rounds began to fall.

The Governor and his men all looked over the block wall at the main building as the mortar rounds fell in twos and threes, exploding the rooftop and starting fires throughout the building. Finally, Cummins heard someone on his radio.

"Governor Cummins, this is Torrence with Critter Company. Are you okay, sir?"

"I'll live," replied the Governor. "How many more mortar rounds do you have?"

"About twenty-five, sir. Should we use them all on the building?"

"Drop another eighteen or so on the building. We need to empty the building of gunmen. Shoot down anyone who does not surrender as they exit. Save a few rounds in case they get reinforcements coming in behind us. And where are Stonewall and Jeb?"

"Roger on the eighteen. Stonewall and Jeb are attacking on the opposite side of the complex," came the reply, as more rounds whistled down, bringing fire and confusion to the Moorish Nation complex. Between the gas fire started in the kitchen and the fires started by the mortar rounds, it was only a few more minutes until the whole building complex was billowing smoke. Some of the Moors surrendered and some ran from the burning building with guns blazing. The later were cut down with rifle fire by the men of Critter, Stonewall and Jeb, while the former were gathered up, hand-cuffed and ankle-shackled.

Cummins had his men gather the bodies of Fazaz and five other Moors into the vehicles. Those who had surrendered were left shackled at the premises, while the dead were mostly left where they lay.

By the time the Moorish reinforcements had arrived from the city of Atlanta, all they found were the shackled or dead Moors lying about the smoking ruins of what had been the Moorish Nation compound. Also by that time the local office of the FBI had responded with several tactical units of their own, all armed with automatic rifles. With Fazaz dead, the remaining Moors were leaderless and surrendered to the feds without another shot.

Chapter Nineteen

Centennial Olympic Park
Downtown Atlanta, Georgia

The Governor's raid on the Moorish Nation terrorists had made for big news, and brought thousands of supporters to the Governor. Cummins called a major press conference to announce the results of the raid on the terrorist compound, displaying both the body of Fazaz as well as the evidence against him. The Superior Court Judge who had signed the warrant against Fazaz was also present.

A rally in support of Cummins had been planned via Facebook and Twitter and was gaining momentum, even with the rolling blackouts that had been imposed due to the economic collapse that had started with the gas-crisis and China's dollar-dump. Thousands had still managed to sign up for the event that was to be held in Centennial Olympic Park.

This was a sprawling park built in downtown Atlanta on the occasion of the Atlanta Olympic Games back in 96.

A big-time political event draws big-time coverage. By the time Cal Limkey of ROX News arrived on the scene, a large crowd had already gathered and more people were streaming into the park every minute. Already it was difficult to navigate one's way through the thousands of protesters, marchers, and various agitators. The Governor obviously had many supporters present, but the opposition had shown up for the event as well.

Limkey had a full compliment of sound and camera people with him, and these trailed him as he made his way through the crowd. He had waved off an offer made by his boss at ROX News to provide security guards for him, dismissing it as an unnecessary waste of News Corp. money.

Though Limkey earned seven figures a year at ROX News, he still believed in pinching the pennies when possible, just as he had learned in his strict Catholic upbringing. But now he was not so sure he should have turned down the offer as he eyed different elements of the crowd. He realized that though this protest had been organized by the friends of Governor Cummins it was sure to draw a vigorous counter-protest by the man's detractors.

Limkey had a keen sense of smell for all things political and he could feel the electricity in the air as he moved about. Things could get heated in a hurry in a setting like this. The Atlanta City Police had promised the public that they would provide a strong show of force to dissuade any trouble makers, but Limkey knew that if either side felt that the police were taking the part of the other side, it would take only a spark to set off real fireworks.

Still, Limkey felt pretty confident. Even though he was a New Yorker, he had always been impressed with most southerners for their well known hospitality. Only in the south had Limkey been regularly greeted as 'Sir' by those who had nothing to gain from him. He respected those kind of manners.

Yet that confidence began to evaporate the moment he spotted the first man with a gun strapped to his belt. At first Limkey thought it was merely a large cell phone or Blackberry in its carry case. But the black steel barrel protruding out of the bottom of the holster told him otherwise.

The veteran newsman began to scan the crowd for more weapons. He quickly spotted another strapped low on a man's hip, the bottom of the holster tied around the man's thigh like a gunslinger from the old west. A big black revolver rested in the holster, a true hand cannon, probably a .44 magnum, judged the newsman. That same man was also carrying a large placard held high on a wooden stake. Limkey recognized the phrase writ large on the placard as Jeffersonian;

Water the Tree of Liberty
With the Blood of
Patriots and Tyrants

Disconcerting to say the least, thought Limkey. Another man standing near by held a placard with pictures of President Soloto and Governor Cummins facing each other, with 'VS' in the middle, between the two faces. Limkey saw that one of his cameramen was stopping to get shots of these armed protestors.

"No time for that Ted, let's move along," he chided the cameraman, who seemed to resent missing such great pictures. Limkey and his crew continued to make their way through the crowd, a crowd growing thicker, its initial small groupings now being forced closer together by the masses of incoming protester flesh.

One protester who did not see Limkey coming through bumped into the tall news anchor. Limkey thought it was intentional and raised his voice at the person.

"Watch out, Bub!" he said in his best New Yorkese. But Limkey then realized it was no man. It was a woman, a large, big boned women dressed in camouflage from boot to hunting cap. The woman gave Limkey a 'drop dead' look, but it was the A.K. 47, with its banana ammo clip, slung over her beefy left shoulder that startled him. Starring wide-eyed, the newsman suddenly remembered that Georgia was an open-carry State. None of these people who had come to this public, outdoor meeting with guns were actually breaking the law. As long as their weapons were not fully automatic they were within their rights.

Limkey walked quickly away from the armed lady in camouflage, giving a backwards glance to make sure she was not following him. He recalled that this was the park which Eric Rudolph had bombed during the Olympic Games of 1996. He tried to dismiss that particular thought from his mind as he led his crew towards the north end of the park where a stage had been erected as a platform for those scheduled to speak to the protesters.

Limkey, being a tall man of over six feet, tried to look above the crowd to see how close he was to the stage, but all he could see was flags.

A sea of flags dominated the area near the stage, flags of every kind and description. He recognized many of them at once, and realized that this protest had quickly become a circus for every extremist under the sun to have their say, whether they knew what the protest was about or not.

There were several American flags, the stars and stripes. There were Confederate flags, six or eight different versions including the Battle Flag with its familiar X filled with stars, the post 1956 Georgia flag dominated by that same design, and the National flag of the Confederacy in its various versions. There was the Roy Barnes Georgia flag that looked like a large blue table place mat. There were several versions of the Gadsden 'Don't Tread On Me' flag with a picture of a rattle snake on it. Then there was a black liberation flag with its stripes of red, black and green.

Then Limkey spotted a Confederate Flag painted solid watermelon green, a strange attempt to combine the Battle flag and Black Liberation flag. There was a flag with a peace symbol that could've come from a Vietnam era protest. There was another flag with the same peace symbol and large picture of Bob Marley on it. There was a Nation of Islam flag as well as a Nazi flag with a large swastika. And right in the middle of all this Limkey saw a large flag flying in the breeze with a Pokemon picture in the center. Thank goodness for a little comic relief Limkey thought, chuckling to himself.

The crowd was thickest nearest the stage, and Limkey had to shove his way through like a blocking fullback leading the way for the runners, in this case his crewmen. Finally, after enduring the curses of several protesters for being shoved aside, Limkey was at the end of the stage where a prime coverage spot had been promised to him and his ROX News Team.

About to mount the stage now, Limkey stopped in his tracks, the look on his face grim indeed. There, in his spot, stood a rival news anchor, Kyle Olgleby. Olgleby had his own news crew gathered about him on the stage; clearly there was no room for the team from ROX. Olgleby caught a glimpse of Limkey.

Limkey was known for his Irish temper and had had many an emotional and verbal blowup on his news commentary show. In fact, it was these occasional blowups that helped keep Limkey's rating in the stratosphere, far above those of the equally smirkey yet less engaging Olgleby.

Olgleby, seeing now the look of utter disgust on Limkey's face, knew that a confrontation was unavoidable. So, he thought, why not make the most of this. Besides, he had been wanting a crack at Limkey for a while. The men had traded barbs and insults for years over the airways. Now it was live and in person. To his cameraman, out of earshot of Limkey, Olgleby said,

"Roll camera." The cameraman was unsure of why he was being ordered to film, but did as he was told, though he went to pains to try and not let Limkey see that he was being filmed. Then Olgleby launched his first verbal volley.

"Well, well, if it isn't Ole Cal the King Of All Liars." Olgleby's jab was a hard one and it hit Limkey right on the button. It was a reference to a title he had used on-air to describe Limkey for years, 'King of Liars.' Limkey's face, which had already been bitter, now turned a darker shade of red, contorting in a bizarre way that made him look like a madman.

"You bag of dirt!" spat Limkey, "I'll rip your heart out!" Heart ripping was one of the analogous threats Limkey sometimes used against people he did not like. Olgleby was a little afraid; Limkey was a big man and looked crazed and ready to explode. Still, the news anchor remained outwardly calm, smiling and chuckling at Limkey's outrage. Time for another well placed verbal punch.

"Why are you here, Cal-boy? Come to cover some of your fellow Fascist friends in down-south Jaw-ja?" Another low blow, for Olgleby's network often referred to ROX News as the 'fascist network,' associating them with Hitler's kind.

Limkey's eyes grew wide and bloodshot. An explosion was not far away.

"You scum bag! You piece of trash, get off that stage right now! You are standing in my spot!" Limkey thought of looking for a stage manager to force the rival crew out of his promised, coveted spot, but that thought evaporated with Olgleby's next comment. Olgleby loved the fact that he could so easily rile Limkey, so he turned up the heat even more.

"Stay down there where you belong with your fellow Nazis, you bottom feeding tabloid journalist. This isn't New York, Cal-boy, and you don't own this stage!"

"Arrrgh!" Limkey growled a strange guttural sound as he rushed the steps to the platform. "I'll destroy you!" he cried. Limkey was in great shape for a man his age, but each step was a full foot in height, and the toe of his Florsheim caught on the top step, tripping him and sending his large frame sprawling across the plywood platform where he came to rest at Olgleby's feet. Olgleby burst into a fit of laughter at his rival's folly.

"Here Cal-li-co, let me help you up," said Olgleby as he grabbed Limkey by the hair of his head, meaning to drag him back down the steps. Olgleby was several years younger than Limkey, but he forgot to account for the strength of a thoroughly humiliated and enraged man. Olgleby felt Limkey grab his outstretched wrist, pulling him downward. Limkey was up on one knee now, and as he had Olgleby bent over him, he planted his shoulder into Olgleby's stomach and stood up with him.

There was Cal Limkey atop the stage, with Olgleby helplessly flayed over his shoulder in a fireman's carry position. Olgleby was stunned at Limkey's strength, but could do nothing about it now.

"What say you now, Kyle my boy!" screamed Limkey, madly grinning now like Jack Nicholson in "The Shining." Limkey humped it to the edge of the stage and tossed the disbelieving Olgleby off and into the crowd below.

Exultant stood Limkey, and tall at the edge of the platform looking down on the now humiliated Olgleby. Kyle had landed belly-down on top of the man carrying the swastika flag, a burly biker-type with a thick beard and bald head. Olgleby thought surely he was in for a terrible beating at the hands of this biker, but instead this biker was a member of the gay community and tried to hold Kyle close to him, not wanting to let go.

Realizing what was happening, Olgleby frantically pushed away from the biker dude. Undaunted, Olgleby rushed the stage and jumped nimbly up and onto it. Limkey saw that his rival was game and determined to answer the bell. Recalling his days as football player, he rushed towards Olgleby. Olgleby squatted, braced for the tackle, but did not know that Limkey had been a kicker in college. Limkey pulled up just shy of Olgleby and delivered a right-footed kick directly into Olgleby's groin. The man doubled over in pain, falling to his knees.

Limkey lifted both hands Rocky-style and began a little victory dance on the stage. By this time, hundreds in the crowd had realized a fight was going on between men in shirts and ties on stage. Many of them recognized the combatants and began to chant for their favorite, leftists favoring Olgleby and rightists pulling for Limkey. The right-wingers had the most to cheer about at the moment, for Limkey was still doing his victory dance as the left-wingers showered him with jeer's and boo's.

Yet Olgleby was made of better stuff than that, and forcing himself to his feet, he caught Limkey off guard with a fisted straight right to the chin. Limkey was knocked backwards, and would have fallen flat if he had not been caught by one of his crewmen. The crewman, like a cornerman in a prize fight, pushed his boss back into the fray, yelling 'get'im Cal!' Cal was stunned by the shot to the chin but proved his own metal with a hard uppercut that sunk into Olgleby's gut. Again, Olgleby found himself doubled over in pain.

Limkey wanted to finish off his foe but was too out of breath to follow up the body blow. By the time he regained his breath, Olgleby had recovered. The two news-gladiators then went toe to toe in the middle of the stage.

Thousands of protesters now became spectators as lusty as those of Old Rome as the fists, teeth and blood flew wildly.

Olgleby was working his left jab to Limkey's face, quickly opening numerous cuts. Limkey was swinging roundhouse lefts and rights, most of them missing. The jabs were taking their toll on the older Limkey. Then he remembered his uppercut. Feinting with a left, Limkey uncorked a sweet uppercut that hit Olgleby on the jaw in a glancing blow.

A solid lick might have finished the rival, but the glancing shot merely stunned him. Olgleby ducked under another roundhouse right, blocked the next upper cut, then delivered a straight right that hit Limkey dead on the nose, breaking it and sending him to the deck, out cold.

Policemen burst onto the stage, corralling Olgleby. Medical help was called for Limkey, but it would be an hour before paramedics could make their way with a gurney through the crowd that was itself about to erupt.

Seeing the police manhandle Olgleby enraged his supporters. Limkey's supporters were equally angered that their boy had been knocked out. Both sides turned on one another and nothing short of bedlam ensued as three hundred uniformed riot police descended on the protest that had become a street brawl. Years of pent-up rage erupted as the two sides went at it, though no one really knew who to fight or which side their neighbor was on. Mostly it was self-defense, a battle royal where the last man standing wins.

It took hours for the police to clear the park. The fight between the two newsmen had been captured by Olgleby's camera-crew. That tape would be suppressed for legal reasons. But this was the age of camera phones and Youtube, Google Video and the internet, and the whole fight, viewed from a hundred different angles, was soon on the web and viewed by hundreds of millions worldwide.

In his penthouse apartment in Manhattan, Don King sat watching on his Television. He suddenly jumped up and screamed in agony as he kicked the flatscreen television to the floor. Rushing in from the kitchen, his wife demanded to be told what was going on.

King replied in a profoundly frustrated voice,

"The greatest pay-per-view opportunity in history just went out to the entire world...for free!"

The Oval Office
The White House
Washington, D.C.

A furious President Soloto called his COS into his office. Along with Brandenburg, NSA Director Click and Attorney General Lawrence Kabill were alone present.

These were the men that the President had trusted with the job of neutralizing Governor Jim Cummins of Georgia, and Cummins had thus far bested them at every turn.

"Gentlemen, the threat from Cummins in Georgia has become intolerable! I will not stand by another moment as he endangers this country! He will bring absolute MAYHEM to the streets if we don't stop him now! Look at this so-called raid on this compound outside of Atlanta. He is claiming that this raid of his destroyed an Islamic terror-cell!" The President was wide-eyed and almost shaking with rage. It took a brave man to speak first after that Presidential outburst.

"Sir," replied Kabill, "I have no doubt that the raid on the Moorish compound was illegally carried out by Cummins. However, I do need to mention that this Moorish Nation group had been suspected of harboring members of either Al Quaeda or Hamas. Our people had a file started on them more than a year ago." Soloto looked blankly at his AG.

"So what, Kabill! It doesn't matter to me if Osama bin Laden's little gay brother was hiding in that compound--we must not let such information leak out! That would only be used to justify Cummins' actions. No one deals with terrorists but this office!" Soloto was livid, but went on.

"Look at everything that this man has done: he has turned my airplane away from Atlanta and blown up a fighter jet, killing the pilot, no matter what the investigators say; he has raided and arrested a federal IPS agent; and he has now entered into a firefight with private citizens on private property, killing scores of people. And yet," said Soloto, pacing about with his arms held out in mock wonder, "the man responsible for all this chaos is still at large! Somebody tell me why!" After an awkward moment of silence, Kabill spoke up.

"Well, sir, we did secure an arrest warrant and attempt to serve it, but the lake-house raid was ill—"

"ILL PLANNED, ILL ADVISED, ILL EXECUTED AND ILL EVERYTHING ELSE!" shouted Soloto at all in the room. "And that is not all that was ill-planned. What about our wonderful mercenaries from BlackSky--got their tales kicked by a bunch of hick-plow boys!" That barb was thrown directly at Click, the man who had first suggested using BlackSky in Georgia. Click knew he was in hot water now with Soloto, and needed to come up with an answer quickly.

"Sir," chanced the NSA Director, "I think it is time to take stronger measures."

"Stronger measures, Director Click? All of your 'stronger measures' have been absolute disasters thus far! What is your great plan for today?"

"Sir, with all due respect, I have done my best under difficult circumstances. Trying to work these things out in the midst of an economic collapse—" But Soloto cut the man off with another angry tirade.

"Of course there is an economic crisis, thanks to those stinking yellow Chinks! They are trying to destroy me, and this Cummins idiot is using the crisis as cover for his rebellion. I'm telling you people right now--if we don't stop this Governor of Georgia, his next move will be for Secession. And because the people are so frightened about the dollar, about gas, about bus-bombs--Cummins just might be successful in taking Georgia out of this Union!"

"We would never let that happen, Mr. President," said Brandenburg reassuringly. "We can simply fall back on the example of our greatest President, Lincoln. Ninety-nine percent of the experts in this country will support you in your Presidential right to keep the Union together."

"Yes, yes, I know all about Lincoln and the Civil War, Eli. But to be *greater* than Lincoln I must avoid a Civil War, can't you see! The last Civil War cost this country two percent of its population. Do you know how many dead that equals in today's numbers? Six million citizens, Eli--six million." The President walked over to a window and looked out across the lawn. When he turned around to face the men, he said,

"Gentlemen, listen closely. If you think I'm going to be the President that lets civil strife break out on my watch, the kind of strife that could claim millions of American lives, then you are sadly mistaken. Now, I want one thing and one thing only--Cummins must be stopped and stopped now, without delay!"

"Stronger measures, Mr. President--stronger, more decisive measures are called for, measures that cannot possibly miss," said Click.

"Go on," said Soloto, his hands folded across his chest.

"The answer to this problem is the same as in Pakistan or Yemen or Afghanistan. Drones, sir, we use the Predator Drones, armed with the most powerful weaponry they can carry. We won't have to worry about a pilot whose scruples won't let him bomb a sitting Governor. The Drones make things much more impersonal, more like a video game."

"But Cummins has not left the Governor's Mansion in days, you said so yourself," injected Brandenburg. "How can we use that kind of weaponry there, with his family with him?"

"No time to be squeamish, Eli," said Click. "Cummins is an enemy of the United States. Our duty is to find him wherever he is and eliminate him. If others are collateralized with him, we simply say he was using them as human shields. Better for a few to die than millions. He brought this on himself, and those around him."

"No American Governor would use his family as a human shield. That's preposterous. No one will believe that," objected Kabill.

"Kabill," replied Click, "we are in the middle of a dollar collapse, and gasoline hit sixteen dollars per gallon today. Do you really think anyone will care?" Kabill felt a chill in the room--he had never heard anything so cold.

"I know he must be stoped, but he *is* a U.S. Citizen—we can't just erase him without due process," replied Kabill.

"We brake no new ground here, we've put hits on citizens before—remember Al-Awlaki in Yemen? And his son, he was only sixteen when we hit him, wasn't he? Besides, we will use NSA Drones, not DOD Drones, to keep it internal."

"But--" Kabill's further objection was cut off by the President.

"Okay," said Soloto, "we use the NSA Predator Drones to take Cummins out. I want all doubt removed, make sure this rogue Governor does not survive this bombing. If he walks away in one piece, they will make him a hero--mark my words."

"He won't walk away from what I'm sending in, Mr. President. The NSA just took delivery of a new Drone that can carry the equivalent of a Daisy Cutter!" Click pulled out his phone to make the necessary call.

"Wait," said Soloto, "don't make those calls from here. I don't want to come in here every day knowing those kinds of orders were made from here." Kabill thought to himself but did not say 'Mr. President, those kinds of orders *were* just made here.'

GEORGIA BURNS

The Governor's Mansion
Outside of Atlanta, Georgia

Governor Jim Cummins was sitting on his sofa reading a book to his children when his secure cell-phone began to ring. The book was called 'Dangerous Journey,' an illustrated children's version of Pilgrim's Progress, and the Cummins kids did not like their Father's reading of their favorite book interrupted.

"Hold on kids, let me get rid of Uncle Wilder and I'll keep reading." But it wasn't the voice of Wilder Fields he heard when he answered the cell-phone.

"Governor Cummins," said the young voice.

"Who is this? How'd you get this—"

"I can't give you my name, but I am an agent with the National Security Agency."

"This is a private, secure line--what are you—"

"I broke the cell-phone's encryption. That's what we do. I'm somewhat familiar with that particular encryption. I' a Yellow Jacket myself, no offense to you Bulldogs."

Cummins realized the man he was talking to was claiming to have graduated from Georgia Tech, which really got the Governor's attention, considering the source of the secure cell-phone.

"Well my friend, I believe you--no one would claim to be a Georgia Tech grad unless they really were one." The young voice on the cell-phone laughed at the inter-state rivalry jab.

"Good one, sir. But there really is no time for that--I'm calling to tell you that I have just sent three fully armed Predator Drones, dressed out with Maximum Penetrating Ordinance, towards your home. I don't believe in killing women and children, so get out now-- you've got less than eight minutes." The cell-phone went dead in the Governor's now-sweaty palm.

Cummins felt his stomach knot first with fear, then anger. *They would hit me here, along with my wife and kids?*

Dropping the compromised phone, Cummins grabbed his children by their hands and yelled for his wife to hurry to the basement. He heard a glass fall and break against the tile kitchen floor and was glad because that meant his wife was wasting no time following his instructions. It took only a minute for the family to make it down the flight of stairs leading to the basement and Cummins was glad he had made them practice just such an emergency plan, although he had had a tornado in mind instead of a trio of Predator Drones.

But the Governor had no plan to stop in the basement. The children watched in confusion as their mother and father each grabbed up a crow bar from a tool rack and began to pry at a large stone that was embedded in the middle of the cobblestone floor of the basement. The older of the two children was a son, and still thinking 'tornado' he shook his head in confusion at the needless actions of his parents. What good would it do to loosen the floor-stone if a tornado hit?

The boy's eyes grew wide though when he saw that there was no earth underneath the large stone his parents had loosened and removed from the floor. He saw a hole in the floor with a small, rusted metal ladder running down.

"You go first and help the children as they come down," said the Governor to his wife. Down she went into the hole in the basement floor, following the ladder down rung by rung.

"Hurry, move faster!" The kids tried to do as their father said but the hole in the floor was small, as were their little hands that clung to the rusty rungs of the ladder.

With both kids and his wife now down the ladder, the Governor quickly got both of his feet into the hole just as the first Compact Penetrating Daisy Cutter hit the mansion roof. Two more identical weapons followed the first in quick succession. Each Predator was armed with two of the weapons, and the next pass saw three more bombs rain down, each making perfect strikes on the Governor's Mansion, bringing the massive house down and setting the remaining rubble on fire.

It would be five hours before the fire burnt itself out. fire and emergency responders were called by the neighbors but were kept at bay by agents of the NSA who flashed their federal badges and automatic weapons to over-rule anyone wanting to get to the scene.

Dennis Click himself arrived on the scene. He had ordered a half-dozen bull-dozers to be trucked onto the property to begin clearing away the ash and debris. He needed to see a body for proof before the body was dumped into the Atlantic. Only a burial at sea would keep a Governor's gravesite from becoming a shrine of rebellion.

But now the six dozers had been at work for nearly ten hours and the only body brought to the Director was that of the family cat.

Click began to worry. What could have gone wrong? He knew that if he did not find Cummins' body in the smoking rubble, he would be lucky if his job was the only thing he lost.

Epilogue

Six Miles Away
Deep In the North Georgia Forest

Darkness had set in, and two very dirty and fatigued children were being hand-led along what was nothing more than a woods deer trail by two parents also covered in dirt and dust. The mother gave glaring, disapproving looks at Jim Cummins--she did not enjoy putting her children through this kind of ordeal. The children had thought it fun at the beginning: first a quick shimmy down a ladder in a hole in the basement floor, then a long crawl through a secret tunnel only to climb up another ladder to emerge from the earth.

But after another five miles of walking through woods so thick a jack-rabbit might not risk it, the children's sense of adventure had run out. Briars and brambles had scratched arms, hands and faces until blood trickled from nasty cuts.

"Where is the road?" demanded the mother, "You said there was a road." Her voice cracked, she was on the verge of despair. Her husband, Jim Cummins, held a flashlight to light the way, but he was not sure why they had not yet found the road that was surely nearby.

Cummins loved his wife dearly but hated the looks she kept giving him. The family had felt the concussions of the bombs that tore through their home. All their possessions were gone. All the lovely antique furnishings that the wife especially had grown to love--all gone in a moment. Even before they emerged from the tunnel they had smelt the acrid smoke and smell made by weapons of war destroying a place once called home.

Cummins hoped they would find the road soon, and hoped against hope that help would be there and find them. But his cell-phone had been compromised, its codes cracked, and now that phone was in the burnt ash-heap six miles away, along with all the family photos that represented so many memories. *Was it worth all this?* Was it worth nearly sacrificing the lives of his wife and children? Had he underestimated the ruthlessness of the powers-that-be?

And even if they made it out of the forest, what kind of life could they expect to have. He wondered about his grown children--had they also been apprehended, taken in 'for questioning?' He had no way of knowing. Now he was a wanted man, but then again, he knew from the start that this was what he was choosing--for himself--for his family.

Lights, up ahead. The sound of a car engine. Cummins broke from the others and moved quickly towards the headlights. He *had* been close to the road after all.

Careful to turn off his flashlight, he could not afford to give away his position until he knew who was in that vehicle.

Then he heard it, a familiar tune on the night air, a tune so dandy and uplifting that even Lincoln included it among his favorites. Cummins began to hum now, to sing in time with the music--Oh I wish I was in the land of cotton, old times there are not forgotten... He turned his flashlight back on, using it to flag down the vehicle.

Wilder Fields pulled the old Jeep Cherokee to a halt, keeping the motor running. Getting out of the vehicle, Fields ran right past the Governor and into the forest, emerging a few moments later with the tired mother and two dirty but unharmed kids.

"Let's get you three into the Jeep and get you out of here. Uncle Wilder's got hot food and cold drinks in the back seat, so let's see who's hungry. They all climbed, like refugees, into the Cherokee to leave the forest. As the kids dug into the burgers and fries, the older man spoke to the younger.

"Close call wasn't it? Had no idea if y'all even made it out. Can't believe they tried that. Came out here like we had planned in case of emergency," said Fields.

"Well, I think this qualifies as an emergency. Glad we remembered the tunnel option," replied the Governor.

"Thank God you're alive, and thank God for that old tunnel! And one more thing," said Fields. "Jim, its starting, a wider resistance is starting to spread across the country. When word hit the internet about the attack on your home, flash protests and riots sprang up in every major city—in New York, L.A., Dallas, Phili-- even a Boston Tea Party broke out in Bean Town."

"And so it begins."

"Yes, it begins." replied Fields. "The White House put out that it served a warrant on you at the Governor's Mansion and that you yourself had set off explosives, determined not to be taken alive. T.V. news is running with that line, but the internet crowd ain't buying it. Most folks know you would not put your own family in that kind of danger. Though most don't know if you're even still alive, some have already started calling you

'America's Governor.' That last bit drew a strange look from Cummins. "Governor, what do you think our next move should be?"

"To get us out of here, Wilder. We need soap and warm water--and soft beds."

THE END...
OF THE BEGINNING

www.ingramcontent.com/pod-product-compliance
Lightning Source LLC
Chambersburg PA
CBHW031247170626
46807CB00001B/20